Ann
The col

THE NATURE OF CONCENTRATION

THE SERMON ON THE MOUNT

PROSPERITY

PRIMARY LESSONS IN CHRISTIAN
LIVING AND HEALING

SPIRITUAL HOUSEKEEPING

ALL THINGS ARE POSSIBLE TO THEM
THAT BELIEVE

ALL THE WAY

CONTENTS

BOOK ONE.
THE NATURE OF CONCENTRATION

FOREWORD

These lessons have been presented to large audiences in various cities of the world with most happy and practical results. The style of the familiar talks has been retained, yet for this book the lessons have been revised, added to, and rearranged. They have been written with sub-heads so as to be made easy to study or to be taught, and, in many ways, to be made convenient for the practical student of spiritual mind to attain the power of concentration he desires.

May all your needs and desires in this direction be met quickly, O Reader! That this little volume be a privileged instrument in setting your feet in the Straight Way forever is the earnest prayer of the author,

Annie Rix Militz

Chapter 1. THE NATURE OF CONCENTRATION

The Common Center

THE simplest definition of concentration is that found in the dictionary, namely, "to gather to one common center," for it defines that which is spiritual as well as that which is material.

We need only to consider what is the common center in order to put concentration into its right place. That common center is within you and its name is One, whether we call it the name of the Lord, as we read in the book of the prophet Malachi, as to the great Manifestation that finally shall be in this world, that "there shall be one Lord and His name One," or whether we call it the mathematical one. It is sufficient that we see the common-center of our spiritual thoughts and of our material thoughts as one thought, one manifestation.

The Way of Creation

Concentration is the formative way of creation. Creation is manifested by the power of divine mind working upon thoughts, ordering them and being obeyed, so that they gather around one common center; thus we have that expression, called the Solar System, or a world.

If we turn to the scientific theories of the formation of this universe, we have that nebulous mass which finds its center in some nucleus about which all is gathered. This formative power of divinity within you is that which brings everything to its essence. The common center of your being is the essence of God, your divine self. To begin to make your eye single to that central self, that divine I, is to feel your mastery.

The reason why people are so disturbed, upset, mixed and lacking in concentration, is because they have forgotten. They have ceased to look to that One, and they must return, and remember the One that is the source of our life; the power that holds us together; the great means by which we can order our lives and manifest the works of God—works of healing, of mastery, of self-control and the restoration of memory. Thus can you be a power like the sun, radiating power to transform your whole world, according to your own idea, to the light that dwells within you, bringing forth all that which is right and that which is a blessing.

A Gauge of Intelligence

The power of concentration has always been a gauge of intelligence. It is an indicator of intelligence, whether it be expressed in the animal realm, or in the human, in the babe or in a Socrates.

When a trainer wishes to select animals of intelligence, he will note their power of concentration. A famous trainer of dogs would gather together a number of these animals from everywhere; sometimes they would be very common dogs, for he found that it was not always dogs of the best breed that showed the most intelligence; sometimes it would be but a yellow cur that would make the best trick dog. After association with their master long enough to become familiar with his voice, it was the practice of this trainer to test their powers of concentration. He would gather them together and holding up some object, would demand the attention of all the dogs to that thing. One by one, the dogs dropped their eyes, turned away their heads and sought some other interest, only a few remained alert and waiting and these were the dogs that the trainer chose to become performers on his stage. And so we can take the babe. The babe that "takes notice" very quickly and very steadily, we count of much intelligence. This is also true of ourselves, we find that the times, when we can hold our mind to certain things, are the times of greatest accomplishment—when we manifest the greatest intelligence—and finally, we shall see this a power so supreme that one might, like another Socrates, stand in the midst of the market place absorbed in a revelation, and even stand for hours. It is said this great philosopher once stood a whole day and night, while the people surged around about him. Were you or I able so to stand, we also might present to the world such a philosophy as he gave. Socrates represents intelligence of the highest degree, and it expresses itself in this power of concentration. There is no greater pursuit than that of the knowledge and understanding by which you can express your intelligence in concentration.

Natural Concentration

It has been found that those who follow the spiritual life, devoting all their time and attention to it, have no difficulty in concentrating. Healers easily center their thought; can easily be at peace, be self-possessed, poised and fearless in some of the hardest problems and the most distracting situations. Therefore if you simply pursue this truth, putting it into practice in your daily living, seeking ever to help people and lighten their burdens by your power of thought, you will manifest concentration without an effort. You are even now exercising that power in centering your minds upon what I am saying. I have had speakers, who have been on the platform with me, express themselves with wonderment at the attention that is given me—the silence, the peace, the freedom from restlessness. It is all a marvelous' expression of concentration, because the subject that I present is so vital and of such power that it naturally unites our thoughts, and you concentrate naturally— without an effort.

Special Concentration

We know the advantages of the ordinary concentration, how it gives you peace and self-control, and the masterly, orderly expression that invites confidence. But there is a special advantage in the concentration that is based upon principle. Have you discovered that what you concentrate upon, you become one with? That it is possible for you to enter into the heart—into the very essence of a thing and get its secret and make it reveal its nature and its meaning? Some of you have had this experience that when you wanted to know a thing, you simply centered your mind steadily on it, and presently it was opened up to you and you found yourself knowing without the ordinary efforts of getting information. One man told me this, as a common experience with himself in school. He was a boy of fine intelligence, but he was lazy, and oftentimes did not have his lesson, but when his turn came to answer the question put to him, he would think toward the Professor, and say (mentally) to him.: "You know the answer; it is right in your mind this moment," and while he would think that, the answer came to him. He did this so often that he knew that he had fulfilled some law.

Again, let me remind you of the little newsboy that I saw guessing the dates on the coins, which another boy held in his hand. Steadily his eye rested upon each copper cent, and three times he gave the correct date, imprinted on the under side, which none of us knew until after each coin was examined.

It is a good illustration of power that is in us which we exercise, even when we do not know the nature of it nor how we have it. You think it is by coincidence or chance. You think that something called your attention to the fact, and you dismiss the experience in a materialistic way, even with doubt. But it is a power called "psychometry," now acknowledged by scientists. Maeterlinck says, "The existence of this faculty is no longer seriously denied." It is orderly; it is right; we have this power, we need only to exercise it. But to do so, we must take care of our thoughts, dismiss certain kinds of thinking and hold to certain other kinds of thinking.

Thoughts of Evil, Rubbish

In the first place, we cannot afford to "clutter" our mentalities with thoughts of evil. It is a homely word but it is literally so. You clutter your mind, filling your brain cells with what the physicians call "dirt," and this is all because of erroneous thinking— thinking upon wrongs and upon evils, revenge, fear and worriment. Everything that has its root in the belief of evil must utterly pass from our mentality and pass forever, and we become like a little child, with pure, clean brain-cells, because we have no false thoughts or ill feelings, but are filled with love, and purity and goodness. So the very organ of your mentality, the brain, can be orderly and free, without congestion of blood, without any piling up of that foreign material which the physician calls "dirt," and when you wish to think upon a thing, you will not have to use your human will power but just wait and rest, and naturally it will spring to the front and you will have wasted no effort, but have concentrated easily and with power.

Memory Restored

This is the way for the restoration of your memory. The reason why people lose their memories and find their mental faculties getting out of order, is because they try to hold thoughts in their minds that do not belong there; they will be so disconcerted if they forget dates, or events that should be counted nothing at all. Why should you remember the old past, and why should you dwell on the things of yesterday? Now is the only time. Live in the present. Dismiss thoughts of yesterday; those thoughts of the past. Be as though you were born this morning. Begin every day anew.

Some may say: "I have been so wronged by everybody; people impose upon me and it will not do for me to forget or I'll be wronged again." There is "a more excellent way," by which these experiences shall not be repeated, than remembering the wrongs of the past. This excellent way is to begin to fill your mind with meditations upon God, the Good. Even though it be so simple as this reasoning—that there is the One that is the source of all and that One is God the good; that One is omnipresent; therefore good is everywhere. Then insist upon seeing it everywhere, upon believing it, dwelling upon it continually—Good is the only real presence. Do this in place of the evil thinking; do it persistently. How do you put out darkness? Not by dealing with darkness! So you cannot put out evil memories by dealing with them. themselves. You put out darkness by bringing in the light, and you put out evil memories by bringing in good ones.

Faithful Practice

This means an exercise as faithfully practiced as the beginning of the study of music. When you began to learn music, you pursued practices that were tiresome, but your teacher said it was necessary. When you began to learn a physical exercise, like rowing a boat, you went through simple actions and pursuits, and some were very wearisome, but these simple things were most essential. Begin your practice of concentration by centering your mind upon the thought that the good is all there really is, and learn to crowd out the opposite thoughts with that one thought. It will prove itself true, presently.

Such was the case of a young boy who had run away from his home in Portland, Ore., and became stranded in San Francisco. Through a lady, who learned his story, he began coming to the Home of Truth. There he learned to hold the thought: Good is all there really is.

He desired to get back home, and a purser on an Oregon steamer told him to be at the dock on the Sunday morning that the steamer would sail, and he, the purser, would come ashore and get him, and he could work his passage home again.

The boy was there but the purser never appeared. The steamer sailed, leaving the boy in rage and despair.

Then he remembered that he was to say, "Good is all." In bitterness, almost sarcasm, he began to repeat the worth. Soon he calmed down and found himself walking toward the Home of Truth. There, on the steps, he met a lady who began to inquire why he had not gone. He reluctantly told her his bad luck, with the result that she handed him the fare to go on the train to Portland, and he arrived there before the steamer reached that city. He proved quickly "the power of the word."

Worldly Success

Worldly success is one of the out-picturings of the power of concentration. Those who have made material success will tell you that it has come by concentration upon their business, and devoting all their strength and time to it. The secret of Paderewski's skill with the piano was this, that he gave himself to eighteen hours' practice at a time. A certain rich man, who was very successful with railway stocks, gave it as his secret, that he studied the manual of railways, night and day; would read it before he world go to sleep, then the first thing in the morning before meals, after meals—all the time. And when some one asked him the secret of his success, he said it was concentration—studying night and day upon that in which he was successful.

Oh, but Paderewski can be thrown off with the injury of a finger; the railway man can receive a little blow on the head, and it all counts for nothing. Those who concentrate upon material things have but a temporal success, for if they try to concentrate upon anything else, they find they have not power in that direction, and it sometimes seems like beginning life over again. This was illustrated in the experience of a man who had been a most successful business man, as a commercial traveler, commanding a high salary and finally becoming a partner in the company, though still pursuing his own efficient line.

Finally, he had accumulated such a snug little fortune, owning a pretty home and ten acres in one of California's loveliest towns, that his wife and daughter persuaded him to retire from business.

What they meant to be freedom and a joy to him proved to be the greatest mistake. He tried to lead a quiet life and, for activity, to become interested in the pursuits of his society-neighbors. But his mind was ever off on the familiar routes that he had followed for over fifty years. He could not center his thoughts on the new life and the result soon was "softening of the brain," the beginning of dissolution.

Fortunately, his wife and daughter understanding Truth, brought his case under spiritual treatment and his mind was saved, and be was able to hew out a new way of concentration, by utterly abandoning the material for the spiritual.

The Oriental Yoga

The Hindus call the practice of spiritual concentration, "Yoga," which means "union," and comes from the same root as our word "yoke" The Aryan language is at the root of all civilized languages, and our word yoke and their word yoga have a common root, and it means to unite—to join.

"Take my yoke upon you, for my yoke is easy and my burden is light." This is the Christ teaching of yoga, that we shall have such a power of concentration that there shall be no burdens at all, but all life shall be full of ease and freedom. The Christian Yoga is "taking on Christ," being one with him, which is the easy way of concentration. Hindu devotees spend whole lives in the study and practice of Yoga, because, by means of right concentration, they look for all power, all knowledge and all bliss here in this life. The text-book of Hindu practice is "The Yoga Aphorisms of Patanjali," in which is displayed most subtle and wonderful understanding of the human mind and its workings, and the way of deliverance from its errors by right knowledge and practice of concentration.

Knowledge and Love

There are two forms of thinking which make the way easy for concentration. One is knowing; keep on knowing; never rest content with ignorance; get knowledge and get understanding. The other is love. Begin with the love of truth; love truth for its own sake. My friends, if you will only "fall in love with truth," you need not have another lesson; you will concentrate and no one can stop you.

There are people who think truth night and day. in their dreams, and in the ordinary things of life, and the consequence is that they are joyously and powerfully in the consciousness of concentration. Of course they are in love with truth. If anybody is in love with another you do not need to tell them to think about the other one; if you are in love with another, you simply cannot help thinking of that one. It would sound ridiculous to say to a real lover, "If you expect to win her, you must think of her night and day." "How can I help it!" says the lover. The advice is not needed. A lover has a wonderful power of concentration, and if there is no mixture of resentment, of hatred or jealousy, there is a perfect feeling of peace and power. Pure love is a power for concentration in itself, and so to be in love with truth is to be able to concentrate without a thought. Love is faithful.

Express your love by obediently practicing this first rule of concentration, the use of the silent word. Often practice saying, "Good is all there really is."

Chapter 2. THE POWER OF REPOSE

Let us unite in silence, taking the words found in Psalms:

"Be still and know that I am God." Be still in every way, relaxing yourself and letting the I AM be your stilling power. Rest in the Divine Mind that knows itself (which is yourself), the great I AM that dwells in the midst of you. We remember that "God" is the name of our good, and what ever your desire may be—for peace, for health, for happiness, for freedom, it is the very desire of your heart that speaks and says, "Be still and know that I am God"—be still and know that I am. This is our silence.

The Effortless Way

TWO great principles are at the root of the power of concentration. One of them is Knowing and the other is Loving. Knowing might be considered the active principle and loving the passive, or still principle, in this that knowing is associated with activity, pursuing, seeking, grasping, and so on, while loving is associated with being. Love comes without effort. It is the effortless way to love, and if you are in love with truth, you concentrate without effort. And this effortless way is the happy way of concentration. By loving truth, you enter true wisdom's ways, which are pleasantness, and you find the path which is peace. So you must love truth with your whole being, seeking it, not for what it will bring you, not for its reward, its healing, its peace, even for its power of concentration, but for it, itself — loving truth for its own self.

This is the orderly, masterful, efficient way of attaining concentration. Learn to concentrate upon truth, and having acquired that power in the realm of reality, you will have no difficulty in centering your mind upon whatever you will in the realm of appearances. For always you will stand upon the Rock of right reasoning; and if you turn aside from concentrating upon exact truth, you can look at symbols, as symbols, and let them hold your attention, so long as you will, because you see the connection between them and truth. Whereas, the things that distract, that break up the mentality and spoil concentration will not invite your attention. You can refuse to center your mind upon evil, fear, worry, foolish ness, for these are the things that distract and they are spoilers of concentration.

No Suppression by Human Will

The worldly methods of thought-control by strenuous effort of the human will are to be put completely aside. Use no will power to concentrate. This mistake has been made by certain young metaphysicians, and even old ones. Those who have been long in this life have practiced and pursued ways that are strenuous and congesting; have inflamed and disturbed even their brain cells by dwelling upon some word which has little or no meaning in itself, repeating it over and over again, thinking that to hold a thought, one must exercise human will. No, the real holding of thought is as a cup holds water; through being still and letting the thought rest in your mind, and the power by which you do that is the power of repose.

Repose is not something you do not already have. It is within you, and it needs only meditation and acknowledgment of it, to bring it forth. The way to uncover it is by, first of all, knowing yourself.

Know Thyself

You cannot know yourself perfectly without knowing God. For this personal self, which has been called yourself, is but a reflection, a shadow of your Real Self which is one with God. Knowing the Real Self, you will understand this shadow, this reflection, just as one, knowing about a material thing will also understand its shadow. Recognizing the power that is in you to cast a shadow, you know how to manage the shadow —that of your hand on the wall, for instance; you can control the shadow because you know how to manage the hand. Thus, if you know your Real Mind and its processes, you will understand its shadow, and, doing what you will with your Real Mind, you can reflect or shadow it forth in appearance, just as you wish it to appear.

The Real Mind is God Mind. It moves upon itself in all manifestations. It is the actor and the one acted upon. It is God, the actor, and God, that which is acted upon— it being all God. The mind that shadows it, which has been called by various names, —the carnal mind, mortal mind, mentality, mind-stuff and so on—also acts upon itself, imaging, reflecting the laws of the divine Mind.

Mentality and Mind-Stuff

Let us call the actor of this mortal mind "mentality," and that which is acted upon, "the mindstuff."- To know how to conform your mentality to the great Actor, the divine One, and to act upon the mind-stuff according to the Divine Law, is to have a power that will heal, and thoughts with which nothing can interfere, so that you need never be con fused nor disturbed, nor lose your poise or your peace, no matter what you face or are passing through.

Sometimes the mind-stuff, which is the great mass of thoughts that are going hither and thither within us and round about us, has been compared to a lake, and the mentality to the breeze that blows upon the lake. When this mind-stuff is still and the mentality is quite at peace, then we have a lake all clear and free to reflect perfectly. Whatever is then held over that lake will be imaged forth as it should be, not distorted nor false, but true. Although inverted, it will be clear and its form correct, a perfect image of that which is held over it.

Upon a still lake, the ship that floats on its sur face will show forth all its beauty, form and graceful movements, giving a perfect image of itself. But when the lake of your thoughts is disturbed and agitated, then your mentality is like the wind that blows and lashes the waves. Then the mind-stuff is thrown into foam and becomes roiled and disturbed and it is not strange that you cannot reflect what you wish. You must become still again. The lake must subside and the wind must calm, that perfect repose may be manifest, that you may reflect what you wish and show forth the concentration which you desire.

Christ in the Ship

The One in you which can still your mentality is the Christ-self. To try to still the wind and waves without the Christ-self is a long process with more or less sense of failure. The Christ may appear to be asleep in the ship, as we read in that story about the disciples, who were crossing the Sea of Galilee and a great storm came upon them and the ship was in danger of sinking; of how they went to the Christ, asleep in the hold of the ship—not Christ really, but the form, Jesus, for the Christ is "the Lord that slumbers not, nor sleeps." It is but the form of that Christ-presence which seems to be hidden and non-active for a time. Your Lord-self never sleeps nor loses consciousness, but if it seems to you that you have no Lord-self, that you cannot think of yourself as divine or spiritual, then you need to arouse and awaken yourself, even with a cry of prayer, "Awake thou that sleepest!" or as the Psalmist calls, "Why sleepest thou, O Lord?" The disciples went and called Jesus from his sleep and he came forward and rebuked the wind and waves and all was still. So, no matter how agitated you seem to be—no matter how roiled the waters are or contrary the wind, in an instant, by remembering your God-self, the whole lake will quiet and you will quickly find yourself at peace.

This Christ-self is your power of repose. It is that part that abides in peace. It is the great immobility by which all things are moved. If you can find that Holy of Holies, that still place within, you will take hold upon a power of concentration which will remain with you forever.

Purity, Essential to Clear Thinking

The lake—the mind-stuff that fills your personality and surrounds it— must not only be still, but clear. Our living true to principle and fulfilling the moral law tends to purify this mind-stuff; sincerity, purity of life, freedom from deceit—freedom from doubleness in action, thought, word and deed— clarify this lake and make it pure. This means a life of freedom from "the three qualities" that the Hindu describes as Tamas, Rajas and Sattvas.

The Three Bonds

The Tamas quality is described thus: it is that state of lethargy and inertia, deadness, dullness and laziness which lies back of stagnation. If you feel spiritually lazy at times, or physically lazy, you can rise above that appearance by remembering the divine life, which is -always alert, active, sparkling, even in its stillness. You are God's active self, full of life, full of alertness, full of power and God. State these things for yourself and put away that stagnation which will make the waters of the mentality grow dark and thick with scum and not able to reflect what is held over them.

The second quality, the Rajas, is that of passion. It is the opposite to the Tamas quality for it stirs and muddies our thought-realm. Greed, jealousy, envy, anger, lust are things that move one to excess and upset one, so as to muddy the water of the mind-stuff, that it cannot reflect. Watch yourself. The moment you begin to find yourself wandering off into this state, being moved by anger and other forms of passion—the power of concentration is needed, the power of self-control, which is the next lesson we will take up especially.

The third quality is Sattvas, a sense of goodness often so personal as to be self-righteousness. The human ego says, "I am good, why should I not have perfect health? I have always done right, why should I suffer?" It feels that certain things are owing to it. This ego longs for praise and approval. It says, "I must be regarded," and again "I have been insulted," or "I have been neglected." Such thoughts are very disturbing. You may be leading a very pure life, may be fulfilling the laws so that you are counted very good and very lovable. Yet, if your face is full of fine wrinkles, or you have nerves unstrung, and there is a trembling or an agitation in your body, you lack in concentration.

The human ego can dwell upon its "rights," its "superiority" and its ambitions and achievements until unbalanced. "Insanity is egotism gone to seed."

Insanity is simply the lack of concentration, reaching its ultimate.

It is the Christ that brings you to yourself, out of the three qualities, giving you perfect peace and repose, as you are in the divine Mind.

Repose a State of Mind

Repose is a state of mind. We commonly associate it with our surroundings, and our relations. We think, "Oh, when I can get into a place where there is no more noise; when I can relax in body; when I can get off on my vacation; when I can have a change, then I shall rest and find repose." These things are but symbols of that which is the real cause of repose, the restful state of mind. All the time it is your mind that gives you the repose, even though it seems to be the bed, or a vacation, or something else external.

If the mind is not at peace, you can have weeks of vacation and be as upset and disturbed at the end as you were in the beginning. If your mind is not at peace, you can lie down upon your bed hour after hour and even go to sleep, and at the end of it you will feel as though you had had no rest. Why? Because the mind did not take hold of the idea. Yet, on the contrary, there are people who have no vacations, but who are just as fresh at the end of the day as in the morning, full of energy, resolution, full of power for work, and they never grow tired. Why? Because their minds are at peace. They love the activity, and there is nothing at cross purposes with them.

The man who has been working hard all day will dance all night, but have no sense of weariness at all. His dancing was according to his mind. There was peace in it, there was a poise, there was a sense of refreshment and rest.

The Art of Decomposing

The philosopher, Delsarte, taught away of acting and living, which he associated with thinking—so much so, that those who are the best students of this philosopher never separate the mind from an exercise, but always associate the mentality with whatever one is doing. Thus, he gives practices for what he called "decomposing"; to relax the muscles; to decompose the strained, fixed expressions, inward or outward. But the decomposing begins in your thought— in your mind—you may shake your hands, like tassels on the end of a whip-cord, but you will not decompose your wrists until your mind relaxes itself.

Practice relaxing every hour of the day, realizing that to be still is just as important as to act; that these two are to be rightly married through all your expressions—stillness and activity, rest and motion. These are to meet and associate perpetually in your life.

There are certain ways of relaxing yourself which you can practice, no matter where you are. Let out the muscles of your face. Have you ever thought of the muscles around your mouth? your lips pressed together, oftentimes strained with thought of precision or rectitude. Relax the muscles around your eyes. Perhaps you are contracting them with the thought that the light is too strong. Realize the power of the spirit to temper the light and to take care of all your affairs.

Whenever you have opportunity, let out the muscles in your body. Perhaps you are sitting in a car, clutching your bundles, when you can just as well lay them down and loosen the muscles of your arms. Perhaps your whole body is tense, and, thinking of the end of your journey, you are pushing the car men tally. If you find yourself growing tense in any of your muscles, loosen them by relaxing your mind and taking the words: "Be still and know that I am God."

Have the same consciousness that the motorman has, as he sits, turns his levers and applies the power, or takes it off. He is not pushing the car, or pulling it, but he is knowing that the greater power is established and fully centralized, and he is in perfect connection with it, and all that he has to do is to turn the lever, on or off, without an effort. This is our true consciousness of ease. It brings us peace and rest and satisfaction in and about our affairs. Go on, you need have no concern about anything.

The Power of Silence

The great philosophy of this silence is, that there is in you a mighty nothing, a quietness that has been from the great forever and always will be. It is the master of goodness, that still place, that Holy of Holies. It is your power of abandonment, your child-likeness, and in that, it rests, waiting for you to move. It is a mighty vacuum, that causes all motion but in itself does not move. O, that being nothing—nothing of yourself! When that feeling of having so much to do, of being so important, and you must do things or they will not be done, rises up, about that time let go and enter into your own sweet nothingness. Stop thinking. You can do it. Just remember there is a power to stop thinking, and if, suddenly, you should find your mind a blank, know then, you are practicing the perfect concentration of repose.

Practice not thinking, non-thinking. Practice being nothing—especially when you feel like asserting yourself. Be like the mirror, as to your human mentality. The mirror is nothing of itself, but it can take in all things. The mirror is a marvelous symbol. In the religion of Japan, the Shinto religion, they have only two symbols in their temples; one is a mirror, the other, a bell. The mirror is the nothing, the wonderful nothing, by which God is reflected.

To be a perfect reflector, a mirror must be still. If you wish to see yourself in a mirror and it is moving back and forth all the time, you have to take hold of it and steady it, in order to get a good reflection. So with your mentality. In order to reflect your Godhead you must be still. True, the mirror must also be clean, it must be true. There are other things besides stillness; nevertheless, even the mentality, to be true and clean, must be well controlled and well trained—you must hold it still and steady

The Christ-Door, the Nothing

"I am the door," said the Master. A door is useful as an entrance, through being nothing. We commonly call that which closes up, "the door," but the door is the empty space; and a door, to be perfect, must be unobstructed —an unobstructed entrance. So, when the Christ says, "I am the door," he is refer ring to that power of being nothing.

When you are perfectly still, you feel the nothing ness; you are not thinking; you cannot even feel your body. There are certain of you that have experienced this lightness, when there was a loss of the sense of being a body, of being a personality, and then came the great cosmic consciousness. You entered the universal. You did not lose consciousness. You gained the great consciousness, beside which the other seems trivial. If you could be perfectly still as to your human thinking, then the great divine consciousness would be your thinking and your life for ever.

It was so with Tennyson. He could enter into cosmic consciousness by centering himself upon his own name and losing all thought of the little self. He entered into the great Idea for which his name stands. He saw only the great immortal self, and he describes it as losing all consciousness of being a body or a personality, a little man among things. It was an entering into the universal mind, feeling himself the whole mind; knowing all things without beginning of time and without limitation of space.

"BE STILL BEFORE GOD AND LET HIM MOULD THEE!"

Chapter 3. SELF-CONTROL

Let us unite in silence with these words: "I, if I be lifted up from the earth, will draw all unto me."

These are the words of Jesus Christ spoken from the central I. For this I to be lifted up from the earthy thoughts, the earthy associations, is to lift up all the thoughts so that they work for peace and not pain, for harmony and not discord. So we take the statement as our very own: "*I, if I be lifted up from the earth, will draw all unto me.*"

The Three Bonds Broken

THE Hindu philosophers are among the deepest students of psychology, understanding the subjective nature so well, that we can take their description of the bonds that hold and rule unregenerate humanity, as sufficiently reliable, for our inquiry into concentration.

Let us briefly review the three great causes of the mortal manifestation. The first of the three bonds that hold humanity is the quality of dullness, deadness, torpor, drifting, blankness, ignorance. Itis the lack of knowledge—inertia, laziness. It is that which causes us to drift along the old lines and take no step progressively, the Tamas quality. It is back of laziness—whether physical, mental or spiritual.

The second quality is just the opposite —passion, that which causes great action, hurrying, struggling, striving, worrying, agitation and disturbance in general, the passionate quality, Rajas.

And the third quality, Sattvas, is that which is counted the best in us, that of which we may be proud, that which is self-assertive, self-righteousness, that in which we feel that we are good. It is called the goodness of the race and by other good names, such as virtue, enlightenment, knowledge, etc. Nevertheless, it acts as a bond with people who claim reward; that think they have earned a right to good things. They may be bound by that feeling, and perhaps filled with self-righteous pity or self-excuses from the basis of their righteousness. They may feel themselves wronged and misunderstood, and suffer from sensitiveness and, worst of all, from egotism, for there is where the ego stands, the I of us, which, seeing from a personal standpoint, believes itself to be the good.

Now, according to the psychology of the Hindus, these three bonds must be broken. The sages among them have learned that they are not broken by violence, but by knowledge. First of all, knowing the nature of them, that they are delusion, that they are not real but are shadows and reflections. They have no real strength and no real place, and by the mind keeping single to the Real back of each, their sub stance and strength in the Spirit, they can be sur mounted and used for the Highest.

Repose not Inertia nor Laziness

The Real of the Tamas quality is the power of repose, of being still and poised and quiet, that of resting in the Lord. Sometimes people condemn that passivity and quietness, and call it by unregenerate names through not understanding it. Let us learn that persons may sit with folded hands, apparently having nothing to engage their action, and yet not be lazy, but be bringing forth a great and wonderful stillness which is back of all the moving of activity. It is the power behind the throne, what the mystic Eckart calls, "that immobility by which all things are moved," and we must learn to cultivate that righteous stillness.

Certain active things may carry out the Tamas quality, such as a being busy doing nothing or foolishness; much talking that is only chatter; a dullness and conventionality that is simply a drifting along with the rest of the race. A number of our activities arise from the thought that we must be doing some thing all of the time, because of this belief that if we are not doing something we are lazy. Yet in this we are wrong, for there is a virtue in not doing, which we must take hold upon for repose. If you find your fingers twitching, that you are chattering and talking too much—about that time, relax and be still.

If we come under the accusation of laziness from ourselves or from others, let us enter into the repose of our spirit and realize that we are not lazy, that in truth, we are not lacking in energy. Our sweet still ness is more powerful and a greater cause of manifestation, than much of the activity round about us that has no principle in it.

The Great Self in Control

Who is the self that controls and what is that which is controlled? Again, the Hindus teach us: "Upraise the self by the self; do not sink the self. For the self is the friend of the self, and even the self is the enemy of the self." —Bhagavad Gita.

Raise, uplift, or "upraise" the self by the self, that is, self-control is control of the self by the Self. Divinity says, "I control myself." The Self that controls is God in the Highest, and the self that is being controlled is that appearance which is called our selves, but which is only the shadow or the reflection of the Great Self.

There is no one that should control you but your self, and, in truth, there has never been any one con trolling you but yourself. If you think that others have controlled you, there is something that has consented to it within you; that is, blindly and weakly consented because there was, to your ignorance, no way out of it, or else you have knowingly consented at the time, even though you afterwards desired to recall your consent.

Therefore, begin with yourself and speak the truth: "I am. the one that controls myself. I am the only one that controls myself."

Soon you will prove that you can no longer ascribe things in your life to anything or anybody outside yourself. Declare, "I am my own Master and I rule myself," and be delivered from the apparent influence of circumstances and people and other outside things.

World Mastery

You begin with your own feelings and thoughts, and see them as your little selves to be ruled by your dominant Self, and, controlling this microcosm or little world, you will exercise your true control upon the outer world, as yourself enlarged, realizing the macrocosm to be yours as well as the microcosm. But this ruling yourself is by love not by force, with knowledge not in ignorance. It is the second quality that we meet with this power of self-control, the Rajas quality, or the passions that seem so active and disturbing. These are to be put into their right place and become subject to ourselves. So we guard against our feelings running away with us; against being confused by the desires and passions of others. Because we have found control over ourselves and our own feelings and thoughts, we cannot be interfered with by the feelings and thoughts of others.

Ruling the Passions

The passions, that are counted the most influential in disturbing one's peace, are anger, lust and hatred. If one will take up these three and put them into their right place by finding the reality of them, and see to it that everything which springs from evil, or the belief in evil, is put under foot, then we shall have broken the bond of that Rajas quality which was interfering with our perfect concentration. You know that when you are agitated, disturbed, or begin to feel the passions of others stealing over you—you are not in the peace and poise of perfect concentration. And it is for you, in the midst of the storm, when things seem to be going against you and there is a rising in you of passion from the uncontrolled nature, to prove yourself master and keep your peace. The way to do this is to begin to understand and control these primitive passions. First of all, we must take the right stand or view point of these passions. We must not condemn our selves when we have repented of our false ways, no matter what we have done. It matters not where you find yourself, or what perverted passions are con trolling you, the moment you discover the condition, it can be brought under control if you will not condemn yourself. Condemning yourself is confusing and weakening.

No Self-Condemnation

Never condemn in yourself what you do not condemn in any one else. You will have the same fruit for yourself that you deal out to others. "With what measure you mete" to others, you will measure to yourself. And whatever attitude you wish others to take toward you, practice it toward others. So, when you find criticism rising within you and you are losing your repose—your feelings are being disturbed on account of the actions and words of others —take warning. Bring yourself quickly to yourself. "Come to yourself" and remember that "there is now no condemnation to them that are in Christ Jesus"— neither condemnation of self nor condemnation of others. So long as we condemn others there is an entering wedge of self-condemnation, and sometimes there is nothing so powerfully bitter and withering as one's own criticism of oneself. Better can you bear the sting of the tongues of others than you can the hateful criticism of yourself. Saints have been spoiled by it in their realization of the kingdom of heaven here. They have thought it right to put the stripes upon their own backs, torment themselves, turn the screws tighter, so long as it was' their own bodies that suffered, and they have spent a whole life-time keeping themselves out of the kingdom of heaven, which was for them and into which they could have entered, if they had not justified this false position.

One way for you to cease from condemnation is to remember that it is not your real self which you condemn, but your shadow or representation, that personality which you call yourself, upon which you have been willing to put your divine I AM. It is to be cared for as tenderly as your little babes; with the same mercy and kindness with which you look after your beast of burden, for it is the vehicle of your life, and it cannot do well if you are at enmity with it. If you are finding fault with it, forgetting it, hating it and mistreating it, all because it is your own, from the feeling "I can do with my own as I choose," what better are you than one who mistreats his wife, or the mother who misuses her child from that same stand point?

Be Merciful to Yourself

Bless your self and do not curse it; uplift, do not degrade it; do not make it your slave, but your good servant. Servants cannot do their best when one is finding fault with them all the time. So, see to it that you look at this which has been called the carnal nature, the mortal mind, with kindly eyes, tolerant and generous, and, best of all, with knowledge. If an animal is natural, you don't condemn it. You simply say it is an animal, and animals will always act that way. So you should see your carnal nature. As long as it is not open to the spiritual overshadowing, it will act its own natural self from its own natural basis, and should not be whipped nor condemned on account of it. But, you may say, tought to know the law, and be obedient. Paul says, "The carnal mind or natural man receiveth not the things of God and is not subject to the law of God, neither indeed can be." (I Cor. 2:14 and Rom. 8:7). Well, if it cannot, why punish it? Why find fault with it? Why condemn it? Be wise. See that nature as it is, and instead of finding fault with it, help it. For truly your carnal nature wants your happiness; wants to be abiding in the peace of your higher nature, and it is your privilege to instruct it on its own plane continually and to exact obedience. And when you see that it repents, that it wishes it had not done that, then let it not accuse itself nor condemn itself, but be at peace.

Not Destruction Nor Suppression

Do not think to have control over your passions by destroying them. You cannot destroy the life of your passions. "Kill out desire" are words, which spring from the belief that the kingdom of heaven can be seized by violence, but the truth is, you never can kill anything, not even "desire." If you think you can kill you are deceived and you will have to do your work over again. So, we do not think of destroying our passions, neither, on the other hand, of suppressing them. For there are people who have a certain amount of self-control through suppressing themselves. Sometimes they suffer great distress through crowding back their desires until they are like a mighty dynamo of power. Sometimes there follows a bursting, an explosion — a lawless act through a mighty desire for freedom, and a crashing fall of a nature overborne with ascetic restraint.

Transmutation

No; transmute your desires. Lift them up to the spirit and have the spirit take hold of them. Trans mute them through the renewing of your mind. The anger that you have held back and crowded down, suppressing your words, pressing your lips together, and yet justifying the cause of your anger, will one day burst out in words most painful, if you do not take it in charge and give it to the spirit. Give no place to righteous indignation—not even as the wrath of God, for there is no such thing. That is a figment of the imagination, making God in the image of the mortal—an idol which men have bowed down to, content in their own lack of peace and power through justifying the wrath of God. There is no place for anger in love, and so, if you find this rising even in the slightest, give it over to the Spirit. Say some little words, like "Thou only" or pray a prayer. Realizing that fear of anger within you, you begin to give it over to divine love. Love takes it. Love uses it. Do not try to think anything else until that old form of "righteous indignation" begins to pass away.

And so with lust. When thoughts that you have counted impure, and desires which you have felt to be unregenerate and unclean rise within you, instead of being filled with self-condemnation, or the false thought that those desires must be gratified because of the ignorant teaching of the world, take hold of the passion and lift it up to God. Whenever you feel the accusation of being impure, immediately hold, "I am pure! I am pure!" Thus will you use this mighty passion for rising to spiritual heights; for getting joy in the life of regeneration; for the mastery over yourself.

In the same way, if you have a revengeful and hateful feeling and a memory of wrongs, and if malice tries to impose itself upon you, remember to pray the Lord's Prayer, "Forgive us our debts as we forgive our debtors." Say, "I let all my feelings be used by the Spirit of Love, by the Almighty God, and no revengeful, hard or bitter thought of hatred can, work through me." This is the stand to take, instead of crowding things back and suppressing them, as though they were realities, and ready to burst forth at any moment.

Counter-Thoughts

We remember that the transforming is all done from the mind, from the inner nature, "Be ye trans formed by the renewing of your mind." Some have used certain external practices, such as holding the breath. Controlling the breath reacts upon the thought, for the breath moves with the thought, and acts by reflection or "reflex action" upon the mentality. Some of these practices have been good up to a certain point, but eventually it is the mind that does the work, even when you control your breath.

These are aids, but they have their limitations. There are other aids— ways of counteracting these thoughts, feelings, words and deeds by setting up counteracting thoughts. Thus, when one is being stirred by some passion which naturally would burst forth in violent words or rough actions, one can say, sing or do something gentle and harmonious. There are some people who, when angered easily, slam doors and throw things. If you feel like stamping your foot (and probably you justify it, it seems so harmless), put that foot down gently.

You who would have perfect control over yourself and always be poised and full of power and peace, manage your mortal nature as a man manages a horse or an engine, or whatever he wills. Use all the devices that come into your mind to get the upper hand of your passionate nature. Remember that passion is not evil in itself.

Texts and Mantrams

The committing of verses and mantrams and reciting them is one of the outward ways to aid in concentration. The Hindu calls them mantrams; we call them texts. There are some that have a pacifying effect and bring a realization very quickly of the control exercised by your divine self. Take a single thought and raise it above your other thoughts, like a Moses in the wilderness raised up to lead the children of Israel out of the old slavery into the land of eternal freedom and happiness. I know one who took, Thou only as her statement, and every time she found herself having thoughts and feelings that were not desirable, she would say, "Thou only."

There are those who have taken "Thy Will is done in me," with the result of giving up the human will and knowing there is but one will working in and through them. Some take the twenty-third Psalm, others the Lord's Prayer. Whatever appeals to you, in verses or single words, use them as Leaders about which to gather your wayward and scattered thoughts.

If you love this life and are pursuing it all the time, some Truth is always presenting itself and you can have a variety in your spiritual diet. As I have said before, whoever is living this life, uplifting others and talking truth, is concentrating without an effort, and I must continually call your attention to this way—this effortless way of loving truth for its

own sake, for when you are in love with truth, you cannot help but think of it night and day, and thus the power of concentration becomes as natural to you as your breath.

Chapter 4. CONCENTRATION IN THE DAILY LIFE

Let us unite in silence, taking with us the words of power found in Zachariah 4:6. "Not by might nor by power, but by my spirit, saith the Lord of Hosts."

We understand that the "might" spoken of here and the "power" refer to the human will and mere external power. This statement is one of the very best to bring you to the consciousness of effort less concentration, that you do all things, not by might nor by power, but by My Spirit, saith the Lord of Hosts or Forces.

Leader Thoughts

BY way of review, I will remind you that in entering into concentration, whether for a few moments or a regular half hour or more, it is well to have a leading thought, just as in the gathering together of people, a leader is most essential—not that the leader is superior, necessarily, but is simply good as a leader.

There are spiritual thoughts that appeal to you and certain thoughts do not; again, there are times when the same thought will appeal to you much more than at other times. Select your leading thought by that divine sense within. You will know when you have found the right word, or the right statement, by the same sense of satisfaction that you have when you taste anything and it tastes just right.

It is the same with the Scriptures, that the mind "trieth words, as the mouth tasteth meat." Thus we try sentences —words of truth —and accept certain statements at the time as the very best to hold. That which we have just held in the silence, "Not by might nor by power, but by my spirit, saith the Lord of Hosts," is an excellent leader almost any time. I

Illustration: Overcoming Worriment

And this is what I mean by taking a leading thought. You may sit down full of worriment, of belief that there is so much to do and so little time to do it in and that much effort is necessary. Then that thought of not by effort "but by my spirit, saith the Lord," dropped among the other thoughts about the necessity of effort and rush and confusion, will pacify and quiet, and give you rest by its cool, calming realization, so essential to do the things necessary to be done in the time that you have.

What is true of worriment in its character of dis traction and confusion, might be said of fear and other perverted passions, like jealousy and hatred. But we will not dwell upon these as positive things — no evil thought is

22

positive. Sometimes one gets an idea about evils, that they are so real and have so much power, that they so interfere and spoil things, that that very thought is followed by panic. A per son is almost afraid to be afraid and worries about worrying. Put away that suggestion this moment by realizing that all these evil thoughts are mere negations, mere emptiness. They have no real power in themselves, only as they are emphasized. Some metaphysicians have so enlarged upon the power of evil thinking that they have made a new devil. I have heard many people say that they would rather believe in the old-fashioned kind of a devil than this kind, known as "m. a. m."—or "malicious animal magnetism." It is for us to prove that such influence has no real power, no real place.

Emptiness of Error-Thoughts

Let us take up these things in the right way as nothingness; worriment is negation, fear is a kind of emptiness. Fill in the place of these negatives (worriment or fear) the opposite thoughts which are positive. Here you will need to use discretion and discernment to select your opposite thought, but the mere act of feeling after God, the seeking of the Word, is itself beneficial. The very attempt to find the opposite sometimes will do the work—just the attempt.

Perhaps, whenever you have, thought of a certain person you have had a sweep of hatred go over you, and you have justified it. You felt you had done right to hate that person for he had been the embodiment of wickedness and vice; there was no good in him. You had made up your mind that he didn't even have a soul and there was nothing to save about him, and he might as well be out of the world as in it. I am describing something that may not apply to any of you, but there are a great many people who think that way. They dwell upon the thing so long that they justify murder, and then some one is killing somebody else.

You have come into the Truth, and if you have had an old hatred for some people, now you have learned to dismiss them from your mind, for they were so uncomfortable to think about. You have learned that you cannot hold them altogether evil, but then you sometimes justify hating the sin because you think that God hates sin, and that wrath against sin is legitimate. But in love, there is no hatred at all. God is love, and love knows no wrath, knows no hatred, not for one second. Therefore there is nothing in hating sin; sin is nothing; what is there to hate?

You reason with yourself and this reasoning is good. It takes you from that distracting thought, that dividing, breaking, insane thought of hatred. For hatred leads to insanity. So when that person comes into mind, you should know a thought that neutralizes the old one of hatred—something just opposite to hatred.

Exercise by the Audience

By way of exercise let all this audience think upon an opposite thought to hatred.

Audience—' 'Love."

Speaker —Perhaps you start with love: "I love you. Love is the only presence and the only power."

It sounds, perhaps, like a lot of words; you don't want to spoil your thought about love, so you drop it.

"It is a little too much," perhaps you are thinking; "I don't see how I ever can love that one."

Then some other thought had better be introduced.

Audience —"Tolerance."

Speaker —"I will be tolerant."

Perhaps you take a little pride in it. Perhaps charity would be better. You are beginning to climb. Charity. Yes, perhaps I can find some excuse. There is a kind of mildness about that charity. It works. Perhaps you begin to find your word empty. Then you think peace, and you grow a little less agitated. Every time that image rises and the thought of hatred and the old sense of justifying it, you say, "Tolerance, Charity, Peace," and you lead up to "Love." Soon you find yourself saying, "God is Love. Love in me for gives," and you go on in power, and presently you can speak the whole truth, for you are large enough to understand the old mortal mind, its nature and why it acted that way, and you have come to your peace. Let us continue this exercise. Supposing that you find yourself full of fear and you are agitated. Now fear is a negation. Give me some opposite word.

Audience— "Faith!" "Confidence!" "Assurance!" "Courage!" "Trust!"

Trust is a very good word. Now give me some thing the opposite to jealousy.

Audience—"Confidence!" "Understanding!"

You understand what I mean. Every one of these evil things are like emptiness; that is all. And you need only to take the opposite —the opposite which appeals to you at the time—to begin and fill in that emptiness.

Concern About Tomorrow

Sometimes you are under a pressure to fill in with the substance of faith for a demonstration that is coming. You find yourself worrying tonight about tomorrow. You don't know what you are going to do tomorrow, and in the old days, you would lie upon your pillow and keep awake, thinking:

"What can I do? Where shall I go? What is the next step?" and perhaps remain awake all night or, if you fell asleep, you would awake exhausted, still with that awful sense of fear and worriment, feeling you had not slept at all.

What is the meaning of it? You need more faith. You are going to have a special demand for the manifestation of your prosperity or protection. Therefore begin to radiate this substance, faith, and meet that thought of worriment with,

"I trust in the great principle of my life. I trust in the All-Good, working in and through my life. My Good is coming to me. I know what to do. I always do the right thing. I speak the right words. I am inspired." Words like that, until you fall asleep. You will wake in the morning without a sense of bur den, with a wonderful calm and peace. Why? Because last night you laid up treasures in heaven.

The landlady comes in for her rent—suppose this was the coming demonstration which was to be made. You are able to face her with, "Will you wait a little while?" There is such a confidence in your voice that she says, "Very well I" Then in some unlooked

for way, as surely as you laid up substance the night before for a manifestation of it at the right time, the money comes. This is the way it works. We have seen it again and again.

Concentrating Where You Are

In this talk I am taking up concentration in the daily life, right where you are—not in some other place or among other people, or by yourself. Where you find yourself, there you are to know concentration, self-control, poise, self-possession, peace and power. The old idea that we must go to a nunnery or to some secluded spot in a mountain, or be by ourselves before we can get control and be at peace, we must dismiss.

It is true, you will have moments when you can go to "The Secret Place," and you must recognize such; even though it be only five minutes, you must thank God for that, when you can get off by yourself and hush everything. It may not come until you are at the point of retiring at night, but take advantage of it and thank God that you can be still and forget every thing for two minutes. It is enough. Such a minute is "like unto the grain of mustard seed." If you can have the Sabbath-consciousness for one minute in the day, it can solve the whole problem of concentration. "Remember the Sabbath to keep it holy." Remind yourself that you have that minute. Don't say, "I have no time for concentration, for meditation." You might as well say, "I have no time to be useful." You have all the time there is and you can do with it what you will.

In the busy life we learn to concentrate by using the things that we are passing through, which we are contacting, as suggestions of concentration. What ever you are employed in must be a means of suggestion to you of some spiritual thought of power and goodness which you desire to realize.

The Practice of the Presence of God

There is a little book that I would recommend to you, called "The Practice of the Presence of God." It is one of the very best treatments for concentration that has passed down to us. It is over two hundred years old, but it is just as meaty, just as full of sub stance as it ever was.

It is about a man, who was a lay brother in the Catholic Church, who had not become a monk because he felt too humble even to apply for such advancement, but was content to act as servant. He entered a monastery to do the cooking, the common work. But he had had a touch of the cosmic consciousness, insight of heaven, and he never forgot it. He learned that he could commune with God at other times besides the stated hours when he entered into the form of prayer. He became very familiar with the Divine Presence and it instructed him so that he learned to do everything he did for the Lord. He said if he picked up a straw off the ground, he did it for the Lord. He tells us that "the best rule of a holy life is to practice the presence of God." This means that there is nothing to recognize but the

Divine One in everybody; that there is nothing but peace; nothing but purity; nothing but blessings.

Practice the presence of your Good. Thus learning to see divinity in and through all things, nothing is impure or unclean to you. Like the poet Herbert, you can pray:

"Teach me, my God and King,

In all things thee to see.

And what I do in anything

To do it as for thee."

George Herbert was inspired, and it is such things as that that make him dear to us. Truth that he saw over one hundred years ago is just as true today.

Practice the presence of God—in that poor, old woman that you are waiting upon; that miserable man, fault-finding, and unkind, that you are serving. These can become divine in your sight and you can realize that you serve the Lord in them—the spirit in them. That very thought will transform her, and she will grow sweet and patient; and he will begin to be kind and considerate, such is the power of right thought. And when this takes place, you will have known a richness and sweetness in your life that cannot be described in words; you concentrate with out any trouble; nothing can distract you. Nothing can move you from your peace when you do every thing for the Spirit, and let the Spirit in you do it.

Spiritual Housekeeping

In the little book which I have written on Spiritual Housekeeping I give the spiritual meaning of the daily life of the housekeeper and show how each day can be a suggestion of some manifestation of the spirit. I take you through the seven days, and many of the points that I have given you in this course on concentration will be found in this book.

Monday is for water—Freedom; Tuesday for fire —Love; Wednesday for sewing—Creation; Thurs day for a general individual work—Grace; Friday for sweeping—Purity, and Saturday for baking and finishing work—Perfection; and Sunday has its own sweet Peace, the word of satisfaction and rest. Each day can bring forward these divine qualities in your selves. It will mean, perhaps, overcoming that impatience; putting away that temper that upsets things so easily; that besetting sin put under foot, as you know yourself and know what it is that distracts you. You will work with that until you walk at peace with yourself.

Your Special Business

While a person might take that little book upon concentration and see one's self a housekeeper, in as much as you are keeping this house—your body, and you are a housekeeper, no matter what you appear to be,—yet some of us would like to be specific as to the business we are in; to know the thought to hold in order to let that business, which perhaps is disliked by you, be a suggestion as to how you can think and feel while, perhaps, this one is calling you to do this, and another that, and another is giving you another piece of work, and you feel you must push and pull and give all your strength and knowledge to things material and foreign to the spirit.

Therefore, let us consider some of the business pursuits that men are in. I know one man that was a carpenter, who was well advanced in the power of con centration, because every time he built a house, he thought, "Every nail I drive home, I drive a spiritual thought home, such as 'now the truth sets you free,' " etc. He was talking silently to somebody all during his work or sending out his word in a general way, and he was full of activity and spiritual thoughts, quick to see and full of business alertness and efficiency.

Thus the man in the shop or the real estate dealer, or the promoter can find that each one of these things has a correspondence in the spirit, which he can learn by saying often, in his heart, "I am about my Father's business. I am here to do the work of the spirit, and to do divine work."

If he is a promoter, for instance, what is he really promoting? He is promoting the good of humanity; promoting opportunities for individuality to express itself; for the spirit to work through these bodies; to manifest to the greatest advantage to everybody with whom he comes in contact, not merely promoting his own purse.

Attracting Your Own

Taking this spiritual position, a man draws to him the very people that should be opened up interiorly. They are ready and waiting, and as truly as those, who have come to this lecture today, have come by the spiritual law, so every man who puts his business under the spiritual law will draw to himself men that mean business, that will not trifle, men that are able, that have substance, that are prosperous and desire what he has to give.

He will draw men that will not try to exploit him, for he is not trying to exploit men. The very best people will be his customers, for they will be like what he thinks about. It may seem at first a slow movement and somewhat mixed, but he will know why. Because he, himself is going on slowly in this spiritual life, and more or less mixed in his thoughts.

This is the way the business life will teach the gospel, will carry it everywhere, and the man who fills himself with spiritual thoughts, no matter what he is engaged in, radiates prosperity and helpfulness, has poise and power and "prospers in whatsoever he puts his hands to." He is inspired and inspires others, being a living Word of God to unite earth with heaven, and usher in the millenial age.

Chapter 5. CONCENTRATION THROUGH DEVOTION

Now let us join in silence, taking the first words of the Psalm 103: "Bless the Lord, O my soul; and all that is within me, bless his holy name."

Most excellent words to remember, whenever you have occasion to drop into the Silence. When, perhaps, no other words can come to your mind, these will center you quickly, not by merely wording them, but through realizing their meaning.

We know that the Lord of all needs no blessing from us. Nothing can be added to, nor taken from, the great divine One. But it is everything to your soul to express itself towards this One in the form of blessing, for when you begin to praise the divine One you center yourself and get into the poise, the peace and the power that belong to right concentration. We are remembering that the Lord is the Good in all and working through all, and to remind yourself of this Good and to be devoted to it is the way of the happiest concentration.

"Bless the Lord, O my soul; and all that is within me"—the demand is not only upon the soul, but upon every faculty that is within you, your mentality, your feeling nature, as well as your soul consciousness. All that is within me, bless his holy name — his holy nature—his whole, pure, true being. With this understanding let us repeat these words in the silence and rest in the spirit of them.

The Power of Blessing

One of the easiest ways to concentrate in your daily life is mentally to bless everything and everybody. And it is not merely a matter of the lips, for when you I speak these words, especially from the heart silently radiating them, you are transforming people. You are transforming things. You are removing the curse and giving everybody and everything opportunity to express themselves in the best way.

If there is anything that is especially cursing you, bless that until you find its meaning, what it is prompting you, or pressing you, to manifest, and thus dis cover the divinity in everything; that all things are working together for good to them that love the Lord. There is nothing that seems to worry and irritate you, and to cross and oppose you, but what is an instrument in the divine hands to bring forward something right and beautiful, fine and noble that lies in your nature waiting to be expressed. Instead of being irritated and feeling at cross-purposes and upset, thus losing your power of concentration, let nothing defeat or overcome you, but make everything an opportunity for rising and expressing more of your divine self, more the conqueror and captain of your soul.

"Bless them that curse you" was the divine direction, "that ye may be the child of your Father which is in heaven, for He is kind unto the unthankful and the evil." This is the divine character and whoever takes upon himself the divine method and nature is in a masterly control, the power of concentration that is back of the universe.

Healing and Being Healed

Everybody and everything that comes into your life is there for one of two reasons and generally both —either to be healed or to heal you—and I am not speaking of disease alone, except in the broadest sense of the word. Disease from "dis" and "ease," means lack of ease, lack of comfort, uncomfortable, and whatever brings discomfort to you could be called disease, whether it is poverty or sorrow, vice or chronic sickness. Whatever is of discomfort comes under the category of disease and can be healed, and your healing is your whole-ing—being made whole, holy, hearty, healthy. Everything and everybody is in your life either to press you into more of holiness, or for you to draw out of them more of this holiness or wholeness.

Therefore we learn not to run away from things, not to resist people, not to grow impatient and fret, but to transform, redeem, wholly save and uplift and bless. Just as soon as you have done that, the thing or person changes or passes out of your daily life; they cannot irritate you; they cannot trouble you. Although they may still appear in your life, they only feel harmony toward you and have nothing but blessing for you, when you have fulfilled your part to wards them. But if you run away or in other ways try to escape, because they seem so evil, you simply put off the day of salvation, that is all. You must take it up in some future form because of your wrong belief about it.

As long as you believe a thing to be evil, that very belief draws that experience into your life until your belief is healed, and you know there is no reality to the evil, that the good is all there really is.

The Way of Devotion

All this is part of the devotion which is one with concentration, because it comes from the love of truth, because you love the true Life, the Source of all good. You love the All Good, you love to express good and are devoted to it, and the first thing you know, you are quite self-possessed, poised and peaceful, and you have never thought about concentration.

The Hindus call concentration "Yoga," and con centration by devotion, Bhakti Yoga. According to their teaching there are four paths which the devotee of right concentration, or "union with God," can take: The path called Bhakti Yoga or the heart way, through loving without reasoning about it, only devoting your whole heart to God; the second way, Raja Yoga, wherein the soul and its psychic powers are given over to devotion, the aspirations and all that is spiritual in us being devoted to the one God; the third, Gnana Yoga, or giving the whole mind, making the union with God through giving all the reasoning or intellect; and the fourth, the way of our strength, our works, called Karma Yoga, wherein one gives one's self to serving the Spirit in our works, doing everything for the Lord, giving all our strength to this Divine One. The Way

The Way of Jesus Christ "But behold, I show you a more excellent way" than these four, and that is a combination of the four, as described in Jesus' presentation of the first of all the Commandments: "Thou shalt love the Lord thy God with all thy heart, and with all thy soul and with all thy mind and with all thy strength." You take the four: heart, soul, mind and strength and devote every one of them to the Spirit of the Lord. Obeying and fulfilling this commandment, you concentrate wherever you are. You are at peace. You are poised. You are free. It matters not what comes to you. This is the power of devotion.

The Convent of Perpetual Adoration

Those who go to nunneries and monasteries have certain practices of devotion which continually recall them from distraction. We read in Victor Hugo's Les Miserables about the nuns of the Convent of the Perpetual Adoration, that they were reminded of the Holy Life every half hour by the ringing of a bell. Then it mattered not what they were doing, or how much they were engaged at that moment, every nun ceased and repeated over an Ave Maria or other prayer. Oftentimes the ring came in the midst of a conversation which was causing a nun to be disturbed, distracted and resisting within herself, but they all dropped their eyes as the bell sounded and repeated over the words, that reminded them of the One of whom they were to think perpetually. You can imagine that sometimes, when a nun was losing her temper, she turned within to the quiet place and was immediately poised; that one, perhaps, was beginning to engage in some foolish occupation or conversation, then she was reminded and quickly came to herself. The description is very beautiful of the Convent of Perpetual Adoration, and there is something very high, and strong and noble in this method which com mends itself to us, though we do not need to go to convents or monasteries in order to get control of ourselves.

Our Convent-Bell

Certain things in your experience can remind you of your deep Self just as that bell reminded those nuns. Is there something in your life that annoys you? Somebody is continually drumming on the table; or when that one is practicing you begin to get worked up? Let that state be the bell and repeat these words:

"Bless the Lord O my soul and all that is within me bless his holy name."

Perhaps you have been thinking you have no control over yourself as you listen to that practicing, and you will have to complain to the landlord; yet you want to give that person liberty to live in his or her way. Let that practicing be the bell to remind you, that now is the moment of your peace and nothing can move you, as you repeat these words, "Bless the Lord O my soul and all that is within me bless his holy name."

The Value of Prayer

It was that man might have this control and self-mastery, to be ready and alert for any emergency in his earthly experiences, that Jesus gave the teaching: "Pray without ceasing, pray always." When we consider prayer in its highest meaning, we see that we can be praying continually by reminding ourselves of the All-Good in everything and in everybody. Learn to enter into your closet, retire within yourself and shut the door of the senses. Learn to speak to your Father in secret and your Father in secret will answer you openly. Thus the Master describes the way of prayer.

Meditate upon Emerson's description of prayer, for it also covers the whole ground and is as inspiring as those words of Jesus Christ. Here is Emerson's definition: "Prayer is the contemplation of the facts of life from the highest point of view; it is the soliloquy of a beholding and jubilant soul; it is the spirit of God pronouncing his work good."

It is a beautiful exposition of prayer, and it takes you from the mere externals into, and up through, your own soul to your Godhood —body, soul and spirit. If you contemplate the facts of life perpetually from the highest point of view, you are ever in prayer according to Emerson. If you lift up your joys into the high places of the soul, then anything that you do, whether you dance or sing, whether you play cards or you run and leap in the sports of the field—your soul can be jubilant, can be talking with God, and there is nothing but what can become a holy action, and a pure and true pastime, as you let your soul uplift it. Prayer is the finishing power and benediction upon the creation of God. It is God in you pronouncing His work good.

Our Desires One With Prayer

Through devotion, all your desires can be turned into declarative power, blessing God that it is so, declaring your desire to be fulfilled now. Sometimes our desires distract us, we are wishing so hard for something and fearing disappointment lest it will not come out just as we want it, and then there is agitation and disturbance. Give all your desires to the Spirit. See that everything—every single desire— is a prayer, and learn to bless God that it is now come to pass. "I thank thee, Father, that thou hast heard me," said Jesus at the tomb of Lazarus, before the work of raising him from the dead was accomplished. Learn to say, "It is so, it is so, it is so," for every wish of your heart, and then do not trouble yourself about it but when you see it come to pass, acknowledge it and be glad. So shall you pray the prayer of the righteous man—the right-thinking man—and your devotion, your "prayer without ceasing" be a perpetual accomplishment.

Those who will remember to declare their wishes already come to pass are placing themselves as the instruments of God to benefit this whole world. There comes a wishing that is so righteous and good, that is such a blessing for everybody, that, when you are wishing for anything, you are simply voicing God's desire. Then you must take the next step for its accomplishment. Declare it is so. It is done now. It is finished. It is, already.

Character, the Garden of the Lord

We are returning to Eden through this devotion, that Eden described in the first chapters of Genesis— the plenty of the Lord. Every time you "contemplate the facts of life from the highest point of view," you are cultivating that garden of the Lord within you, your blissful state, your union with God. You can bring forward that Eden-consciousness by sim ply remembering it, putting fresh plants into it and cultivating it. If there be weeds in it, fears, doubts or unspirituality, or a serpent still among the trees of subtle suggestion of something else beside God's good, it is in your power to lift that serpent up and to redeem the weeds. As Emerson says, "A weed is only a flower whose use has not been found." When you have unworthy thoughts or suggestions that do not belong to the Eden peace, instead of finding fault with yourselves, by saying, "How can I have such thoughts?" rise up and give them to the Spirit, and declare the truth, "I am pure, I am true, I am divine," and your weeds will come under the hand of a spiritual Burbank, who knows how to find use for weeds and to cultivate the best in all.

Seed Thoughts

One way to practice concentration is to see thoughts as seeds and, if you desire certain thoughts, take them and deliberately plant them in your mind. Some seed you have to watch over very carefully, very tenderly, that they may root and start growing. A strong stream of water must not play upon them,

because it will uproot the new plant. It will not do for the sun to come too directly upon some of these tender little plants. There is a wisdom, a marvelous good judgment in planting seeds of truth.

When you want to be healed of certain tendencies, or to develop certain traits, give the work over to the Spirit to cultivate. You will find yourself growing wise and tender and kind to yourself; not finding fault and lashing yourself, feeling that you are so far wrong; such is letting the sun beat down upon your tender plants and pouring the water upon them, when there should be a gentle spray and tender sunlight to those young thoughts, those budding trees that are just coming to their manifestation.

The Practice of Mental Planting

One way to plant these seed thoughts is described in Primary Lessons in Christian Living and Healing, sixth chapter, where a method of concentration is described thus: You take a thought that you wish to cultivate. Say that you desire to manifest Faith— more Faith. Suppose you are feeling shaky about something, some position you desire; you don't know how things are going to turn out, keeping you on tenter-hooks, as it were; you are not as self-possessed as you ought to be when going out to take a position, or to undertake a piece of work; you feel nervous and you see you must have more faith and more trust.

Therefore you begin to meditate upon Faith, letting that be your seed thought. It appears nothing but a word to you at first, just a dry seed and you wonder if it will amount to anything, but you proceed to plant that thought of Faith and this is the way you do it:

You mentally repeat the word seven times (I take seven because that is the perfect number) . To avoid counting, you repeat it three times, and three times and then once. Then going within yourself you shut the door of the senses and repeat it in your heart:

Faith, faith, faith—faith, faith, faith—faith. Thoughts will begin to rise, you may remember certain texts of scripture; you may begin to feel stronger because it is the law that what you meditate upon you gravitate to. You begin to draw all the mentalities that are filled with faith. You are launched upon a stream of faith. You are contacting the mentalities that have confidence, strength and trust and your faith in yourself grows stronger. Some doubt falls down, some unbelief takes to itself wings. There rises up in you a new consciousness.

This may not take place at first, for sometimes your mind begins to go off into lines that have little or no connection with faith. But so long as your mind is upon a spiritual thought, you are in right meditation. The stems, leaves, branches and fruit may not look like the seed, but eventually there is a seed at the end that is just like the first. It comes as the divine promise. First the seed of the vine, then the root, stem, branch, flower and fruit, and within the grape is the seed again, complete and perfect. If you find your mind going off into other channels, not altogether good, bring yourself back to that first thought, just as though you were beginning again. After a while you will be able to cut off those branches that do not bear fruit, with the Word. Keep your vine growing in an orderly way and by the time you have finished your meditation, you will enter into a new consciousness of your seed-thought, whatever it was. If it was Faith, you will be the stronger and the truer and clearer in your consciousness, as to confidence and trust, and ready to express a greater faith than you have ever yet experienced.

Soul Culture

This is soul culture. It is fulfilling the work that Adam was created for. "And there was not a man to till the ground," so the Lord God formed man of the dust of the ground, and breathed inspiration into him and he became an immortal soul. And he was there to till the ground. This Bible story is a description of the work of the Spirit in you every day. Every day there is something in you moulded by the Divine Hands; a character coming forth from you that is spiritual, strong, intelligent, loving; and that character is there to cultivate this ground, the earth-consciousness, to till this soil and make the most of it and show it to be an Eden of God.

In your flesh you shall see God; with that body that you have now, you can see all that belongs to heaven, peace, health, freedom and every good. This is what you are called to do. It is not merely a privilege, it is a commandment: "Let them have dominion over all the earth."

You are here to do the work which the spirit has given you to do, and that is to be happy, healthy, true, an angel on earth, drawing into the kingdom of heaven just as many as you possibly can. That is the glorious work that you are appointed to do.

Here, to Prove God, the Only Self

In devoting yourself to the Great Self, I would have you remember that it is not a Lord far away, nor a God in opposition to you, but the Great Heart that dwells within you. You are to love your Self, as God. This is the true interpretation of that first commandment, "Thou shalt love the Lord thy God with all thy heart and with all thy soul and with all thy mind and with all thy strength." But you cannot love yourself when you think it is this personality. For that is not your true Self. It sometimes seems that in this earthly ego you had taken up your enemy and were working with your enemy. That is why people hate themselves. But you must make friends with yourself, make friends with your enemies, learning to love your enemy-self in the Christ-way and you will heal it and redeem it.

This one Self is the same God that they are bowing to in India, in China and in the isles of the sea, in the temples of our City. It is You that they worship, and it is the Self of us all, and we are to prove that we are that Self; that there is nothing to us but our great Godhood and we are to prove it in the midst of the flesh, while yet we walk humbly, meekly and in lowly spirit upon this planet.

It is not an occasion for pride, for self-glorification, nor conceit, not that state where they feel their I Am is the little personality; that is gross egotism, a form of insanity. No, your Great Self is the Self of the meanest as well as the highest, it is the Self of us all, whom you worship in that other personality just as well as in this, your own, and you are to face it in your neighbor. The second commandment, "Thou shalt love thy neighbor as thyself," is the same as the first. Thou shalt love the Lord thy God in thy neighbor as well as in thyself.

Devote yourself to the All-Good in all. Take the idea of Eden and fulfill it in yourself; learn to con template the common facts of life from the highest point of view; let your soul talk to itself, a beholding and jubilant soliloquy; see that the one that we are praising in you is God, and ours is the prayer of affirmation, not beseeching but pronouncing all things good and very good.

Chapter 6. PEACE AND BLISS

Let our meditation be the closing words of Psalm 19.

There is no better book of the Bible, wherein to find leading, spiritual thoughts that are good for meditation, than the Book of Psalms. These words were studied by the old Hebrews with the understanding that they had spiritual powers which would ward off trouble and deliver from any predicament in which they might find themselves.

The words Jesus Christ spoke on the cross were almost every one to be found in the Psalms. His closing words, "Into thy hands I commend my spirit" are in the 31st Psalm; "My God, why hast thou forsaken me?" the first verse of the 22nd Psalm was the word that loosened up his interior from his exterior body. Death is always the ultimate expression of the sense of separation, and Jesus expressed a sense of separation from his Source and the result was death, but he entered into death only to conquer it by repudiating that thought of separation in his heart, and he rose triumphant over death.

The words which we will take today are affirmations, three-fold. "Thou wilt shew me the path of life. In thy presence is fullness of joy. At thy right hand are pleasures forever more." The spirit within us is showing us the path of life; that in this great omnipresence is the fullness of joy; on the right hand or power of the Spirit are pleasures, eternal and unlimited. This was the inspiration of the Psalmist. Let us take it for ourselves.

We Make Our World

WE live in a great world of our own creating, for what we meditate upon determines first of all our mental world, and this determines our outer world. Therefore it is exceedingly important what we meditate upon, since meditations upon peace and bliss determine whether we shall walk in peace and bliss; and, on the other hand, meditations upon evil may fill our whole world with evil images.

Wise are we to cease utterly and forever from meditating upon injuries; from meditating upon this little self; from meditating upon poverty. These three are important subjects to eliminate utterly from our consciousness— injuries, the little, false self, and poverty. For if we meditate upon these long enough it means insanity. Meditation upon evil is disintegrating. Not only distracting, but disintegrating. And if we meditate upon this little self, its injuries, its rights and so on, we develop a false ego, and as some one has said, "Insanity is egotism gone to seed." And that third meditation upon poverty lies back of many of the cases in the insane asylums. People thinking that thieves are after them, that their property has been taken from them, although they may be wealthy; that losses are crowding upon them, and that every man's hand is against them—this is un healthy meditation, distracting and spoiling.

Therefore we take our stand to repudiate utterly all meditation upon evil or injuries or upon this little, mortal, conceited self or our poverty-ills or lack. We learn to put in their place the good, the beautiful, and the true. This Platonic trinity of the good and the beautiful and the true can counteract all the false meditations that have been set up.

Memory Restored

Your memory is purified by the truth as you learn to dismiss from your mentality all memories of injury, mistakes, sins and sorrows. You deliberately forget these, that your memory may be clean and free and strong and true. It is written, "Thou shalt for get thy misery and remember it as waters that pass away." This is the divine promise and it is fulfilled in the man of right meditation.

Instead of being disturbed because you cannot re member certain dates, names, faces or other temporal, passing things, count them all nothing and you will soon find that you will easily remember just what you should. That list, that date, those evil memories are absolutely non-essential and must be forgotten sometime. Why not now? And as you cease to be agitated and do not congest your brain cells over things, they can slip into your mentality just when they should; and if you are to remember a date, you will remember it quickly; if a number, it will come in good time, and names will come quickly by not worrying over your memory.

The suggestions that you are weak or old or losing some of your faculties, dismiss immediately. They are not fit companions to entertain. You did not invite them and they have intruded themselves upon you. Learn to shut the door to such thoughts and say, "I never knew you. I know you not nor whence you came." This is the power of the Christ—the Master of the House (Luke 13:25) who shuts the door upon all these things that would claim place and power in the name of your good.

No suggestion that you are losing your memory should be entertained for a moment, for it is not true. That which is to be remembered by you is there for ever and you can call it up at will. This is the truth, and if you will not be deceived into believing that you are losing your memory, you will co-operate with your own Spirit so as to have the inspired memory —always thinking the right thing at the right time. Conscientiously dismiss all the false thoughts, the tramps, beggars and impostors that would clutter your mentality. By refusing such thinking you give room for the operation of the true thoughts. This is one of the secrets of peace, that quiet joy that belongs to one who is in the true life.

Serenity by Right Memory

Serenity is yours by right, and for you to demonstrate while yet you walk in the flesh, so that no one can take your peace from you. No one can do that if you will not do it yourself. Therefore never concern yourself about remembering injuries or wrongs. Sometimes people make the mistake of taxing themselves with such thoughts as, "Now I must remember that I made a mistake that time and so not repeat it." What you are to remember is that which is not the mistake but the truth, and declare to yourself, "I must remember to walk true here, to speak right there, to act wisely always," etc. Put it into the right affirmation, not the false negative, for what you keep your eye single to, you manifest. If, when Peter started to walk the waves (Matt. 14:29, 30) he had kept his eye on the Christ and had not begun to observe the wind and the waves, he could have walked all the way. It was because he looked down at the seething water and thought of the storm that he began to sink. That was the manifestation of his limited faith, so the Master said, "Why did you doubt—O ye of little faith?"

"They who observe lying vanities, forsake their own mercies." Let us not observe lying vanities, but keep our eye single to our God at all times and under all circumstances. And so it is when we speak to warn others, little ones and people coming to ask counsel of us. Learn to draw their attention to the way of safety, not the way of liability. If you were to cross a muddy street, would you look out for the mud? No, you would keep your eyes away from it, looking for the dry places where you could put your foot safely and avoid the mud. Keep your eye single to the good, and the beautiful and the true, and you will avoid their opposites without care.

Freedom From Personality

The second false meditation to be avoided is thinking upon personality. Oh, to have your mind taken off from this little personality! Why, that is the key of self-possession. It is the secret of the little child. It means that you shall not think of this little personality as your self, but look at your great Spirit and remember it; to be able to hear anything about one's personality and not be moved —whether it be praise or blame. There are some people, who are immune to blame, and can harden themselves and

feel quite at peace when fault is found with them, but who become quite elated and fairly unbalanced when they are praised. And sometimes they get so puffed up, that there comes the pride that goes before a fall, because they are so out of balance. On the other hand, there are people who can stand praise, it seems so natural, but when one little fault in them is pointed out, one little condemnation, they "go all to pieces." They are so sensitive, they grow weak as water before criticism.

Neither praise nor blame "should move us. The praise you receive, you can ascribe to your divine Self and silently say, "I give all glory to the universal Life —the Holy Spirit. I am nothing of myself. I am nothing except by this power." Thus you will keep your modesty and your peace, and praise will not be able to move you. And when, on the other hand, you are condemned or blamed, you will not be moved either, because you remember this, that the carnal self can never be anything of itself. Only as the power of the universal Spirit fills it, can it be anything. Why blame it? Why find fault with it?

Simply take every one of these things as a help to further expression of your divinity—as a means of correction, just as artists love to have the master give them "a criticism." They know they advance by it and it does not hurt them, even when he speaks quite sharply and is very sweeping in his condemnation and his general view of their work. It only means that they will correct this and go on further.

Sense of Limitation Lost

As you meditate upon your divine I Am—the Great Self that you are—you may find yourself growing so impersonal that you lose all feeling of this body. If you should have the sense at any time when in meditation, as though you had no body at all and you were very large and very universal, be not concerned. At that time you are entering into your greater consciousness and it is good; and, instead of hurrying back to the small consciousness, sit still and grow accustomed to it, for you will observe that you do not lose consciousness but have a more acute sense of being real.

I know one lady who once felt that her material beliefs were standing in her way as a healer, and she determined to have a less material mind. So one day she lay down on her couch and began to hold,

"All is Mind! All is Mind! There is no matter. All is Mind!" And as things would come up before her mentality she would say,

"Mind—not matter! That is Mind! Nothing is matter."

As she went on with this, she suddenly found herself to be pure mentality. She could not feel her body; the room had no walls about it; she was one with the whole earth; there was no time—neither past nor future. She knew things to come; she could see the people that she was going to meet as right in the present; she knew the things of the future that would take place in her life.

About that time, somebody knocked at the door * suddenly, and she was back in the old consciousness. She had learned the secrets of the prophet, that it was because he had entered into the universal consciousness that he knew no time nor space, and could know what things would take place.

The Cosmic Consciousness

There is nothing that seems to break the limits of the carnal senses so quickly as the denial of matter. For matter is a limited view. That is all. It is nothing per se, only a view. Even the material scientists have come to that conclusion, that there is no matter of itself, it is a mode of thinking. Both matter and motion are modes of thinking. And the way to recover from those methods of thinking is to break down the material limitations which one has put upon oneself and upon others. Abiding in this peace and giving yourself to spiritual pursuits and living the life, you find yourself rising to a greater conscious ness and a more pleasing realization until suddenly there comes to you the Lord —the Glory of the Lord, called the Cosmic Consciousness.

The Cosmic Consciousness is an actual experience, a realization, a joy. It is a taste of your universal knowing, feeling, being. Anyone who has ever tasted of this can never doubt that there is more than the physical sense can testify. Everything in our spiritual experience is preparing us for this baptism, so that when it shall come upon us we shall be able to contain it and be normal. If you are instructed about it, when it comes upon you, you will walk in peace, knowing yourself and the realm of appearances and able to handle things, at the same time abiding in this peace and bliss, the Way of Jesus Christ.

The Heavenly Anaesthetic

In the closing days of Jesus' earthly career, He walked through the sorrows and the strife, the ignominy and the crucifixion, calm and serene as one who has taken an anaesthetic. The earthly anaesthetic is a symbol of this super-conscious state, in which you can pass through anything and everything and be absolutely unmoved and unhurt. But it has none of the deadening effects associated with the material anaesthetic, for you have perfect and conscious control over yourself. You are poised, peaceful and blissful—in the world, but not of it—healing, teaching, uplifting and delivering your fellow-beings and yet not implicated in any of these things.

Those who have never heard of Cosmic Conscious ness, and yet arrive there may, either through fear or ignorance, do that against which the

Buddhists, in these words warn us: "Drive not back the ecstasy of contemplation." Through being instructed about this state, you will not drive back this blissful conscious ness by thinking that something is going wrong, but rather will see that you are only just entering into heaven, while yet you walk upon the earth.

The Escape From Insanity

Anyone who meditates upon the beautiful, the good and the true need never fear insanity, for he keeps the mind single to the All-Good, to the Divine Self. When people have seemed to go insane on account of religion, it is because they have had some belief in evil, which they did not eliminate from their consciousness as they went on in the spiritual life, and therefore that little grain of dust spoiled their vision.

I saw this illustrated in the case of a woman who had been unbalanced twice before I saw her in this third attack. Religious mania they called it.

A friend of hers, a student of Truth who came to my classes, asked her to come and stay with her, and one day, this student was very much concerned, because it seemed as though her friend were on the verge of being unbalanced, so she brought her to my Bible Lesson.

She sat and listened to this lesson, and at the close she rose up in the midst of the students, her face very white, and began to speak words of Scripture. I had not been told anything about her case, but I saw what the trouble was, and the whole class began to hold her in the One Mind, the Divine Mind.

She said, in a soft, plaintive voice: "They are all lost, they are all lost, and only I am saved! O my friends! Where are they gone?"

Her friend tried to reassure her with the words, "We are all here!" but she did not hear.

Then I spoke up and said, "I am here!"

And she turned to me, "Yes, but where are the rest?"

I said, "They are eternally safe."

"No," she said, "they are lost forever."

I saw the mania in a moment—that old dogma that some are elected to salvation, but the greater part are to be lost forever. I was able to keep myself in her sight as one who was saved, until she came to herself, standing by my side and began to receive the assurances that everybody was absolutely safe in life. The outcome of understanding her was, that instead of antagonizing her brothers, who wished her to be placed in a private sanitarium for a while, she agreed with them. It had always been her antagonism that would throw her off her balance. She agreed with them and in perfect co-operation did as they wished, and was afterward dismissed by the physicians of the sanitarium as perfectly sane and of sound mind. I received a letter from her not very long ago, in which she told me that she has always been poised and peaceful from that day, and she now knows she is absolutely safe through the power of the Truth.

We need never fear that we shall be unbalanced so long as we keep the good before us and our eye single to the good. It is the same with our friends that seem to be going aside from the balanced state. Remind them there is but one presence and power working in and through them and everything, and you will make yourself a vehicle—a bridge over which they may pass out of the false, disintegrating concentration into the true.

Openness to the Holy Spirit

It is for each one of us to know the bliss of heaven while we walk upon the earth, and the way is to be instructed by the Holy Spirit within us and learn to hear the little Voice—"the still, small Voice"—and receive its guidance. The object of Jesus' teaching was this very end, that you might be open to your own heavenly Voice and always be able to know just the step to take, when to move, when to be still, how to walk the straight way in peace and poise and power, the Path of Life—"Thou wilt show me the path of life" is what we can declare of the Spirit with in us. For there is where the prophets found the Spirit—within—the Lord in themselves, telling them these great truths: "Thou wilt shew me the path of life. In thy presence is fullness of joy. At thy right hand are pleasures forever more."

If there has been any earthly sense of ecstasy, whether of seeing or hearing or any other sense, be sure it is as a toy to the real thing, only a taste of the perfect and supreme satisfaction compared to the fullness of the joys that await you. It is written that it has not entered into the heart of man (into our meditation) to know the joys that are prepared for them that love God. But we must dismiss the old satisfactions that we are clinging to, in order to receive the new feelings, as a mother is not a perfect mother, who still clings to her dolls after the little babe has come to her. Many of our pleasures are only toys compared to the real bliss which is ours forever and ever.

Living by Inspiration

You rise above all fear concerning your circumstances, and enter into the inspired life, wherein every step is shown you and you cannot make a mistake. You do not need to plan your life, it is already planned and you slip into the divine way which has been arranged for you, as a car goes on the track smoothly and does not need to lay its own track, because everything is already prepared.

This means that you live, putting away all objects —not living even with a purpose or a mission, but like a child. A child has no mission. It is not living for something. It is just living. And so the highest consciousness is planless, objectless, without purpose, and without a mission. And yet it will seem to be fulfilling the greatest mission and the greatest purpose and the most divine plan that could be devised by human beings. This is the highest consciousness of the daily life that is without anxiety.

Be not anxious for anything; not about tomorrow; not anxious to live, to get well, to demonstrate anything. To be without anxiety is the way to get all these. Then your hearing can come easily; that healing comes along without an effort; prosperity and other manifestations of good are as natural as your breath. Whenever you have to make an effort to breathe, you are not very healthy, and when you are breathing with an object in view, you may find yourself in a very weary state. The highest expression is where you have no object. You simply are yourself

—the great Divine Self, without an effort. This is the way of bliss, of peace. Walk in this, day by day, for walking with God is abiding in this joy, this full ness of joy forever.

In closing, let us take that meditation which came to Isaiah in a cosmic moment, when he rose to the High Consciousness and heard the angels sing, "Holy! Holy! Holy!" We will enter into the silence and hold these words, finishing with

"The whole earth is full of His Glory!"

"Holy! Holy! Holy! Lord God Almighty!

The whole earth is full of His Glory."

The End.

BOOK TWO.
THE SERMON ON THE MOUNT

PREFACE

EMERSON says in his essay on History: There is one mind common to all individual men. Every man is an inlet to the same and to all of the same. . . . Who hath access to this universal mind is a party to all that is or can be done, for this is the only and sovereign agent."

This is the Mind of the Spirit, the same Mind that was in Christ Jesus. From It comes all inspiration and by It alone can Its utterances be interpreted.

Believing that the divine Mind is the same to-day that it was in the ages past, and that it is no respecter of persons, I have applied myself to receive interpretations of all the holy words which have come to my notice and which I believe to be inspired, since they cause men to live holier and happier lives. Thus have I studied the scriptures of the Hindus, the Chinese, the Egyptians and the Persians, as well as those of the Hebrews, and of the Christians.

Someone has said of certain writings in the Bible: "I know that they are inspired because they inspire me." This seems a safe criterion of inspiration. The result of my faith in the Spirit of Interpretation being one with the Spirit of Inspiration, and the consequent daily application of heart and mind to receiving its light, has been the opening to me of the flood-gates of scriptural understanding, so that the fullness of blessed knowledge that has already been received would take years to record.

The following commentaries were written at the request of the editor of Universal Truth, and appeared in that magazine in the year eighteen hundred and ninety-three. They are condensed and brief, the writer believing that the reader also has the Spirit of Interpretation, and often needs but a hint to light his torch and give him the joy of receiving directly from the Spirit without the intermediary of a teacher.

When you study this little volume, my prayer is that you may feel the presence of the Master whose words have so transformed this world, even as He promised, "where two or three are gathered together in my name, there am I in the midst of them." You are one, the little book another, met in his name, therefore the spirit of our Lord Jesus Christ is upon you.

A. R. M. HOME OF TRUTH, ALAMEDA, CAL., Sep 20, 1904.

My doctrine is not mine, but his that sent me.

FOREWORD. JESUS CHRIST

EVERY man is an Idea of God, a thought of the divine Mind, sent into the world upon a great mission. In proportion as he carries out that Idea a man becomes universal, and is immortalized in the recognition of mankind, which claims him for its own; for he has ceased to belong to any one race or people, or to live in any one time or place.

Jesus Christ represents the crowning Idea of man and God, the Truth that saves man from sickness, sin, sorrow, and death. He is that Truth within us that says: I am the Son of the Most High God. I am spiritual, not material; immortal, not mortal; holy, not sinful: and all dominion over the whole universe is given unto me, and all things that my Father hath are mine."

As this truth gains ground in the heart, and becomes master over the carnal and lower self, Man proves his divinity; and the history of Its ongoing within man is depicted in the life of Jesus Christ, from Its immaculate conception to Its ascension and identification with God, the universal Good.

The many years of Jesus' life that are unknown typify the silent, invisible workings of the divine Man within.

The coming forward of Jesus to minister openly signifies the stirring of the inner nature that is beginning to be recognized by the outer self. Then many thoughts begin to run to and fro in the mind in pursuit of this one great Idea; or, as it is said in the Gospel, "and there followed him great multitudes of people from Galilee, and from Decapolis, and from Jerusalem, and from Judea, and from beyond Jordan."

THE SERMON ON THE MOUNT

(From the Gospel according to St. Matthew)

Chapter 5: verse 1. And seeing the multitudes, he went up into a mountain: and when he was set, his disciples came unto him:

Mountains are symbols of exalted states of mind. When our thoughts are concentrated upon a great truth we are lifted up in mind preparatory to an outpouring of divine revelation and instruction.

2. And he opened his mouth, and taught them., saying,

THE BEATITUDES

The nine blessings called the Beatitudes are divine announcements of the presence of the Good in the midst of evil, of joy in the place of mourning, and happiness in the place of misery; " to give unto them beauty for ashes, the oil of joy for mourning, the garment of praise for the spirit of heaviness " (Is. Ixi: 3) .

Hear, O children of the Most High, says the Truth to all you that appear so desolate, destitute, and abandoned; so humiliated, grief -stricken, hungry, and persecuted: "The Lord shall give thee rest from thy sorrow, and from thy fear, and from the hard bondage wherein thou wast made to serve" (Is. xiv:3).

The word "blessed" is makarios in the Greek, and should be translated "happy," as it is in Romans xiv:22: "Happy is he that condemneth not himself in that thing which he alloweth." By substituting the word "blessed" for "happy" in this last text one can discern its true significance in the Beatitudes.

These blessings are not arbitrary awards,

but they are the result of the coming of Truth to the soul, and its recognition by men upon the earth.

3. Blessed are the poor in spirit: for theirs is the kingdom of heaven.

He is poor in spirit who realizes that as a mortal and a man of flesh he is nothing. He makes no claims or pretensions as a man of the earth, calling himself neither good nor evil, but simply nothing.

Jesus was poor in spirit. As a human being he never laid claims to either good or evil. He denied goodness: "Why callest thou me good?" he asked. He denied evil: "Which of you convinceth me [convicts me] of sin?" he asked.

In every thought, word, and deed he denied himself when looking from the standpoint of the mortal. "I do nothing of myself," he says; "I speak not of myself; but the Father that dwelleth in me, he doeth the works."

True self-denial brings the clean, free, empty sense of being that is preparatory to being filled with the Holy Spirit.

Whatever is receptive or whatever is to take in must be naked and empty. It is the vacuum that causes the water to flow. A cup being perfectly empty, even of air, would forget itself and be drawn into heaven. Therefore when the spirit is free, in right loneliness, it forces God. Eckart.

It is that emptiness that causes, through its irresistible drawing power, the substance of God to pour forth into the divine manifestation called His beloved Son. This emptiness is realized through complete self-denial and willingness to ascribe all your goodness to your God, the true Self, and claiming nothing as a being separate from God.

The soul that is completely empty of all that is not of God is called the Virgin Mary. Hear her sing: "My soul doth magnify the Lord, and my spirit hath rejoiced in God, my Savior. For he hath exalted them of low degree. He hath regarded the low estate of his handmaiden: for, behold, from henceforth all generations shall call me blessed."

I declare by good truth and truth everlasting, that in every man who hath utterly abandoned self, God must communicate Himself, according to all His power, so completely that He retains nothing in His life, in His essence, in His nature, and in His Godhead; He must communicate all to the bringing forth of fruit. Eckart.

4. Blessed are they that mourn: for they shall be comforted.

Now are the mourners blessed, not because of their mourning, but because of the comfort that the Truth is bringing to them. Here is a paraphrase of this beatitude which may be explanatory of it: Blessed are the sick, for they shall be healed. They are blessed, not because they have been sick, but because health is coming to them.

Truth reveals to the mourners that their loved ones are not lost, but are safe in the omnipresence of the Good, who lets not even a sparrow fall to the ground without receiving its little life into His own. They that mourn for their sins see themselves freed from the bondage through the Truth that sin has no power in itself, and is a delusion that can no longer deceive them.

5. Blessed are the meek: for they shall inherit the earth.

Meekness is freedom from pride, ambition, and covetousness. It is that spirit in man that cares nothing for honors, riches, glory, or power, and thus receives them all. It knows no jealousy or envy, seeks obscurity and oblivion, and does not shun annihilation.

Moses was once requested by Joshua to stop some young men among the Israelites from prophesying, but he replied to him: "Enviest thou for my sake? would God that all the Lord's people were prophets, and that the Lord would put his spirit upon them."

"Moses was very meek, above all the men which were upon the face of the earth," therefore he inherited the earth. By his word were millions of people clothed, fed, and sheltered for years in a barren desert.

Meekness claims nothing for its own apart from its fellow beings, therefore meekness never steals even in thought.

When abstinence from theft, in mind and act, is complete in the yogee, he has the power to obtain all material wealth. Pantajali

Meekness is the divine cure for poverty.

6. Blessed are they which do hunger and thirst after righteousness: for they shall be filled.

All hunger and thirst is, in reality, after righteousness. He that thinks it is material bread and wine he desires is under a delusion, and must be undeceived by hearing the truth about himself. Eating meat and drinking wine bring temporal satisfaction only, to be followed by hunger again. But to realize that the word of Truth satisfies all appetites is the complete healing of all forms of drunkenness and lust.

In Christ appetites are not destroyed nor desires killed, but all are redeemed by getting satisfaction in God, instead of in material things.

7. Blessed are the merciful: for they shall obtain mercy.

Whoever will never give another pain either

by thought, word, or deed, is exempt from pain forever. He who will not punish another, whether he merits it or not, is freed from all affliction.

8. Blessed are the pure in heart: for they shall see God.

The pure in heart are they who see the Divine only in all. The Pure One in us is the one who, from the beginning, always beholds the face of God. It is our first and real nature, knowing neither good nor evil, but only God. It is our childlikeness. The purely childlike never see impurity, for to the pure all things are pure. He who sees God in everyone and in everything is pure in heart.

9. Blessed are the peacemakers: for they shall be called the children of God.

Peace is God. Peacemakers are the manifestors of God. The manifestor of God is his child, the Son.

10. Blessed are they which are persecuted for righteousness' sake: for theirs is the kingdom of heaven.

11. Blessed are ye, when men shall revile you, and persecute you, and shall say all manner of evil against you falsely, for my sake.

12. Rejoice, and be exceeding glad: for great is your reward in heaven: for so persecuted theythe prophets which were before you.

Learn this of the Truth, O man: that under all circumstances you are blessed; not only when they are harmonious and your lot plainly happy, but also in the midst of evils. Your rejoicing is not in the persecutions or because of the torment, but because you know how to rise above them all, and take all the sting out of insult and accusation. True Christianity never sorrows,

nor is sad, for it sees all affliction and persecution to be nothing, and powerless to harm those that will not acknowledge their power because of allegiance to the true power Good, the one God. Such attitudes of mind toward evil carry one through all things triumphant and without pain.

Prove that you can keep your joy in the midst of sorrow and hold your peace in the midst of torment, and you know from thenceforth that no man can take your joy from you. You have the fountain in yourself.

THE SALT AND THE LIGHT

13. Ye are the salt of the earth: but if the salt have lost his savor, wherewith shall it be salted? it is thenceforth good for nothing, but to be cast out, and to be trodden under foot of men.

Salt preserves and purifies. It not only has a taste of its own, but it enhances the taste of everything else. As the minister of Truth, man purifies the earth of sin and disease, and preserves life, health, and holiness. All talent, genius, and every form of Good is uplifted and enhanced by salting it with Truth.

The savor or taste of salt is its spirit. Those ministers who give the theory or doctrine of Jesus Christ without doing the works are salt without savor. They become as the salt that the Jews used to gather at the Lake Asphaltites, and put upon the floor of the temple to prevent slipping in wet weather. They are not useless, they keep the people's feet from slipping; but there is a higher office yet for them.

14. Ye are the light of the world.

I AM the light of the world. One light in all, even God.

A city that is set on an hill cannot be hid.

15. Neither do men light a candle, and put it under a bushel, but on a candlestick; and it giveth light unto all that are in the house.

16. Let your light so shine before men, that they may see your good works, and glorify your Father which is in heaven.

One who has the Truth cannot be concealed. Let no man hide the revelations of God given to him. A light is not to be put under a cornmeasurer (a bushel), so the Truth is not to be hidden, but is to be given in appropriate and useful language (the candlestick) to the world, so as to light all those in the house, the state of mind ready to be benefited by it. Fear has too long kept many of the great truths from people's understanding. Now are all things being revealed.

THE LAW

17. Think not that I am come to destroy the law, or the prophets: I am not come to destroy, but to fulfill.

18. For verily I say unto you, Till heaven and earth pass, one jot or tittle shall in no wise pass from the law, till all be fulfilled.

19. Whosoever therefore shall break one of these least commandments, and shall teach men so, he shall be called the least in the kingdom of heaven: but whosoever shall do and teach them, the same shall be called great in the kingdom of heaven.

20. For I say unto you, That except your righteousness shall exceed the righteousness of the scribes and Pharisees, ye shall in no case enter into the kingdom of heaven.

The Pharisees were the people of the church who were very strict in fulfilling the letter of the law, but who were not entering into the promises which had been given to those who should keep the law. They had been promised immunity from all diseases, famines, and poverty. They were to be free from every bondage, and to be honored and enriched without limit. But they were filled with sickness, leprosy, and devils, and in bondage to a people that worshiped strange gods. Many of their number, realizing this, made the mistake of thinking more laws, and stricter, were required in order to get the favor of Jehovah, and they made harder laws and bound more burdens on themselves, until they were in abject bondage in every way, and saw not how to get out of their condition; all this because they were ignorant of their own miraculous powers.

The law had been given to Moses to lead men out of their sorrows and privations, and not to put them into bondage; and this is true of all the teaching of any great master of life. The laws of Jesus Christ are for the freeing of the race. But men's own false interpretations of his words have attached penalties and condemnations to them.

"Do not think I will accuse you to the Father. I judge no man. The word that I have spoken shall judge him," through the meaning which he shall give it.

The law is fulfilled and passes away when the spirit of it is understood and obeyed. The whole teaching of Jesus is *how to think in the heart*, how to fulfill the law in the mind and heart. If a man will never be angry in his heart or destroy with his mind he will not kill outwardly. If a man ceases to have lustful thoughts he will not commit adultery. This is true of every law; fulfill it in spirit and you will surely fulfill it in letter. But the letter of the law is not abolished until all both the spirit and the letteris fulfilled. He who thus fulfills them is as the

Christ, a law unto himself, and above the law.

The statement made in the nineteenth verse is one of the most mystical and wonderful of Jesus' declarations. Ponder it well in your heart. Who is he that is in the Kingdom of Heaven? It is the Son of God, your divine Self. "No man hath ascended up to heaven, but he that came down from heaven, even the Son of man which is in heaven" (John iii:13).

Who, then, is least in the Kingdom? The Son of God.

And who is the greatest? The Son of God; "I am Alpha and Omega, the beginning and the end, the first and the last" (the latest, the least).

Who, then, teaches men to break the commandments, and who to fulfill them? Even the same one, the Son of God. Jesus showed men how to break the law of the Sabbath in fulfilling it, and somewhere in his life he has taught how to break the bondage and limitation of every law by right fulfillment.

How does Jesus testify that the Son of God is the least in the Kingdom of Heaven? By his words: "Among them that are born of women there hath not risen a greater than John the Baptist: notwithstanding he that is least in the kingdom of heaven is greater than he" (Matt. xi:ll).

Combining these statements of Jesus we have: Whosoever therefore shall break one of these least commandments, and shall teach men so, he shall be called greater than John the Baptist.

The Scripture cannot be broken but by the master hand who knows how to fulfill in abolishing.

The righteousness that exceeds the righteousness of the Pharisees is that goodness which is above external form, and independent of it. It is that understanding of right thinking which is the Way. It is knowing neither good nor evil, but God alone.

When one thinks he cannot walk in the righteousness of Jesus Christ, then let him fulfill the righteousness of Moses.

When Tau [the Way] is lost, virtue comes after; when virtue is lost, benevolence comes; when benevolence is lost, justice comes after; when justice is lost, propriety comes after. For propriety is the mere skeleton

[the attenuation] of fidelity and faith, and the precursor of confusion. Lao-tsze, with translator's comments.

This applies to every act of one's life. If you cannot do it in the perfect way, do it in the virtuous way; if not for virtue's sake, then for charity's sake; if not for charity, then for justice; if not for justice, then for the sake of propriety. It is the least, but it is better than no good motive at all.

The parable of the Worldly Steward, in Luke, sixteenth chapter, carries the same instruction.

The highest justice or righteousness is after the manner of Jesus Christ, but there is a justice or righteousness of the world. If you cannot attain the first, follow the last.

The righteousness of the world brings temporal happiness, but the righteousness of Jesus Christ is the entrance into the Kingdom of Heaven here and now. The righteousness of the world, or the Pharisees, as Jesus expressed it, is an outward keeping of the moral or ethical laws. But in order to enter into the Kingdom of Heaven one must know how to keep the law inwardly, which is a righteousness that exceeds the old way, and is as high above it as the heavens are above the earth. This inward fulfilling of the law is the subject of the remainder of Jesus' discourse upon the mount.

SALVATION FROM ANGER

21. Ye have heard that it was said by them of old time, Thou shalt not kill; and whosoever shall kill shall be in danger of the judgment:

"Ye have heard." Jesus is speaking to men who have heard, and been trained under the Moral Law. Those who, in the world, have been educated, either by themselves or by others, to follow a code of ethics or any laws of morality are, spiritually speaking, Israelites, or Jews.

The Christ doctrine is always preached first to Israel (Matt. x:5, 6; xv:24), those having some kind of an understanding of what is lawful and right, and to a certain extent following it. "Salvation is of the Jews" (John iv:22) signifies that the steps that lead up to the Way consist in keeping the letter of the Moral Law. But to walk along the Way is to know how to fulfill the spirit of these same laws, and then to fulfill them.

Jesus does not give any new laws, but takes those that the people already have, and shows the spiritual fulfillment of them.

Many people would not kill with their hands, or by any external act break that law: "Thou shalt not kill," yet justify themselves in holding angry and revengeful thoughts toward others.

22. But I say unto you, That whosoever is angry with his brother shall be in danger of the judgment: (Revised Version).

The old version has the phrase "without a cause," which is now considered an interpolation, and should be omitted. It destroyed completely the force of Jesus' injunction, for there never was an angry man but what thought he had cause for his anger at the time of his passion.

The instruction of Jesus is that one who is angry is just as much liable to the judgment as one who kills outright. It is not sufficient to refrain from angry deeds or words; one must be perfectly free from angry thoughts.

What is the judgment to which man is liable? Does Jesus refer to a day some time in the faraway future, or to some one great act of doom? Not at all; for he says, "Now is the judgment of this world: now shall the prince of this world be cast out" (John xii:31), thus declaring judgment to be already established in the world, and to be a matter of daily occurrence and not a future event.

What is the judgment anger brings to man? Confusion and inharmony, both in his circumstances and in his body. Why cannot men see the close connection between the thoughts of the mind and the organs of the body? When strong passion fills the heart and mind, see how the circulation of the blood is changed; how it rushes to or recedes from the face; how it chills with fear or renders feverish; how it interferes with the digestion, blurs the eyes, deafens the ears, and so forth. This we see plainly when passions are strong; but when they are of a weakly though persistent nature, their immediate effect is not so plain. But let the blood be inflamed day after day for many months, then men begin to see the congested and inflamed result to some organ in the body. Continued anger produces disease, and there is no healing of certain chronic ailments but by the cleansing of the heart of all angry thoughts and tendencies.

Spiritual student, are you obliged continually to suppress anger? are you impatient? do you allow your temper to foam and ferment within? Perhaps you seldom speak an angry word, rarely act impatiently. If you have gained control of your tongue and your hands, it is well; you are fulfilling the letter of the law: now you must know how to fulfill the spirit. The inward irritation must be removed in order that you may be healed.

This is the healing of anger: Remember that your heavenly Father is Love, and you, the child of Love, are made, spiritually, in the image and likeness of unchangeable Love; therefore angry thoughts have no real place in you, and do not belong to you at all. They are a false creation, and have no real life, force, or strength. When they begin to rise in your .heart, say to them quietly and lovingly, "You are nothing, and have no place in me. I am the child of Love, and only Love thoughts can live in me." Watch and pray without ceasing, and deliverance is yours.

and whosoever shall say to his brother, Raca, shall be in danger of the council: but whosoever shall say, Thou fool, shall be in danger of hell fire.

The Christ instructs us to call no one a worthless or common fellow (raca), or a fool. In the eyes of God, all are equally precious, wise, and divine. One who views his fellow being as a body of flesh, or a mortal creature, makes a mistake, and is apt to fall into confusion and blindness because of his ignorance. He is liable (in danger of) to make a wall which will keep him from his divine inheritance if he thinks a man a fool. The Pharisees thought Jesus a fool, and, by disregarding his words, missed their opportunity. Call no one a crank or a fool because you do not agree with him. The wise man listens quietly to all without prejudice or contempt, and is not hasty to accept or reject, seeing that there is some truth back of every statement that can be made, and knowing that from those who are sincere and earnest in their search for Truth, the error will fall away for very lack of nourishment.

So also never deem anyone outside the pale of salvation. No one is worthless; nothing can equal the value of the immortal soul, which is the true Self of all them that men have called "raca."

The judgment, the council, and hell fire are three symbolical terms used to indicate three stages or states of mind, the result of holding false thoughts in the heart. The first word refers to a common court, consisting of twentythree men, which the Jews had, and which possessed the power of sentencing men to death either by beheading or strangling. The second is the Sanhedrin, consisting of seventy -two men, before which the highest crimes were tried, and which alone had the power to put to death by stoning, considered more terrible than the other death penalties. The third is gehenna, a valley without the walls of Jerusalem in which a fire was kept burning continually to consume the refuse of the city, the carcasses of beasts, and the unburied bodies of criminals who had been executed. All these words are used allegorically by Jesus and do not refer to places to which one is going after death, but to experiences which men are passing through all about us because of uncontrolled passions, and from which Truth, our savior, has come to deliver us.

23. Therefore if thou bring thy gift to the altar,, and there rememberest that thy brother hath ought against thee;

24. Leave there thy gift before the altar, and go thy way; first be reconciled to thy brother, and then come and offer thy gift.

Since "the hour cometh, and now is, when the true worshipers shall worship the Father in spirit and in truth," and not in temples made of stone, therefore the altar here referred to must be spiritual and not material. That altar is the heart, the within, and the gifts we bring to our God are all our desires, thoughts, prayers, deeds, sacrifices, and joys. By offering them to the

Great Good we identify ourselves with it, and draw down upon ourselves the harmony, joy, peace, life, and health which are the Kingdom of Heaven. Why is it that many have so often brought their gifts to God, and apparently have not been accepted? They have given away in charity hundreds of dollars, and yet suffer poverty; they have prayed many prayers, but see little return. It is because they have not studied the Master's instructions closely enough; for he has given a perfect guide into the right life, and somewhere among his sayings we shall be sure to find the key that will solve every puzzle that lies in human experience.

Right in these two verses lies one of the solutions to the oft-repeated questions, "Why is not my prayer answered?" "Why are my treatments so ineffectual?"

When you enter the silence to commune with your Good, and suddenly remember that some one is angry with you, or has something against you, first go and be reconciled with thy brother; then return, and all will be well.

Here Jesus shows that it will not do to have any one angry at us. No matter how little cause he may have for his stand, our part must be done toward bringing forth the true reconciliation.

"But suppose he will not be conciliated?" says one. There is no such thing as failure with the true Love. Be as fervent about that, then, as you have been in other things. Pray to God; all things are possible to them that believe. The inharmonious wall of your brother's anger or revenge must be pierced by your all-conquering love. One enemy reconciled becomes a mighty host to carry you into higher and greater realization of the divine Kingdom here.

Reconciliation commences in the heart, and when one's love and desire go out to another for harmony and peace between you often the Spirit brings back the sweet assurance that it is done, even when that one is over seas and far away from personal communion, such is the power of right thinking.

25. Agree with thine adversary quickly, whiles thou art in the way with him; lest at any time the adversary deliver thee to the judge, and the judge deliver thee to the officer, and thou be cast into prison.

26. Verily I say unto thee, Thou shall by no means come out thence, till thou hast paid the uttermost farthing.

The adversary (literally, opponent-at-law) is the accuser, sometimes called Satan, disease, pain, condemnation, affliction, death, and so forth.

This instruction of agreement is given us by Jesus Christ in order to escape from our adversary, and not become slave to or subject of the evil, as would result if we should oppose it. Here is taught one of the great tactics of the Spirit, the wisdom of the serpent combined with the harmlessness of the dove. Many an evil is escaped through ignoring it, or not caring about it.

But wise is he whose non-resistance is grounded upon knowledge of what is real and what is false. He does not fight evil, seeing it would be as a man who fights shadows and wars with darkness. Wisdom teaches her children to scatter the darkness by bringing in the light, and to overcome evil through not resisting it.

Your adversary is not necessarily an enemy. Your accuser may be your best friend. He perhaps accuses you of selfishness, deception, impurity, or some other false trait, and it may seem to you most unjust. But do not resent it. Ponder it in your heart, and you may discover some subtle error which has hitherto been too concealed to be visible to yourself. By your non-resistance you may be delivered from some

secret foe. "A man's foes shall be they of his own household."

Had this trait been left to increase it would finally have brought you under the Mosaic Law ("the judge"), and you would be delivered up to the "officer" (experience), and be cast into bondage of mind and body, like to a prison house. There you would remain until you had paid the last farthing that is, until the cause of your bondage, certain false thinking, had been completely canceled and replaced by true thoughts. It is always Christ (the Truth) that pays the last farthing, and frees one finally from the clutches of the law. "If the Son therefore shall make you free, ye shall be free indeed" (John viii:36).

PURITY

27. Ye have heard that it was said by them of old time, Thou shall not commit adultery:

28. But I say unto you, That whosoever looketh on a woman to lust after her hath committed adultery with her already in his heart.

Not only must man be chaste in word and deed, but also in his most secret thoughts. Thinking is the source of action, and to cleanse a fountain one must begin at its source.

Lust has no place in the spiritual mind. Whatever feeling is not high and holy is adulterous that is, idolatrous and must be cast out of the heart by the Truth. Freedom from adultery and impure thinking comes from loving God alone. When a man loves God, the Spirit, only, in a woman, then no carnal desire can enter his heart, even though she be his lawful wife. Jesus does not make any exception in this statement; there should be no lust in the heart of a man toward any woman --not toward his wife even; for the truth is that there is but one marriage the union with God. The true bride of every man is the Holy Spirit, and Christ is the true bridegroom of every woman.

"All men cannot receive this saying, save they to whom it is given" (Matt, xix:11). Those who follow close upon the Christ put away every sensual appetite, that its true spiritual correspondent may be made manifest in them.

29. And if thy right eye offend thee, pluck it out, and cast it from thee: for it is profitable for thee that one of thy members should perish, and not that thy whole body should be cast into hell.

30. And if thy right hand offend thee, cut it off, and cast it from thee: for it is profitable for thee that one of thy members should perish,, and not that thy whole body should be cast into hell.

The word "right," used in the Scripture, signifies our belief in what is good and right; and the word "left," our belief in what is evil and mysterious. For example, God, reasoning with Jonah, says: "Should not I spare Nineveh, that great city, wherein are more than sixscore thousand people that cannot discern between their right hand and their left hand?" (Jonah iv:ll). They were like those children described in Deuteronomy, first chapter, thirty-ninth verse, who could not discern between good and evil, yet be-, cause of their innocence entered into the promised land.

The "right eye" is the perception of what is good and right. If your sense of what is righteous and lawful stands in the way of your spiritual advancement ("offend you"), put it away from you. It may be a relationship which according to the law is right and just; but "whosoever he be of you that forsaketh not all that he hath, he cannot be my disciple" (Luke xiv: 33).

The plucking out and casting away is a heart process. Right self-denial taken in season saves the wise man from being submerged in mental and physical gehenna, some vice or sickness, sorrow or mistake.

The "right hand" is a deed or a power that one believes to be righteous and conducive, or necessary, to one's happiness. When Jesus told the young man who had great possessions that in order for him to advance further in the spiritual life he must sell all that he had and give to the poor, it was the same advice as the cutting off the right hand.

Whatever pleasure, lawful or otherwise, causes us to forget God and our spiritual nature is a stumbling-block, and the Truth must remove it. Better to cast away a temporal joy than to remain without the consciousness of our eternal happiness.

31. It hath been said. Whosoever shall put away his wife., let him give her a writing of divorcement:

32. But I say unto you, That whosoever shall put away his wife, saving for the cause of fornication, causeth her to commit adultery: and whosoever shall marry her that is divorced committeth adultery.

There is no divorce in the spiritual mind. True marriage is of the spirit and not of the flesh, and in the divine marriage, as in the divine life, there is no beginning and no end. Divorce is death; and going from one married state into another is like going from one plane of existence (physical) into another (psychical), neither of them being the true state, as is shown by their having beginning and ending. They who look to divorce to free them from a false marriage are like one who looks for death to release him from life. It may bring temporary relief, but it leaves the problem unsolved. In the Christ knowledge, that to God only you are married, is freedom from the woes of a carnal marriage.

Jesus gives no cause for divorce. It is Moses alone that justifies divorce. Men have said that Jesus allowed divorce when the cause was adultery, saying that in verse thirty-second he meant adultery by the word "fornication"; but that is not so. He carefully used his words, and porneia (fornication) is very different from moicheuo (to commit adultery). The first is the act of an unmarried person, the second of one who is married. In what sense, then, can this word, used of the unmarried, be applied to married individuals? In one sense only the spiritual.

One who consecrates his or her generative powers to God enters into the regenerative state, and thenceforth generates spiritually and no longer physically. Such a one, whether married (after the world) or unmarried, becomes a virgin or eunuch, one who is unmarried (Matt. xix:10-12). If such a one puts away his wife that he may refrain from fornication, he is exempt from causing his wife to commit adultery.

Impure thinking is put away from the heart and mind by continually remembering that you are not a fleshly being in your real nature, but spiritual, like unto your Father, God. The flesh is not yourself. You are spirit, not created by carnal or sensual laws, but created by pure and holy Love; and only chaste and pure thoughts can enter your mind or go forth from your heart. "Blessed are the pure in heart, for they shall see God."

SWEAR NOT AT ALL

33. Again, ye have heard that it hath been said by them of old time, Thou shall not forswear thyself, but shall perform unto the Lord thine oaths:

34. But I say unto you, Swear not at all; neither by heaven; for it is God's throne:

35. Nor by the earth; for it is his footstool: neither by Jerusalem; for it is the city of the great King.

36. Neither shalt thou swear by thy head, because thou canst not make one hair white or black.

37. But let your communication be, Yea, yea; Nay, nay: for whatsoever is more than these cometh of evil.

Whoever swears to anything, makes a vow, takes an oath, gives a promise, makes a resolution, or in any way binds himself by his word places himself under the Mosaic Law, and is liable to incur penalty through breaking the law he has made for himself.

Swearing, promising, and vowing arise from two common errors: first, belief in the future; second, distrust and lack of faith. There is only the eternal "now" in which we should live, and all that we affirm should be of the present. The Wise One says, "It is," and it is so; "It is not," and of a surety it is not: whatever is more than plain and direct affirmation or denial comes from belief in evil.

He who trusts his fellow beings needs no promises or vows. He who trusts the divine Spirit within himself knows his word to be as good as gold, and that it needs no indorsement of oath, vow, or promise; and he is willing to let it go forth in all its simplicity, trusting the

Truth in it to give it acceptability and substance.

Heaven is the throne of God. Heaven is within you, therefore God is enthroned now in your heart, and always has been; for God, the unchangeable, does not come and go, but remains ever in the same state or place. "Lo, I am with thee always" "I will never leave thee nor forsake thee."

The earth is his footstool. The "earth" is the great negative state in which is included all that is material, evil, and inimical to God. It is the state that is to be overcome, or come over, and to be put under foot. Man, following after God, must learn to have dominion over the earth, and to put all that is earthly under his feet. "Sit thou at my right hand [in the power of the good], until I make thine enemies thy footstool."

"Thou canst not make one hair white or black" by using false words, which oaths are. Only true words have the real magical powers. He who desires all his words to be magical, and to bring forth that which he wishes, must be careful always to speak words that are absolutely true, and which are based upon divine principles.

Let your communication be "Yea, yea," to all that is everlastingly good and holy, and "Nay, nay," to all that is not of God-evil, and of the carnal or fleshly nature. Ever honest, straightforward, fearless, and loving, the simpler and more direct the speech, the more Godlike is your manifestation.

THE DOCTRINE OF NON-RESISTANCE

38. Ye have heard that it hath been said, An eye for an eye, and a tooth for a tooth:

39. But I say unto you, That ye resist not evil:

According to the justice of the world evil must be returned for evil in order that evil may be diminished. This is the highest teaching that the world can give; and most of the law-givers have seen justice only in returning good for good and evil for evil. "Thine eye shall not pity," says Moses, "but life shall go for life, eye for eye, tooth for tooth, hand for hand, foot for foot" (Deut. xix:21). To-day these same old laws are still in force, and men who call themselves Christians think they are doing God service, and that it is for the good of the people to murder murderers, and if a man steal to steal from him his liberty, and in every way recompense evil with evil; whereas their Master's teachings are very clear and plain: " That ye resist not evil."

The old laws of compensation, evil for evil, were based upon the belief that evil is a great reality; in fact, to most people the greatest reality in the world: more so, even, than the existence of God. When the premise, or root, of a law is false, then its enaction is false, and all its fruits worse than useless. "Therefore every tree which bringeth not forth good fruit is hewn down, and cast into the fire." "For the tree is known by his fruits." The old Mosaic laws have never abolished evil, but every evil (punishment) which has been returned for evil contained within itself the seeds of more evils, and the last state of the average punished criminal is worse than the first. But these laws are the best man can follow until the coming of the Christ to him; then he is a law unto himself, for he sees the inwardness of all law, and knows how to fulfill it in spirit and in truth.

The Christ reveals to a man that God, the Good, is all there really is, and that evil is but negation, like darkness, having no real substance or place, and is not to be fought any more than phantoms or shadows are to be resisted. When a man understands that evil is delusion, and has no real power or presence, he will adopt the Christ method of simple non-resistance toward it, and turn upon it the light of pure goodness, and keep it there persistently until its darkness is converted into light.

The philosophy of non-resistance of evil consists in reasoning that evil is nothing and cannot be anything to anyone except he gives it substance by his belief in it and consequent fighting of it. Every word or act that recognizes an evil serves to give it an extended existence, and the way to counteract it is either by ignoring it and being indifferent to it, or, best of all, to return an active, heart-felt good for it, and it will fly as shadows disappear before the sun.

but whosoever shall smite thee on thy right cheek, turn to him the other also.

The right side of the body represents our positive beliefs, what we believe to be right and good, and which we put forward into manifestation. The left side of the body represents our negative beliefs, the unknown or secret part of our nature, that which is hidden and under cover. The word "right" has thus come to mean good, and the word "left," that which is negative in character not always evil, but generally -considered so. Thus a morganatic wife is called a "left-handed wife," and an illegitimate son a "left-handed son," and so forth.

With this understanding of the symbolism of right and left we can see why Jesus said "upon the right cheek" instead of upon the left. If any one attacks you in that wherein you know you are good and in the right, mentally turn the negative, or secret, side of your nature, and let it receive the blow. When one is smitten upon the left cheek, or accused of that which can plainly be seen (the cheek is in plain sight) to be an error or fault, then it is no effort to be non-resistant, but rather it is the policy or politeness of the world to offer the right cheek, which is to apologize and make good. But it is Christlike to be silent under undeserved assault, and even to count it deserved, in that no flesh is justified in the sight of the law .(Ps. cxliii:2; Ecc.

vii: 20). By turning the other cheek to him that smites you with the true spirit and a prayer in your heart for your assailant you will not receive a second blow, but, instead, take the sting out of the first blow, and convert an enemy into your friend.

40. And if any man will sue thee at the law,, and take away thy coat, let him have thy cloke also.

"And him who is desiring thee to be judged and to take thy tunic, let him have thy mantle also." --*Rotherhants Translation*. The coat, or tunic, is a small woolen shirt worn next the body; of small value, but necessary for warmth, cleanliness, and comfort. It signifies anything that is a necessity and comfort to a person. The cloak, or mantle, is an outer garment, not so necessary in warm Palestine, but often ornamental and of considerable pecuniary value. It signifies the beautiful and valuable among our possessions. So if any one wishes, by process of law, to take from you the very necessities of your earthly life, instead of resisting your prosecutor, rather add something richer and fairer. "For a man's life consisteth not in the abundance of the things which he possesseth" (Luke xii:15).

There is no "mine" and "thine" in the Spirit. All things belong to all, for God is the one possessor, and we, as his Son, say, "All things that the Father hath are mine" (John xvi:15), and we are all one. The early Christians understood and practiced this teaching of Christ: "And the multitude of them that believed were of one heart and of one soul: neither said any of them that aught of the things which he possessed was his own; but they had all things common" (Acts iv:32).

41. And whosoever shall compel thee to go a mile, go with him twain.

This refers to a custom of the Roman couriers, who had authority to impress into their service men, horses, and ships, or anything that came in their way and which might serve to accelerate their journey. Jesus reveals to us how to treat those who would climb up by our shoulders, or use us for their good, and who would even impose upon, tyrannize, or domineer over us. Resent it not in your heart or outwardly. Even when in your spiritual progress babes in the Way cling to you and demand your spiritual aid, and so seem to hinder your upward flight, do not avoid them or refuse them, but lend a hand, and instead of being detained you will be accelerated in your spiritual speed. Resist no imposition, but cancel it from your life by always giving it more than it demands. Recognize nothing as imposition, but only as opportunities to render divine service, and finally, by perfect non-resistance, all form of imposition shall be overcome and pass utterly out of your life.

42. Give to him that asketh thee,

"Give to every man that asketh of thee" (Luke vi:30) without discrimination or question as' to whether he be worthy or not. Does God consider whether we are worthy in giving us life? If worthiness were the gauge of our receiving, then no flesh could receive the divine benefits. But there is one in us that is worthy, and to that one, His Son, God gives everything. All our dealings should be with the Christ man in our fellow beings. If we recognize only the divine in our neighbor, then we will give quickly and without question. We shall not consider as

to how he will use the gift. "What is that to thee? follow thou me." We shall not be giving to the tramp-nature or the beggar-man or the drunkard, but to the divine in each of these, and the gift will carry something else besides material benefit -a spiritual quality that will cause the recipient to hear the voice of his inner Self, and often be the opening of the door into the higher and holier life. Give as unto the Lord, for "I was an hungered," says the Christ within, "and ye gave me meat: I was thirsty and ye gave me drink: . . . for inasmuch as ye have done it unto one of the least of these my brethren, ye have done it unto me."

You give nobody anything but what belongs to him, and is his right; and if we withhold from another what belongs to him, what better are we than a thief?

Nothing is more thorough than Jesus' teachings concerning possessions. Instead of resisting theft, he says, "Of him that taketh away thy goods, ask them not again" (Luke vi:30); instead of asking for rightful division of inheritance, he warns his followers (Luke xii:15) to "Take heed, and beware of covetousness." Place no valuation upon any material thing, and all thieving will pass out of your life. Care neither for riches nor poverty, and you will never be in want.

and from him that would borrow of thee turn not thou away.

Not only this, but "lend, hoping for nothing again" (Luke vi:35). Look for neither interest nor capital. Forgive your debtors absolutely; hold no one, not even in thought, as owing you anything. Cease to be men's creditor and you will cease to be their debtor. For as you forgive men their debts, so shall your indebtedness, both material and spiritual, be canceled. Forget that you ever gave to anybody. God, who balances and adjusts all things, will remember, and "thy Father which seeth in secret, shall reward thee openly."

OVERCOME EVIL WITH GOOD

43. Ye have heard that it hath been said, Thou shall love thy neighbor, and hate thine enemy. **44.** But I say unto you, Love your enemies,

Both these laws have the same object the destruction of the enemies. The Christ way is to transmute enemies into friends by the alchemy of the holy love-fire. Divine love operating in the heart of a man causes him to seek the spiritual Self in his enemy, and to think about that one, and to try and love the Holy One within his foe. Such love forces the better nature of his enemy into manifestation, and the victory is won. King Ptolemy was one day reproached for rewarding instead of destroying his enemies. "What!" said the noble-minded monarch, "do I not destroy my enemies when I make them my friends?"

Jesus, in inculcating this doctrine, indorsed and accented an old teaching. Buddha says:

A man who foolishly does me wrong, I will return to him the protection of my ungrudging love; the more evil comes from him, the more good shall go from me. Hatred does not cease by hatred at any time; hatred ceases by love: this is an old rule.

Lao-tsze says:

The good I would meet with goodness. The notgood I would meet with goodness also. The faithful I would meet with faith. The not-faithful I would meet with faith also. Virtue is faithful. Recompense injury with kindness.

A man's enemies are not always people.

Whatever is of evil can be your enemy --disease, sin, pain, poverty, and so forth. Even these we are not to hate, but seek God within them all, and love the God-side; for everything has a true side that can be found by them that seek. "If I make my bed in hell, behold thou art there" (Ps. cxxxix:8).

It will be seen that the Christ doctrine is even more than non-resistance. Beyond the negative, still attitude toward evil it swings you into a most active, positive, supreme, supernatural attitude toward all evil, overcoming everything with the omnipresence and omnipotence of Good. *bless them that curse you,*

This does not mean mere lip -blessing. Those who understand the power of their words, realize that to bless another with right affirmations is to bring great good to him! The ancients knew the value of their blessings, and when once their word had gone forth nothing could recall it, as when Esau bewailed his lost blessing and cried to his father, Isaac, "Hast thou but one blessing, my father? bless me, even me also, O my father" (Gen. xxvii:38).

When blessings meet curses, the evil words can have no effect. Curses are evil speakings of any kind.

Give a silent affirmation of Good for every evil word you hear, thus meeting every curse with a blessing.

do good to them that hate you, inwardly -as well as outwardly, in secret as well as openly. Kant says that "Love thy neighbor as thyself" does not contemplate doing our neighbor good in consequence of our inward affection for him, but it looks to our acquiring the affection for him by doing him good.

To do good for goodness' sake is to fire the heart with love; for we cannot help loving those whom we willingly serve.

and pray for them which despitefully use you, and persecute you;

And when ye pray, believe that ye receive, and ye shall have. Meet every sneer and insult from people, all contemptuous and scornful treatment, all tormenting and hateful conduct toward you, with an earnest, silent appeal to their high and holy nature to manifest itself. Invoke their God-being to come forth with a persistency that will not take "no" for an answer, and verily you shall win the day; for the gates of hell cannot hold out against such faith.

45. That ye may be the children of your Father which is in heaven:

That you may be your Father's child, not only in Principle, but also in manifestation; not only in the realm of Reality, but also in the realm of appearances. You are indeed His child; prove your divine character by being like your Father. for he maketh his sun to rise on the evil and on the good, and sendeth rain on the just and on the unjust.

"And ye shall be the children of the Highest: for he is kind unto the unthankful and to the evil" (Luke vi:35). There is nothing but goodness in our God; no revenge there, no punishment. He returns good for evil ever and forever. Our Holy Father is absolutely good, and in him is no evil at all. He never sends disease or death, sorrow or sin, misfortune or poverty, or any evil thing. He resists not evil, but loves his enemies; blesses them that curse him, and does good to them that hate him. The world's righteousness has been "good for good" and "evil for evil," but the righteousness of our God is Good for good and Good for evil ever and always Good.

46. For if ye love them which love you, what reward have ye? do not even the publicans the same?

47. And if ye salute your brethren only, what do ye more than others? do not even the publicans so?

Except your goodness exceed the righteousness of the world, ye can in no wise enter into your divine inheritance. Anyone can give good for good. It is natural to be loving and kind to those who treat us well. It is human to bless those who bless us, and speak well of those who are our friends. All these things we will do naturally just in living in the old earth-life. But how do we advance in the Way by such walking in a circle? It is but the old treadmill practice of the world, that leaves a man and his race at the close of his earthly career just where it found him.

It is easy to be an angel among angels, but God demands that you be a Christ among mortals; that you prove your divinity in the midst of humanity, your Godhood in the midst of demons.

48. Be ye therefore perfect, even as your Father which is in heaven is perfect.

The perfection of God has always been perfection. God did not become perfect, but always was, is now, and always will be perfect. Therefore to be as perfect as God, one must always have been perfect. This is true of the real Self. It was perfect in the beginning and is so now. It has never fallen, or sinned, or been imperfect in any measure. Return to your divine Self. BE YOUR SELF ---this is the gist of the Christ-teaching.

IN THE SECRET PLACE

The realm of causation is in secrecy. All the Father's causative work is done in secret, but its fruit, or manifestation, is open. This truth is symbolized throughout nature, and even also in the arts of men.

The seed works underground, sometimes a long time, before it puts forth its green leaf, and throughout its growth its laboratory is still most secret. The embryo babe is hid from sight. Both the land and the sea cover thousands of treasures diamonds, pearls, gold, coal, coral, still in process of formation, preparing for manifestation which may be ages hence.

In the arts of men they continually hide the mechanism that produces the fair showing the works of a watch, the dynamo that lights, the kitchen that produces the banquet; there is not a work of man's hands but has its secret region of causation.

In order to be master of any work of art or nature one must go right into its secret place. So, herewith, Jesus would show us how to get into the secret place of the Most High, the realm of causation. Act as God acts, who does not care to what men ascribe His good deeds. Let your religious acts (verse one) be most secret; your charitable works (verse three), your praying (verse six), your self-denial (verse eighteen) all must have their root in the secret Presence, that their fruit may be of the everlasting and heavenly nature.

Chapter vi: verse 1. Take heed that ye do not your alms before men, to be seen of them: otherwise ye have no reward of your Father which is in heaven.

The word "alms" should be "righteousness." It is a different Greek word from the one used in verses second, third, and fourth. It signifies devotional acts and observances.

Make no parade of your religion. Do nothing, religious or secular, "to be seen of men." Draw as little attention as possible to your personality. Do not advertise your demonstrations so as to make your personality conspicuous. Those who do this get an earthly reward, but miss the highest, which is the eternal power to demonstrate belonging to the true Self.

"Reward with [not of] your Father which is in heaven" is reaping the same results in unison with God. "My Father worketh hitherto, and I work."

Again, this instruction of the Master will keep us from doing things in order to be an example to somebody. It takes away all human selfconsciousness, and our deeds are without affectation, just like the little child who simply does a thing because it is natural. There is one example for all, even God, and no human being is our example, or should set himself up to be one. God in Jesus is the one to follow; God in me, and God in you, and none other. This direction to do nothing to be seen of men is another way (the negative) of presenting the idea embodied in verse sixteen, chapter five. Let your light so shine that men will glorify your Father which is in Heaven, and riot you personally. After performing a great cure or other good work, if you can succeed, like Jesus (Luke xviii: 43), in turning the gratitude of the beneficiary away from yourself to God the same will come to pass in you that was promised to Moses (Ex. vii:l) and the house of David (Zech. xii:8), and manifested in Jesus, the becoming as God to the people.

2. Therefore when thou doest thine alms, do not sound a trumpet before thee, as the hypocrites do in the synagogues and in the streets, that they may have glory of men. Verily I say unto you, They have their reward.

The word "hypocrite" is from the Greek hupokrites, meaning a stage-actor or masked player. It was the custom in those days for performers to herald their coming (like the circus of to-day) with advertisement through trumpet and pageant, or parade of some kind. The word hupokrite was not used in the evil sense then that it is now, but could be an epithet of praise or blame according to the individual judgment of the hearer. Call a man "a good actor" to-day and all will depend upon the connection of the words as to whether it is a compliment or a term of approbrium.

Taken in its largest sense we see that all human beings are actors (hypocrites). "All the world's a stage and all the men and women merely hupokrites," to paraphrase Shakespeare. The Latin persona, from which comes "personality," is identical in meaning with hupokrites. Thus we see that the word "hypocrite" could be applied to any personality, which is but a mask of the true Self. As sinful beings we appear to be what we are not; for are we not in reality pure, holy beings, and yet seem to be weak, sickly mortals? Be not as the hypocrites, but appear as you are; act your true character, which is perfect.

Sound no trumpet before you. "I receive not honor from men," says the Christ. It is human nature to love the praise of men, but it is divine to love the praise of God only. In all ways Jesus would have us lift up our human loves into the divine; for the human is temporal and unsatisfying, while the divine is eternal and allsatisfying.

3. But when thou doest alms, let not thy left hand know what thy right hand doeth:

"Thine alms" are your forgiving, loving, charitable good deeds. Not only are we to be careful so that they shall not be seen by the world, but they are even to be secret to our own selves. Do not, even in your most secret thoughts, claim the slightest credit for them, or congratulate yourself, or give yourself one particle of praise. The tendency of the mortal is to whisper to its left hand what its right hand has done, to condone its delinquencies (the left hand stands for our negative acts, deeds of omission, evils, and so forth) by remembering its meritable deeds. As long as this is done there is not the realization of the commonest conduct of our spiritual Self.

Good actions must be our natural habit. As we do not go about telling people we breathe, or taking credit to ourselves that we eat, so also we should realize that our goodness should be as spontaneous and as unassuming and as free from self -consciousness as every function of the physical organs.

Jesus advises us to look upon all our highest and noblest actions as just what we ought to do ---"So likewise ye, when ye shall have done all those things which are commanded you, say, We are unprofitable servants: we have done that which was our duty to do." We are "unprofitable" because nothing the mortal can do brings any gain to our master Self. Never do anything for reward, but all things regardless of fruit or consequence. More than this, Jesus teaches us to avoid earthly recompense as much as possible (Luke xiv: 12-14).

4. That thine alms may be in secret: and thy Father which seeth in secret himself shall reward thee openly.

Nothing is secret that shall not be made manifest. No spiritual treatment is ever lost, no good work is ever wasted. And the more secret it is, the more it is within, at the source of good, the greater and more complete is the manifestation.

The Father does not reward secretly, but always openly.

PRAYER

5. And when thou prayest, thou shall not be as the hypocrites are: for they love to pray standing in the synagogues and in the corners of the streets, that they may be seen of men. Verily I say unto you, They have their reward.

The hypocrite (actor) is one who pays attention to the external and neglects the internal; who follows the letter of a doctrine, but omits its spirit; who is exacting as to the form of words (prayers, ordinances, laws, statements, and so forth), but who either forgets or ignores their power and substance, "Having the form of godliness, but denying the power thereof" (2 Tim. iii:5).

The hypocrite in us talks much, but does little; theorizes and has opinions, but bears none of the fruits of the Spirit; nor yet its leaves,

which are for the healing of the nations^ body, mind, and soul.

In true prayer there is no consciousness of the presence of men, but only of God; this is also true of spiritual treatment, which is declarative prayer.

Prayer is communion with God, and is the means by which power is transmitted from the universal to the particular. All men are continually praying to some one or some thing, but prayer to God is recognition of the power and the presence of the Almighty Good alone. It is not for the changing of God; it is only the mortal that changes. True prayer from the heart of the devotee is THE WORD which manifests all that ever is manifested.

6. But thou, when thou prayest, enter into thy closet, and when thou hast shut thy door, pray to thy Father which is in secret; and thy Father which seeth in secret shall reward thee openly.

"Enter into thy closet," or inner chamber.

That this direction is to be taken in its spiritual sense is shown by the actions of Jesus, who did not seek any literal closet when he prayed. The inner chamber is the interior consciousness. When you pray, turn within, or retire within yourself, and shut the door by keeping out all worldly, wandering, and idle thoughts. When learning to pray, this may require steady watching. Brother Lawrence, who lived two hundred years ago, in telling how he learned to commune consciously with God, says:

That useless thoughts spoil all; that the mischief began there; but that we ought to reject them as soon as we perceived their impertinence to the matter in hand, or our salvation; and return to our communion with God. That at the beginning he had of ten passed his time appointed for prayer in rejecting wandering thoughts and falling back into them. Practice of the Presence of God.

"Thy Father which is in secret." God is within you, for Heaven is within (Luke xvii: 21) , and to address our Father which is in Heaven we must know God to be in us, and not away off, as children have been so ignorantly taught to believe in the blue sky, or some other indefinite, unreachable place. Therefore let the mind seek the peaceful center of being by causing the thoughts steadily to dwell upon the presence and power of God's kingdom.

7. But when ye pray use not vain repetitions, as the heathen do: for they think that they shall be heard for their much speaking.

The heathen, those who do not know God, repeat prayers without feeling them, using words that are but an empty form, and therefore are not heard, that is, responded to.

Repetition is all right; Jesus himself repeated the same prayer three times on one occasion. But it is vain repetition that the disciple is warned against.

Better to speak one sentence in which is faith and confidence, and warm, loving realization than many statements that carry no conviction of their truth to you, but still sound like empty words, though you know them, intellectually, to be true. "Hold fast the form of sound words" (2 Tim. i:13), and then fill the form with the substance of strong faith and warm love, and such a prayer is its own answer, for it is the very Word itself which brings to pass the thing desired.

8. Be not ye therefore like unto them: for your Father knoweth what things ye have need of, before ye ask him.

Prayer is not for the purpose of informing God of your needs. Your Father knows just what spiritual realities you need to bring forth the desire of your heart. The object of prayer is to place ourselves and those we pray for in a receptive state to receive the divine blessings that are ever being outpoured.

THE LORD'S PRAYER

9. After this manner therefore pray ye: Our Father which art in heaven, Hallowcd bc thy name.

10. Thy kingdom come. Thy will be done in earth, as it is in heaven.

11. Give us this day our daily bread.

12. And forgive us our debts, as we forgive our debtors.

13. And lead us not into temptation, but deliver us from evil: For thine is the kingdom, and the power, and the glory, for ever. Amen.

"After this manner" we are to pray, not necessarily using the same words or expressing the same desires, but to observe the general form and substance of the communion.

There are many points of resemblance in this prayer to David's found in 1 Chronicles, twenty-ninth chapter, tenth to nineteenth verses. But whereas David, in common with all the Old Testament prophets and lawgivers, calls upon God as Lord, it is Jesus who first addresses Him as "Father" not alone "my Father," but "your Father" and "our Father."

What greater baptism of spirituality and of uplifting could there be than a realization of the import of those first two words, "Our Father"?

The first step in right prayer is the raising of the thoughts to God by devoting the first part of the prayer to praises and blessings upon the character and power of the great Spirit. The mind, though cold and fearful at first, is often filled with faith and inspiration by simply remembering the divine nature through praising it. All this is for man's benefit, to set his mind aright not that it in any way affects the loving Almighty Father.

"Which art in heaven" within us. The Spirit of God dwells in you your very life, health, love, purity, and all-goodness. Within is the storehouse of all bounty and the fountain of life, and prayer opens the storehouse, and sets the fountain flowing in whatsoever direction you will.

"Hallowed be thy name." Holy is thy Being without blemish, pure and undefiled.

The man who exalts and reveres the name of

his deity, though he be a heathen, shall come finally to the true magical Name of God, which is no longer hidden from those whose will has become identified with the divine will. Those who use any deific name lightly or in vanity are like children who play with gunpowder. Strong feelings of any kind are fire, and they are as liable to touch the name as sparks to come to the gunpowder. To the spiritually wise and loving THE NAME is revealed because they have hallowed every name of deity. "Thou hast been faithful over a few things, I will make thee ruler over many things" (Matt. xxv:23).

"Thy kingdom come." "All things whatsoever ye shall ask in prayer, believing, ye shall receive" (Matt. xxi:22), therefore believe that God's kingdom is come, and it shall be unto you even as you believe. Changing the prayers from the form of petition and asking to the affirmative and declarative form of expression often brings realization to the mind. Thus, to pray, "Hallowed is thy name; thy kingdom is come; thy will is done; thou dost give us our daily bread; thou dost forgive; thou dost lead us," carries out Jesus' direction of praying as though we had already received our answers, and thereby brings them to pass.

"Thy will be done in earth as it is in heaven." The earth is the outer man, Heaven is the inner man. The will of God done in Heaven produces peace and prosperity, health and freedom. When doubts come into the mind as to whether our prayer is according to God's will, let us remember how His will is done in Heaven.

Does the divine will done in Heaven bring forth sickness or sorrow, poverty or death? No. Then His will done in earth will not result in these. When Jesus prayed for the cup to pass away, his prayer was granted, for the Father never refused him anything. But it was the method of its passing away that he refers to when he says: "Not as I will but as Thou wilt," knowing that the Father's way would be the easiest and the quickest, and would bring the greatest good to all, whereas the human way would be the hardest and the least desirable in the end. "If this cup may not pass away from me, except I drink it, thy will be done." Not by resistance could the evil be overcome, but by the redeeming act of identifying himself with the cup. This was the Father's way.

When in doubt as to how the divine will in granting your prayer is to be accomplished always use Jesus' words, trusting the Father's way to be the easiest, quickest, and grandest way of bringing to pass your desire, not only bringing you good, but also bringing the highest good to all.

The simple utterance of "Thy will be done in earth as it is in heaven" continued faithfully from day to day will cleanse us from every unheavenly thought, and bring forward that One in us who is the everlasting habitant of the divine regions.

"Give us this day our daily bread." One of the offices of prayer is to cause us to acknowledge the source of our Good. He who realizes that it is God that gives us even our literal bread and riches will never be in want, for he will not turn his mind to other gods, such as human intellect, material work, personalities, for his support, but will continually acknowledge the true Source, and thus make himself receptive to divine supply.

The spiritual significance of "day" is season of illumination and manifestation; "bread" is Truth, or Word of God (Deut. viii:3). "Give us for this manifestation the Truth, or Word, belonging to it."

"Forgive us our debts" can have as literal fruit as the preceding petition. Material debts are canceled by God, just as physical hunger is satisfied and physical diseases are healed.

Indebtedness of all kinds, physical or moral, is canceled in the same proportion and in the same manner as we cancel the debts that others owe us, for this is the outworking of the law and the prophets: that whatsoever ye do unto men, even so will your Father do unto you.

The invocation for forgiveness is the central point of the prayer, the apex of the prayerpyramid, therefore Jesus dwells upon it after finishing (verses fourteen and fifteen, which see), and through explaining the reciprocal law of forgiveness he gives one of the secrets of prayer-answering, which is: "Give, and it shall be given unto you."

"And lead us not into temptation, but deliver us from evil." In leading us into spiritual heights, save us from the temptations that shadow them. God tempts no man, yet the outpouring of the gifts of the Spirit may seem to bring new phases of life that will cause the disciple to fear a falling away from the Spirit. Now this closing petition is a provision for that fear. The one who prays for a gift of God may suddenly have the thought: "Perhaps if God grants this I shall be led into sin, or some great evil may follow." If it is health he prays for he thinks: "If God makes me well, perhaps I may return to my old excesses; "if it is prosperity, the adversary may whisper: "You will forget God if you are prospered." To all these suggestions this is the reply: "Lead me, my Father, away from the evil of this, into thy safety," and we are then to remember to leave the issue with God, trusting him to grant our heart's desire, and at the same time deliver us from its snare.

After being baptized with the Holy Spirit, there came to Jesus his first testing, through which he passed unscathed. The good men receive may seem to bring them into evil experiences, just as light seems to bring shadows. Yet as shadows are no part of the light, so these temptations are no part of the spiritual life, and are to be dealt with as we deal with shadows pass safely through them by carrying the lamp of the Lord. "Thy word is a lamp unto my feet, and a light unto my path" (Ps. cxix:105).

"For thine is the kingdom." The ruling, the dominion, the control is all thine not Satan's, or the devil's. "Thine is the power," Almighty Life; not disease or death, sin or sorrow. "Thine is the glory" and the honor; it is never to be given to mortal man, or to any personality.

Jesus' prayer closes in the same way that

David's begins (1 Chron. xxix:ll), the same Spirit being the alpha and omega of both.

FORGIVENESS

14. For if ye forgive men their trespasses, your heavenly Father will also forgive you:

15. But if ye forgive not men their trespasses, neither will your Father forgive your trespasses.

Being forgiven is a state of mind, and no one is forgiven unless he thinks he is. By exercising kindness and mercy toward another who has sinned we can realize how that same feeling may be extended toward us when sinful. And the more lenient we grow toward others, the more we come out from the bondage of condemning and being condemned, and consequently out of its effect or symbol, physical pain, disease, and death, until finally we stand where no thought of vengeance or punishment for an offender can enter our heart, even when the sin is against our beloved and those who are helpless and innocent. Then we enter into full freedom. He who forgives all receives full forgiveness.

NO SAD APPEARANCES

16. Moreover when ye fast, be not as the hypocrites, of a sad countenance: for they disfigure their faces, that they may appear unto men to fast. Verily I say unto you, They have their reward.

17. But thou, when thou fastest, anoint thine head, and wash thy face;

18. That thou appear not unto men to fast, but unto thy Father which is in secret: and thy Father, which seeth in secret, shall reward thee openly.

"Is it such a fast that I have chosen? a day for a man to afflict his soul? is it to bow down his head as a bulrush and to spread sack-cloth and ashes under him? wilt thou call this a fast, and an acceptable day to the Lord?" asks Isaiah (lviii:5), and then he proceeds to show that true fasting is loosing the bands of wickedness, undoing heavy burdens, breaking yokes, and so forth. The word of denial spoken in heart and mind, and carried out in speech and action, breaks every chain, and" loosens every bond, and unfastens every yoke that enslaves mankind. This is the fast the Good has chosen.

There are conditions in human experience that require more such fasting than others. They are when poverty besets the disciple, and pain, and persecution; when he comes face to face with loss and deprivation, failure and death. Then he must faithfully hold to the truth of the unreality of evil and the omnipotence of Good. Then be not of sad countenance, but "the Lord make his face shine upon thee, . . . the Lord lift up his countenance upon thee, and give thee peace" (Num. vi:25, 26). You live, move, and have your being in the Kingdom of Heaven, and there are no gloomy faces there, or sorrowful mouths, or tearful eyes.

Put away from you every sign of woe. The true Christian puts away all mourning clothes and other symbols of grief. He who realizes that there is no death, and that his beloved is immortal, would but contradict this truth and repudiate it by assuming apparel that testifies to the presence and power of death. Those who wear sad countenances and garments of woe are magnets to draw that kind of thoughts and conditions to themselves, and in that way they make it hard for themselves to break through the gloom and sorrow of the world when they most wish to do so.

It is a mistake to think that in order to get sympathy and help it is necessary to make people realize how much pain we are in, or what hardships of poverty we are enduring, or how sick we are, or how persecuted.

"Abstain from all appearance of evil," that thou appear not unto men to fast, but carry all these things to the secret place, and your Father will be your sure and lasting relief.

TRUE VALUATION

19. Lay not up for yourselves treasures upon earth, where moth and rust doth corrupt, and where thieves break through and steal:

Herein Jesus shows how to fulfill the spirit of the commandment, "Thou shalt not steal," and also, "Thou shalt not covet."

Cease from giving any value to earthly things. The material world is without real substance in itself, and is altogether an imaginary existence. It is an error to place value upon it, and this error bears false fruit, like every other mistaken belief. "Beware of the illusions of matter," says Buddha.

God is spirit, and his kingdom spiritual. "My kingdom is not of this world, my treasures are not material," says the One who knows. Divine supply is introduced into the earth by man's adopting the economics of Heaven no saving up, no "laying by for a rainy day," no frugality, but following the law of divine abundance, "Give, and it shall be given unto you."

The sage does not lay up treasures. The more he does for others the more he has of his own. The more he gives to others the more he is increased. Tao-tehking.

There are no "private property rights" in God's world. Jesus reveals that there is to be no claiming earthly property, even that which is counted by the world legal and legitimate. This is shown by his word to the young man who asked him to direct his brother to divide the inheritance with him. "Beware of covetousness," is the Master's reply.

Material supply is limited by man's belief in limitation, manifested as waste and parsimony. Whoever believes that substance can be wasted is the wasteful one of the earth, whether he throws away or hoards up. Lavish nature knows no waste, yet produces bushels of fruit that are never eaten and thousands of flowers that are never seen.

Giving value to material things is mental thieving taking from spirit and giving to matter and people who do this are stolen from. He who cares nothing for earthly treasures is exempt from the ravages of the thief.

Not prizing things hard to procure keeps the people from theft.

If men would abandon their skill and forego their gains, thieves would have no more existence. Lao-Tsze.

When abstinence from theft in mind and act is complete in the yogee, he has power to obtain all material wealth. Patanjali.

Selfishness, covetousness, competition, are the moths in the garments of false living; acquisitiveness, avarice, fear of poverty, are the rust that stiffens the joints -of old age. The thieves are whatever may seem to steal away our peace, our health, our joy, or our life.

20. But lay up for yourselves treasures in heaven, where neither moth nor rust doth corrupt, and where thieves do not break through nor steal:

Fill your hearts with right thoughts and desires, fill your lives with unselfish deeds and actions based upon the knowledge that all things belong to all, and that we give to others only what belongs to them, and receive from others what has been ours from the beginning.

The charity of the world is an abomination in the sight of God (Luke xvi:14, 15). Love, the charity of God, knows not "mine and thine," but holds all things in common.

21. For where your treasure is, there will your heart be also.

We become like that which we think most about.

What thou lovest, man, become thou must; God, if thou lovest God; dust, if thou lovest dust. Johannes Scheffler[x]

If our love is centered upon some mortal, our heart shows forth mortality. If we treasure up things belonging to the past, like relics, mementoes, old letters, and so forth, we become like the past, and presently are, to sense, no more. The true Christian lets the dead past bury its dead. He remembers Lot's wife, and does not get into a rut. We will not show the effects of time if we cease to think about time, and live in the eternal Now.

CONCENTRATION UPON GOD

22. The light of the body is the eye: if therefore thine eye be single, thy whole body shall be full of light.

The lamp of the body is the eye, the illuminating power of the soul is its perceptive, intuitive faculty. "If thine eye be single," if all your intuitions be focused upon God and his manifestation, then your whole soul is filled with Truth. Our eye is single when we believe in God as the only power and presence. Our eye is double when we see two powers, good and evil, or have two loves, God and the world, or in any way believe in the reality of two opposing beings or powers.

Concentration of all the faculties upon God drives every particle of darkness from us body, mind, and soul. According to the first and great commandment, we are not to have any thought in our mind but of God. Thou shalt love the Lord, thy God, with all thy mind. We are not to have any feeling, affection, or emotion but for God. Thou shalt love the Lord thy God with all thy heart; and our whole vitality ("all thy strength") and every aspiration ("all thy soul") is to be given to God, and God alone. This is the "one-pointed" mind spoken of in the Bhagavad Gita that overcomes the world and captures the heavenly Kingdom.

23. But if thine eye be evil, thy whole body shall be full of darkness. If therefore the light that is in thee be darkness, how great is that darkness!

The better translation is, "How dark is the darkness!"

Of the true Man it is written, he "shutteth his eyes from seeing evil" (Is. xxxiii:15), and of God, "Thou art of purer eyes than to behold evil" (Hab. i:13). Therefore, following our great example, God, we must have the pure eye, the single eye, that beholds only Good, the everlasting God.

If evil comes into the mind, then there is an adulterous mixture, followed by confusion and darkness in proportion as evil is entertained and believed in as reality.

To believe that God is a God of wrath, or that He sends both evil and good, is to have a light that is darkness. There is no cheer in its ray, no healing in its beams, no life in its shining. Therefore to such a one darkness is very dark, evil most evil, sin very black, and all the shadows of man's life gloomy and fraught with ill-omen.

24. No man can serve two masters: for either he will hate the one, and love the other; or else he will hold to the one, and despise the other. Ye cannot serve God and mammon.

The man who is the greatest success in any pursuit is the one who devotes his whole being to it, and makes all things bend to that end. We cannot serve God and worldly riches, and make a success of both. Nothing but whole-hearted service to God can win full God-powers and manifestation.

What we acknowledge to be our master, to that we are servants. No man should acknowledge two masters, for one is his master, even God. To own to the dominion of other powers beside God is idolatry. Abandon all material seeking forever, for matter is without substance and real-, ity; it is vanity and nothingness, and he who pursues it follows illusion, and forsakes his own good.

NO THOUGHT FOR WORLDLY WELFARE

25. Therefore I say unto you, Take no thought for your life, what ye shall eat, or what ye shall drink; nor yet for your body, what ye shall put on. Is not the life more than meat, and the body than raiment?

Anxiety and worriment about support and supply are acts of unfaith, and many a disease has its source in such thinking.

All external food and raiment are symbols of the true substance upon which the soul is fed and with which it is clothed. Feed the soul with heavenly nourishment and the earthly food will follow just as surely as a shadow follows the thing that casts it.

Clothe the mind with right thoughts and Godwords, and the outward raiment will be forthcoming, most appropriate and efficient. Meditate upon the true life-is it not more than meat? and the spiritual body --is it not more than raiment?

Make no laws as to what you ought to eat, or to drink, or to wear. Nothing without a man can affect him, but the thoughts he has about these things, and all things, are what affect him (Mark vii:15-21). If a man believes his food will hurt him or make him less spiritual, it will be unto him according to his faith. If he takes care of his thoughts and desires, to keep them pure and spiritual, then he can follow Jesus' instructions "to eat such things as are set before you" (Luke x:8), and can claim the divine promise, "If they drink any deadly thing, it shall not hurt them" (Mark xvi:18).

26. Behold the fowls of the air: for they sow not, neither do they reap, nor gather into barns; yet your heavenly Father feedeth them. Are ye not much better than they?

27. Which of you by taking thought can add one cubit unto his stature?

28. And why take ye thought for raiment? Consider the lilies of the field, how they grow; they toil not, neither do they spin:

29. And yet I say unto you, That even Solomon in all his glory was not arrayed like one of these.

30. Wherefore, if God so clothe the grass of the field, which to-day is, and to-morrow is cast into the oven, shall he not much more clothe you., O ye of little faith?

Live like the birds, the flowers, and the grass. Abandon yourself wholly to trusting in your God for all things.

Which of you by taking anxious thought can add one particle to his stature, or change in the least degree the material world? Anxiety and material desire accomplish nothing. It is only as thought is spiritual and God-trustful that it has power over the material universe.

"Labor not for the meat which perisheth," but work only for love's sake. Unselfishness and absolute God-trust are the cure for poverty. Christ frees man from the Adam curse of work by showing there is but one work to do, "my Father's business." Banish fear from the mind, and every man will gravitate to that work which will be most congenial to himself, and which will render most loving and able service to his neighbor. Man, like God, loves to work his joy is in carrying out his ideas.

By realizing the spiritual correspondent of the earthly work which a man is engaged in, he knows how to work for the Lord, and that it is the Lord that works in him, and then no work can tire him, or make him feel material and separate from his God. If he is a carpenter, he will remember that he is ever building the temple of God for all for whom he works; if she is a housekeeper, she is ever cleansing and preparing a place for the Lord in the hearts of the people she is giving them the bread of Truth, and it is as easy to supply the symbol when one is giving the substance as it was for Jesus to feed the thousands with material food because he had first given them the real food of life.

God both feeds the ravens and clothes the grass by being Himself, and by radiating His supply to whatever and to whomsoever will let Its presence come.

31. Therefore take no thought, saying, What shall we eat? or, What shall we drink? or, Wherewithal shall we be clothed?

32. (For after all these things do the Gentiles seek:) for your heavenly Father knoweth that ye have need of all these things.

33. But seek ye first the kingdom of God, and his righteousness; and all these things shall be added unto you.

The kingdom of God is here in all its beauty and power, just where the earthly kingdom seems to be. Seek Its presence alone. Seek to bring forth the beauty of your character and soul, and the external beauty will be added. "The king's daughter is all glorious within" and thus it follows that "her clothing is of wrought gold" (Ps. xlv:13).

It is useless work, vanity of vanities, to try to beautify the outside when one is not, first of all, looking after the within, the reality (Matt, xxiii: 25).

Harmony and spirituality in the family is the substance of the beautiful home, and makes its beauty lasting.

Beauty of soul remodels the body, and confers upon it youth and strength commensurate with the desire of its owner.

As with beauty, so with knowledge, and all the arts and sciences. He who seeks to know God will have all earthly knowledge added. He who seeks the harmonies of spirit will unfold his true musical genius, and have added the earthly power to express music.

In all things both great and small seek first the spiritual reality, and the symbol will be added without a single thought or effort upon the part of the recipient.

34. Take therefore no thought for the morrow: for the morrow shall take thought for the things of itself. Sufficient unto the day is the evil thereof.

Give no thought to the future, because there is no future. Fears concerning coming days and speculations about the "'hereafter" are vain imaginings. We never live except in the present. Consider all thoughts that dwell upon. the future (whether they are evil or good) as present unbelief, to be redeemed by the Truth of what now is. Whatever is to be is now. Only the Good really is.

Sufficient to meet every evil is the day (the light or understanding) for it. "As thy days [according to their character and needs], so shall thy strength [knowledge, faith, and power] be" (Deut. xxxiii:25).

FREE FROM JUDGING

Chapter viii: verse 1. Judge not, that ye be not judged.

2. For with what judgment ye judge, ye shall be judged: and with what measure ye mete, it shall be measured to you again.

The word "judgment" (krisis) is not the same as the word "condemnation" (kata-krisis) , neither does "to judge" (krino) always mean "to damn" (kata-krino) . A judge may pronounce a thing good, and may give his word in favor of the one brought before him. This distinction between judgment and condemnation has not always been regarded by the translators of the Bible; often they have used "condemnation" and

"damnation" whcrc thc truc word is "judgmcnt." Scc John v:29, Mark iii:29, 2 Thessalonians ii:12, where "damnation" should be "judgment"; and John v:24, also iii:17, 18, 19, where "condemnation" should be "judgment."

Not only are we not to condemn to pronounce evil against any one or any thing, and to mete out punishment but also we are not to sit in judgment, neither to declare for nor against. In other words, we are to cease eating of that forbidden tree which causes us to see double, the tree of the knowledge of good and evil. We are to know only that Good which has no opposite. We stop our ears from hearing of evil, and shut our eyes from seeing it (Is. xxxiii:15). We judge not after the sight of mortal eyes, neither reprove after the hearing of the ears (Is. xi:3). We judge not according to appearances, but judge righteous judgment, which is to see all things with those pure eyes that behold only God.

There is no judgment in the Kingdom of Heaven. The Father judgeth no man, but hath committed all judgment unto the Son, who says of himself, "I judge no man." "I came not to judge the world, but to save the world."

Who then judges the world? "There is one that seeketh and judgeth;" men's interpretation of Jesus' words judge them (John xii:48), and men's own words about themselves and others (Matt. xii:37). The Christ accuses no man, but Moses (John v:45) is that austere judge who says, "Out of thine own mouth will I judge thee" (Luke xix:22).

"Neither do I condemn thee" is ever the verdict of the Christ-man, and to him that wishes to judge he says, "Let him that is without sin first cast the stone," for that stone will not hurt nor destroy, but transform and redeem, as it is described in Daniel, second chapter, thirty-fifth and forty-fourth verses, as the stone that smote the image and became a great mountain that filled the whole earth.

3. And why beholdest thou the mote that is in thy brother's eye, but considerest not the beam that is in thine own eye?

4. Or how wilt thou say to thy brother, Let me pull out the mote out of thine eye; and, behold, a beam is in thine own eye?

5. Thou hypocrite, first cast out the beam out of thine own eye; and then shall thou see clearly to cast out the mote out of thy brother's eye.

"Therefore thou art inexcusable, O man, whosoever thou art that judgest: for wherein thou judgest another, thou condemnest thyself; for thou that judgest doest the same things," says Paul (Rom. ii:1).

Everything we do to our neighbor* we do to ourselves, for what we see in our neighbor is in ourselves, and one should look at his neighbor as he looks at his mirror; if he sees a spot upon the countenance in the mirror he knows he must wash his own face in order to remove the blemish in the mirror.

Thus if we will remove the beam from our own eyes we will see clearly that there is no mote in our brother's, it having been dissolved simultaneously with our own cleansing. For in lifting up ourselves, we have lifted up our brother; in purifying our own mind and heart our clear sight "looks away" the error in our brother, as it is written: "A king that sitteth in the throne of judgment scattereth away all evil with his eyes" (Prov. xx:8).

There is a saying ascribed to Jesus by one of the early Christians, said to be Matthias, the apostle. It is consistent with the rest of Christ's teachings, in which he shows the unity of man that we are all one: "If the neighbor of an elect man sin, the elect sinned himself."

According to this, if the elect would realize his own sinlessness, let him see the reality of his neighbor to be the Sinless One. Then he, too,

can say with Christ, "I, if I be lifted up, will draw all men unto me."

To cancel our neighbor's sin is to lift up ourselves. All humanity rises together. Redemption, like forgiveness, is reciprocal. The day comes, and is now here, when a man will be more concerned in bringing his neighbor to the realization of the Truth than in advancing himself. Just as the strong men upon a sinking ship see to the safety of the weak and helpless first, so the Christ-man seeks ever to save that which is lost, and does not say, "It is finished," until he has spoken the word of pardon for the greatest sinners of all " Father, forgive them, for they know not what they do."

Never will I seek nor receive private individual salvation; never enter into final peace alone; but forever and everywhere will I live and strive for the universal redemption of every creature throughout the world.

Kwhan Yin.

GOOD JUDGMENT IN MINISTERING

6. Give not that which is holy unto the dogs, neither cast ye your pearls before swine, lest they trample them under their feet, and turn again and rend you.

Every man is a world in himself, and contains within all that he sees in the world without. The description of man, the manifestation or expression of God, is the entire content of the first chapter of Genesis. In man's true state, the herbs and the sea, the animals and the lights of the firmament, and all things from the least unto the greatest, are pronounced good, and very good.

The animals of the Scripture represent natural traits of character, and according to the unfoldment of a characteristic the animal is wild and undesirable, or tame and held in esteem. Anger, malice, greed, and the rest of men's unredeemed characteristics are symbolized by wild beasts, and as man overcomes these carnal propensities it is said that he treads upon the lion and adder, and is given power over serpents and scorpions. As he advances in the Christ-life, every poisonous plant and wild animal is redeemed in his world. Of him it is written that he shall take up serpents, when the wolf shall dwell with the lamb, the lion shall eat hay like the ox, the child shall play with the asp, and "They shall not hurt nor destroy in all my holy mountain; for the earth shall be full of the knowledge of the Lord, as the waters cover the sea" (Is. xi:6~9).

Man can appear to be what he wills God or devil, angel or beast. This is his marvelous power and privilege. Therefore whatever state of mind he identifies himself with, that he will represent. If he comes seeking the Truth in a docile, non-resistant state of mind, he will be one of those babes to whom the mysteries of the kingdom are revealed (Luke x: 21) . But if he comes the same man even the next hour filled with malice and covetousness, he may hear words that are darkness to him, and not light: "Ye serpents, ye generation of vipers, how can ye escape the damnation of hell?" (Matt. xxiii:33).

Use divine judgment in dispensing Truth. "Be ye therefore wise as serpents, and harmless as doves," and "render therefore unto Caesar the things which are Caesar's; and unto God the things that are God's."

When one who is approached with the Truth receives it in a sneering way, waiting only to tear it to pieces; or laughs contemptuously at it, giving low and impure replies; or is sullen, sarcastic, or in any way cynical (cynic, from the Greek, meaning dog): such a one is called a dog. He has no use for the deeper mysteries called the holiest, and they should not be forced upon him. When the dog within him becomes subservient to the Master, and a guardian and protection, like the faithful shepherd dog, to the precious things of God, then will he be ready to receive, and be blessed.

The swinish nature in us is that which comes to Truth only for its material comforts and enjoyments. If we try to satisfy this nature with absolute statements and spiritual revelations it will feel itself being fed with stones when it is crying out for bread. The Christ has corn for even the swine, and feeds this nature in its due season, not despising it. But he is not an unfaithful steward (Luke xvi), wasting his Lord's goods, by administering Truth in forms inappropriate and unwelcome.

Great discretion and discernment is given the faithful one that he may give corn to them that are asking for corn, and pearls to them that ask for pearls. Nevertheless, he, too, like Jesus, may see that though a man has come seeking only loaves and fishes, yet he is ready for the pearl of great price. Then fearlessly he gives it, though offenses come, and men rend him even to crucifixion (John vi:26-66).

Of such it is written: "Behold, I lay in Sion a stumblingstone and rock of offense: and whosoever belie veth on him shall not be ashamed" (Rom. ix:33); he "is set for the fall and rising again of many in Israel; and for a sign which shall be spoken against" (Luke ii:34); "and blessed is he whosoever shall not be offended in me" (Matt. xi:6).

DIVINE PERSISTENCY

7. Ask, and it shall be given you; seek, and ye shall find; knock, and it shall be opened unto you.

8. For every one that asketh receiveth; and he that seeketh findeth; and to him that knocketh it shall be opened.

One of the most marked teachings of Jesus Christ is that the spiritual student must be divinely persistent in his demands upon the Spirit for his spiritual rights, the virtues and the gifts of the true Self.

The Master of Life here impresses upon the mind the omnipotence of persistency. "Men ought always to pray, and not to faint" (Luke xviii:!).

Jacob, when wrestling with God, would not take "no" for an answer. "I will not let thee go except thou bless me," he prayed, and then he was blessed, and a new name (character and power) was given him "Israel," signifying a man who could prevail with God.

Jesus teaches that when, even as the friend of God, you could not get your desire, yet you could accomplish it by determined importunity: "I say unto you, Though he will not rise and give him, because he is his friend, yet because of his importunity he will rise and give him as many as he needeth" (Lukexi:8).

Answers to prayer go not by favor, but by the law that equalizes the supply to the demand. Again, Jesus shows that though no human idea of justice or right or reward can prevail with God, yet persistency will gain the day: "Because this widow importunes me, I will do her justice, lest at last her coming should weary me" (Luke xviii:5, Wilson's Translation).

There is a pressure born of superhuman trust and love, and sublime belief in the right of one's desire, that, when brought to bear upon the Fountain of Life, makes it yield up its treasure.

There is a persistency that is the indomitable God Himself, and God cannot resist Himself.

In the life of Jesus this attitude of mind is portrayed in the Greek woman (Mark vii:2530) who so believed in the goodness and power of God that nothing could stop her prayers. The disciples could not hush her, and even Jesus could not argue her off from her faith. The great Spirit within her gave her words that answered his, and won the day. She would have reasoned with God Himself, and, like Jacob, she would have won.

The Spirit that knows no failure nor discouragement is the Spirit of God. "He shall not fail nor be discouraged, until he have set judgment in the earth" (Is. xlii:4). "To him that overcometh will I grant to sit with me in my throne" (Rev. iii:21).

All the Masters of Truth have taught the power of persistency.

Gautama's priests, the Bikshus, asked, "By what power of resolution and fixed determination the WorldHonored had obtained perfection?" Buddha replied, "I remember in years gone by that I was a merchant prince who went to sea in order to gather precious gems, and whilst so engaged I obtained one manigem of inestimable value, but I let it fall into the sea, and lost it. Then taking a ladle I began with fixed determination to bale out the water of the ocean to recover my gem. The sea-god said, 'How can this foolish man empty the wide and boundless ocean?' I replied, 'My resolution shall never flag; I will bale out the ocean and get my precious gem; you watch me, and do not grieve and fret at the long delay.' The sea-god, hearing these words, was filled with anxiety for the safety of his realm, and gave me back my gem."

"To the persevering mortal," says Zoroaster, "the blessed Immortals are swift."

THE WILL OF GOD

One of the commonest causes of men's weakening in their pursuit after their Good is the insinuating, treacherous doubt, "Perhaps it is not the will of God." Knowing this, Jesus proceeds to reveal to mortals the character of the divine Father by comparing Him to an earthly father.

The minds of mortals cannot comprehend

God; it is the divine Mind in us that knows God. But mortals must reason by analogy from what they do comprehend to what they do not, therefore the Christ reveals to us that we may judge of the character of God by the qualities of a just and loving earthly being.

Or what man is there of you,, whom if his son ask bread, will he give him a stone?

Or if he ask a fish, will he give him a serpent?

If ye then, being evil, know how to give good gifts unto your children, how much more shall your Father which is in heaven give good things to them that ask him?

Is God any less good than you? Then if you would not consign any being to everlasting torment, do you think God will? If you, being a good and all-wise physician, would not give people sickness and deformity, do you think God will?

Carry Jesus' reasoning to the greatest extreme of goodness, and realize that "of a verity the will of the just man is the will of God."

The will of our Father is to give us every good thing we ask. "But how shall we know that our desire is a good thing?" asks the doubtful one. How do we know that bread and fish are good to eat, and not stones and serpents? Just as we have sense and judgment to know our bodily good, so we have perception and discernment to know our soul good.

The heart that truly seeks God has good judgment, and knows that what is good for God is

good for himself. "He shall have whatsoever he saith."

A wise criterion for us to have in asking "good things" of our Father is to ask for that only which we are willing that all humanity shall receive equally with us. For as we are willing to give to men, so do we realize our Father's willingness to give to us.

As you would have God act toward you, so act toward all men. All thoughts, words, and deeds that we send forth to men return to us, coming directly from men, or indirectly as a decree or dispensation of our God. Therefore Jesus summarizes all things in the great Golden Rule.

THE GOLDEN RULE

12. Therefore all things whatsoever ye would that men should do to you, do ye even so to them: for this is the law and the prophets.

"For this is the law." As long as we are un

der the law (and whoever believes in sinning and being sinned against is under it) we must know it to be absolutely exact and sure. Its principle is the same one that lies back of every mechanical law of action and reaction, of balancing, of reflection, of reciprocity. Jesus gave it in many other forms: "With what measure ye mete, it shall be measured to you," "Give, and it shall be given unto you," "Forgive, and ye shall be forgiven," "Blessed are the merciful: for they shall obtain mercy," "Judge not, and you shall not be judged," "Condemn not, and you shall not be condemned," "For with what judgment ye judge, ye shall be judged," "They that take the sword shall perish with the sword."

Inexorable Law is cold, accurate, and unchangeable as the laws of mathematics. No begging nor pleading can change its regular and legitimate course. Paul gives it in full terms in the words: "Whatsoever a man soweth, that shall he also reap."

"And it is easier for heaven and earth to pass, than one tittle of the law to fail," says Jesus.

Therefore, while under the law, it behooves us to sow only that seed which we are willing to reap, to think of others as we would have them think of us, to speak to all as we would be spoken to, to do to others only what we would have done to us.

The Golden Rule was not announced by Jesus as a new law. Many have given it, because the Christ speaks the same truth in all men:

Do not to others what you would not like others to do to you. Hillel, 50 B. c.

Act toward others as you would desire them to act toward you. Isocrates, 338 B. c.

Do not to your neighbor what you would take ill from him. Pittacus, 650 B. c.

We should conduct, ourselves toward others as we would have them act toward us. Aristotle, 385 B. c.

What you wish your neighbors to be to you, such be you to them. Sextus, 406 B. c.

Avoid doing what you would blame others for doing. Tholes , 464 B. c.

Do unto another what you would have him do unto you, and do not unto another what you would not have him do unto you. Thou needest this law alone. It is the foundation of all the rest. Confucius, 500 B. c.

"This is the law and the prophets." But "ye are not under the law, but under grace" (Rom. vi:14), and though the laws be as inevitable and irrevocable as the famous laws of the Medes and Persians, yet He who can make "the heavens and the earth to pass" can also cause these laws to fail. He is the Son of God.

He who identifies himself with the Son of God is free from the law, and is therefore neither rewarded nor condemned, but comes into the grace of Truth, which is freedom from the laws of good and evil.

As Christ, Lord of Heaven and earth, can overrule physical laws, so also, when he is dominant in our hearts, can he overrule the Mosaic laws and the laws of heredity, destiny, and karma, and we can enter into our inheritance, not because we deserve it or have earned it, but because we are the returned heir, the Son of the Most High God.

He who knows God is free from the law of destiny, and is not subject to the evil one. Hermes Trismegistus.

THE WAY AND THE DOOR

Enter ye in at the strait gate: for wide is the gate, and broad is the way, that leadeth to destruction, and many there be which go in thereat:

Because strait is the gate, and narrow is the way, which leadeth unto life, and few there be that find it.

"The shortest distance between two points is measured upon the straight line that joins them." Between God and the devotee lies the one road that joins them. It turns neither to the right nor to the left (Deut. v: 32; Josh. i:7; Prov. iv:26, 27) , that is, neither to the good of the world, nor to the evil. It knows neither good nor evil, but God alone, and it is the only road by which the traveler may come to the Gate which opens into everlasting happiness.

The name of this road is Regeneration, the orderly unfoldment, progress, and development of the spiritual nature. Every step of the way is identification with God a continuously advancing consciousness and realization that ALL is GOD. These steps are taken by daily, hourly, practice of the presence of God, walking often by faith and not by sight, and keeping the spiritual senses ever on the alert to perceive and recognize the Gate.

Although the Way seems a succession of stages and degrees, yet the devotee must faithfully deny the need, desirability, or reality of growth, development, and all process of becoming, for the Gate is reached by ceasing to believe in progression. There is no becoming with God, not even as the Son does God become. To appearance he was born and grew to manhood, yet even then he knew I AM that I AM, and "Before Abraham was, I AM." Being is the true state of the Self, therefore I AM is the Gate,

and not I was, or I shall be. I AM the way (John xiv:6), and I AM the door (John x:9), and I AM the one who goes through the door. "He that entereth in by the door is the shepherd of the sheep" (John x:2). "I AM the good shepherd" (John x:11) .

No one can enter into the Heaven state of mind and abide there at will, but he who knows, as Jesus did, I AM the Son of God. Yes, knows it, not by the intellect, nor by hearsay, but even as God knows I AM God.

You, in your true Self, the Christ of you, are the Way, and the Door, and the One walking the Way and entering the Door. The Truth shows us that we are all that one Son, the only begotten Son of God. There are not many sons of God. It appears so, but it is a delusion, the same kind as believing in "gods many, and lords many."

In the false belief that we are "many," separate from each other and apart from God, we are walking the road that leads to destruction, that is, death. But this sense of separation is destroyed as we walk the Way of the Christ, and we have but one consciousness as we pass through the Gate: my neighbor and I are one, Christ and I are one, the Father and I are one, for God is all in all. "In that day there shall be one Lord, and his name one" (Zech. xiv:9).

"By Me if any man enter in, he shall be saved, and go in and out and find pasture" (John x:9). Whoever enters into the realization of Heaven through the knowledge, "I am the Son of God," can walk in perpetual joy and power to do all the works of God when and where he wills.

Many of us are entering from time to time into ecstasies and temporal realizations of Heaven, but are not going in at the Door. Climbing up some other way, we do not stay in the fold, but soon find ourselves thrust out like intruders, and we know not how we got in or how we fell out. So also many have performed great healing works, but they cannot tell how they did them, nor can they do them again, for they entered not in at the strait gate, absolute knowledge of the Principle of their being, and how to work by it.

"Wide is the gate, and broad is the way, that leadeth to destruction." Every thought that condemns is destructive. Sins destroy. 'Belief in sickness and death lead to destruction. Schisms lie in this way, and all the sects that are founded upon quarrels and Pharisaical separatism are in this false way, whose end is the grave. All truth is one, therefore whatever disunites and separates has in it the elements of error, and lies in the broad way that leads from one sense of destroying to another a continuous dead march.

The ways of death are hard (Prov. xiii:15), and whoever is walking in them will never reach Heaven until he leaves them. All roads do not lead to Heaven. Men say "All roads lead to Rome," but that is a fallacy. No racetrack will take you there. Also he who rides the circle of sin and sickness, death and birth, may keep on indefinitely, but he will never reach Heaven by that road.

"The Way to Heaven is Heaven," and we may know the road by its peace and its pleasantness (Prov. iii:17). No temptation to be sorrowful, to commit sin, or to believe in the reality of any evil should draw us off from it.

The carnal mind and the spiritual mind are seen to act in this way: the carnal always detects differences while the spiritual notes similarities. Max Muller.

If you are moved from the calm, holy, healing, loving center of your being, you may know you are upon a side track.

Quickly step back into Heaven.

How far from here to heaven? Not very far, my friend.

A single hearty step will all Thy journey end. Scheffler.

FAIR WORDS AND FALSE THINKING

15. Beware of false prophets, which come to you in sheep's clothing, but inwardly they are ravening wolves.

"Beware" (literally, "hold towards yourself") is translated in other texts, "Take heed to yourselves" (Matt. vi:l; Luke xvii:3, xxi:34, and so forth), and signifies a fearless, careful watchfulness.

A prophet, in the Hebrew understanding of the word, means not only one who foretells, but one who exhorts, and publicly expounds and preaches.

Of all the kinds of false preachers, Jesus draws attention to only one as needing especial watchfulness, the kind that speaks fair words, but whose inward thoughts are not one with the utterances of his lips. They come with the clothing, the outward form of the Lamb, symbol of meekness, docility, harmlessness, purity, and nonresistance; but covetousness, pride, lust, ambition, and cruelty are the untamed animals within, the ravening wolves which you, as the good shepherd, should quickly discern if you would keep your flock, spiritual thoughts, intact.

The words, "Take heed to yourselves," show that the act concerns one's self principally. Look out for the false prophets, evil thoughts, and worldly beliefs in yourself. Be able to deal with your own thoughts and suggestions, and you will know how to look upon those of others.

By not allowing personal sense, or desire, to have one's own will and way, or fear, or policy, or greed of fame and gain, or any other false motive to prompt us to use the arguments of Truth, we become wakeful and discerning disciples, and cannot be misled by the sophistries and wrong deductions of others.

He who never deceives cannot be deceived. He who seeks Truth with all his heart, just for Truth's sake, will receive only the Truth, no matter how false the lips that speak to him.

The spirit of Truth within opens the spiritual senses to read the inmost thoughts of men, so that the spiritual student knows all men, and needs not that any should testify of man, for he knows what is in man (John ii:24, 25)
.

Nevertheless, to those who feel themselves still liable to be led astray by false teachers the Master says:

Ye shall know them by their fruits. Do men gather grapes of thorns, or figs of thistles?

Even so every good tree bringeth forth good fruit; but a corrupt tree bringeth forth evil fruit.

A good tree cannot bring forth evil fruit, neither can a corrupt tree bring forth good fruit.

Every tree that bringeth not forth good fruit is hewn down, and cast into the fire.

Wherefore by their fruits ye shall know them.

The fruits of a man's thinking and speaking are his actions.

Comparing him to a tree, his thoughts are the roots, his words are the leaves, and his deeds are the fruit. One may not be able to tell the character of two plants whose leaves are alike by examining the leaves, as, for instance, the deadly nightshade and the tomato plant; but he can turn to their fruits, and there he is at once able to distinguish them.

What are the actions we should expect from the true man? Paul tells us that the fruits of the spirit are love, peace, patience, gentleness, goodness, faith, meekness, temperance (Gal. v: 22, 23). Then the actions should be loving, peaceful, patient, meek, temperate, and so forth.

So when a fair doctrine is preached, then let us look to the lives of the preachers.

How does the prophet act when opposed or interfered with? Is he then gentle and nonresistant, as the Christ doctrine he teaches? or do thorny-words and thistle-deeds follow?

Is he alike to all, and at all times? or does he lead a double life, acting one way in public and the opposite in private?

Does he exalt himself and depreciate others?

Does he in any way advocate or embody in his life the works of the flesh enumerated so fully by the apostle (Gal. v:19-21), such as adultery, fornication, witchcraft, hatred, envyings, drunkenness, and so forth?

Again, there are other fruits that the Christ bids us to expect of the true preacher of the gospel. "These signs shall follow them that believe in my name shall they cast out devils; they shall speak with new tongues; they shall take up serpents; and if they drink any deadly thing, it shall not hurt them; they shall lay hands on the sick, and they shall recover" (Mark xvi:17, 18). Are these Christ-works following their doctrine? or do they say these are not expected of us, and belong to a past age? Have they the goal of the full round life of Jesus here on earth, or do they have simply "a form of godliness but denying the power therof"? Read 2 Timothy, third chapter, first to seventh verses.

The sins or errors of omission of the works of Christ are the same deadly fruit as the sins of commission of the works of evil. They may not have the same active poison in them, but they are like apples of Sodom, dust and ashes in the mouth, a starvation diet that in the end produces the same result as sins of commission spiritual deadness.

Whatever produces evil has its root in evil, and whatever produces good is good. Good does not come from evil, neither is evil undeveloped good. Whatever is truly good always has been good and always will be good, for Good is God, the unchangeable One. So also all evil had its origin in evil, and its end is evil, that is, pure nothingness and annihilation.

The good of every prophet is preserved, but the false must be consumed. Every tree (thought, word, and deed) that does not bear good fruit is continually being cut down and cast into the love-fire of God, and being returned to the void from whence it came. "The fire shall try every man's work of what sort it is. ... If any man's work shall be burned, he shall suffer loss: but he himself shall be saved; yet so as by fire" (1 Cor. iii:13, 15).

For no form of evil comes from God; they are all plants which He has not planted. "Every plant which my heavenly Father hath not planted shall be rooted up" (Matt. xv:13) .

21. Not every one that saith unto me, Lord, Lord, shall enter into the kingdom of heaven; but he that doeth the will of my Father which is in heaven.

Not everyone who is declaring Jesus Christ to be his savior or his teacher shall enter into the

Kingdom of Heaven. For the Kingdom of

Heaven is a state of mind and heart, a consciousness of peace and freedom, of eternal health and life, of unlimited wisdom and changeless love. "The kingdom of God cometh not with observation [or outward show]: neither shall they say, Lo here! or, lo there! for, behold, the kingdom of God is within you" (Luke xvii:20, 21).

Simply talking about Truth, or making statements of Truth, is not sufficient to bring one into this divine realization, this state of bliss called the Kingdom of Heaven. One must live the life of Truth, and do the will of God, in order to be perfectly healed, and enjoy continuous peace and prosperity.

Jesus Christ, by his life and teaching, reveals to us the will of God. He says, "I came down from heaven, not to do mine own will, but the will of him that sent me."

God, being unchangeable, has the same will forever. Being no respecter of persons, he has the same will for you and me that he had for Jesus and the disciples. It is, to live the immaculate life of love through obeying every direction given by Jesus, and doing all the works he did, healing, raising the dead, freeing people from their sins, commanding the earthly elements, exercising our spiritual senses and finishing our earthly existence by submerging it, without death, into its divine reality. Your meat is to do the will of him that sent you, and to finish his work (John iv: 34) .

WORKS WITHOUT LOVE

Many will say to me in that day, Lord, Lord, have we not prophesied in thy name? and in thy name have cast out devils? and in thy name done many wonderful works?

And then will I profess unto them, I never knew you: depart from me, ye that work iniquity.

"In that day." In this earthly school of experience examination-day comes to each aspirant for heavenly honors; and to pass our examination, and not be sent back to the old grade of experiences to re-learn our lesson, we must be well equipped with the one thing needful LOVE that good part which cannot be taken from us.

The Highest Consciousness (Christ) cannot enter into the disciple who omits love from his aims, even though he be an adept in works of healing and in miracles. This is enlarged upon by Paul in his wonderful discourse upon Love (1 Cor. xiii). He there reveals that one could have the greatest eloquence, and yet, not having love, be only like a beautiful musical instrument, without any life in itself.

One may have occult knowledge so as "to understand all mysteries"; one may have a faith that could heal case after case, "moving mountains," and yet if he is neglecting to develop the love-nature, these powers will fail him, and he will need to return to the simplest study of the life of love in order to enter into that joy of his Lord to which his heart is aspiring.

It is prophesied (Joel ii:28) that "it shall come to pass in the last days that I will pour out my spirit upon all flesh." Already a mighty spiritual wave is rolling over us, and increasing rapidly in volume and power, and as a result we may begin to look for great and wonderful works upon all sides. But unless these signs be accompanied with that love that thinketh no evil, they will count for nothing to the discerning Truth student.

Love will be the great test; the love that is no respecter of creeds or sects, that judges no man and comes not to condemn the world, but that the world through it might be saved.

Love is the Way.

Love is the Door, and no man can enter into the Kingdom of Heaven but by Love.

HEARING AND DOING

Therefore whosoever heareth these sayings of mine, and doeth them, I will liken him unto a wise man, which built his house upon a rock:

And the rain descended, and the floods came, and the winds blew, and beat upon that house; and it fell not: for it was founded upon a rock.

And every one that heareth these sayings of mine, and doeth them not, shall be likened unto a foolish man, which built his house upon the sand:

And the rain descended, and the floods came, and the winds blew, and beat upon that house; and it fell: and great was the fall of it.

"Whosoever heareth these sayings." The spiritual significance of "hearing" is understanding and accepting. All those disciples of Truth who are receiving its divine principles, and putting them into practice in every department of their daily lives, are building up a faith whose foundation is solid, reliable, and substantial. For it is a rock of demonstrated doctrine Truth that has been proven true.

The follower of Truth who has built his belief

upon that rock will not be overcome by the winds and floods of adversity, or sickness, or death. When trials and tribulations assail him he will be like a man in a secure house, who feels all the more his safety, peace, and comfort when storms rage around. "These things have I spoken unto you, that in me ye may have peace. In the world ye have tribulation: but be of good cheer; I have overcome the world" (John xvi:33, Revised Version).

While walking the Way of regeneration, we may be tempted at times to believe in the reality of evil, being assailed by the errors that were once believed in the sins, diseases, hardships of the old earth-life. But whoever fulfills all the commandments of Jesus Christ will come out of every spiritual examination accredited with a high mark, and instead of fearing or dreading the problems of life, will see them only as opportunities for proving where he stands, how much he knows and can do by the grace and omnipotence of God.

The science of God must be practiced as faithfully and efficiently as any material science. No Christian should consider his spiritual education finished unless he can do all the works of Christ.

A good mathematician is not content to rest in a theory of his science; he not only acquaints himself with all the principles of his science, but he examines into the rules and methods discovered and invented by other mathematicians and experts, especially if he is to be a master in it, so as to be able to do every problem that has ever been worked by anyone, and, if possible, more. The aspiration of every true Christian should be the same.

Can you raise the dead? Can you control the elements, stilling the winds and the waves with your word? If we cannot heal every case that is brought to us, let us not supinely mesmerize ourselves into the thought that it is not expected of us, but let us get more understanding, more faith, more love, more application. All things are possible to him that believeth.

He is but a theoretical Truth-seeker who is saying of Jesus' commands that any are too transcendental or impracticable. Such a one is building his religious life upon a poor foundation, that will fail him when he needs it most.

The comparison which Jesus makes between the two kinds of followers of Truth is again made in the parable of the Ten Virgins. The foolish man who hears and does not, is like the foolish virgins who had their lamps but were unprovided with sufficient oil.

Many are now hearing the words of Christ and are expecting to demonstrate all that he did? even to the overcoming of death. But how can we do all the works unless we obey all the directions? How can you, earnest healer, expect to heal every patient and still hold hatred in your heart toward anyone or anything, and even justify it in yourself? How can you, wise teacher though you be, expect to overcome death when you do not take Christ's teachings of living a sexless life, which is the very keystone of that attainment (Luke xx: 35, 36; Matt, xix: 12)?

Jesus Christ has given us every essential direction that must be known and obeyed in order to be completely emancipated from the mistakes, sorrows, and sufferings of the realm of delusion. He indorsed many of the teachings of the sages that had preceded him, and where spiritual masters seem to disagree or to be obscure he has forever settled each important point so that there may be no uncertainty in the minds of those who have ears to hear.

Under the name of Christ every impersonal, universal follower of Truth who seeks It for Its own sake is willing and ready to rally, that there may be perfect unity among all those who worship the true God.

The wise men of all generations and races are the powers that are ruling the nations of the earth, and they have chosen One to represent them, Jesus Christ, who is to be the central standard about which every other independent -one is gathering through concentrating upon His name, life, and words.

The Truth is being presented in all ways and by all means to reach the hearts of even the dullest, and each, as he rises in the scale of understanding, and becomes universal in love and wisdom, will know and appreciate Jesus Christ as God-with-us in fullness of manifestation, even as he, himself, prophesied: "It is written in the prophets, And they shall be all taught of God. Every man therefore that hath heard, and hath learned of the Father, cometh unto me" (John vi: 45).

Then when all have been gathered together under one name, Jesus Christ's work will have been done, and even that name, which has been above every other name, will be erased, that the Lord whose name is One may be all in all (Zech. xiv:9).

"Then cometh the end, when he shall have delivered up the kingdom to God, even the Father; when he shall have put down all rule and all authority and power. For he must reign, till he hath put all enemies under his feet. The last enemy that shall be destroyed is death. . . . And when all things shall be subdued unto him, then shall the Son also himself be subject unto him that put all things under him, that God may be all in all"5(1 Cor. xv: 24-28).

THE END.

BOOK THREE.
PRIMARY LESSONS IN CHRISTIAN LIVING AND HEALING

A Textbook of Healing by the Power of Truth As Taught and Demonstrated by the Lord Jesus Christ

PREFACE

FOR over twelve years these lessons have been given to spiritual students, hundreds of whom are living demonstrations of their efficacy in healing.

Not only have the sick been healed by the practice of these teachings, but characters have been redeemed from vice and weakness, and prosperity has come to those who had never dreamed that there is a law of mind that gives fortune and freedom from debt. Therefore these teachings are not theoretical or chimerical, but proven Truth, that Truth which is more valuable than any earthly treasure that could be named, and for which no exchange would even be considered by the one who has learned and realized It.

The lessons were first brought out as a serial in the metaphysical magazine Unity, of Kansas City, Mo., and through its wide circulation they have reached thousands whose loving testimonials are coming to the writer every day.

As numbers of public teachers and healers have been the fruitage of the oral deliverance of these lectures, the same blessed harvest is anticipated through their dissemination in printing. Already the good news has come from different localities of groups gathering day after day and listening to the reading of the lessons by some one of their number, whose enthusiasm and faith baptizes the letter of the reading with that Spirit which is the essential goodness of oral instruction.

Whoever wishes to use these lessons in teaching is welcome to do so, without referring to the author of them. No greater praise could be given than to quote them as impersonal Truth.

For the benefit of those who wish to make a study of the Bible with the true understanding of spiritual things there has been added an index of all the Bible references used in the book. Many obscure texts will be found among them whose interpretation is given clearly in the context of the book where the passage is quoted.

Teachers and speakers who wish to give sermons and Bible readings will find this index of much assistance.

Go, little book, and if in the great galaxy of spiritual lights that shall crown this century as the Spiritual Renaissance of the world thou canst be the polar star to even one weary mariner, lost upon the ocean of delusion, by which Truth may guide him to his Home, thine existence will have been well accounted for, and thy mission blessed.

CHICAGO, January, 1900. A. R. M.

INTRODUCTORY DIRECTIONS TO STUDENTS.

IN taking up the study of pure Truth it is well for the student to understand what is the best attitude of mind to keep in order to receive the greatest good in the easiest way and in the shortest possible time.

Be as nearly like a child as you know how. For the time being put aside the old ways of thinking, former prejudices, and unbeliefs, and listen quietly to all that is presented to you. Do not try to reconcile your old ideas with these that are given you here, neither look for differences. Sit calmly and quietly as the judge sits upon his bench, and listen with impartiality and without fear.

Do not feel obliged to accept or reject what is given you, but trust the Truth in yourself to adjust all things, and to give to you and retain in you only that which is indeed true.

Do not argue about any statement given you, either for it or against it. You do not need to defend the Truth, for Truth is sufficient unto itself. And if a statement seems untrue leave it alone. If it is not of God it cannot live.

It is well to talk these teachings over with one who is harmonious, but if either feels any disturbance or inharmony then let silence reign, for then indeed is silence golden.

These lessons are healing, and as you eat and digest and assimilate these truths you will find false physical conditions dropping away, and false and disturbing thoughts passing utterly from your mind forever.

While you are being healed do not be surprised or discouraged if there are days when you seem worse, either in body or mind, than usual. At such times read those parts of the lessons that help you many times over, and you will be lifted right up into peace and health speedily.

Repetition and reiteration are purposely adhered to, for this course is a study, not a diversion.

Just before studying each lesson, sit for a few moments in silence and declare for yourself:

"Truth is my God. I love the Truth. Therefore I trust the Truth to guide me into all Truth, the whole Truth, and nothing but the Truth."

PART I.

LESSON I. FIRST PRINCIPLES.

The Pursuit of Happiness

AS with our mental eyes we look forth over the world and consider its people, and what they are living for, and what they are most earnestly desiring, we find that all mankind have one common pursuit, and all are desirous of but one thing, and that is Happiness.

No matter by what name they are calling their desire, whether it is power, honors, riches, health, peace, love, or knowledge, everyone and all can be summed up and brought under the one name, Happiness.

Not only does everyone pursue happiness, but everyone at some time believes that he can have it, and at all times he believes that he has a right to have it.

Some think that they have ceased to look for happiness—the word seems too large to them, but there is one word that represents what they think they can have here and now, and happiness, that word is Satisfaction.

"Oh, to be satisfied!" they cry, "Oh, to be at rest!" Yes, it is true all can have satisfaction, and not only may we be passively, quietly satisfied, but it is our right and our privilege to be happy—actively, joyously happy—here and now, with not a sorrow to mar our joy, not one thing that can interfere with our happiness. In other words, we can enter into eternal, unchanging bliss now, in this time, and it is right for us to believe so—to believe that all good is for us to-day, and to ask, to seek, to knock until we are consciously one with our own true state of being, pure happiness.

Knowledge of Truth

All along the ages have arisen great souls, grand masters of life, who have believed in man's right to happiness, and, believing so, have given all they had, their whole lives, all their energy, love, and whatever they prized into the service of finding how this happiness may be attained, and, with one accord, we find them saying that to know the Truth and to live the Truth is the one and the only Way to eternal happiness, and he who once knows the whole Truth, need never know sickness, sorrow, evil, death, poverty, or any other wretchedness ever again. "Ye shall know the truth, and the truth shall make you free."-—John 8:32. Free from what? Free from every evil condition; free from every material limitation to which mortals seem so in bondage. And if we are not free, if something still prevents us from having what we desire or doing that which we wish to do, then we may know that we must rise up out of some ignorance, and we must seek and receive the whole Truth, for it must be the whole Truth that shall set us wholly free.

It has been argued that when we have found the whole Truth we shall know it, in that it fulfills three conditions of perfect happiness. It should give us (1) Health of body, (2) Peace of mind, (3) The key to all knowledge. Since these three conditions have been fulfilled in students by these teachings we see that we can truly call this gospel, Truth.

The Foundation

In order that we may walk the Way with understanding and profit we must, in this first lesson, see that we start from the same point—that is, that we all stand together upon one Foundation Principle, and standing together there, we shall see that we cannot but walk together from principle to principle, and every deduction and conclusion must be taken from alpha to omega. We shall know that if we have not believed in all these principles, and not only believed them but lived them, that it will not be hard for us to understand why we have not had that happiness we desire, or manifested that perfection we would show forth.

The first principle of Truth is: God is good and God is omnipresent. Upon the acceptance of this principle depends your receptivity to all that follows. "Come now, let us reason together, saith the Lord." —Is. 1:18. There are three statements in the wording of this principle which may be called the first axioms of Truth, viz:

1. God is.

2. God is the Good.

3. God is omnipresent.

An axiom is defined as a self-evident truth. Taking this definition in its highest sense we can see why the truth "God is" can be called axiomatic. No external evidence or human argument can prove to you that God is. Such can be corroborative witness to what you have already received from within, but let us rest forever in this understanding that only God can prove to you that God is, and that proof comes from the divine within yourself.

Every thinker believes in a cause back of all that he observes about him. Some call this great cause Force, some, Nature, some, Law, some, The Great First Cause, some, The Unknowable, but by far the greater part of those who have most earnestly pondered upon the idea have given it the name of some deity. In these teachings we have chosen to use the name God, because it includes all that is in the other names and more. The name Force would seem to exclude the attribute of love, Nature seems often strangely blind and merciless, while with the name God it is not difficult with most people to associate those higher qualities omitted from the others. Another advantage accruing to the name God is that it is one in its Anglo-Saxon root with the word Good.

God is the Good

Let us now consider our second axiom, "God is the Good." It is agreed by all the wise that have most blessed the world that the First Cause is good. Those who call it Force, or Law, agree that it is good, as evidenced in the theory of "the survival of the fittest," or best, in all species. The devotee of Nature believes that all her efforts are towards Good- bringing forth health, beauty, and good in manifold ways. It is not difficult for us to agree that God is good. Let us enlarge upon this basic statement, God is the Good. What do we mean by the Good?

The highest goodness must be that which is so good that it is never anything else. It is that which is everlastingly, unchangeably, universally good—in other words, the Absolute Good.

God is that which is good for all people at all times and in all places. It is not that which is good for one race and not for another, or for one sex and not for another, or for one age and not for another; that is only relative goodness, passing shadows finally swallowed up by that sun of righteousness—the Great Good of All.

If we begin to consider that which everyone believes is good for himself we shall enter upon infinity, for the good things of God cannot be numbered. We will state a few in order to lay our foundation stones:

1. HEALTH is GOOD. Everyone believes that health is good for himself and good for his loved one. Always, everywhere, health is good. Listen to this simple logic, this syllogism:

Since God is Good,

And Health is Good,

Therefore God is Health And Health is God.

"For I shall yet praise him, who is the health of my countenance, and my God."— Ps.42:11.

2. LIFE is GOOD. By Life is not meant that condition of earthly affairs between birth and death—not many see that good—but that Principle, that Power that lies back of the sparkle in the eye and the glow on the cheek, that great Essence and Presence whose beginnings materialists have, all in vain, so ardently sought. No mortal has ever touched Life or confined It to form or definition, but all agree that It is as unknowable and undefinable

as God, and, like Deity, only appreciable through Its effects or manifestations. Listen to our reasoning:

Since God is Good And Life is Good,

Therefore God is Life And Life is God.

SUBSTANCE is GOOD. What is Substance? Metaphysicians define it as that which is the reality of being, that which is the genuine, indestructible presence that is back of the appearance called "matter." Its essence is unchangeability. It is eternal, incorruptible, infinite, and unlimited. It is Being, of which materiality is the shadow. What is Substance with the metaphysician is Spirit with the theologian, and in these teachings Substance and Spirit are synonymous terms used interchangeably. Again we reason:

Since God is Good,

And Substance is Good,

Therefore God is Substance And Substance is God.

"God is Spirit," says Jesus (Wilson's Emphatic Diaglot). God is one Spirit, in, and through, and the reality of all manifestation—the beauty, grandeur, and glory of the universe. By this time the observing student will be cognizant of our methods of meditation and deduction, and can himself start with correct premises and arrive at true conclusions, proving to his own satisfaction that God is all that is pure Goodness— universally, eternally, impartially good. Practice meditating upon what is good for all people at all times and in all places, and then see how God is that, and your foundation is sure.

4. LOVE is GOOD. Unselfish, pure, unchangeable Love is good for all. God is Love.

5. INTELLIGENCE is GOOD. God is Intelligence— Wisdom.

6. TRUTH is GOOD. God is Truth. We need not put any limit to our enumeration of the Goodness that is God. God is Peace, Prosperity, Purity, Strength, Trust, Faith, Rest, Power, Freedom, and so on to infinity. But it is enough for our foundation Statement of Being to dwell upon certain thoughts of God now, and charge our minds with one short statement only: God is Health, Life, Love, Truth, Substance, and Intelligence.

God is Omnipresent

Let us now consider our third axiom, "God is Omnipresent."

God is everywhere. God fills all, and is the very being of all that is. God is All in All. Let us see to what conclusions the acknowledgment that God is omnipresent will lead us. Since God is good and God is omnipresent, then

Good is omnipresent, Good is everywhere. Since God is Health and God is omnipresent, health is omnipresent, health is in and through all things. Life is omnipresent, love is omnipresent, truth is omnipresent, substance is omnipresent, intelligence is omnipresent.

All that can be predicated of God can be declared true of all that is good. God is Omnipotence, therefore health is omnipotent, and so also is life and love.

Repetition of these truths in every conceivable form is the mental method of hammering, "driving home," stamping, and solidifying the foundation of that building which is to be the center and headquarters of all our coming demonstrations. Too much attention cannot be paid to this first lesson. A student that is well grounded upon the basic principles will find all the subsequent lessons easy to comprehend and practice.

The truth about yourself

Who are you? "Know thyself" has ever been the inspired injunction. Every sage has expressed this thought in some manner: "If man would only study himself and know himself, then he would know all things—nothing would be unknown to him." This is true. If man knows the true Self of him, then he must know God, for the true Self is one with God.

Moses spoke of Man's oneness with God as Man being made in the image and likeness of God. Jesus spoke of Man's oneness with God as the Son being one with the Father. "I and the Father are one."

God is divine Mind. Man is its Idea. God creates or thinks Man. God thinks upon Himself, images Himself, speaks the word, "I am." Man is that Word.

You are the thought of God, the idea of the divine Mind. You have no existence apart from God. The perfect Mind never loses one of its thoughts; so you, God's thought, cannot be lost out of His mind. "In him we live, and move, and have our being."

The thought is always like the thinker, therefore Scripture says Man, who is the thought, is like God, who is the thinker.

Therefore this is the truth which you must speak for yourself and realize is true: Since God is Health, I, who am the image of God, must be healthy— not sick. It is true that I am, in reality, strong and well.

Since God is Spirit, I am Spirit. I am, in reality, spiritual, immortal, healthy, and harmonious.

I am Divine, not mortal; I am Holy, not sinful; I am Wise, not ignorant, Because God is All, And beside Him there is none else.

The Idea of God is one with God. Since God is All in the universe, there is only God—only God and His Idea, His Son, and that Idea is God. For since God is All, there is only God for God to think upon. "This is life eternal, that they might know thee, the only true God [the Father] and Jesus Christ [Man, the Son] whom thou hast sent."

The real Self of you is the Christ, one with the Father. You are not a mortal, sickly, weak, and foolish being, as it would seem you are. In reality you are all that is everlastingly divine and perfect. This is the truth about yourself.

The Practice

It is not enough to listen to these teachings only, they must be practiced. These truths must be used in order that they may be proven good and desirable. We know that with music, one will not be proficient who only listens to the theories, but does not apply them. So it is with the Life. We must live its principles every day—every hour, every moment thinking some good thought, some God-thought.

If one hears, that is, listens carefully and obediently to these lessons, and then practices them all he can, he has built his house upon a rock, and no matter how he may be assailed by sickness or trouble, it can get no hold upon him, but he will stand, and the more the storm beats about his house the more secure he will feel himself within.

But he that hears, be he ever so attentive and pleased with the doctrine, but does not do may know why some problems seem too hard for him, and sickness and disaster undermine him.

Build upon rock by continual practice of the Word. Jesus called this "praying always."

In the interim between the study of this lesson and the next hold this statement in mind, often silently repeating it: Only the Good is true.

Copy the following, and mentally repeat it every night and morning: God is Health, Life, Love, Truth, Substance, Intelligence. God is All.

God is Omnipresence, Omnipotence, and Omniscience.

I am the Thought of God, the Idea of the divine Mind. In Him I live, move, and have my being. I am spiritual, harmonious, fearless, and free. I am governed by the law of God, the everlasting Good, and I am not subject to the law of sin, sickness, and death.

I know the Truth, and the Truth makes me free from evil in every form and from all material bondage, now and forever.

God works through me to will and to do whatever ought to be done by me. I am happy. I am holy. I am loving. I am wise. I and the Father are one. Amen.

LESSON II. THE REAL AND THE UNREAL

THE first lesson the student of Truth must learn is summed up in the answer of Jesus Christ to the scribe who asked him what was the first commandment, or rule, for right living:

"And Jesus answered him, The first of all the commandments is, Hear, O Israel; The Lord our God is one Lord: And thou shalt love the Lord thy God with all thy heart, and with all thy soul, and with all thy mind, and with all thy strength: this is the first commandment. And the second is like, namely this, Thou shalt love thy neighbor as thyself"—Mark 12:29-31.

God must be loved with the whole nature, and this is only possible as we know that God is all that really is. God is the One Good, everywhere present. God is the One Spirit, the One Mind in everybody. God is the One Substance in the universe. God is the One Life, Health, Love, Truth, Substance, and Intelligence.

God is the only Self in us and in our neighbor. Therefore the second commandment is just the same as the first, for if we love God with all our heart, soul, mind, and strength, what love have we left for ourselves or our neighbor unless the real Self in us be God? There is only God. There is no reality in anything that is not God.

The Whole Truth

It is written, "Ye shall know the truth, and the truth shall make you free." This is true, and as we look about us and see the human race so in bondage to evil we have but one conclusion in our minds—it must be that they do not know the Truth. Some seem free from one thing but are in bondage to another; others are almost entirely free, yet something still limits and binds, and in the case of these we must conclude that they have received but part of the Truth, or have been contented with a mixture of Truth and error, for when once they know the whole Truth, and practice it, they must be wholly free. Parttruths heal us only in part.

Contradictions in Preaching

Why is it that men who are preaching what they believe to be the Truth are sick and poor, weak and full of sorrow and trouble?

This is the reason: While they declare God to be good and to be omnipotent, in the same breath they begin to talk of another power called evil, the devil, as very strong and powerful, which is continually warring against God, and most of the time prevailing.

At the same time that men have said God is omnipresent, everywhere present, they talk of another being, exactly opposite to God, the Good, as a real presence, and even ascribe to it the All-presence that belongs to God. Thus they break their first commandment: "Thou shalt have no other gods [powers] before me."

To give evil even the smallest presence is to put it in the place where God should be—yes, where God really is. They should know the omnipresence of the Good only, and acknowledge that in order to be free from the evil in which they have so long been believing.

Ignorance the cause of error

Gautama Buddha, the great Eastern sage, after days of prayer and fasting, desiring above all things to know why his people suffered so, received this word from the Divine Spirit: "The reason of suffering is ignorance. Teach the people the truth, and they shall be free." It is ignorance of God that we must rise out of in order to be set free from those ills that are the results of it. And this ignorance is expressed by the people as a belief in the universal presence of evil. From this error every mind must be set free by being imbued with the idea of the universal presence of God.

Is it reasonable to say that God is good and all-powerful, and then say that evil has any power at all? Is it reasonable to believe in the omnipresence of God and at the same time think the devil has any real presence? Come, let God in you speak to you the whole Truth!

Denials deduced

Since God is the Good and God is everywhere, Good must be everywhere, and there is no real presence to evil at all. Since God is all and He is the one creator, He must create all out of His own substance, which is Good. God creates Good only. "And God saw that it was good."

"And God saw everything that he had made, and, behold, it was very good."—Gen. 1:31. Good is all that really is made. There is, in reality, no place for evil in God's universe. Evil has no real presence, or power, or law, and all that can be classed under the head of evils are delusions and unrealities, and should be recognized as only such.

Sin, sickness, sorrow, death, have no place in the omnipresence of God.

God does not think impure, unholy thoughts, therefore sinful desires, words, and deeds have no part or place in the true Self. There is no reality in sin; it is without power, law, or substance.

God is omnipresent Health. There is no pain, no sickness, no disease in God. There is nothing in God to be sick or out of which to make disease, therefore He does not make pain, sickness or disease. There is no reality in disease.

God is immortal, changeless Life, omnipresent Life. Life does not end. There is no reality in death. Absence of life is an appearance, and no one ever really dies. Death has no real place or power in God's world.

God is Spirit—pure, holy, unlimited, eternal, perfect Substance. Since God is all, His creation must be in and of Himself, in and of His substance, therefore the world of God must be Spiritual and not material. Matter is not the real substance of the universe, for the qualities of matter—change, decay, limitation, mortality, and imperfection—have no place in divine manifestation. Materiality is negation.

All the beauty, grandeur, life, and goodness of creation are Spiritual, not material, and therefore they are eternal to the mind that truly knows and to the eyes that really see.

Absolute belief in God

Not only must we believe in the omnipresence and omnipotence of God, but we must carry that belief to its ultimate extent, which is to believe that there can be no reality in any other presence or power. We cannot allow the claim of any presence other than Good and Spirit to take hold upon our minds in order to be loyal to the greatest command of all: "Thou shalt love the Lord thy God with all thy mind." "In all thy ways acknowledge him."—Prov. 3:6. "Look unto me and be ye saved, all the ends of the earth: for I am God, and there is none else."—Is. 45:22.

Unlearning errors

The Greek philosopher Zeno says: "The most necessary part of learning is to unlearn our errors." The mind that comes up to the fountain of Truth to partake of its blessings must first be placed in a receptive condition, must first be cleansed of its belief in the reality of evil and materiality, in order that it may receive the full Truth and this cleansing process is accomplished by the word of negation.

Every negative word erases, and to erase false thoughts from the mind the word of denial must be spoken.

In the first chapter of Genesis the mind that awaits the coming of Truth is spoken of in the language of symbolism as the earth, without form and void—"and darkness was upon the face of the deep." Darkness is the symbol of ignorance, and light is the symbol of Truth. "And God said [to the waiting mind], Let there be light [Truth]: and there was light."

Denial makes us receptive. "And God said. Let there be," as though the earth must let the light shine. And so it is. The mind must let the Truth come in. "Prepare ye the way of the Lord, make his paths straight," by beginning to clear out the rubbish of false thinking— pulling up the "plants which my Father hath not planted."

People who have sick bodies, or vices, or inharmonious surroundings are like pupils who have worked their problems incorrectly, and before they begin to work them aright they must first erase their old work, then begin the working anew with true principles for their bases of operations.

Right denial pulls down old, false structures built by vain imaginings, and leaves the mind ready to build anew.

The doctrine of denial

Every religion has taught denial in some form. All fasting is but the symbol of the denying which is going on in mind. Sacrifices represent the putting away, or the denying of the power of "the world, the flesh, and the devil." Fanatics have cut and lacerated their bodies, and sat in sackcloth and ashes, to signify their realization of the vanity or unreality of the earthly body and worldly life. In truth, the real denial was all the time in mind, and no external ceremony could make them, realize the nothingness of the worldly life and ways if they were not trying in all sincerity to realize it in heart and mind. We see this proven by people going through long fasts and other external forms of denial, and yet not realizing any more spirituality after them than before. All real denial begins in the heart and mind.

John the Baptist

The process of denial is represented in the Scriptures by John the Baptist, who, it was prophesied, must come first in order to prepare the way of the Lord, the full Gospel.

"Repent ye! Repent ye!" was John's cry. The literal translation of the Greek metamoia (mistranslated "repent ye") is "Change your mind." In other words, stop thinking about sin, and so stop the doing and speaking it. Change your mind as to what are the realities of life, .and seek the things of the Spirit. "Except ye become converted [turned right about] and become as little children [who know no evil] ye cannot enter into the kingdom of heaven."

Self-denial

"If any man will come after me, let him deny himself." How is it that Jesus denied himself? By beginning in heart and mind to set aside the fleshly man. He says, "If I honor myself, my honor is nothing;" "I speak not of myself, it is the Father that dwelleth in me, he doeth the works." He denied his personality, for he knew that that was not the real Self. He knew Himself to be Spirit, not flesh. "The flesh profiteth nothing," he said. He knew himself to be Immortal, not mortal as he seemed to be. He said, "Judge not by the appearance, but judge righteous judgment." We, too, are Spiritual, not material; divine Immortals, not carnal and mortal. We deny the reality of the carnal mind and body under the name "personality." It is a good term to express all the collective errors that man has held about himself. The word "person" (from the Latin per and sona, to sound through) was originally applied to a mask which ancient actors wore upon the stage. Most personalities seem to hide the real nature of the individual—beautiful natures obscured by ugly forms and features, great souls curtained by diminutive bodies. Denial of personality draws aside the curtain, dissolves the imperfect, and reveals the translucent body through which the Spirit shines and works untrammeled.

The fleshly body is not yourself, and nothing done to it can hurt you. Mentally look at all personality as you would look through darkness to the light. Deny its actions, its foolishness, its sickness, its weakness, its meanness, its wickedness, and these will melt before your true word like mist before the sun.

Evil, a lie.

To remember to meet every evil claim, suggestion or appearance with the silent assertion, "There is no evil," is to be a light in the midst of darkness, causing the evil to fly and the real good that was there all the time to come forward in all its strength and power.

You are like one who continually says to false report, "That is not so," and it cannot influence you because you will not believe in it. All evil is a lie, a delusion, and it has power to those only who believe in it. Thus Jesus defines evil and its author: "He was a murderer from the beginning and abode not in the truth, because there is no truth in him. When he speaketh a lie, he speaketh of his own: for he is a liar and the father of it." No matter how true a statement may seem to be, if it is not true of God, then it must be known as a relative truth or a lie, and we are not to be deceived by it. One way to lift the mind from believing in evil is to look at the falsities squarely and fearlessly, and say: "You are not real, you are not true. It is nothing. It has no real and true creator, and I will not believe in it any longer." But the most terse, effective, even drastic, denial that one can speak is embodied in those words, "There is no evil."

If you believe the mirage on the desert is a reality, a real lake of waters surrounded by trees, then you will pursue it as long as you are deceived, and endure many sufferings and hardships through your ignorance. But the traveler who knows it to be nothing, says so, and cannot be deluded into following it nor led out of his way, no matter how fair it may be to look upon. So should we regard all evil and all this dream-world which passes away continually, and which all prophets have pronounced "vanity of vanities," and "its nations as nothing in the eyes of the Lord."

Sense Evidence

"But can I not believe my senses?" the mortal cries. Surely not, since the senses are continually contradicting each other, as has been proven both by experiments and natural experiences. Even material science contradicts the senses. For example, the sun seems to rise and set, but astronomy tells us that that is but an appearance, and it is the earth that moves and not the sun. The senses say the moon is a flat disc, astronomy declares it to be a sphere; the stars seem points of light, whereas it is said that some are suns many thousand times greater than our sun.

We are not now looking to our senses for Truth, but to the divine Reason within us, and to our Intuition, "that light which lighteth every man that cometh into the world." When thy senses affirm that which thy reason denies, reject the testimony of thy senses, and listen only to thy reason. Maimonides.

The effect of denials

The mind that is determined to believe in God alone faithfully takes up the denial of all that is not God, and, as he walks along the Way, he soon begins to see that Truth proves itself true. What is the result of persistently holding, right in the face of appearances, to the thought, "There is no reality to sin; no real power, presence, or law to sin?"

It is to see vice and impure thinking drop right out of your own mind and life, and not only yours, but out of those for whom you speak the words. Does the denial of the reality of sin cause license, making people more sinful and wicked? Not at all. On the contrary it causes them to see that there is no pleasure in it, that there is no satisfaction in it, and a great realization of the uselessness and powerlessness of sin comes to the faithful student. For the saying is true, and Truth, boldly spoken though in silence, is a living power in itself capable of freeing from every bondage.—even of sin itself.

When the mind that dwells in the consciousness of God sends forth its word denying any place or power to sickness, pain, disease, then we see health spring- forth as flowers spring up when a crushing weight has been removed.

The right denial of personality causes egotism to fall from one with its pride and vanity, its sensitiveness and stupidity, and the universal Self to be revealed.

He who holds to the thought, "There is no real substance to matter, the Spirit is the only true substance," finds himself no longer burdened and limited by material things. His body seems light, the things of the world do not tire him. "They that wait upon the Lord shall renew their strength; they shall mount up with wings as eagles; they shall run, and not be weary; and they shall walk, and not faint."—Is. 40:31.

The effect of right words of denial is like water, for they cleanse, loosen, free, wash away, and dissolve false appearances. The effect of right affirmations is to fill in (fulfill), to make substantial, to build up, to establish, and cause to come into appearance that which is real and true.

Real baptism with water

The realization of true denial in thought, word, and deed is called being "born of water," and the realization of true affirmation is being "born of Spirit." This is the beginning of regeneration. He that is continually being cleansed by the word of denial—"Now are ye clean through the words which I have spoken unto you"—is being baptized with water. Water is the symbol of the cleansing power of repentance, change of mind, conversion, all of which come through the right denial of the world, the flesh, and the devil, or, as we have said, materiality (the world), the personal self (the flesh), and evil the devil).

The practice

To every suggestion of evil in your daily life mentally declare, "There is no evil." To all talk of people about evil, such as scandals, descriptions of diseases, accounts of deaths, disasters, fears, discouragements and dangers, silently say, "That is not true." Many cases have been healed by that simple, silent message.

Do not feel obliged to join in conversations that dwell upon the dark side of humanity. Courtesy and good judgment will cause you to reply in ways wherein there is no offense, and yet you make no concession to evil. Silence is better than assent to error. Learn the virtue of stillness.

Copy and learn the following denials, and repeat them night and morning in conjunction with the affirmations at the close of the preceding lesson:

Since in God there is no evil, I deny that there is any reality to evil at all. There is no real power in sin or death. There is no real substance to sickness or disease. There is no true cause for sorrow. There is nothing to fear.

God's world is Spiritual, not material. There is no matter, Spirit is the only substance.

Personality is not the real Self. The true Individual is Spirit, not flesh.

I am the free and fearless, impersonal, selfless child of God, and what I am so are you, my neighbor, as myself. Amen.

One of the happiest ways of denying for one's self is to begin your sentences with, "I am free," such as "I am free from doubt," "I am free from care," and so forth.

The denial of your personality does not destroy your Individuality, but, to the contrary, establishes it. Fear not; "He that loseth his life [loses the limited personal conception of life] for my sake [the Truth's sake] shall find it [the true Individual life]."—Matt. 10:39.

LESSON III. WORDS, THEIR USE AND POWER.

Mind, the great cause

GOD is supreme Intelligence, Wisdom, Understanding, Reason, all of which can be comprehended in the one word, Mind. God is Mind, and since God is the great first cause, therefore Mind is the great first cause. Divine Mind is the one creative power and source of all true manifestation.

What can be predicated of God is true of Man, who is the image and likeness of God. Man's mind is the cause of all that is in his life. Solo- on says, "As he thinketh in his heart, so is he" (Prov. 23:7), and the Dhammapada expresses the same idea in the following words:

All that we are is the result of what we have thought; it is founded on our thoughts, it is made up of our thoughts. If a man speaks or acts with an evil thought, pain follows him as the wheel follows the ox that draws the cart. If a man speaks or acts with a pure thought, happiness follows him like a shadow that never leaves him.

Thoughts are the product of Mind, and the means through which Mind works. The thoughts of divine Mind are pure and good, true, and full of life and health, and they produce heavenly conditions. In the measure that man's mind dwells upon the pure and the good, he enters into health and happiness. The only real thoughts that man has are those from the Mind of God, in which is no evil imagination, memory, or production. "To think the thoughts of God after Him," as the great Kepler said, is to have a mind filled with noble, wise, loving thoughts in which there is no mixture of error or evil.

Discord and disease arise from a mixed mentality in which is belief in both good and evil as real. Pure thoughts result in pure manifestations, but mixed thoughts show forth as a mixture, an adulteration, in the bodies and circumstances of the thinkers.

Orderly thinking

The mind of man is set in order by the science of God, and all the good thoughts are gathered and ascribed to their divine source, while the beliefs in evil are separated, as the tares were taken out of the wheat in the parable (Matt. 13: 30), and cast out into nothingness.

Divine Science and logic systematize and arrange thoughts, so that their nature is known, and name and place are given to them.

Life proves to man that a mind filled with good imagery, with peaceful, loving, gentle, trustful thoughts, is in Heaven, while one who dwells upon evil, malice, revenge, injustice, pain, and misery is in hell. For Heaven and hell are states of mind. "A good man out of the good treasure of his heart bring- eth forth good things: and an evil man out of the evil treasure bringeth forth evil things."—Matt. 12:35

All the health and happiness you have is the result of your belief in Good, which, in order to persist, must have its foundation in the true knowledge of God. If you would be constantly happy, that is, manifest your true Being which is at peace, strong and healthy, prosperous and full of love and knowledge, you must think good thoughts not only "now and then" but perpetually, which means the casting out of every other kind of thought.

We must begin to put out of our minds miserable, gloomy thoughts, not letting memories of injuries, sorrows, and mistakes possess us, and allow only those thoughts which give power and presence to Good remain in our mentality. We must put from us every doubt and fear, all discouraging thoughts of every kind, and hold fast only to those thoughts that God thinks.

The Kingdom of Heaven

Whoever is in a state of happiness is in Heaven, no matter what his surroundings may be, for Heaven is a consciousness, not a place. The Kingdom may be represented by a place filled with joy, beauty, and goodness, but primarily it is within our hearts and minds, and does not depend upon externals for perpetuation. We must find Heaven within ourselves, regardless of our associates and environments. As soon as we identify ourselves with the Divine within we become powers to externalize our inward happiness in forms which fitly symbolize God's creation. "And when he [Jesus] was demanded of the Pharisees, when the kingdom of God should come, he answered them and said, The kingdom of God cometh not with observation: neither shall they say, Lo, here! or, lo there! for, behold, the kingdom of God is within you."—Luke 17: 21.

Jesus Christ came to teach men to look for Heaven right in their midst. He called his teaching "Preaching the Kingdom of Heaven," which is, in other words, declaring the ruling of the Good. At one time he contrasts it to the old preaching: "The law and the prophets were until John: since that time the kingdom of God is preached, and every man presseth into it."—Luke 16:16. He declared that every nation must hear of this teaching before the end of the old conditions could come (Matt. 24:14), and he has but one instruction to all his followers as to their preaching: "As ye go, preach, saying, The kingdom of heaven is at hand."—Matt. 10:7. What does the phrase "at hand" mean? What do you mean when in writing a letter in answer to a correspondent you say, "Your letter is at hand?" Do you mean that it is coming by and by? No. You mean that it is in this place at this present moment—here now. So also Jesus meant: The Kingdom of Heaven is here now. Is not this the good news—the gospel we are to proclaim the world over? The Christ still says to you, "Go, preach the Kingdom of Heaven is at hand."

Preach goodness and happiness as the only real presence and power (kingdom) in all the universe.

Must we speak contrary to the senses? Did not Jesus do so? With thousands of poor, hungry, sick, miserable creatures around him he still declared the true Kingdom. And while he spoke Heaven came to one after another of those cripples and miserable beings—he proved his doctrine by his works.

Does it seem to you that you are telling a lie to say these things? Then remember that you are speaking of everlasting things only, and you will see that your words are true. The student of divine things ceases to think or talk about worldly and temporal appearances as though they were realities, but he lets his "conversation" be "in heaven," and enlarges upon the bright side of life, and learns to meditate upon and discuss the enduring things of Being.

When you say there is no evil, sin, sickness or death you are speaking of the real World ("My kingdom is not of this world"), where none of these things have any place. When you say, "I am pure and holy," "I am strong and well," you are speaking of the real I, the true Self, and not of the personality called by an earthly name, and which but represents you for the time being.

Is it not written in the Scripture, "Let the weak say, I am strong" (Joel 3:10)? Ignore the personal claims of sickness, believe only in the Son of God, and identify your I AM with the pure and holy, healthy, immortal Son of God. So also when speaking to others address the Real in them, and you will no longer feel that you are saying that which is not true in denying the senses, and declaring your neighbor well and strong. "Speak ye every man truth to his neighbor . . . and let none of you imagine evil in your hearts against his neighbor."—Zech. 8: 16, 17. "He that speaketh truth sheweth forth righteousness. ... the tongue of the wise is health."- Prov. 12:17, 18

Invisible Good made visible

The Good is all about us and in us. We live, move, and have our being in Health, Life, and

Love. Good fills a11 things as thoughts fill the mind. But nothing comes forth without the Word. "All things were made by him [the Word]; and without him was not anything made that was made." — John 1:3.

Words are the expression of Mind. Words are thoughts made visible, or brought to consciousness and realization.

We are continually speaking words, but not always aloud, for there are silent or mental words as well as audible. These words are forming and reforming, un- forming and deforming all the conditions and manifestations in and around us. If our silent or audible words dwell upon evil, then evil conditions "show forth;" if upon good, then good is manifest. "But I say unto you, That every idle [even the lightest, vainest] word that men shall speak, they shall give an account thereof ... for by thy words thou shalt be justified [established in Good] and by thy words thou shalt be condemned" [continue in ignorance and misery]. — Matt. 12:36, 37.

If one says, "I am sick," "I can't understand," "I am tired," and so forth, he will continue subject to sickness, to be in ignorance, be weary, and so forth, until Truth causes him to cease from such utterances through a true change of heart.

If one says, "I will fear no evil for thou art with me," when faced by danger; or, "I love you," before the darts of hatred and persecution; or, "The child of God knows no failure or discouragement," he shall be established in fearlessness, in omnipotent love, in success, in just the measure that he realizes the truth of the words he utters.

The Word is the divine means by which God creates, and Man, following in the footsteps of God, uses the same means, words, to bring into manifestation what God has already created.

The original intention and use of language was not to convey thought, but for the purpose of creation. Spiritual magicians can decree a thing, and it shall be established unto them (Job 22:28).

In the Golden Age all men shall work after the manner of Christ, who did all things by his word—healing the sick, raising the dead, stilling the storm, feeding the multitudes.

Jesus declared, "What things soever he [the Father] doeth, these also doeth the Son, likewise" (John 5:i9), and inspiration revealed to the writer of Genesis that previous to every manifestation "God said."

"And God said, Let there be light: and there was light." "And God said, Let there be a firmament . . . and it was so."

"And God said, Let the earth bring forth grass . . . and it was so." "And God said, Let there be lights ... and it was so."

"And God said, Let the waters bring forth." "And God said, Let us make man in our image."

Whoever follows in the footsteps of Jesus will work as he saw the Father work, speaking forth all that is to be manifest by the power of decree.

The Scripture

Throughout the Bible are references to God's word, its delight, and its power. Men have missed the meaning of those texts by thinking that it was the written book that was referred to, whereas the Bible itself teaches that we are to look within our hearts for the word of God and not to externals. "It is not in heaven, that thou shouldst say, Who shall go up for us to heaven, and bring it unto us, that we may hear it, and do it? Neither is it beyond the sea, that thou shouldst say, Who shall go over the sea for us, and bring it unto us, that we may hear it, and do it? But the word is very nigh unto thee, in thy mouth, and in thy heart that thou mayst do it."— Deut. 30:12-14.

It has been the inspired custom of wise men of the most spiritual nations to teach the people the holy utterances of others, that their hearts and tongues might become receptive to the divine Voice within themselves, that "well of water springing up to everlasting life." "[My words] are life unto those that find them, and health to all their flesh."—Prov. 4:22.

Whoever learns where to look for divine words and believes in the holy source of inspiration within himself will realize with Jeremiah: "Thy words were found, and I did eat them, and thy word was unto me the joy and rejoicing of mine heart: for I am called by thy name, O Lord God of hosts."— Jer. 15:16.

If one will read the one hundred and nineteenth Psalm with this new understanding that God's word is the Truth—a living, healing presence in his own mind—and that he can speak it, and so bring forth divine works, then the Scripture will become unsealed to him in many parts.

Prayer

One of the forms of "speaking the word" is Prayer. As all modes of conversing unite one, more or less, according to the nature of the communication, with those whom we address, so it is with prayer. It is one means of making connection with universal Mind. A law of communion is fulfilled by right prayer, as exact a law as the one governing the transmission of electric force, or the centralizing of energy through any mechanical device.

The Soul's aspiration combined with the Mind's knowledge that what is desired is already an accomplished fact constitutes the "prayer of the righteous man that availeth much."

By prayer man acknowledges the true source of that which he desires, and the belief is turned away from its false props to the real helper.

The divine child does not beg or beseech its Heavenly Father, knowing His holy will is to give him every good thing. Prayer is not for the changing of God, who is the same yesterday, to-day, and forever, but it is for the changing of the mortal from an unbelieving and false-believing state to a consciousness like the true Mind, which knows all things to be possible to him who believes.

Thanksgiving, praise of the omnipotence and omnipresence of Good, and acknowledgment of God, lift the mind out of doubts and fears, and prepare it to cooperate in bringing to pass the very thing desired.

In order that prayer may be realization it is well to put it into an affirmative form instead of a petition. By this method the direction of Jesus is most easily fulfilled that, "What things soever ye desire, when ye pray, believe that ye receive them, and ye shall have them."—Mark 11 -.24.

Practice

Bring the tongue under absolute and perfect control. No one can advance in spiritual unfoldment who permits the tongue to voice evil. So essential is it that the student control his lips that the very first practice enjoined by Pythagoras was a silence of five years.

James says, "If any man offend not in word, the same is a perfect man, and able also to bridle the whole body." The easiest way to bring all the body under subjection is to put a guard upon the lips, that no utterance be other than happy, peaceful, harmless, loving, kind. "I said, I will take heed to my ways, that I sin not with my tongue: I will keep my mouth with a bridle, while the wicked is before me."—Ps. 39:1. "Set a watch, O Lord, before my mouth; keep the door of my lips."—Ps. 14113. "To him that ordereth his conversation aright will I shew the salvation of God." —Ps. 50:23.

Our spoken words are the result of our silent words, therefore the thoughts must be watched continuously in order that our conversation be orderly and right. See that you do not criticize in secret, that you cease from mentally finding fault with another.

Put away all sarcasm from your speech. Never complain. Do not prophesy evil— the Greeks called that blasphemy ("speaking injury" to another), and they avoided a grumbler or one who foretold misfortune because they believed he brought them bad luck.

Refrain from accusing others of hypnotism, adultery, or any other evil practices. Withdraw all accusation from yourself. Says the Bhagavad Gita:

Upraise the self by the self, do not sink the self; for the self is the friend of the self, and even the self is the enemy of the self.

Do not let your lips form such utterances as, "I am stupid," "I hate" this and that, "I have no strength," "I am always unlucky."

Again, see that you cease from petty, false statements about your associates. It is folly to depreciate any one, for instance calling your boy "bad," or referring to the delinquencies of your partner, or calling attention to the awkwardness and rudeness of those whom we would gladly see graceful and courteous. Have a good word for every one or else keep silent.

Pray Without Ceasing

Accustom yourself to praying "without ceasing" by silently communing with the Good in all. Prayer is letting God think and speak through you, it is thinking God, it is God thinking. This communion with God is your very life, and the more one's mind can be filled with holy thoughts and desires the more manifestation there will be in and through one of health, prosperity, knowledge, and love.

Often breathe this prayer: "Let the words of my mouth, and the meditation of my heart, be acceptable in thy sight, O Lord, my strength, and my redeemer." —Ps. 19:14. Add these words to the evening and morning repetition of affirmations and denials given in the previous lessons.

That prayer may be natural let it be free from ritualistic forms. Constancy in prayer precludes the necessity of certain external attitudes, such as kneeling, and reveals that a life filled with God-desires and God-works is more acceptable to Deity than much prostration and the recitation of many formal orisons.

"Watch ye therefore, and pray always, that ye may be accounted worthy [able] to escape all these things that shall come to pass [every calamity, disaster, disease, and death], and to stand before the Son of man" [the realization of your own sublime Divinity].— Luke 21 36.

LESSON IV. FAITH.

ONCE when the disciples of Jesus Christ were unsuccessful in healing a case that was brought to them they asked the Master what was the reason of their failure. His answer was brief, but in it lies the clue to all inability to solve the problems of life when one knows the great principles of Being, and ought to understand their application. "Jesus said unto them, Because of your unbelief: for verily I say unto you, If ye have faith as a grain of mustard seed, ye shall say unto this mountain, Remove hence to yonder place; and it shall remove; and nothing shall be impossible unto you."— Matt. 17:20.

Unbelief in One's Self

What is the unbelief that seems to prevent the disciples of Truth from accomplishing the works? It is unbelief in one's self, in the divine power to work through one, in the presence and power of Good, of Health, and Life, and Love. It is belief in the opposites of God, in disease, death, failure, and evil generally.

The young student beginning to learn the principles of the science of God is like one who takes up the study of mathematics or music. He believes heartily in the cause which he has espoused and applies himself with assiduity to understanding and remembering its rules, but he does not expect to do well, or to be a master in his science, but by determined, faithful practice.

Nothing is promised to half-hearted service, or to a faith that is divided between Good and evil, or between Mind and matter. "He that doubteth is like the surge of the sea, driven by the wind and tossed. For let not that man think that he shall receive any thing of the Lord." — Jas. 1:6, 7 (Revised Version).

Faith That Wins

The faith that wins is that which is placed wholly in God, Spirit, Mind, as the only real substance and power. In the proportion that the student turns away from believing in the reality of evil, disease, pain, and sorrow, and from believing in the power of sin, death, and materiality, he will be able to prove the healing, freeing efficacy of divine Mind.

Whoever begins to work out life's problems by divine rule is a pioneer in his own mental realm, and indeed, at the present stage of human unfoldment, he is a pioneer in the racemind, and will need to advance with the same bravery and fidelity that distinguished those men and women who have been the first settlers and reclaimers of unknown lands in the physical sphere. The race-thoughts concerning the reality of evil are like the rocks and wild growth upon uncultivated ground — the unbelieving, bigoted, malicious resistance of ignorance like the heathen Amorites and Hittites who were in possession of the fair land that was to be developed by the race obedient to God.

Steadfastness to Principle, especially in the face of the oppositions of sense and material belief, will meet the false suppositions of the race-mind, as the persistent shining of the sun upon a block of ice at last overcomes its coldness and hardness.

All your faith must be placed in God, and God alone. It will not do to have faith in the power of Good and, at the same time, believe there is some power in evil. It will not do to look to the word of God for our healing and at the same time lean upon some material aid. Continually the word of the Lord is coming to us, "Choose ye this day whom ye will serve"—that is, what ye will acknowledge as the power, Good or evil, God or devil, Mind or matter, and continually we choose.

"Ye cannot serve two masters." Ye cannot serve both God and mammon. So, taking the uncompromising stand that God the Spirit is all-sufficient, the one healer, the one support and supply, the one defender and deliverer, you establish your faith, and then, no matter what comes to you, you are carried through it all- victorious.

True faith is a firm, persistent, determined belief in Almighty Good— changeless, deathless, substantial Spirit—as the All in All. Faith is the substance of everything that you desire. Out of your own believing is formed, that is, brought into manifestation, that which you are wishing to have. Jesus understood this law of mind, so all his teachings were to have faith, or, as he often expressed it, to believe. "Have faith in God," he said. The better translation is "Have the faith of God."—Mark 11:22 (see the margin).

"For verily I say unto you, That whosoever shall say unto this mountain, Be thou removed, and be thou cast into the sea; and shall not doubt in his heart, but shall believe that those things which he saith shall come to pass; he shall have whatsoever he saith."— Mark 11:23.

"All things are possible to him that believeth." And what is this believing? Is it believing in the historical character, Jesus of Nazareth? Is it believing in a creed? No. It is believing in your own divinity, even as Jesus believed in his. It is believing in your own words—it is believing in God in you, just as Jesus believed in the Father, our God, in him.

He who would see the mountains move at his word, who would see loaves and fishes increase, and waters firm under his feet, and winds obey him, diseases fly away, sins dissolve, death succumb to his word, must not have one doubt in his heart of his divine power, must see himself one with God, so that when he speaks he sees that it is God speaking. Then indeed shall he believe that those things that he saith shall come to pass, because he lets God speak the word in him—he does not look at the personality as himself—and true indeed is it of him that he shall have whatsoever he saith.

Have the Faith of God

What is God's faith? It is faith in Himself, because He knows there is none else in whom to have faith. Have faith in yourself. Have faith in God in you. God is your own true Self. God, the Son, and God, the Father, are one and the same. God in you is the only power and presence. God in all is the Reality of all. God is the only one in your neighbor. God is the only one you trust.

There are times in the on-going of the spiritual student when he is brought face to face with hard problems and strange situations. Then it may be that evil seems more real to you than usual, that here is a place where the Word does not seem to act with its customary effect, and doubts begin to creep in, and you feel that you are being forsaken. Then is the time when you show your steadfastness, then you prove yourself to yourself, then, just at such times, you show your faith in Good as the only real presence and divine Mind as the all-sufficient power. Such times in the Truth- seeker's experience have been described as a clashing of Truth and error, the error trying to hold its ground while the Truth steadily and firmly establishes itself. It is the warring of the flesh against the Spirit, and the Spirit overcoming. The Truth does not fight, neither does the Spirit, but it is error apparently struggling as though it feels that its time is short, and the student must keep still and see the bloodless, silent, sure victory of the Good, of Health, of Life, of Truth.

It has always been in the history of the world that whenever a great truth has been given to it, the world fights it; but those who do not let themselves be influenced by fear or doubt, but have the courage of their convictions and stand by their principles, no matter who wars against them, finally find themselves upon the victorious side.

Even in what are called material truths there is seldom any great discovery given to the world that it will accept at once. How Galileo was fought! How Columbus was laughed at and talked to to discourage him! And how he held out! The last days of his voyage, just before the discovery, when the sailors were very desperate and threatening mutiny if Columbus would not turn back, are a good example of those days that sometimes seem to come to the student of Truth when he is urged by circumstances, by doubts, by his senses, by personality, to give up his stand and throw aside his principles; then is he to have faith in his God, even as Columbus had in himself and his expedition, and God who promises all things to them that trust Him will never fail him.

All Have Faith

If one says he has no faith, he is mistaken. All have faith, for Faith is God. The only question is, what have you been having faith in? Has it been in disease, that it is strong and persistent, and will require years to heal, or else is incurable?

When seeking satisfaction, what have you put your faith in? Whisky? When looking for power, what have you believed in? Money? Our faith has been scattered and dissipated amongst a thousand false gods, and all that we have been putting into evils and into material things must be gathered and concentrated in God.

There is no unbelief— Whoever plants a seed beneath the sod, And waits to see it push away the clod, Trusts he in God.

There is no unbelief—

The heart that looks on when the eyelids close, And dares to live when life has only woes, God's comfort knows.

There is no unbelief,

And still by day and night, unconsciously,

The heart lives by that faith the lips deny— God knoweth why.

Lizzie York Case.

Faith is Your Life.

Your faith is your life. If one's faith is in a power that is limited then the life seems limited, and why place your faith in anything less than omnipotence? All that the Truth teaches is to put your faith in the Supreme and not in any thing or any power less than God. You take the faith which you have placed in medicines, opiates, liniments, canes and crutches, eye-glasses, trusses, tonics, and so forth ("gods of wood and stone"), and give it to Spirit alone, believing God supports you, God invigorates you, God is your seeing power and health; and then you do not compromise in any way. To try to serve two masters, trusting the Spirit to heal you, and looking to the smallest particle of matter, even to a glass of water, for your healing is that mistake which is called in the Scripture "idolatry." And the result is only partial healing, or being healed only to get sick again.

Now we wish absolute healing; we desire only that healing which is of God, the Highest, that healing that is everlasting. Looking to powers that are unreliable and changeable brings results that are unreliable and changeable. That is the reason why the practice of medicine can never be a science. It is largely theoretical and experimental—"empiricism" they call it.

There is but One Physician that never fails when we trust Him completely. We place all our trust in the unlimited Healer, and the result to us is unlimited Health.

If any look to a limited power for healing, such as materia medica, substance less than the divine Substance, material which is not God; or mesmerism, a will-power less than the divine Will, and even contrary to it; or magnetism, an emanation said to be from the human body, but limited, often evil—in other words, an emanation less than the divine Essence; or to mediumship, a control by what are called spirits, said to be inferior to the Most High, the One Spirit, these will be but slightly healed. "They have healed also the hurt of the daughter of my people slightly" (Jer. 6:i4), because they look to other gods than the One God.

"And Asa in the thirty and ninth year of his reign was diseased in his feet, until his disease was exceeding great: yet in his disease he sought not to the Lord, but to the physicians. And Asa slept with his fathers, and died in the one and fortieth year of his reign."— 2 Chron. 16:12, 13.

The Word, the healing power

"He sent his word and healed them."—Ps. 107:20. The Word of God is the one healing power, the universal panacea, the elixir of life, the fountain of youth, that men have been searching for all these years. And that the Word of God may heal every The Word the time we must trust in it, and it alone, healing power. It will not do to trust in the Word of God one moment and in aconite the next, to look to the Will of God one day and to the personal will another. Let that will which says it can be weakened and grow exhausted be utterly nothing, and let the Will of God be the only acknowledged power.

Look not to personality for healing, whether in the flesh or out of the flesh. Look to no magnetism, mesmerism, or mediumship for your healing, but "Look unto me, and be ye saved [healed], all the ends of the earth: for I am God, and there is none else."—Is. 45 22.

"But," you may say, "are not these things the means by which health comes? Does not

God use means?" Yes, God uses means, but His means are spiritual like Himself—divine Mind and its ideas. And though it seems as if it is the material medicine that heals, yet it is the spiritual idea of which the drug is a symbol that really does the healing. Every material thing is the shadow or reflection of some divine thought, and we who know can take the thought direct without the interference of symbol, and we must do so in order to receive the full blessing of perfect health.

Symbolic or material means are only for the minds that do not take the whole Truth and are not seeking the Highest. There is no virtue in material things themselves, but the power is in the mentalities that have concentrated their thought upon them, thus endowing them with a reflected potency.

The question rises, why did Jesus once use the clay and spittle (John 9:6), and Elisha tell the leper to bathe in Jordan (2 Kings 5:10)? If one understands the symbolism of material things, then he uses them without falsely ascribing power to them. Thus Jesus used the clay and spittle symbolically, knowing that the mixture had no power in itself. It was his mind that did the work, even while resorting to symbolism to assist the feeble faith of the man born blind. So also when Naaman was told to bathe in Jordan, Elisha knew that Jordan water of itself could heal no one, but the meek and obedient act of Naaman would effect his healing when backed by the mighty faith of the man of God.

Until our minds become thoroughly imbued with the understanding that Mind is the only causative power, and that there is no causation in matter, let us not use symbols, but put all our trust in the Word of Truth. We have faith in God's Word because we understand its nature and unlimited power. This is the secret of true faith—to know in whom we believe.

True prayer

"And the prayer of faith shall save the sick."—Jas. 5:15 True prayer is believing that all things are now yours; all good is now come to pass—not looking into the future for the answer to your prayer, not saying, "To-morrow (or next week) I shall be well," but holding fast to the thought: "Now I am well; now I am free; now all is accomplished." For this is the truth concerning real Being. God is your health. Now you live, move, and have your being in the health that is God. Realize this. You breathe health. Health attends your every step. Health is omnipresent. This is the believing which is the substance of your prayer. "And all things, whatsoever ye shall ask in prayer, believing, ye shall receive,"— Matt. 21:19.

Do not think it may not be the will of God to give you that good thing you desire. Honor God. Trust the divine Love. If an earthly father who had the power would give you that gift you wish, will not your Heavenly Father give it to you (Matt. 7:11)?

If you ask God for life and healing, will He send death and disease? Do you think it is His will that evil should be your portion? What a misunderstanding of God that would be! Jesus did the will of his Father, and we see how that will worked, in healing and giving more life and blessing every way.

The will of God done in Heaven produces happiness only, therefore when it is done on the earth, as it is in Heaven, it will never bring forth misery, sickness, or any other evil.

Trust the will of God that it works you good and good only. Then you will not be paralyzed in your prayers—you will not stop in your praying— you will pray and not faint, just as Jesus gave directions (Luke 18:1).

Persistency in prayer

Persistency in prayer is prevailing with God. Speak the word of God— the word of believing that ye have received—in season and out of season. Let no doubt rebuff you. Let no word of Scripture, of the Angel of the Lord, yea, the very Christ himself, discourage you or cause you to move away from your faith that God is with you and Good is for you. Remember how Jacob would not let the Angel of the Lord go from him until he blessed him (Gen. 32:26). Remember how the Syro-Phoenician woman would not take "No" to her prayers, though it would seem as though Jesus himself wrestled with her (Mark 7:26; Matt. 15:21-28).

God loves you to trust in His goodness. "Prove me now," He says continually. "Prove me now herewith, saith the Lord of Hosts, if I will not open you the windows of heaven, and pour out a blessing, that there shall not be room enough to receive it."—Mai. 3:10.

We trust God not only as our physician, but as our banker, our defender, as our husband, our father, our all in all; therefore we do not acknowledge anything or anyone as our support but God. Wherever we have said "healing" and "health," we know it to mean the same as saving and salvation, or redemption—these are all one in God.

This is the prayer of faith that heals the sick: to know God, to trust the goodness of God, to believe in the mercy, the indulgence of God, who gives good always and forever, and never withholds any good that his child asks.

And then we must be constant in this knowledge and not let our senses argue us off our base, or circumstances move us to doubt the presence of God, but to believe despite everything to the contrary. According to your faith it shall be done unto you. "If ye abide in me, and my words abide in you, ye shall ask what ye will, and it shall be done unto you."—John 15 7.

Practice

Practice concentrating all your faith in God, Good, Health, Life, Prosperity. When doubts, or fears, or discouragement creep into the mind, remember it is a trial of faith. Stand firm. Declare the power of God. Assert your divine nature, that there is no fear in you. There is no cause for doubt and discouragement, ever, in God's world. Your mind is fixed and centered upon the Almighty Good whose changeless will is to establish the Kingdom of Heaven in man's heart and upon the earth. It is the will of your God that you shall manifest health, long life, prosperity, and perfect happiness through living a sinless, loving, unselfish life.

Trust God to the uttermost, as you would an earthly lover who would move Heaven and earth to bless you and set you free from pain and misery.

Practice the constant silent prayer of thanksgiving and acknowledgment that all the good your heart is desiring is now come to pass.

THE LORD'S PRAYER.

Affirmed as one prays who believes that already he has received.

Our Father who art in heaven, Hallowed is Thy name;

Thy kingdom is come, Thy will is done in earth, as it is in heaven.

Thou dost give us this day, our daily bread;

Thou dost forgive us our debts as we forgive our debtors;

Thou dost lead us, not into temptation, but dost deliver us from evil. For Thine is the kingdom and the power and the glory forever.

IT IS SO.

LESSON V. KNOWLEDGE AND GOOD JUDGMENT.

FAITH and understanding go hand in hand when the works of the Christ are made manifest. Whenever either appears alone there comes a limitation in healing, for each is essential to the full manifestation of the other.

The belief in faith alone, commonly called "blind faith," in which the disciple does not seek knowledge, degenerates into superstition and eventually becomes barren. Increase of faith comes through increase of knowledge ("I know whom I have believed"—2 Tim. 1:12), and the student who seeks to add to his consciousness of healing power must apply himself to a fervent and systematic study of divine Mind and its idea.

Misunderstanding of the character and office of God and His child, Man, is the cause of impotency in accomplishing divine works. Many a faith-healer has lost a case because of this lack of knowledge of God's wish concerning the one for whom he is praying. Perhaps he has prayed earnestly, and is near the state of consciousness whereby the false claim of disease can be met and vanquished when a tempting doubt begins to insinuate itself into his mind:

"Perhaps it is not the will of God that this one shall be healed; perhaps his time has come to die."

Then the ardor of the petitioner begins to cool. He is shaken. He fears to proceed lest he be doing that which is contrary to the divine will. He weakens, he ceases to pray, and the patient goes "the way of all flesh."

"The prayer of faith shall save the sick, and the Lord shall raise him up."—Jas. 5:15. But the faith that always succeeds must be founded upon the knowledge that it is not the will of God that any man shall die. The world has hypnotized itself too long upon this subject, and must now be awakened to the truth that God does not send death any more than He sends sin. "The wages of sin is death; but the gift of God is eternal life."—Rom. 6123. "I have no pleasure in the death of him that dieth, saith the Lord God: wherefore turn yourselves, and live ye."—Eze. 18:32.

"God is not the author of confusion, but of peace." —I Cor. 14:33. God is not the author of discord, such as disease and death. Ignorance is the cause of all evil manifestations, and the grossest ignorance of all is to ascribe their origin to God. Let us be healed of this ignorance.

Wisdom

Solomon says, "Wisdom is the principal thing; therefore get wisdom: and with all thy getting get understanding."—Prov. 4:7.

"This is life eternal, that they might know thee the only true God, and Jesus Christ, whom thou hast sent" (John 17:3), breathed that Master of knowledge who had the key to all power—the only true God and perfect Man, His child. All true knowledge takes its rise in this primum mobile of understanding, the Unity of God and the Divinity of Man.

God and Man are to be studied and thoroughly known, and thus shall the problems of life be solved, and eternal health and happiness be ours.

The mind must be fully imbued with the foundation principles of this teaching in order to receive and assimilate the lessons that are their logical sequence.

The basic propositions, briefly reviewed, can be stated as follows:

Since God, the Good, is all, evil has no real place or power.

Since Man, God's child, is divine, the carnal self has no real place or power.

Since God's World is spiritual substance, materiality has no real place or power. Those semblances of consciousness called "carnal sense" and the "human intellect" naturally rebel against one or more of these statements, for spiritual things are spiritually discerned. But there is an inner teacher called the Intuition that will calmly and steadily hold to their truth until at last fretting, resisting mortal will yields, and the God-wisdom (the divine sophia of Paul, Solomon, and the other wise ones) has its way. Paul expresses this very clearly in Corinthians, second chapter, and also James, in James, third chapter, thirteenth to eighteenth verses, which passages the student will please read and ponder.

The teacher within.

True understanding comes from within. "There is a spirit in man: and the inspiration of the Almighty giveth them understanding."—Job 32:8. Only God can teach us Truth. And since Man is the image of Omniscience, within him is all knowledge, and the Spirit of Truth is his true instructor. The most that an external teacher can do is to point to this inner teacher and train the student to become receptive to instruction from his own Soul.

The best educators of the day tell us that all one will ever know is already in him— was in him even as a child, as the oak is in the acorn. Books, travel, and other externals are but suggestions which serve to uncover and draw out the knowledge that is within.

By seeking the highest wisdom of all, that of divine Mind, all other knowledge will be added. Being filled with spiritual knowledge does not exclude an understanding of the things of the world, just as knowing about the sun does not prevent our knowing about its reflection in the sea.

Through prayer men and women have come, even suddenly, to the ability to read, to compute numbers, to understand foreign tongues. By faithfully believing in the inner Teacher students have had the arts of worldly wisdom given them, becoming correct in speech, astute in reasoning, excelling in music and painting, through seeking the Highest. "And the Jews marveled, saying, How knoweth this man letters, having never learned?"— John 7:15. "And all that heard him [Jesus] were astonished at his understanding and answers."—Luke 2:47. "Daniel answered and said, Blessed be the name of God forever and ever: for wisdom and might are his: ... he giveth wisdom unto the wise, and knowledge to them that know understanding."—Dan. 2:20, 21.

Divine knowledge is self-increasing. He who claims knowledge for himself will have knowledge added, but he who reiterates, "I don't know," and "I can't understand," thus denying Wisdom, will be denied (Matt. 10:33).

"Take heed therefore how ye hear: for whosoever hath, to him shall be given."— Luke 8:18. Let us get more understanding by dwelling often upon what we do already know, and to every question that comes into mind respond silently, "I understand, I know the answer." Then it will come to pass that the faithful student will find his teachers coming to him, books will open to the places wherein the information lies, and he can learn from everybody and everything, finding . ..tongues in trees, books in the running brooks, Sermons in stones, and good in everything.

The Truth student who does not depend upon external teachers and books finds all life in collusion to advance him in the understanding of things real and unreal, educating him both within and without.

Scriptures, an open book.

The Scriptures become an open book to those who listen to the Spirit of Truth.

Inspiration is not limited to a few souls- All are inspired, for inspiration is the breath of God, by which man lives. Every good thought is an inspiration, no matter how commonplace and trite it may be.

True prophets and spiritual seers are the result of ardent search after spiritual light. To breathe in and forth thoughts of good continually manifests the mind of Christ and gives the power to interpret Scripture, causing it to bless, feed, and instruct in divine things, according to its holy intention.

The Bible is a rich storehouse of Truth, but it takes the Mind that inspired it to give its meaning. Therefore intellectual effort cannot remove the veil without the co-operation of the spiritual Mind.

Biblical correspondence

There is a Correspondence between things natural and things spiritual which is revealed to the wise one, and this not only opens the eyes to a right reading of Scripture, but also causes all nature to reveal herself as a great symbolism of the processes of thought and the laws of Mind.

In symbolism men and women represent dominant ideas in the mind; divisions of the earth, mountains, islands, seas, signify states of mind; trees, rocks, animals, stand for traits of character.

The Bible from Genesis to Revelation is an account of man's spiritual ongoing as a race and as an individual from the time he rises above the "dust of the ground" (Gen. 2:7), or from the common lot of humanity, to the day in which he is given a name above every earthly name (Rev. 2:17; 22:4) and stands a proven Son of the Most High.

The divine science of correspondence has been greatly uncovered through the light of the seer, Swedenborg. It has always been the language of the prophets (Jer. 1:1-14; Eze. 37:16-21; Heb. 8:5; Gal. 4: 22-31), and of poets and sages. "And without a parable spake he not unto them."—Matt. 13:34. "When he, the Spirit of truth, is come, he shall guide you into all truth ... for he shall receive of mine and shew it unto you."—John 16:13, 14.

Spiritual transactions must be translated into the language of mortal-sense that they be understood, so as to be of practical benefit to mortals who desire to be redeemed from mortality.

The Truth has always been in the world, but the fear and intolerance of men have kept it hid; also the intoxication of earthly pursuits has blinded their eyes to its holy joys. But now the race is rapidly awakening from its dream that satisfaction can be found in worldly pleasures, and the age is ripe for the fullest presentation of God's Truth.

Good judgment

The mind that accepts the whole Truth regardless of consequences and independent of the fears of man comes to judgment, that divine faculty by which he discriminates between good and evil, the spiritual and material, the divine and carnal. The process of separating the false from the true begins in his mentality and life, and he has the good sense or good judgment to hold fast to the eternally good and utterly refuse the evil.

The Day of Judgment is revealed to be a continuous day, now ruling our lives and casting out error. "Now is the judgment of this world: now shall the prince of this world be cast out."—John 12:31. "Because the prince of this world is judged."— John 16:11. It is the presence of God's good judgment in the heart of the devotee.

The wheat is separated from the tares, the truth from the error, the sheep from the goats, the spiritual traits from the carnal, the positive from the negative, each being put in its true place.

The day of judgment is a welcome day, for by good judgment comes knowledge of this mixed world of appearances in which good and evil seem so commingled, the divine and the human so interwoven, truth and error so confused as to justly merit the appellation, an "adulterous [or adulterated] generation" (Mark 8:38). All uncertainty vanishes before this divine ability to distinguish the real from the unreal, the genuine from the counterfeit.

It is promised that the Christ will work with us until this power of judgment is established in the heart of each, for when that is accomplished, then righteousness shall reign without end. "He shall not fail nor be discouraged, till he have set judgment in the earth." "For when thy judgments are in the earth, the inhabitants of the world will learn righteousness." "And the work of righteousness shall be peace; and the effect of righteousness quietness and assurance forever." —Is. 42:4; 26:9; 32:17.

Socrates says, "If you would teach the people to act rightly, teach them to form correct judgments." In this world of opposites we must know that the good is the positive and the evil is the negative; the first is the real, the second is the opposite to real.

The origin of evil.

To the question, "What is the origin of evil?" there is but one direct answer: It has no origin. It is nothing, and it came from nothing. It has no substance, it is without principle, it is pure negation.

If we give evil origin and reality, then we must say that God created it, for He made all things that are made. In a sense we can say that that which is the origin of good is the cause of its opposite, just as the carpenter who builds a house is the cause of the shadow which the house casts. In that sense the prophet, who seeing evil as much a reality as good was not in the full Truth, declares, "I form the light and create darkness: I make peace and create evil: I the Lord do all these things" (Is. 457), but the highest revelation says, "This then is the message which we have heard of him, and declare unto you, that God is light, and in him is no darkness at all."—1 John 1:5.

Evil is darkness, without being or law except to the mind not fully instructed in Truth. This mind, still in the valley of shadows, reasons from a basis of relative truths in which there is satisfaction for a time, but soon new questions as baffling as the old arise, and no complete satisfaction comes until the wise one takes the absolute stand: Evil is pure nothingness; absolutely without place, law, or origin.

In the childhood of our spiritual advancement the mind is content with such explanations as: "A lie is but a truth perverted; evil is but undeveloped good." But the maturer student soon demands, "How can the Good that is God have ever been imperfect or undeveloped? Good has always been good, it never was evil. Either make the tree good and its fruit good, or make it evil and its fruit evil (Matt. 12:33). Who is this that lies? or perverts good? Who is this that makes mistakes, and is in ignorance?"

Absolute Truth compels its adherent to acknowledge that since God, the one Mind, is the only real thinker such error-thinking is but supposition and truly un- thought. As a prophet of the new age has voiced it:

The dreamer and dream are one, for neither is true or real. Mrs. M. B. G. Eddy.

The unknowable

God is not the unknowable, but that which is the opposite of God, the realm of evil, sin, sickness, sorrow, and death is the unknowable. It has been decreed from eternity that evil shall not be known, and to attempt to know it is the first delusion of mortal minds. The belief of Adam and Eve that they could disobey and thwart, or prevent, the fulfillment of God's will represents the first step of self-deception, followed by others until the delinquent reaches the climax of delusions, death.

The tree of the knowledge of good and evil is like the mirage of the desert, fair to look upon and harmless as long as one knows its nature to be illusion, a play, a game, nothing in itself. But when one does not listen to the inner Guide, but begins to make something out of nothing, he thinks he can eat of this tree. He never does eat of it. God's law is never broken—he who thinks he can break it thinks he can suffer, grow sick, and die, which he does again and again, until after bitter experience he turns to the Truth and begins his journey out of the land of dreams.

The best that can be known of evil is that it is not to be known, and that to try to know it is fruitless and useless.

As soon as a shadow is understood in its relation to the thing casting it the mind quickly dismisses all thought about it. It excites no wonder, it brings no fear. The way to make it disappear or change form and place is understood, and the mind applies its study and mastery in the right direction.

Shadows and reflections

Materiality is the shadow of spirituality. Physical manifestation at its best is but the reflection of the real substantial creation of God. This reflection is good or ill according to the state of the reflector, the human mind, which, if clear and still like a calm, limpid lake, can give forth an image worthy of the divine Reality.

"The world is what we make it," and "We take out of the world what we put into it," are sayings of wisdom.

Clearness and the power to be still become the properties of the human mind as it conforms itself to the divine Mind, and confesses it to be the only real Mind. Then comes the true negativeness in which is reflected the true Self as it is in God.

Nature is the mirror of God; the receptivity of manifestation; the deep over which the Spirit of God ever moves, bringing forth His image; the "emptiness" or vacuum; the nothing being perpetually filled with the All.

The true Kingdom, which is the fullness of manifestation, is here in all its completeness. Whoever seeks its joys and treasures, and strives to understand its laws and purposes, will also come into the knowledge and possessions of this world which shadows it. "Seek ye the kingdom of God; and all these things shall be added unto you."—Luke 12:31.

To follow after the riches and wisdom of a world of change and decay is the act of one who tries to possess and control a shadow without any knowledge of or hold upon the object back of it. Read 1 Kings, third chapter, ninth to fourteenth verses.

Personality

Right judgment teaches to divide the true Self from the carnal. The wisdom of God guides us to seek first the real Man in every person, to hold that one ever in mind, to love that one and believe in him. Then we know how to regard the performances of the fleshly self, the persona. We are not surprised, or pained, or disappointed by it. We neither criticize unjustly nor condemn. We see no personality as wholly bad, or believe in total depravity.

Our judgment is just, and the false is uncovered but for the purpose of causing it to disappear under the -healing influences of the Sun of Truth.

The Eastern sage traces all false appearance to what he calls "nescience," not-knowing or ignorance.

True knowledge combines in it every divine manifestation, such as love, faith, goodness, power, and therefore contains the secret of all healing and redeeming. "The wisdom that is from above is first pure, then peaceable, gentle, and easy to be entreated, full of mercy and good fruits, without partiality, and without hypocrisy."—Jas. 3:17.

Practice

Meditate upon Scriptural passages while holding that you have the Mind of God and that He makes you understand what He has inspired.

Watch that your lips and your thoughts do not assert, "I don't know," and "I can't understand." It is true that the carnal mind does not know the things of God and "not that we are sufficient of ourselves to think anything" (2 Cor. 3:5) if we are speaking from the earthly standpoint. But we are not. Our purpose is to train our believing into our divine Self and keep our "I" lifted up above the earth.

Learn to look upon all things material, personal, or evil as but signs and symbols back of which lie the Real, to be found and expressed, or drawn out, by the God-Man in us.

Some mentalities seem to leap quickly out of their former errors into the Truth. It is because of the difference in beliefs that the unfolding appears so different. Some let go of their errors immediately, and some cling to old thoughts even though earnestly desiring to drop them, fear, conventionality, or one of the causes mentioned by Jesus (Matt. 13:21; Luke 8:14) seeming to prevent their progress.

Be true and possess your souls in patience. Realization will come. Only be faithful. What you consciously hold to-day sinks deep into the sub-conscious realm where lie these false memories and habits of thinking, and persistent right believing will at last displace the old mind and substitute for the untrue the true.

The renewing of our minds may be compared to the change which comes to one who has been journeying for months upon the sea, until his senses are charged with the motion of the ship. When he steps upon terra firma it may be for days that the land will seem to rock and roll, but he continually remembers the truth concerning his environment and himself, until at last his consciousness is normal, and he is at rest.

LESSON VI. UNITY AND CONCENTRATION.

Unity of true and good

THE pursuit of Truth uncovers the spiritual discernment by which men clearly see that all real good is one, and this intuitive perception of the unity of the true is confirmed by the logical processes of reason. These two witnesses, Intellect and Intuition, establish the Truth in our hearts, and wherever inspiration is corroborated by reason there is the Rock against which no doubts or fears of mortal sense can prevail.

All Good is one and the same. In the highest, love, wisdom, health, purity, and every manifestation of Good are one in essence and in being. It is only to mortal sense and its misconceptions of life that love and wisdom ever seem separate, that justice and mercy stand apart, that innocence and knowledge are disunited, that health and goodness are not companions.

Perfect Good includes all good. The true Life is a whole life with nothing in it of death or disease. Divine Health is wholeness, or holiness, in Spirit, soul and body.

Absolute Truth is one—there cannot be two truths contradicting each other, else one of them would not be the whole truth.

All good can be gathered under one name, God, who is all that is good and the good of all. The one God of us all is the one good of us all, to which men have given an infinite variety of names, such as Intelligence, Prosperity, Right, Freedom, besides deific names, such as Brahm, Jupiter, and Jehovah. "That which exists is one: sages call it variously."— Rigveda. "There shall be one Lord, and his name one."—Zech. 14:9.

Spiritual mind ever uniting

The spiritual Mind is ever uniting. It seeks God in everybody and everything, and makes that the point of oneness with all. It operates by love. "I drew them with bands of love."— Hos. 11:4. Whenever there is dislike or inharmony, its source can be found in the carnal mind. According to Max Miller this is the way we can know which mind is operating in us:

The carnal mind and the spiritual mind are seen to act in this way: the carnal always detects differences while the spiritual notes similarities.

The tendency of the human intellect is to differentiate, and this tendency can be checked by not enlarging upon the differences between those manifestations of God which in essence are one, such as Spirit, Soul, and Mind. If we see the identity of these in the Highest we can clearly analyze the appearance of difference to the human mind, and disclose that it is but a matter of the point of view from which these things are seen, or perhaps a difference in the use of terms.

The broad, deep mind can see the unity of all religions and expressions of Truth. It is waste of time and distracting to thought to seek and tell the differences between the beliefs of mankind. Let us be content to find the good and the true in every teacher and his teaching. Then if it ever devolves upon us to point out a stumbling stone we can, like Jesus, do it impersonally and with authority.

Universal tolerance finds Truth omnipresent, and has no respect of persons, creeds, or institutions, yet gives true deference to the real of each.

Purpose of religion

The purpose of religion is to unite God and Man, and that is the true religion which breaks down the barriers between man and his fellow-beings, and brings to him the consciousness of the eternal union between the Heavenly Father and His Child. The origin of the word "religion" is two Latin words meaning "to bind together again." The power of reconciliation which is in the true religion is without limit, joining together those which have seemed hopelessly apart, even at enmity, such as the higher and lower natures. It is the Christ-truth that breaks down "the middle wall of partition" between the human nature and the divine by causing the mortal to become obedient to the true Self. Then, overshadowed by the real Man, the earthly is "adopted" into the same inheritance of health and age-lasting life.

It is Truth that forms the universal brotherhood by showing we are all one Body and one Spirit (Eph. 4:4) in God, and that what is done to the least in that Body is done to the whole. The great atonement (at- one-ment) is brought about by the sacrifice of the old nature, the selfish one, and the glorifying of the true Self, who ever seeks the good of the whole.

The true Self of man is God, for since God is All in All and there is none else, man has no being but God. The Mind of God and its Idea are one. For, since God is the only mind, there can be no thought or idea in it but what is God, and He, Himself, all there is to think upon.

As mortals, men can only reflect God. Reflectors of a light are not the light itself. A reflection has no substance and is not the thing it reflects, so that mortal man cannot say, "I am God."

Divine Man is identical with God. "I and my Father are one," says Christ, the divine Man (John 10:30), but "I go unto the Father: for my Father is greater than I," says Jesus, the perfect human concept and the reflection of the Christ (John 14:28).

Jesus Christ

Jesus Christ combined in himself all the steps, the teachings, and the means by which humanity can perfectly reflect God, and by which the real Man may be proven identical with its divine source. The Christ is the Lord, the God of the whole earth and Spirit of us all; Jesus was the man in whom was out-pictured the true relation between the human ego and the divine. In him was portrayed the crucifixion (the crossing-out or cancellation) of the old man followed by the vindication and resurrection of the regenerate or new Man, which is finally transmuted and absorbed into its original Self, God and very God.

Through an impersonal, selfless life Jesus became identified with humanity as a whole, and his history is prophecy and promise of its achievement, both in the individuals and in the race. Whoever unites himself in heart and mind with Jesus Christ will find out the shortest and most direct route to unity with his own true being, the Self who is his god, and the God of all of us.

Concentration

Concentration is the divine art of centering the mind upon what we please for as long as we please. This power is only attained by making God, spiritual realties, the continual object of our thoughts. The appearance of concentration which seems to be developed when one has a standard less than the Most High is only the acquirement of a fixed habit of thinking which is the reverse of true concentration, for it lacks the pliability and elasticity which is essential to the well-rounded thinking and which only comes through focusing on the Universal.

Men concentrate on money so that their faculties are very acute and alert respecting money-making. But take their business away from them, as is generally done some time in their lives either through circumstances, or because of old age, or someone's loving through mistaken zeal to bless them with leisure and with other pursuits, and dissolution begins both mentally and physically, for they cannot center upon anything else. Thus it is with the professor, the artist, the actor, the society woman, the busy housewife, or anyone of ardent temperament who intensely concentrates all his energies and desires upon anything less than the absolute Truth. So also with the religionist who mixes error with his Truth; nevertheless if he be sincere, fearless, and meek he will be led to the Great Truth, God, which to meditate upon and love with your whole being clarifies the mind, purifies the passions, and gives that power of self-management that knows no limit in usefulness, peace, and happiness.

Truth has its science and its art, and concentration is that art. There is no religion extant but has its methods of concentration. The Hindu calls it yoga; the Christian, "prayer." Christ gives it as a command: "Watch ye therefore, and pray always."—Luke 21 -.36.

Practical Christianity requires complete devotion, entire consecration of all you are and all you have to the cause and manifestation of Truth. Concentration is the method by which this is accomplished.

Everything that appears to be external to you should suggest to you Spirit, God, Good, Heaven, Truth. Learn to translate all your employments, your instruments, the people you meet, the things you see, into the spiritual ideas for which they stand.

Human beings are each symbols of Truth—one a personification of Joy, another of Strength, another of Peace, another of Prosperity, according to the relationships they are bearing to you at the time you meet them. Your employments represent the operations that your Spirit is engaged in at the time you are working. If you are sweeping a room, meditate upon the Truth that sweeps error from your mental house. If you are sewing a garment, think of the manifestation of right and good which your Spirit desires shall clothe the Soul for whom you are working. If you are building a house, image the true temple, and with every nail drive home a truth that will show forth the Kingdom of Heaven. If you are teaching children, see them as precious expressions of Mind, your own thoughts being trained as fit habitants of the divine realm. If you deal with people in buying and selling, meet them as representatives of the Christ, and so develop patience, sweetness, genuine deference, and integrity. Knead love into the bread you bake, wrap strength and courage in the parcel you tie for the woman with the weary face, hand trust and candor with the coin which you pay the man with the suspicious eyes.

Preach the gospel with your every gesture and glance through right practice of concentration.

The human mind in which every thought is purified and directed with clearness upon the one theme, God, becomes like a clear, calm lake, which reflects perfectly whatever is upon its surface. Then any thought that is held before it can be imaged with exactness and truth, as one sees oneself in a flawless mirror.

Perfect concentration is having the "single eye" spoken of by Jesus—"If thine eye be single thy whole body shall be full of light" (Matt. 6:22), and the "one- pointed" mind described by Krishna (Bhagavad Gita 6:12).

The great-souled ones, united to godlike nature, knowing Me to be the exhaustless origin of all things, worship Me with mind that turns to nothing else. Bhagavad Gita 9:13.

There are many methods of practicing spiritual concentration; some are external and others internal, but all have for their nucleus the idea of God. Sages agree that the easiest and most direct practice is the internal, through governing the thoughts and desires with silent words of Spirit.

True concentration results in the restoration of the memory, for the mind then has the power to select what thoughts it desires and to hold them as long as it wills. By ability to focus the thoughts comes the power to focus the eyes, and the sight is renewed; through mastery over the faculty of attention the mechanism of the ears again obeys the will, and hearing is regained.

We become like that which we concentrate upon, and the more at-one we are with it the more we know it. All study is concentration, and true education gives us power to know a thing by our becoming it for the time being—the essence and very heart of it.

Sir Isaac Newton when asked by what means he had been able to develop his system of the universe said: "By making it incessantly the subject of my thoughts."

Enthusiasm is one of the essential concomitants to successful concentration, that is, that which manifests in works of Christ. No one can be too enthusiastic in seeking divine knowledge and believing in the possibilities of the true One within him.

Every great and commanding movement in the annals of the world is the triumph of enthusiasm. Emerson.

"If ye know these things, happy are ye if ye do them."—John 13:17.

That Christianity is but theoretical which puts off the fruits of Truth until a future life. Too long has the great doctrine of Jesus been betrayed by those who declare his inspired injunctions, such as "Be ye perfect," "Resist not evil," "Love your enemies," too transcendental and impracticable. He meant what he said, and he knew the fulfillment to be possible and inseparable from the complete Christ life. He drew no limit at any command as to thought, speech, or works, but expected that all who believed in the Truth would do the same as he did.

Manifestation

We have an example in the life of Jesus Christ of what are the fruits of a unity with God. He who enters a life of practical Christianity should expect to comply with all the directions Christ gives to his followers, among which are: "Preach the gospel, heal the sick, cleanse the lepers, raise the dead, cast out devils: freely ye have received, freely give."—Matt. 10:7, 8.

The goal that Truth places before us is the same attainment reached by Jesus Christ. And if we cannot yet do all the works he did, because of our ignorance or our unbelief, let us at least have the loyalty of the devoted students of an earthly art or science, such as music or mathematics, who do not deny that man can accomplish the great things of their study, and who judge of their own proficiency and knowledge by their ability to put into practice the principles they have espoused.

Among the first works to be performed by a student of Christ are those of bodily healing.

While there is an A B C of this divine art there is also an X Y Z, and Jesus shows us that some cases yield easily, while others require closer practice and greater realization, as in the case of the obsessed child (Matt. 17). In mathematics the power to count and to add belongs to its infant study, but even the most complicated problem includes these first practices. In the same way healing runs throughout the whole process of regeneration, and we shall never be finished with these primary steps until we have ceased altogether to function in the realm of mortal problems.

All divine manifestation is allied to healing, and he who masters the principles and practices of the healing of the body through the word of Truth will also have the key to soul-healing, called "salvation," and healing of circumstances, called "prosperity." The Hebrew and Greek words translated "salvation" and "health" in the Bible are often the same. Paul taught the three-fold healing, and prayed for his converts that "your whole spirit and soul and body be preserved blameless unto the coming of our Lord Jesus Christ."—1 Thes. 5:23.

Permanent health comes through freeing the mind from its ignorance and sin. Unless one ceases from sin he cannot be free from sickness, and if men do not know the Principle (God) of Healing, their cure will be temporal, or they will fall into some other disease. The dependence of the body upon the soul for its health is an old teaching. We find Plato telling the Greek physicians that the cause of their failure to heal was in their ignorance of the needs of the soul.

Neither ought you to attempt to cure the body without the soul; for the reason why the cure of many diseases is unknown to the physicians of Hellas is because they are ignorant of the whole, which ought to be studied also, for the part can never be well unless the whole is well.

146

For over three hundred years after the advent of Jesus his followers combined healing works with their preaching, and considered them to be the signs which should follow (Mark 16:17, 18) and confirm the truth of the doctrines (Mark 16:20). But when quarrels and schisms began to disrupt the church, then pride, worldly ambition, and covetousness seemed to hide the simple teachings of the meek and lowly One. Nevertheless the healing has never been quite abolished, and now that its principle is being grasped by reason as well as faith, it has come to abide forever, and will shine "more and more unto the perfect day."—Prov. 4:18.

Every lover of Truth who embodies in himself the unity of the principles and the works of Christ is one who is a center of healing for all the world, the light of the world, the salt of the earth. Universal healing radiates from him as rays from the sun, and many are healed by simply looking towards him for healing. Virtue goes forth from him even when personally he is not conscious of it.

Success in healing is proportionate to the knowledge you have of Truth, the depth of your love, and the true- ness of your life. Cases are healed quickly or slowly according to the receptivity of the patient, the nature of your own beliefs, and your realization of the Truth you are giving.

The daily living in spiritual concentration is working for "that meat which endureth unto everlasting life" (John 6:27), and "laying up treasures in heaven" (Matt. 6:20). "Therefore every scribe which is instructed unto the kingdom of heaven is like unto a man that is an householder, which bringeth forth out of his treasure things new and old."—Matt. 13:52.

Practice

The realm in which lie the spiritual treasures of the Christ-living and healing is called by the Psalmist, The Secret Place of the Most High (Ps. 91). The modern name that has been given to it is The Silence. Jesus refers to it in the words "in' secret," used in Matthew, sixth chapter, fourth, sixth, and eighteenth verses. It is there we are enjoined to commune with the Father, and what He hears in secret He will manifest openly.

The student should be able to dwell in the secret place ever, even when outwardly living a most ordinary life. Many saints attained this power. Brother Lawrence, who lived two centuries ago, had the key to this peace, and gave it very plainly to those who sought him, as we read in the booklet, The Practice of the Presence of God.

In order to develop this power of meditation it is recommended to the student to make an appointment with your inner Self at a regular time each day and enter into the silence of your heart and mind, shutting the doors of the senses (Matt. 6:6), and to meditate upon some spiritual truth with which you especially desire to be at-one.

When once the joy of this peace-bringing practice is realized new methods of soul-communion will be revealed to you by the Spirit of Truth within which you evoke by this devotion, and which is itself the inexhaustible well of Truth.

For a beginner a half-hour daily meditation, such as is herewith suggested, will be sufficient:

Select a spiritual theme, such as Love, Peace, Purity, or some other name of Good. It need not be the same one every day.

Mentally repeat it seven times. To avoid counting divide the seven thus: three, and three, and one. The theme is a seed and you plant it in the mental soil of your human thinking by this process of repetition.

Then let your thoughts go. Let the thought-seed send out rootlets into your mind and grow. As long as your mind dwells upon spiritual things you are in right meditation, which leads to concentration. The stems, branches, leaves, flowers, and fruit may not resemble the seed, but they are all one, and united by the one life. So are all spiritual thoughts one with each other, because Divinity is one.

But if your vine begins to put out a branch that does not bear fruit to the Good, or to

Spirituality, you must cut it off. That is, if the mind begins to wander to material things, or to evil, or to unspiritual events and people, or to sleep, these are branches you cut off instantly by repeating the word which is your theme seven times, as in 2, and again letting your mind go, as in 3.

Write in a blank book kept for the purpose some of the principal thoughts that come to you in the silence, or, if you keep this half-hour in company with other Truth-seekers express aloud the Truths (not visions or speculations) that you have received, as Jesus said (Matt. 10:27). For if you express what Truth you receive, you will receive more Truth to express. "For whomsoever hath, to him shall be given."—Luke 8:18.

PART II.

LESSON VII. OUR HEREDITY AND FREEDOM FROM SENSUALITY .

HEREIN is my Father glorified, that ye bear much fruit."—John 15:8. One of the fruits of the Tree of Life (Rev. 22:2) is Healing, and among the glories of practical Christianity are the thousands of sick and pain-stricken humanity that are being healed through its ministry every day.

These lessons are to make healers, and everyone who receives these teachings thoroughly and practices faithfully the exercises given must ever hold himself in readiness to heal whoever applies to him in a true spirit and shows a willingness to do his part.

All can heal. Whoever can speak Truth can heal. Every true word spoken is a healing force sent out into the world, and specific healing is simply a gathering together of healing words, and sending them in the direction that one pleases (Luke 7:8, 9), charging them with an especial mission in bringing forth a definite result, just as steam is generated by the universal action of the sun upon water, but does not do an exact work for man until it is concentrated, held, and given direction by some mechanism which is the result of man's inventive genius or discovery.

Love makes the truest, most successful healers, and wherever we find "natural healers" we find lovers of humanity. Their power has its source in the same spring whence flows every good, and it is because of their great love-nature that certain students are such powers for healing from their very entrance into life. Its warm radiance has been called "magnetism," but when they turn from looking to their personal presence to do the healing and look to their word they find the quality that healed was mental, not physical.

All healing is from God, whether the means used have been the relics of superstition or the skill of the most advanced practitioner in medical arts. We shall learn that the material means and other methods in which there is no recognition of God were but an interference, and caused the health to seem temporal instead of eternal, as it should be.

If we look into the secret causes of the success of worldly doctors and nurses we shall find them to be either love or faith, and generally both. The physician who grows old in a practice that is an honor to him is, deep down in his heart, an earnest lover of his fellow- beings, one whose love has caused him to make many a sacrifice of his own comfort and pleasure, and often to give faithful service where he knew there was no money to pay him. Happy is that physician if he discovers the true power that has been back of his work. Other successful physicians, though seeming to have little love, have great faith— faith in their method, their school, themselves. So it is with spiritual healers— love and faith are the two principal elements of success in their practice. But in order to continue in love and faith one must have understanding. Then love will not grow cold in the presence of ingratitude nor faith wax dim before appearances of failure.

Three methods of healing

The next six lessons of this Primary Course deal with the special application of Truth to healing people of their beliefs in the reality of physical diseases and bodily weaknesses and limitations.

There may be said to be three general methods of healing by speaking the word of Truth: (1) the Argumentative; (2) the Intuitive; (3) by Spiritual Perception.

The Argumentative Method is a kind of silent teaching by which false impressions and errors are erased from the mind (carnal) and correct ideas and true conclusions, which are already in the true Mind of the patient, are brought forward, uncovered, and made to manifest in place of the false beliefs formerly held, just as when one is reasoned with to bring him out of believing in a lie, or fearing an apparition, or resting under a mesmeric spell.

The Intuitive Method is used by those who realize the inner guide, their impressional nature, and listen to the Truth within themselves. By the intuition the healer knows just what expressions of Truth will reach the case. He may use argument, but will not be confined to any set formula. He will know when he should talk upon the Truth aloud to the patient and when to keep still. He exercises spiritual tact, and yet uncovers error fearlessly. He feels with true sympathy the needs of the patient and gives the meat or the milk of the Word according to the receptivity of his hearer and his degree of unfoldment.

Whoever is faithful to his intuitions in his treatments is that servant described by Jesus, "faithful and wise . . . whom his Lord hath made ruler over his household, to give them meat in due season." To him is promised, if he only continues faithful, that he shall rule "over all his goods."—Matt. 24: 45-47

In the method of Spiritual Perception no argument is used and often no word is spoken, either silently or audibly. The healer simply knows and his knowing becomes manifest. There is a flash of realization or a deep, still consciousness, indescribable with words, that this one is now perfectly well and whole, and this very cognition is like a great light that instantly destroys the error, called the disease, and immediately the healing is done. This was the principal method used by Jesus .Christ, although at times he argued (Matt. 15: 23-28), and needed to speak the word more than once in certain cases (Mark 8:23-25). He used many methods, according to the exigency, but the same Spirit was in all his healing.

Students begin with the argumentative method, and as they become one with the truths of the teaching, they learn to follow their own impressions as to what they should say and do for individual cases. And many a new practitioner in mental healing has a holy baptism of realization (the third method) with his very first patients, so that he heals instantly one after another. It is not experience that produces the ablest mental healers but faithfulness to Principle in the daily life and realization of the truths he speaks for another.

Truth is so powerful that many times just mechanically expressing it is sufficient, but each healer must endeavor to feel what he says. One statement felt with deep, warm conviction is worth more than a dozen statements that are not realized.

As a definite aid to beginners a regular course of treatment will be described in the following six lessons, each lesson dealing with a set of errors to be overcome when a patient goes gradually, day by day, from his negative state, called disease, to his positive state, perfect health. The course is a Creative Week of manifestation, six days of work, or unfoldment, and a seventh day of rest, or full realization.

As Naaman, the leper, was dipped seven times in the river Jordan and came healed; as the children of Israel compassed Jericho seven days before its walls fell; as the child whom Elisha brought back to life is said to have sneezed seven times in coming to consciousness, so it has seemed an orderly procedure to give most cases a course of seven treatments to wash away the errors of mortality, to raze to the ground delusion's structures, and cast out the false claims of personal sense.

Time has nothing to do with the healing, some taking their steps quickly and being healed in a few days, others not letting go their false thinking for weeks, though steadily gaining in the meanwhile. Let us never say, "It takes time to accomplish the healing." It is not time but realization, both on the part of the healer and the patient.

Our heredity

The first realization that one who would "pass from death unto life" (John 5124), from disease to wholeness, must have is the truth about our real parentage, our inheritance and our generation.

God is the one Creator, the source of all true Being, and Man, His child, is made in His image and likeness. Therefore we are Spirit, since God is Spirit, and our Father and Mother is God. Our one Parent is the Holy One, who is perfect life and health—pure, loving, and all-wise.

Accepting this as the truth of our origin and parentage, then we must conclude that from our divine Parent we can inherit only health and goodness, and the claim that we have an earthly parentage and are inheriting diseases and sinful habits is but a passing dream and without true foundation. Henceforth we repudiate and deny all these appearances of an evil physical and mental heritage.

We are not flesh, nor are we the children of mortal man, subject to the false beliefs of an earthly ancestry. We deny the reality of the flesh and its laws, and take our stand that the spiritual Self only is the child of God. "They which are the children of the flesh, these are not the children of God."—Rom. 9:8.

The real law of inheritance is "Good comes from Good." The child of God, the Good, inherits perfect and unchangeable health, strength, purity, and holiness.

Counterfeit laws of evil

All so-called laws of evil are the shadow of divine laws. When evil is acknowledged as a power and presence it seems to echo the spiritual law of inheritance, "Good comes from Good," with the delusion, "Evil comes from evil." This false law is annulled through the knowledge of the truth that evil has no life or intelligence, no creator, and no place in Being. Disease cannot propagate itself. Sin has no real strength or power to increase. Weakness is a negative, and has no power to pass from one to another. Foolishness and mistakes have no law of reproduction or power of perpetuation. It is men's belief in these things as real and as having laws of their own that has caused them to have their seeming dominion. The whole baseless fabric can dissolve, and be made void by any child of God speaking the truth about it.

"All flesh is grass and all the goodliness thereof is as the flower of the field: the grass withereth, the flower fadeth: because the spirit of the Lord bloweth upon it." "All nations before him are as nothing; and they are counted to him less than nothing, and vanity." — Is. 40:6, 7, 17. "The spirit is that which makes alive; the flesh profits nothing."—John 6:63 (Wilson's Emphatic Diaglot).

"Call no man your father upon the earth: for one is your Father, which is in heaven."— Matt. 23:9. By these words Jesus instructs us to make the same claim of heavenly parentage that he does.

The fear of heredity is sometimes the only error that needs to be removed from a patient's mind in order to heal him. Then, with this one treatment, he is set free.

Many are they who can testify to their release from the bondage of some disease or sin which was said to be their lot because of earthly parentage through denying the reality of a fleshly father and mother.

Why should good, Christian people—patient, loving characters—suffer from inherited affliction? Why do they not accept the promise? Why do they live under the law of Moses, as we read it in Exodus, twentieth chapter, fifth verse? Do they hate God, or Good? No. Then why should they apply that text "visiting the iniquity of the fathers upon the children unto the third and fourth generation of them that hate me" to themselves when they believe they love Good, and are trying to serve Good all they can?

Even under the old dispensation the curse is removed, as it is written: "The word of the Lord came unto me again, saying, What mean ye, that ye use this proverb concerning the land of Israel, saying The fathers have eaten sour grapes, and the children's teeth are set on edge? As I live, saith the Lord God, ye shall not have occasion any more to use this proverb in Israel."—Eze. 18:1-3.

The curse of the inheritance of evil is removed forevermore by the Christ within, who says, "I am the Son of God," and "All things whatsoever thou hast given me are of thee."—John 17:7.

Your health is perfect and sure. Your life is the life of God, immortal. You inherit only strength and purity. Your body is spiritual, therefore not corrupt, or weak, or paralyzed. God gives you nothing but what is in His own Being.

Universal statements, denials, and affirmations must be particularized in some cases in order to be realized. This is especially true in self-treatment. Therefore the healer must be patient and faithful to the word of Truth, and not be discouraged if the walls of Jericho do not fall at the first blasts. "Let us not be weary in well doing: for in due season we shall reap, if we faint not."—Gal. 6:9.

The Holy Family

While denying the earthliness of our parentage, the Christ-born student will not fail to "honor his father and mother," but will love and respect the Spirit in them as he does the Spirit in all. They are the representatives of a great office in God. So also are all other earthly claims of relationship. God in everyone is our relative. We are all one holy family, of whom God is the Life and true Being.

The family circle is for the purpose of forming a nucleus where love can center and pour forth into avenues lawful and useful. When the family fulfills its part, it is like the little fence built about a growing tree of love to keep it from being trampled on while unfolding. But our love should not be confined to those called ours; we are not to love them less, but we increase our love towards all the rest of our Family, thereby fulfilling the demands of our Christ-nature which has no respect of persons, but sees the Divine in all, the ideal which every true lover sees in his beloved.

Universal Brotherhood is based upon the principle of One Life in all the nations, "one body and one Spirit, . . . one God and Father of all, who is above all, and through all, and in you all."—Eph. 4 -.4, 6. With God there is no bias as to race or nation. The Truth destroys all the barriers, such as pride, hatred, and exclusiveness between you and all races and nations, and you recognize but one people, the spiritual race in the Kingdom of Heaven.

Pre-existence

God is without beginning and without end. Therefore, Man, His image, is also without beginning and without end. Always you have been. You did not begin at the appearance called your birth in the flesh. Being immortal, your soul has existed throughout the ages, and will, forevermore. Pre-existence is not a new teaching; the Pharisees had it among their tenets, and many of the blessings and curses of this life they ascribed to the virtues and sins of a previous existence.

Pre-existence is a truth, but the suppositions which have been attached to it, such as reincarnation, metempsychosis, and evolution are still open questions. Though they may be among the facts or relative truths of this realm of appearances, yet they are not true of God. Therefore, let us leave them in the theoretical department of our mentalities, or, at most, use them only as "provisional hypotheses," which we can drop as readily as we take them up. It is sufficient for us to deal with the present fleshly problem, finishing all ignorance and misery in the body which we have now, and in this present age.

Divine experiences go hand in hand with divine consciousness, and these we shall always have. But the experiences which are not in the Life of God have no place or real power in our manifesting. The belief that one is in disease and pain because of the sins of a previous life must be cancelled. Your life has evermore been in God, as it is now. Let no claim of an evil past delude you into sickness.

You are Self-causing, Self-existent Being like God, all that you are being the result of what you have thought, and every moment you are thinking that which is the cause of the next moment's manifestation. Remember your God-origin and you thereby profit by it.

Freedom from sensuality

Side by side with the understanding of the true law of our inheritance goes the understanding of the true law of our generation. God is the one creator, not earthly man or woman. Since you are not flesh, you are not created by laws of flesh. Here we face the race-error of mortal man, belief that he or she can create— the error which has been called "the original sin," thinking that flesh can generate and conceive.

There is but one conception, the Immaculate Conception—that manifestation in the conceiving of Jesus Christ, which is type of the true origin of every child. At every conception the Spirit of God moves upon the face of the deep. Each one is sent of God.

You are Spirit, eternally conceived of God and born of God—not in time, but in eternity. You have always lived, and always will live; you were never born into materiality or time, and you will never die. Realization of this truth is that process spoken of in Scripture as being "born of the Spirit" (John 3).

You are the child of purity and holy love. The love of God knows no lustful desire. There is nothing that degrades or shames in divine generation. In God, no enjoyment is carnal. All enjoyment is of the Spirit, spiritual, and not until man ceases to believe in sensual passions and carnal appetites can he know the real ecstasy of the Spirit, of which these are but the shadow. To love these things or to hate them is error, to uphold or to condemn them arises from ignorance. The true attitude is to know these appetites as non-existent to your higher Self and powerless to him that is free from delusion. The soul's pleasure, the holy delights of Spirit, are all in all to you.

False beliefs in fleshly and sensual gratification must be erased from the mind before their symbolic diseases can disappear. Speak the truth concerning the real Man: "Your desires are Spiritual, not carnal. All sensation is of the Mind, of the Spirit, and you do not look to the flesh for gratification. You are satisfied in God. Your joy is in the Lord. You are holy, pure, sweet, and clean in all your thoughts. God is your Purity. God is your holy Love and you desire only God."

Before pure and holy words no corrupt, unclean disease can stay.

Drunkenness healed

As you speak the truth concerning one sensual appetite, you will see that it applies to all. Drunkenness, smoking, morphine habit—all these are but out- picturings of mental hunger and thirst, which are never satisfied, but continually increased by material, temporal appeasings.

Such hunger and thirst are but the shadows of those spiritual desires which in the divine Mind are receiving perpetual satisfaction. "Blessed are they which do hunger and thirst after righteousness: for they shall be filled."—Matt. 5:6.

Feed the drunkard with right thoughts about his true Self and he will be so satisfied that no saloon can tempt him, and no liquor can longer have any charms. Never treat him as a drunkard, by upbraiding or finding fault, or with impatience or disrespect. Act always as though he were himself and address him as One who is all-powerful to overcome. Recognize only the Christ in him, then you can understand that "inasmuch as ye have done it unto one of the least of these my brethren, ye have done it unto me." Mat. 25:40.

By commencing with the thoughts and desires of the drunkard "the ax is laid unto the root of the tree."— Matt. 3:10. The old method of working on the outside — signing the pledge, avoiding the saloon, keeping the wine bottle out of sight, scolding, blaming, condemning, is like pulling off the leaves of the tree to destroy it.

The true method strikes right at the root, or cause, which is interior—the thinking, the carnal mind. The desire must be overcome, then the work is finished. Working externally is working in the letter, working internally is working in the Spirit. The letter and the Spirit can be fulfilled together, and this is harmonious and easy salvation.

Let us continually remember that the personal man can do nothing of himself, but God is the One that overcomes. Let God work in you and with you, and let the personal step aside. So shall every appetite be redeemed, and what have been stumbling blocks in our life may be made stepping stones to heaven.

St. Augustine! well hast thou said,

That of our vices we can frame

A ladder, if we but tread Practice.

Beneath our feet each deed of shame. Longfellow.

Practice

Daily consecrate yourself to God to be used in His service as a Christian mental healer. Let your soul often voice the words of Mary, "Behold the handmaid of the Lord; be it unto me according to thy word."—Luke 1138. By taking this attitude of mind faithfully you will be preparing yourself, and the Spirit in you will be drawing to you just those to be healed by you.

When any ask you to give them treatment do not refuse on the ground that another can do the work better than yourself. Such an attitude would be untrue to Principle, and a denial of the Lord within yourself.

It is well to wait until you are asked, and in some cases there should be a very earnest desire before any treatment is given.

Never treat anyone against his or her will. The exceptions to this rule are cases of insanity or vice, where a perverted will is the first error to be corrected.

The faith that the patient should have is simply that of not taking any other remedies— not dieting or doing any other thing for his health, nor looking to any other physician or healer while under this treatment.

It is not necessary for you always to be in the personal presence of the patient. There is no distance or space with Mind, and the word of Truth reaches those who are absent as to the flesh just as easily as those present. Jesus shows this in two instances: John, fourth chapter, forty-sixth to fifty-second verses, and Matthew, eighth chapter, fifth to thirteenth verses.

By studying Christ's methods we shall have explained to us many points that we have observed in a true practice.

A few general suggestions can be given to you as a healer, but no fixed rules, for no two cases are treated just alike, though the principles are always the same.

Usually take the patient alone, not allowing any that are skeptical or unsympathetic to the method to be present.

It is advisable not to touch the patient. Do not diagnose the disease or talk about it as a reality. It is not even necessary that you know what the disease is.

Talk little to him at first. Give him the great principles of the teaching, but do not look for him to use the Word for himself until further instructed, and you see that self-work is required to complete the healing.

The following is a good order of proceeding in giving treatment. Remember, the speaking is all silent.

Consecrate yourself.

Mentally address the patient by name.

Apply yourself to reassure him mentally that there is nothing to fear.

Tell him the truth about God and himself.

Make such denials and affirmations as are appropriate to the case. In a six-day course of treatment the first day you deny the belief in an evil inheritance and the reality and power of sensual desires and carnal appetites, and you affirm the truth about the divine inheritance and the pure and holy origin and desires.

Close with invoking a benediction upon yourself, the patient, and your Word of Truth, thus, "So shall my word be that goeth forth out of my mouth: it shall not return unto me void, but it shall accomplish that which I please, and it shall prosper in the thing whereto I sent it."—Is. 55:11.

LESSON VIII. FREEDOM FROM DELUSIONS AND DECEPTIONS.

The true laws

THE laws of the Kingdom of Heaven are the true laws, and the only ones that govern us in reality. It is because of ignorance that men feel themselves under the limitations and control of evil influences and laws. The truth, that Good is the only real presence and power, sets man free from the deceptions of evil and the delusions of matter.

Universal statements of Truth are often too abstract to be grasped by the mind that is struggling for freedom. Therefore we need to be specific in dealing with the errors that appear to face the student daily in his journey out of ignorance into the realm of the true. For there seem to be beliefs in evil that are held to unconsciously until attention is called to them, and measures taken to undeceive the mind that has been so falsely trained.

The true Mind is not deceived by evil appearances nor deluded by material laws, but the claim-to-intelligence, called the "carnal mind," is the one in error which needs to be undeceived, and freed from delusions. It is saved from its own false imaginings by giving up its claim and letting the divine Mind be its thinking.

The race, starting with the erroneous premise that Man is fleshly and mortal, and that materiality is true substance, seems to have involved itself in a maze of false conclusions. From childhood humanity is taught to believe in the evil influences of climate, the likelihood of accidents, the contagion of diseases, the contamination of associates, the limitations of physical laws. Fears, anxieties, distrust of men and animals, dread of future punishment, preparations and provisions for sickness, death, and old age— these have all been considered legitimate states of mind by deluded mortals, and such errors must not be entertained in the mind that desires to manifest perfect health in self and others. We do not need to seek out these false beliefs, but when they seem to present themselves let us be alert not to give them place and power by unconsciously assenting to them as lawful and true.

Small mistakes

To mortal sense some errors, such as those called sins, are greater than others, and yet there is no rank in error if one judges it by results, for the mental physician who diagnoses mind often traces the source of the most aggravating and painful diseases to such common beliefs in evil as worriment and anxiety, distrust, fears, small gossip, impatience, and petty sensitiveness. By neglecting to correct these insignificant errors many an otherwise good man or woman seems slow in being healed, while some flagrant sinner comes quickly to health because he repents and completely renounces the sin that lies back of his disease.

A slight mistake at the beginning of the solution of a problem may cause the answer to be far from true.

"Whatsoever is not of faith is sin" (Rom. 14:23), and the trifling admissions of the presence and power of evil are "the little foxes that spoil the vines."—S. of S. 2:15. These must be eradicated utterly, for they have no part in the Divine Presence. The woman who frets, either secretly or openly, has no abiding place in the Kingdom of Heaven, but has all she can do to drive away headaches and dyspepsia, the natural outcome of her states of mind. The man who is filled with doubts and distrust concerning his fellowmen, or indulges either silently or aloud in sarcasm and criticism, cannot rest in the realm of heavenly peace—he must look after his rheumatism. Only the one who faithfully holds to the power and law of the Good can remain in perpetual happiness.

God's government universal.

The government of God is universal and omnipotent. Its laws are altogether spiritual and good. The true Man governs all things by the power of Mind, and being the image of God is subject to nothing but God, or Good.

The Child of the Most High is not influenced by the opinions of people or the advice of false counselors. He reflects only that which is highest and best in all mentalities. In your true Being you never "take on" diseases or become subject to contagion. "He shall deliver thee from the noisome pestilence. . . . There shall no evil befall thee, neither shall any plague come nigh thy dwelling."—Ps. 9113, 10. While yet you seem in closest contact with associates who are unregenerate, you can remain wholly free from every taint.

If your loved ones are meeting companions whose influences seem hurtful remember the power of your silent Word to cause their true Self to be dominant, so that their goodness manifests many times more influence than all the vices of the others. In the divine economy positive virtue is continually brought in touch with negative characters to purify and vivify their mental atmospheres, and give them opportunity for reformation.

Hypnotism

No one can be moved by the false in others except those who are not positive by reason of a knowledge of the Truth, and those who believe in the power of an evil mind.

The error that is at the root of hypnotic practice is the believing in more than one mind, and that one mind can impose an untruth upon the mind of another.

True mental practice never breathes a statement that is a falsehood, or suggests a state of being or an action unworthy of God.

Truth heals by de-hypnotizing the patient, thus freeing him from the mesmerisms of mortal sense.

The Truth student who is true to his principles never hypnotizes anyone, but speaks what he devoutly believes to be true of the God-Man, and so, as it were, awakens the patient to true consciousness—not depriving him of self- consciousness as is done in ordinary hypnosis.

If we do not deceive ourselves by our own personal desires or fears of evil we cannot fall under the hypnotic spell of another. Never hypnotize others, and so keep yourself exempt from all its claims to influence. For, truly, hypnotism has no real power—all its apparent control comes through some one's belief in it, not always under its modern name, but under such terms as fascination, charm, bewitchery, etc. It is the shadow-side of divine influence, and is now on its way out of superstition into science, to be lifted up and wholly redeemed through humanity ceasing to be swayed by its fears and passions.

The Law of God sets you free from every evil influence, and you realize that there is really no power in evil association for anyone. God, the Good, is the One Influence in all and through all. You cannot be contaminated by any evil at all. Though in the world you do not partake of the world. Instead of being affected by evil influences, you are the salt of the earth, and all are salted by God in you, and made to feel clean, and pure, and healthy by your very presence, even if you do not say a word.

Meet all the malpractice of those who use their minds against you with fearless lovethoughts, and turn every curse into a blessing. "No weapon that is formed against thee shall prosper."—Is. 54:17. "Thou shalt be hid from the scourge of the tongue: neither shalt thou be afraid of destruction when it cometh."—Job 5:2i. No poisonous thought can affect those who meet all malice with the antidote of love.

One, only, has any right to control you—God. No human will should be allowed to usurp the throne of your mind, whether it claims to be in the flesh or out of it. Mediumship and hypnotism have the same mistaken basis, and their effects upon their victims are the best arguments against their false rule. Our divine birthright is Individuality, which may be manifest in the flesh by our being true to our God, and by acknowledging His right only to control us, and govern our minds and actions.

Those who practice with Truth grow clearer in mind, purer in character, healthier and stronger in body the more they use it, and live by it. They do not grow exhausted in their healing power, but gain continually by giving. By this the true practice may be known.

Laws of health

The laws of health are Spiritual, not material, and they cannot be broken, for they are of God. Whoever abides by them will never know any limitation to his strength in doing good, nor lose his health or life while in unselfish service for others. The first law of health in which your consciousness must be well rooted is: God is your health, and the source and cause of your health. Your health and strength do not depend upon what you eat, neither can they be affected by anything you eat. Man does not live by material bread, but Man lives by the Word of God. To realize that the Thoughts of God and not material things feed us is to find ourselves freed from anxiety about eating and drinking.

It is not what we eat that poisons the blood or weakens the system, but our thoughts of evil. "There is nothing from without a man that entering into him can defile him: but the things which come out of him, those are they that defile the man" (Mark 7:15), said Jesus, and when his disciples asked him to explain, he told them plainly the sources of corruption, whether physical or mental:

"And he said, That which cometh out of the man, that defileth the man. For from within, out of the heart of men, proceed evil thoughts, adulteries, fornications, murders, thefts, covetousness, wickedness, deceit, lasciviousness, an evil eye, blasphemy, pride, foolishness: all these evil things come from within, and defile the man."—Mark 7 -20-22.

Eating and drinking represent mental appropriation of ideas, and what we eat and drink symbolizes the kind of thoughts we are taking. Eat and drink of the words of Christ, Truth, and nothing can hurt you. Eat the divine Word and you will never starve.

Make no laws for yourself as to what you shall eat and what you shall drink, or as to how you shall dress, or about bathing, or exercise, or any of those things that the worldly physician thinks are the all-important factors of right living.

No great master of life has ever given any physiological laws to the world. No such law is fixed and certain, or of universal application. To the contrary, they who endeavor to make so-called laws of health agree that "one man's meat is another man's poison"— that is, what is good law for one man will kill another.

Instead of giving laws concerning the external treatment of the body, the great Master, Jesus Christ, says, "Therefore take no thought, saying, What shall we eat or what shall we drink or wherewithal shall we be clothed?"—Matt. 6:31. This is the advice of one who knew all about right living.

"Eat such things as are set before you" (Luke 10:8), he says to his disciples. "And these signs shall follow them that believe ... if they drink any deadly thing it shall not hurt them."—Mark 16:17, J8. "Nothing shall by any means hurt you."—Luke 10:19. This is because "your names are written in heaven" (Luke 10:20)—that is, you realize your being and character (name) is established and under the law (written in) of the spiritual kingdom (Heaven).

You are Spirit, governed by the law of Spirit, and no earthly thing can affect you. You cannot be fatigued by material things. "They that wait upon the Lord . . . shall run and not be weary; and they shall walk, and not faint."—Is. 40:31.

Whoever believes himself to be Spirit, and that matter is unreal, will not test the Truth ("tempt the Lord") by such thinking and acting as, "I will put my hand in the fire and see if God will keep it from burning." Such words come not from trust in God and realization that no earthly element can destroy Man, but from doubt of God, and assumption of the possibility of materiality to harm one. You are not tempting God when you go forward about your "Father's business" of doing good, fearless of every material law and evil condition. You cannot be overworked in doing good, or be in danger from pestilence or evil men when abroad upon an errand for Christ. (*For meditation read carefully and learn Psalm 91, remembering that "he" and "him" in verses 1, 14, 15 and 16 refer to you; also the "I" in verse 2 and the "thee" and "thou" in verses from 3 to 13, inclusive.)

You live in the spiritual world where nothing can hurt you or injure you; water cannot drown you, nor fire burn you, nor the air bring you disease, pestilence, "colds," impurities, and so forth; where the weather is never too warm or too cold, and the climate is ever healthy. Let us cease talking about the evils of the weather and the dangers from the elements, "for our conversation is in heaven" (Phil. 3:20), and "for every idle word that men shall speak they shall give account." —Matt. 12:36. Speak the word for others, as well as for yourself, that these things cannot harm them. Mentally deny their fears and prognostications of calamity.

God, our defense

God is our defense is the understanding that brings deliverance from all disasters and accidents, and protects the lover of Good from all enmity, whether among animate or inanimate things. By this knowledge Daniel was protected from the lions, the "three children" delivered from the flames, and thousands of God's saints and sages rescued and defended when no earthly power could have saved. Examples of earthly experiences taken from incidents in the lives of students where Truth has kept them from danger, and delivered them out of accidents unharmed, could be multiplied. But no testimony is so effectual as one's own demonstrations of the power of the Word of Safety. Let the student learn to stop runaway horses by silently, firmly addressing the Intelligence in them, even though at a distance from them. Say, "You have nothing to fear. Peace, be Still! All is well." Discover for yourself the power of the Word to prevent children from falling down dangerous places, by speaking the true word: "God holds you in perfect safety." They will seem to cling to their places like steel-filings to a magnet. To anyone who seems in jeopardy, breathe trustingly the silent word, "God takes care of you."

Warnings of danger

All warnings of danger and presentiments should be used to make you firm and faithful to speak for the safety of those whom the evil prophecy concerns. Let such prophecies be to you what the danger signal is to the locomotive engineer, a sign to bring in the saving principle of the Almighty, and not let the ones in danger go on to destruction.

Instead of being frightened or dismayed, you should realize that such things are only helps to those who believe in the power of the good word. There is no certainty in any prophecy of evil. At any moment the true word can annul it, even though the evil prophecy were uttered by a prophet sent of God.

Jonah was sent of God, and though he prophesied the terrible downfall of Nineveh within forty days, because of its sins, yet it did not come to pass. Why? Because it took advantage of Jonah's prophecy and repented, and the Good prevailed with the people, and the way was prepared for God to save them from the consequences of their own misdeeds. Thus Jonah's prophecy defeated itself, and was really a divine success.

No decree of evil is sure. No curse can stand before the true Word—the Divine Blessing. For every word of evil, do you send forth a word of good, and though a thousand evil words were spoken, one good word can put them all to flight. "And five of you shall chase an hundred, and an hundred of you put ten thousand to flight."—Lev. 26:8. "One chase a thousand and two put ten thousand to flight."— Deut. 32:30.

Sensitiveness

The Truth delivers you from inner attacks, such as morbid sensitiveness which arises from mistaking the personality for one's true Self. By denying your personality you will see you cannot be moved by either praise or blame. You immediately give all praise to God, and you are not touched by blame, because God is the only One in you, and God is not moved by fault-finding, or neglect, or insult.

To resent insult or neglect, or to feel hurt because of anyone's actions or speech, comes from the error of regarding the mortal man as the Self, when in reality you are above every petty meanness, and are not disturbed any more than God is.

God, our support

God is our Prosperity. Knowledge of the power of Mind sets us free from the idea that money is our support or that it is by personal effort that we are prospered. We learn to look away from people to supply our needs and towards the One who is the power back of the people, the money, and the work.

"God that giveth to all men liberally" (Jas. 1:5) is your supply, and in Him there is no poverty at all. It is no part of the Christ-life to be poor any more than it is to sin or to be sick. Jesus was not poor nor did he lack for any good thing. He had command of all the riches of the whole earth. Could not he who increased loaves and fishes have increased money likewise? Could not he who could bring forth money from a fish's mouth to pay his taxes (Matt. 17:27) bring it forth from any place? He who could make the fisherman's trade a great success by making such draughts of fish that they could hardly land them (Luke 5; John 21), was he a failure financially? Not so. Let no man deceive himself into thinking poverty a Christian virtue.

Why misunderstand Jesus' saying, "The Son of man hath not where to lay his head?"* Were not the disciples' homes open to him? Do we not read of his head lying upon a pillow in one of their ships (Mark 4:38)? How could this saying be literally true of a man upon whom "women and many others ministered of their substance" (Luke 8:3), and who could command the rooms and tables of rich men?—"Zacchæus, make haste, and come down; for to-day I must abide at thy house. And he made haste and came down and received him joyfully."—Luke 19:5, 6. Was he not continually invited to feasts, and to partake of hospitality at almost every place he went, and his disciples with him?

Jesus believed everything would be provided by God, and he sent his disciples out with nothing in their purses just to prove to them how God provides, as is shown by his question, "When I sent you without purse, and scrip, and shoes, lacked ye anything? And they said, Nothing."—Luke 22:35.

Far from expecting his disciples to be poor, he promised them, "There is no man that hath left house, or brethren, or sisters, or father, or mother, or wife, or children, or lands, for my sake, and the gospel's, but he shall receive an hundred- fold now in this time, houses, and brethren, and sisters, and mothers, and children, and lands, with persecutions; and in the world to come eternal life."— Mark 10:29, 30.

*When Jesus said to the young man who wished to follow him: "Foxes have holes, and the birds of the air have nests; but the Son of man hath not where to lay his head" (Luke 9:58), he was simply referring to the state of that man's mind. Cunning thoughts (foxes) burrowed and rested in his mind, and fanciful thoughts (birds of the air) flitted hither and thither and lodged there, but the Christ Idea (the Son of man) had not yet been given place. Thus Jesus described the man's lack of preparation. He must first "prepare the way of the Lord" (Luke 3:4; Psalm 132:4, 6) before he could follow Christ as he should. Jesus spoke in parable to him just as he did to the next one (Luke 9:60), and to the next (verse 62).

"The meek [dispassionate] shall inherit the earth." —Matt. 5:5. "But thou shalt remember the Lord thy God: for it is he that giveth thee power to get wealth." — Deut. 8:18. "If ye be willing and obedient ye shall eat of the good of the land."—Is. 1:19. "Yea, the Almighty shall be thy defense, and thou shalt have plenty of silver."—Job 22:25.

There is no "saving up for a rainy day" with God. There is no expectation of want or penury. "Take no thought for the morrow for the morrow shall take thought for the things of itself."—Matt. 6:34. God takes care of you in the future as well as in the present—it is not necessary to lay up treasures on earth (Matt. 6:19, 20). Lay up the treasures of pure, true thoughts in the heart, and then you "shall not want for any good thing."—Ps. 34:10.

Man, master of natural law

Knowledge of spiritual law gives us also knowledge of its shadow, called "natural law." Mind decides the character of natural laws by ruling the thoughts that form them. Material appearances are formed, reformed, made to appear or disappear, by dealing with their causes, just as men govern the pictures cast upon a magic- lantern screen by their handling of the light and slides, or as we cast a shadow upon the wall or a reflection in the mirror by our management of the objects we wish to be reflected. All nature is a great parable of the processes of Mind. Man, master of natural law. Man must have dominion over the earth, as it is commanded (Gen. 1126), and this dominion is manifest as he proves his power over all false thinking. By ruling the elements within himself he governs those without; by mastery over his passions, and by the understanding of the law of love all the animal world becomes subject to his word. He takes all the poison out of plant and reptile, all cruelty and rapacity from the beasts, and then is fulfilled the prophet's words: "The wolf also shall dwell with the lamb . . . the lion shall eat straw like the ox ... they shall not hurt nor destroy in all my holy mountain: for the earth shall be full of the knowledge of the Lord, as the waters cover the sea."—Is. 11:6-9.

Because Jesus knew the law of Spirit and had overcome worldly thinking he knew that power of Mind by which he could walk on the water as well as on the land (John 6:19). He understood the law of levitation as well as the law of gravitation. He knew how to speak the word that should manifest harmony even among the winds and the waves (Matt. 8:26). He realized the nothingness of materiality so well that he could cause it to appear to increase, as in the case of the loaves and fishes, or to decrease, as in that of the fig tree; to disappear, as when he passed from their midst (Luke 4130; John 8159), or to reveal himself, as when he passed through closed doors (John 20:19). Knowledge of spiritual law gave him that hearing and seeing that neither distance nor material obstruction could interfere with, as when he heard the disciples' discussion, though apparently they were secret about it (Mark 9:33, 34), and saw Nathaniel under the fig tree, a wonderful thing in his eyes (John 1:48-50). All that Jesus did, we can do if we will but believe ourselves into the same Mind, for "He that believeth on [into] me, the works that I do shall he do also; and greater."—John 14:12.

The divine Self, the real Man, is ever saying, "All power is given unto me in heaven and in earth."— Matt. 28:18. Because of the errors held concerning man, that he is flesh and a sinner, he seems to be subject to the laws of evil and matter. Even the so-called religious man does not think he can be exempt from these worldly laws—therefore those that take this free and exalted stand must remember always to make their claim from the Highest, the divine I AM. You must make the secret place of the Most High your abiding place, speaking your words of dominion silently, and thereby not arousing the antagonism of the race. "All men cannot receive this saying, save they to whom it is given" (Matt. 19:11), for some men desire power above seeking the good of the whole, and no one can rule the earth except the one who loves with the love of Jesus Christ. "If any man will do his will, he shall know of the doctrine, whether it be of God, or whether I speak of myself."—John 7:17.

Practice.

The special application of this lesson in the healing of patients is as follows: When giving one a regular "week's course" of treatments, the realization which you have for him upon the second day is that of freedom.

Proceed as upon the previous day (see the Practice at close of Lesson 7), following the general directions with the exception of No. 5, which for this treatment should be:

Make such denials and affirmations as are appropriate to the case. In the six-day course of treatment, the second day you deny the claims of the laws of matter, the influences of evil, and the "mesmerisms" of personalities, and affirm Man's freedom because he is Spirit, Mind, and governed only by the law of God, the Good.

Additional hints for healers:

Never be in a hurry. If you feel excited or disturbed in any way, first treat yourself until you are again calm and trustful. In the meanwhile your patient will be receiving the benefit of your self-treatment, because you are doing so for his sake.

It may seem sometimes as though you were touched by the evil thoughts of those near you. Never think that the reflection of another's error need remain with you for a moment. Deny that you can reflect evil— you are the image, the reflection, of the Good only. If a pain is felt—the same the patient has—when treating, do not fear, but just look upon it as a sign that the pain has left the one for whom you are speaking Truth, and it cannot possibly stay with you, you know its nothingness so well.

In healing children, or those who are looking to others for support— mental, moral or physical—give your treatments principally to those who are thinking most about them, such as the father and mother, or other relative, denying especially their anxiety and fear.

It is said of little children that they are like little mirrors, reflecting the thoughts of those nearest them, particularly the mother, or the one who takes her place toward them. If there is inharmony between the father and mother, or they are in trouble, or fear for their children, the little ones are apt to show it in feverish conditions, colds, and so forth.

In truth, little children reflect God only, and it is very easy for them to realize the true teaching. They are excellent healers, and apprehend the great principles of God without the necessity of argument. Whoever will approach them with this trust in their intuition will prove that they do not need to be taught so much as to be given freedom to let their own Spirit express itself as it wills.

LESSON IX. FORGIVENESS, THE CURE OF SIN.

A slight knowledge heals

EVEN a slight knowledge of God's Truth has healed case after case through removing fear and restoring confidence in life and health as greater powers than disease and death.

Many a captive has been set free from the bonds of sickness and sorrow, misery and poverty, just through the realization that these things are subject to mind and that they are not necessary evils, since they have no part or place in the true Life.

To begin to be conscious of our freedom from the law of an evil and fleshly inheritance (Lesson 7), and that we are not in bondage to the laws of physical causation (Lesson 8), is sufficient to cast off multitudes of the ills to which flesh seems to be heir, and day after day the student sees himself released from daily afflictions and annoyances. He does not catch cold now through fears of draft or damp, knowing that he is Spirit, and cannot be affected by material changes. He does not suffer from indigestion, for he has ceased to give power to his food. He no longer thinks he must have heart disease or consumption, cancer or rheumatism, because his earthly parents suffered from it. Many evils vanish from his life through the very first shining of the rays of knowledge. With the prophet he has learned, "My people are destroyed for lack of knowledge" (Hos. 4:6), and that even a superficial knowledge has great restoring power in it.

But there are some conditions which do not seem to yield so readily as others - conditions which are called chronic, and these, we must know, leave only upon the erasure of sin, or some secret belief in evil called sin, by the one who is showing forth the inharmonious, chronic condition.

Chronic cases

Most chronic cases are caused by belief in sin on some one's part; they are the outpicturing of a belief in sinning or in being sinned against, usually both.

"Why do good people so often suffer with chronic diseases?" will naturally be asked. It is true they seem to be perfect in character, but ask them whether they are without sin and they will tell you they are far from sinless—no matter how peaceful they may seem externally, there is often a fierce battle raging within. An accusing conscience lies at the root of their disease, and not until they stop condemning themselves can they be free from the law of condemnation, which is always delivering the accused to the judge, who delivers to the officer, who casts into prison (Matt. 5:25).

As mortals we cannot say we are without sin. "If we say we have no sin, we deceive ourselves" (I John 1:8), as even Paul says, "For I know that in me (that is, in my flesh) dwelleth no good thing."—Rom. 7:18. It is only as the Son of the Most High, God's image, that we can say, "I am holy, sanctified, perfect as my Heavenly Father, and cannot sin."

Good men and women are suffering because, while they are doing good outwardly, they have not been able to do good within. They are fulfilling the letter of the moral law, but not its spirit.

Letter and spirit of law.

Not only must a man put away evil from his acts and words, but also he must put it away from his thoughts. The invalid who, while calm and patient outwardly, is attacked in thought with impatience and bitterness must learn a law by which he can control his thoughts, and be as serene and kind within as he is without, and then shall his "health spring forth speedily." The man who "cannot forget," even while he claims to forgive, is not on the road that leads to immortal health.

Jesus came to a religious nation which was most punctilious in fulfilling the letter of the Mosaic law, but its people's thoughts were not in Truth. Few of them had realized the power of their minds, therefore they needed One who was in active knowledge and demonstration of the power of thinking to show them how to live so as to bring to pass the results of wholehearted obedience to the laws which they had received from Moses and the prophets.

In the Sermon on the Mount Jesus shows that a man must cease to kill in mind as well as in deed, that he must be chaste in thought as well as outwardly, that he must not steal mentally, such as envy and covetousness, nor return evil for good even in thought. The good people of to-day who are in pain and trouble and want are learning to take these experiences as signs that something is wrong. They cry, "I do not steal, I do not lie, I do not commit adultery, I do by my neighbor as I would be done by. Why is it, then, that I am so afflicted?" And again the Truth is sounding, "Except your righteousness shall exceed the righteousness of the scribes and Pharisees, ye shall in no case enter into the kingdom of heaven."— Matt. 5:20.

Anger overcome

Let us consider some of the directions for right living which Jesus gave in the Great Discourse. He says, "Ye have heard that it was said by them of old time, Thou shalt not kill, and whosoever shall kill shall be in danger of the judgment: but I say unto you, That whosoever is angry with his brother is in danger of the judgment."—Matt. 5:21, 22.

The phrase "without a cause" in the old translation of the New Testament is an interpolation. Those who have given us the New Version have omitted this phrase, deciding after careful research that it has no place there.

That is, not only must a man refrain from killing with his hands and his words, but also he must refrain from all angry thinking. Are you impatient? Must you continually suppress anger? Do you allow your temper to foam and ferment within? Where do you think such force goes? It is plain to be seen how the character and circulation of the blood is influenced by angry thinking—how the face pales or flushes under such emotion. And when it is considered how blood is becoming tissue and fiber of organs, muscles, and bones one can readily see how angry blood makes angry organs, muscles, and bones, which then show forth tumors, cancers, and irritating and inflamed diseases of all kinds.

This is the judgment of which we are in danger.

Our judgment is not put off until some future Day of Judgment. Every day the false thoughts are being separated from the true, the false joining the conditions of evil, torment, pain, disease, and so forth, and the true entering into the rest of their Lord, the Good. If we let our consciousness be identified with the untrue, then it will seem to be ourselves that are tormented, and suffer with pain and sorrow. We cannot be angry at all, else we come under the old Law of Moses, which condemns and punishes.

God is Love, and in Him is no anger at all. You, as the child of God, are the image of pure, changeless Love, and in your true nature no evil temper can abide. We delude ourselves if we ever justify anger in ourselves or in others. It rises from a belief in the reality of evil and from believing in our impotency to cope with it. Trueness to our principle, "Good is the only real power," will strike right at the root of every false emotion, and heal us forever of all anger.

In so far that you do not speak angry words, or commit angry deeds, well and good. This is fulfilling the letter of the law, and now you are ready to fulfill the spirit of the law by not thinking angry thoughts.

To put away from us all angry thinking is to put out all malice, revenge, resentment, impatience, hatred, spitefulness, and all the murderous brood forever. Watch your thoughts continuously, and let only the Christ-love reign in your heart and mind. To every angry thought say, "I know you not," or "You are not of me," or "No," or "There is no evil," or "It is nothing"— some form of true denial which "prepares the way of the Lord," and thus gets the mind ready to entertain the true thought, the Christ—"Love is all," "Peace," "Almighty Good reigns," affirmations of the true.

The Spirit will inspire you with some word or sentence to which you can always resort the instant the temper begins to rise. One student was healed by using the sentence, "Love is patient and kind;" another found great help in "All is Good;" a third would watch her breath and heart and say, "Peace! be still," over and over until unmoved.

Also the word of Truth must be spoken for your neighbor that needs to be redeemed from angry passions. In order that you may be wholly forgiven (be given the Christ-thought in place of evil-thinking) you must forgive others, which is, to give them the Christ- thought in place of evil-thinking. Has someone you know an evil temper? Does someone continually scold, and fret, and find fault? Tell him the Truth about himself— tell it mentally: "You are the child of Love, and Love rules your every thought. You are, in your real Self, gentle and loving, patient and kind. God is your peace. Christ reigns in your heart. You love to be kind and gentle. God bless you."

Give people this bread of life at all times, and never withhold your hand. God shows you how to forgive, for it is God in you who is really forgiving.

Many people are healed of old, chronic diseases just by getting rid of their tempers, or some old, secret, re- vengefulness or resentment, or some poisonous hatred.

Lust cast out

The next commandment Jesus refers to is, "Thou shalt not commit adultery." He then proceeds to show that lustful thoughts must be rooted out of the heart in order that one be free from adulterous consequences— disease in the body and disorder in affairs.

Our thinking must be pure and holy. "Ye shall be holy, for I am holy."— Lev. 11:44. To cleanse the mind of impure thoughts realize that they are not yours, that they are not real, that they are nothing. The only One who thinks in us is God, and God is pure, and thoughts which He does not have are vanity and nothingness. Do not fight them. Do not condemn yourself or another for them. But continually think, "Christ thinks in me now— I am pure, I am holy, I am clean. God is the only presence in my heart."

If others seem to be possessed by impure thinking, speak the same words for them. Do not feel that you can be contaminated by their presence. Jesus Christ touched the lepers, contrary to the Hebrew law, and he was not harmed, whereas they were cleansed. Do not condemn. Remember Jesus' words to the adulteress, "Neither do I condemn thee: go, and sin no more."—John 8:11. This is "casting out devils." A man may be so possessed of a false idea that he seems the walking personification of that idea, and so misers, fanatics, people "out of their mind," are said to be obsessed, or possessed of devils. The healing of such is through the healer realizing that there is but one idea to be possessed of, and that is the Christ. See everyone as pure in God. See the holy One in all. Do not dwell upon the actions and speech of the personality, but think of the pure One. "Blessed are the pure in heart, for they shall see God."—Matt. 5:8.

Injury and imposition overcome

"Ye have heard that it hath been said, An eye for an eye, and a tooth for a tooth: but I say unto you, That ye resist not evil."—Matt. 5 138, 39. Evil has never been destroyed by meeting it with evil. Good is the only power that can annihilate evil. As long as we are sensitive to evil, and recognize it as a power, it will seem to come into our lives. By meeting the hand that is raised to strike you with loving, fearless knowledge that you cannot be injured, and your assailant does not really wish to hurt you, the threatening hand cannot touch you. By meeting the arrows of sarcasm and criticism with active love-thoughts, even though not a word is spoken by you, the unkind remarks will fall flat and sting less. Deny all sense of injury, imposition, and wrong which you may seem to have, and look faithfully for the false appearances to be taken out of your life. They may seem to remain as long as you can feel them evil; the instant you cease to care about them, they will seem, almost miraculously, to fade out of your life.

Love your enemies (Matt. 5 144) by seeking for God, who is your friend, in them. Meet them in soul, and realize that in Spirit each understands and loves the other. Personal actions and evil ways do not count, and cannot deceive you. Convert all your enemies into friends by steadfastly remembering their divine Son- ship, and what they are to God, who is their life and power to be, as well as yours.

"Judge not, that ye be not judged."—Matt. 7:1. Do not talk about the evil in others. Do not call attention to the evils in another. The word of the Christ is, "I judge no man."—John 8:15. Your word is, "I judge no man."

Have that love for all that sees no faults. If you would not speak about the faults of your best beloved, then do not speak of the faults of any. It is said, "Love is blind," because love sees no evil in the loved one. Love has the true sight, for it sees only the Good. "Love thinketh no evil."—I Cor. 13 -.5. You are one with love in thinking no evil. (*For further commentaries upon Jesus Christ's doctrines as to law see Sermon on the Mount, by Annie Rix Militz.)

Selfishness

The one head under which all false beliefs called sins are said to come is "selfishness."

And the error of selfishness arises from thinking there is another self besides God. "Hear, O Israel, the Lord our God is one Lord."—Mark 12:29. There is only one Self—God. And

God owns all things, and nothing can be taken from Him. There is no stealing from God. All happiness, all possessions, are His, therefore yours, you being in Him. There is no envy with God, no covetousness, for all is His. To be desirous of the world's goods, which are vanity, is the error called "covetousness."

God gives freely of His love and His honors and His glory. There is no jealousy with God. He who is afraid of losing his rightful share of love, or his rightful praise, is in the error of jealousy and a false self- love. Let him learn that the love that changes is not real, nor the praise that is misplaced lasting. He is truly healed of jealousy as he realizes that love given to another does not lessen his share, and praise given to another does not take from him. There is only One who is glorified in all expression of appreciation—the great Life and Spirit of us all.

Ignorance causes sin.

Ignorance is the cause of sinning. In the Bible the word "sin" means "missing the mark," a term applied to an archer whose arrow has failed in its flight. We are all aiming at the mark Happiness, and whoever is not attaining eternal happiness is "missing the mark." All sin is ignorance. Ignorance of what is sin? No; not ignorance of what is evil or sin. The veriest savage has his ideas of a right and a wrong, and holds something as a sin for which there should be a punishing. The ignorance is the false idea of what will bring happiness or, at least, satisfaction.

The murderer thinks it is to his satisfaction to kill. He soon proves how ignorant he has been through the sufferings, either within or without, that he has brought upon himself. The embezzler sees no way out of some dilemma but to steal. Here is ignorance of the fact that God is his salvation, and that faithfulness to Principle, God, can lift him out of any trouble, no matter how complicated.

Forgiveness of sin

The only way to set the sinner free is to dissolve him in each one by the pure words of Truth, declaring the unreality of the sinner and the sin, and the reality of the sinless one—the Son of God. This is done by the mind putting away from the human heart and recognition all thought of committing sin, all accusing others of sin, and all meditation upon sin as a real presence and power.

The divine gift of dissolving sinful desires and intents of the heart, and destroying their consequences (misery in body, mind, and circumstances), is called in the Gospel, "the forgiveness of sin." This God-power is now vested in you as the manifestation of God in the flesh, called the "Son of man" in the Scriptures. "That ye may know that the Son of man hath power on earth to forgive sins" (Matt. 9:6) Jesus proved by freeing a man whom sin had bound with palsy. "For the Father judgeth no man, but hath committed all judgment unto the Son . . . and hath given him authority to execute judgment also, because he is the Son of man." — John 5:22, 27.

For every error, mistake, sin, which comes to any of our senses we are to give the Truth, that is, just the opposite. The derivation of the word "forgive," "to give for," will serve to keep one in mind of its original power. It substitutes for a sin the opposite virtue. Thus to forgive adultery in others is to cleanse them of adulterous desires and call forth the purity in them; to forgive hate is to cause love to spring up in its place.

True forgiveness is just as substantial an act as the giving of money is said to be, and as God works through man to carry out His benevolent designs towards the weak and poor, so He erases sin by working through the mind of man to send healing, loving thoughts towards those who seem in the delusion of sinful, unwholesome minds and lives.

We are not only to forgive (1) those who sin against us personally, but also (2) those who sin against our beloved, and (3) those who sin against the lovable and innocent anywhere upon the earth.

There must be no limit to our forgiveness. Some errors seem so deeply rooted that it requires angelic patience and deific persistency in order to eradicate them. Therefore when Peter asked Jesus how often he should forgive his brother—"till seven times? Jesus saith unto him, I say not unto thee, Until seven times: but, Until seventy times seven."— Matt. 18: 21, 22.

True forgiveness cleanses and sanctifies those who are receptive to it. And the outpicturing of this divine process is in being cleansed of the corrupting disease which was caused by the sin, and in having purer, holier motives and thoughts.

"Forgive us our debts, as we forgive our debtors." —Matt. 6:12. "If ye do not forgive, neither will your Father which is in heaven forgive your trespasses."— Mark 11126. As you give to others true, righteous thoughts and see them good, spiritual, and lovable, you will make yourself receptive to the same thoughts that are ever radiating from the Father's presence. God does not cease to forgive; it is wayward man that ceases to receive. We must be receptive to the Divine Presence, else it will not seem to exist for us.

If you wish to be forgiven a certain vice, you must silently and faithfully speak the word that sets others free from that same vice. It is God in you—the Good, Truth, in you—that is the forgiving power.

As long as one believes in sin, so long will he believe in punishment for sin, and no one can escape the effect of sin, suffering, but by the putting away from him of all sinful thinking, speaking, and doing.

If we believe another ought to be punished for sin, that punishment is as likely to come to us as to the other, although we may not consider ourselves as deserving of punishment. So the only true attitude of mind is to be glad and willing to see everyone set free from punishment, and to be an instrument in the divine hands for the consummation of this great work by being glad and willing to give the Truth to all who will receive it in place of the error which they seem to be holding. For the only freedom from punishment is in knowing the Truth.

Men and women who are leading sinful lives and are not suffering for it are free thus far because they have not yet come under their own condemnation, nor care for the condemnation of others. There will come a time when they will desire to rise above their present limitations—someone will come into their lives whose love and respect they will begin to desire—then there must be a change, and, alas! for them, if perversity and unbelief, because of much iniquity, will cause them to be long in accepting the Truth that will make them free.

People who are suffering keenly are often nearer the Truth than those who are content with selfish, impure living. And those are not the greatest sinners who have the most diseases. No one knows established health but the sinless One. "Those eighteen, upon whom the tower in Siloam fell, and slew them, think ye that they were sinners above all men that dwelt in Jerusalem? I tell you, Nay: but, except ye repent, ye shall all likewise perish."—Luke 13:4, 5.

Pity and indignation.

Pity and indignation at the manifestation of a wrong are strong powers which must be turned to usefulness in thwarting the injurious effects that seem imminent. These two forces have their source in the sense of love and justice, and therefore should be used to accomplish these ends. If you see an animal receiving cruel blows, instead of letting your pity be wasted in a feeling of impotence and misery, send your love in warm, living currents to the Life in the creature, declaring: "Your life is the life of God, protected and kept from all harm. No blows can hurt you. Good is the only power in you and around you;" and to the master say: "The wisdom and love of God work through you to bring forth the Good you wish," or words of like nature. Your word will take away all the sting from the lash, and bring the inflictor to true consciousness.

If you see a widow being defrauded by a dishonest money-grabber, do not let your indignation be wasted in anger and powerless denunciation. You may be mistaken in your judgment of the whole affair. Instead of dwelling upon the evil of the situation, say to him: "You desire only Good, and in your true Self you work for her highest Good as well as yours, and find your joy in it," and to her you say: "Everything, he does is a blessing, a help, and an advantage to you; God protects you," and your word shall not return to you void

Wherever there appears to be a sinner or one sinned against, there is your opportunity for the exercise of your divinely ordained task of forgiveness through Almighty Love.

Practice

Proceed with your patient as in the two previous treatments, with the exception of the fifth step, which upon this day is the denial of the power of sin and affirmation of the omnipotence of Love.

Intuition will reveal to you what particular belief in sin you are to dissolve with the word of Truth; but if you are not yet cognizant of this impressional nature, then you can about cover the ground by denying the reality and power of selfishness, pride, avarice, envy, jealousy, and malice.

One method of treatment is that of continually realizing the Divine Character and Man's unity with It. Remember, it is what you realize that counts. Avoid superfluity of words and vain repetition. Feel the Truth of what you say.

SELF-TREATMENT.

God is Love. I am the child of Love, and, like my Father, all-loving and forgiving. God is my loving patience; no anger can control me. God is my meekness; pride has no place in me.

God is my forgiving spirit; I cannot hold malice or revenge in my heart. I am one with God, and possess all things; therefore I covet nothing. Like God, I freely give all things to all; I know no selfishness. I am filled with love; I breathe love; I radiate love. I receive love from all, and no sinful thought can touch me. I cannot be moved by another's anger or pride. No one's selfishness, revenge, avarice, envy, or jealousy can affect me, or cause me to suffer; therefore I am free from all disease and sickness.

I now lovingly, fearlessly, and freely forgive all my fellowmen all sins committed against me and against the world, and I thank my Heavenly Father that I am now fully forgiven, and I henceforth manifest perfect life, strength, and health forever. Amen.

LESSON X. OVERCOMING FEAR.

SALVATION consists in being saved from sinning and from its results—sickness, sorrow, and death. There is no escape from the exact consequences of sinful deeds and thoughts but through the knowledge of Truth, by which comes the forgiveness which destroys sin and all its unhappy fruits.

The highest God-knowledge and power is needful sometimes to make restitution and reparation to others whom we have sinned against, and with mortals it would seem impossible, but to the Divine within you all things are possible.

The Mosaic law was a revelation to the Hebrews of moral causes and their physical effects. "Whatsoever a man soweth that shall he also reap" (Gal. 6:7) is the tenor of the whole Levitical law. To Cain it was revealed that he who kills will be killed again and again ("Everyone that findeth me shall slay me"—Gen. 4:14) unless placed under the protection of the Lord, as it is written, "Therefore whosoever slayeth Cain, vengeance shall be taken on him sevenfold."—Gen. 4:15. He who defrauds and cheats will suffer loss either in this age or in some other. He who deceives will be deceived. He who slanders will, in his turn, be bitten—it may not be by a slander but by a scourging, physical disease.

Divine metaphysics prove the logic and law back of the Golden Rule—"All things whatsoever ye would that men should do to you, do ye even so to them: for this is the law and the prophets."—Matt. 7:12. For if we are not under the law of the Christ every word and deed will bring forth after its kind, and as it is with plants, the fruits will often far exceed the small seeds sown. "It is easier for heaven and earth to pass, than one tittle of the law to fail."—Luke 16:17. But if we have the simplest knowledge of the Christ-truth, then can the heavens and the earth (the old conceptions) be rolled together like a scroll, and be clean dissolved to our consciousness, and we live in the new heavens and the new earth, exempt from the karmic laws of good for good and evil for evil.

Fate, destiny, astrological laws, and karma are all under the control of him who knows his Christhood. "Though his sins be as scarlet, they shall be as white as snow" (Is. 1:18), and not one seed need to bring forth an evil harvest, but "every plant, which my heavenly Father hath not planted, shall be rooted up."— Matt. 15:13.

Remorse and evil memories

When one has thoroughly repented of an error and turned from it, he should let it pass completely out of mind. Continued remorse is contrary to the principle, "Only the Good is true." Regrets and sorrows over the past must be banished wholly from consciousness.

"Thou shalt forget thy misery, and remember it as waters that pass away."—Job 11:16.

The memory is renewed and revived by righteous forgetting—forgetting the evils and the nothings, the vanities of existence, and remembering only its eternal verities, the Good and the Divine.

True repentance is our flight from some burning Sodom and Gomorrah, and when we have once left an evil state let us not look back upon it. "Remember Lot's wife."—Luke 17:32. Those who dwell in past experiences grow fossilized, and age early. There is only the eternal present, the Now-Good, for us to live in. Whatever joys and happiness we have had in the past belong to the Kingdom of Heaven, and we shall know them again, for they are eternal.

Even though we appear to fall into sin again and again, yet each time we should rise up as though we had not fallen. No one is beaten unless he thinks he is. There is no backsliding in Truth. If a person seems to fall away, then you may know that one was not as advanced as appearances indicated. Never think you have "gone back" from Truth. You may seem to be in the valley many days, not seeing the Way as plainly as when you were on the mountain-tops, yet you are nearer your goal. While you are going through extreme experiences you are in mountainous regions of mind, and progression will be marked by many ups and downs, going into valleys as well as ascending mountain peaks. The spokes of a wheel cannot always remain up if the wheel is to go forward. They go down before they come up again, and when they are down they are further along than when up before.

Onward and upward is the law of the Good in the realm of growth and change, and the Truth follower is ever progressing, never really going backward but for the purpose of gathering force to go forward.

The Word is like leaven

As leaven or yeast works in the midst of flour so the Word of Truth works among the thoughts and desires of man, a kind of mental, chemical action setting in wherein there seems to be disturbance and disorder, but to the eyes of the one who knows, a most desirable state preparatory to a new and useful manifestation. In many cases the "working" is deep and quiet, and where there is quick healing or realization of Truth, there is a momentary thrill or a strange, pleasant feeling not easy to describe. Every atom of the being is readjusted and bears new relation to every other atom. While this adjusting is going on one needs to be firm and true to Principle, that the work of casting out false beliefs may be thoroughly accomplished, and the birth into the new consciousness be quick and free from useless experiences.

When liquor is fermenting many foreign things are thrown to the surface which are then easily skimmed off. So the leaven of the Word will seem to bring hidden errors to the surface, and instead of being alarmed if a character seems to be worse after the Truth has begun its work, or a case of healing shows sudden and unusual symptoms of pain or change, the student must recognize this stage that comes between the old and the new, and carry the case quickly past its crisis into perfect relief and cure.

This stage has been described as the warring between Truth and error, the latter being slow to give up its claim, and possessed with fear of losing its life and being, so that the patient thinks himself to be in danger, and afraid of unknown consequences. Therefore fear is the principal error to be met at this time, and not another step is to be taken until fear is eliminated from the mind.

Often a denial of evil will seem to make the evil more real to one's self, but if the student will persist, denying the specific forms of evil that keep coming to the surface, soon the crisis will be passed, and he will come into a new and beautiful consciousness of Truth which was formerly hidden by the fogs of his erroneous belief.

If, when denying matter, new and unusual experiences begin to come, then deny fear calmly and slowly, and when the fear is brushed aside old material chains will also fall, and the omnipotence and omnipresence of Mind be more of a reality than ever.

The Word is like a broom sweeping our house (the body) and often a great dust is raised in the process. Uninstructed minds often stop, through fear, when their work is only partly done. But he who trusts in Life, in

Health, in Good, will press right on to the finish, knowing that "in due season we shall reap if we faint not."— Gal. 6:9.

Confession

Every error must be uncovered and its secret claims met fearlessly by the very name that mortals have given it, and be proven without place, power, or intelligence. To mention a secret belief in the presence of one who realizes its nothingness is sufficient to erase the whole thing from mind. This is the reason why the heart desires to confess to one in whom it has confidence, and feels such relief in confessing. Whenever you feel that you must tell your troubles to someone, select some strong, loving mentality who will make nothing of the evils you tell, and your wisdom will be rewarded with a perfect unburdening and sense of freedom peculiar to candor and innocence. Then you will know the reason of the advice, "Confess your faults one to another, and pray one for another, that ye may be healed."—Jas. 5:16.

As a healer many sins and sorrows may be told you that have never been breathed to anyone. But you should never whisper such confidences to another. The honor that governs the priest and the doctor should be yours. And more than this, you would be untrue to your principles were you to repeat the tales of evil that are poured into your ears. Forget them as quickly as possible, or if they remain in your memory, let them be a suggestion to silently breathe a blessing to the one who has confessed, couching the blessing in words especially appropriate for their realization of the complete absolving of the wrong doing.

Fear cast out

God is Love, inspiring fullness of confidence in His goodness, and bringing unlimited trust in His perfect protection and defense. There is no fear in the Divine Presence. Fear is carnal and has no place in the spiritual nature. "Perfect love casteth out fear; because fear hath torment. He that feareth is not made perfect in love."—1 John 4:18 There is no fear in love, and if we seem to have the slightest fear remaining, whether of God or man, beast or devil, we may know there is a vacuum in us demanding the in-filling of divine Love.

"The fear of the Lord," spoken of in Proverbs, ninth chapter, tenth verse, means reverence for the Lord, without which there cannot be either divine Wisdom or divine Love. Perfect love of God reveals to us that we have absolutely nothing to fear from the Author of All-goodness, in whom there is no evil thing, and that we can trust to His presence and power in everything that lives and has being. "For God hath not given us the spirit of fear; but of power and of love and of a sound mind."—2 Tim. 1: 7.

The fearful are classified with murderers and liars in Revelations, twenty-first chapter, eighth verse, as having no part in the realm of the True, but as being destined to pass through purging fires, that the false may be consumed, and all that is worth anything may be refined and set free from its tormenting presence. Therefore there is no justification for retaining fear of anything or anybody, and every student should be in training to cast out every fear from his being through the power of Trust and Almighty Love.

"Put on the whole armor of God" (Eph. 6:11), and realize the promises extended to all who are fearless because of complete trust in omnipotent Good. A large percentage of diseases rise from fears, either conscious or latent. Especially is this manifest among children, who are often thoughtlessly frightened with hobgoblin stories, and untrue threats of harm, and cruel tricks of the ignorant parents who little know that they are sowing the seeds of the disease that may bereave their household. Every child should learn the protecting presence of God to keep it from all injury and harm.

"He shall deliver thee in six troubles: yea, in seven there shall no evil touch thee. In famine he shall redeem thee from death: and in war from the power of the sword. Thou shalt be hid from the scourge of the tongue: neither shalt thou be afraid of destruction when it cometh. At destruction and famine thou shalt laugh: neither shalt thou be afraid of the beasts of the earth. For thou shalt be in league with the stones of the field: and the beasts of the field shall be at peace with thee."—Job 5:19-23.

All the animal world is harmless before true love and fearlessness. Truth forms an aura of protection about its devotee more impenetrable than walls of stone. It is authentic history that many of the early Christians could not be made the prey of the hungry lions and tigers turned loose upon them, but some beasts would even go and lie down at the feet of those lovers of God like domestic animals to which the savage instinct is foreign. It was by this law that Daniel was delivered from the lions. The rattlesnake will never strike where there is freedom from both fear and harmfulness. "Blessed is the man who is afraid of nothing and of whom nothing is afraid."

If there is any animal which you hate or fear, be it mouse, cat, dog, cow, snake, or any other, see to it that you purge your heart wholly from such feelings by the power of love which makes you one with the life of everything, and able to discern that Presence in them which the naturalist and the holy man find, and respect too highly to have a vain or foolish thought concerning.

Fear of people leaves us as we regard all as our brothers, and radiate to them the love that disarms their enmity. The thief could not then steal from you, nor the libertine insult you. Your life would be as safe with the savage as his very own. It would be as impossible for him to kill you as to cut off his own hand.

No domineering mentality can cause you to cower, nor wound you with tongue or any other weapon.

Fear of death, of the dark, of unknown powers and nameless things are all negations, or blanks, to be filled in with positive and definite expressions of trust and faith.

Every intimation of fear is a little flag of warning, telling us where our faith must be increased and strengthened, and we must never fear fear itself, but make use of its appearance to speak rousing, steadying words of the supremacy of Good.

The practice

When a patient is going from stage to stage, daily, through a six days' course of treatment, he will grow better each day, receiving evidence continually of the power of the Word in healing him. After an effectual treatment against belief in sinning and being sinned against, there follows a mental stage of activity comparable to the effervescence in a liquid wherein an acid and an alkali come together. The patient comes to judgment, mentally and physically, and there begins to be a casting out of false conditions and states of mind preparatory to entering the new, normal, and healthy state of body and of thinking. The commonest physical method of casting out will be through the bowels and the pores of the skin, unless obstructed by fears on the part of the patient or those interested.

When a patient passes quietly and non-resistingly from disease into health this intermediary stage will hardly be noticed, it being signified only by a slight mental disturbance, a sort of unreasonable irritation at things and people, accompanied by a few aches and "growing pains" in different parts of the body, especially those parts formerly diseased. These are but echoes of a past that is rapidly passing away from the patient's consciousness, and they are nothing in themselves, and the less the patient and healer notice them the better for the case.

The mental casting out will be marked by a confidential talk which may include secrets never divulged before. It may even be a sort of confessional, and the penitent may be filled with guilty remorse, and repentant tears flow freely. Let them flow, seeking only to check them by the true denial of the whole matter, silently given.

Confession to the healer is not necessary, and no healer should urge it, for to demand it is to assume the presence of evil, which assumption would decrease the effectiveness of your treatments.

Acute cases

Should there be an unconscious resistance to the Truth on the part of the patient there may appear to be fever and acute pains. This is because of fear, and to allay the fever and pain the healer speaks, coolly and calmly, true words of comfort: "There is nothing to fear. Peace! be still," putting the soothing reassuring statements in silent utterances especially adapted to the mentality of the one needing help.

This is the treatment, the first one, given to all acute cases, such as pneumonia, and in accidents and sudden sharp pains. Wherever the condition is excitable and feverish speak slowly, softly, and soothingly, whether your word is silent or audible. Where the condition is fainting, dazed, or lethargic let your word be expressed vigorously, like a rousing command. In acute cases the fever or the pain should yield while the patient is in the presence of the healer, or, if it is an absent case, the healer should receive inward assurance that the case is reached.

Do not treat the case continuously, but let there be intervals of time the same length as the treatments. If there have been twenty minutes of silent treatment, then let there be twenty minutes of relaxation and trust, in which you turn your mind completely from the patient to restful, trustful subjects of attention. Then again give yourself to faithful prayer until the case begins to show response. When this is assured, then the case can be carried forward just as in chronic diseases.

Remember to be free from fear yourself. Meet every mental suggestion of evil with Truth, bearing in mind that every word spoken for yourself is helping the patient. You may be reflecting the fears of others, in which case they will come into mind, and a silent word to them will release you. Sometimes it will be well to have someone else treat you, especially if you are personally interested in your case.

God calls you to it.

In cases of children, deny the influence of the parents' or guardians' fears, and address these parties individually with the Truth that disperses fears, doubts, and unbeliefs.

Do not be moved by groans, or screams, or evil sights. Let no appearance of evil cause you to "lose your head" or grow faint-hearted, but under all circumstances keep your self-possession by remembering what is the Self and Who has charge of the case. It is God who has called you to it, and God is taking care of His own.

Everyone who turns to Truth for his healing, or through the love of another is brought under its influence, is the subject of a special Providence, and though all things were against him he can truly say, "The Lord is the strength of my life; of whom shall I be afraid?"-—Ps. 27:1.

A healer may have mental pictures while giving treatment. They should be looked upon as symbolical, and either disregarded or used as indicators of what statements will be most helpful to the case. Thus, if a coffin were seen, or some other symbol of death, it should mean that the healer speak fervent words for the manifestation of Life and Life more abundant. The sign means that error is dying—not the patient, who is being called forth from the sepulcher of the old existence into the new Life and Health.

Painless childbirth

Painless childbirth is one of the blessings now manifest through the power and knowledge of Truth. To realize that the matrix is a most normal organ in its office and capable of great elasticity and muscular power is helpful in removing the false beliefs associated with the efforts of child-bearing.

Woman is under the law of Christ and no longer under the Adamic curse of multiplied conceptions and sorrowful travail. Babes represent spiritual ideas, and they can be brought forth without a struggle and in fullness of joy. The Christian world has been long in realizing this emancipation of woman expressed by Paul in 1 Timothy, second chapter, fifteenth verse: "She shall be saved in child- bearing, if they continue in faith and charity and holiness with sobriety."

The banishment of fear insures painless parturition by allowing all the organs to adjust themselves. Therefore let the same treatment be given in such cases as with any crisis, seeing all painful manifestations as only indicators that new ideas and expressions are seeking externalization, and need only our co-operation to cause the pain to vanish, and the true condition to be made a triumphant and happy visibility.

When giving the regular "week's treatment" proceed as upon the first day, substituting for the fifth step the following:

Make such denials and affirmations as are appropriate to the case. In the six-day course of treatment, the fourth day you deny that there is anything to fear, or any cause for guilt or remorse, or that there is any influence in the fears of others, and you affirm the protection of the Love of God and the presence of Almighty Trust in the power of Good, Life, Health, Peace, and Prosperity.

Sudden attacks of disease

Sudden and painful attacks of disease are among the easiest of the problems to be solved by mental healers. They almost invariably yield instantaneously, and are among the best proofs of the power of the Word to those who seek testimony through the senses.

A few such instances will be very helpful to the young healer in giving confidence in his or her word. And this very confidence will be a healing power in itself. When you have gained this, you will find that your very entrance into the sick room will allay pain. More than this, the moment their cases enter your mind they will begin to be better, and you will find that often for them simply to turn to you will relieve them. Cases have been healed when the healer has received no message and given no special treatment. There has been a silent union and communion made even when the personalities of either healer or patient have not known it.

Lay up heavenly treasures of faith and love, and you will be an inexhaustible bank to draw upon for healing and help in every way.

LESSON XI. DIVINE UNDERSTANDING, OUR STRENGTH.

Discouragement

THE well-balanced mind manifests as evenness in temperament, wherein are no seasons of moodiness or moments of discouragement, down-heartedness, or gloom in any form. Students who have times when they feel melancholy—have a "fit of the blues," hearts that are heavy when days are gray, bodies that feel themselves cumbersome and weary—all these are the effects of believing oneself subject to ignorance and liable to foolishness. Such minds must be set free from self-depreciation, which rises from believing in superiority and inferiority. Contentment and self-sufficiency must be manifest through realizing the Lord to be our very Self.

Divine understanding gives strength and independence. He who turns to the secret place in his own nature for all knowledge will walk with God, and not be lame or halt in his mental going. "Stand upright on thy feet!" Learn to stand upon your own power of knowing Truth and interpreting life and Scripture, then your mental feet can walk, run, skip, dance, and go through every other performance, and yet keep their grace and selfmastery, for "the center of gravity will not fall without the base," the mind become unbalanced, or the feelings grow stolid and glum.

Discontent and the sense of uselessness are overcome by the power of Self- centering and ceasing to look outside for satisfaction and knowledge.

"Be strong and of a good courage," said Jehovah again and again to the children of Israel as they were preparing to enter into the promised land of Canaan (Deut. 31:6, 7, 23; Josh. I: 6, 9, 18). "Be strong and of a good courage, fear not nor be afraid of them: for the Lord thy God, he it is that doth go with thee; he will not fail thee, nor forsake thee."

Learn to associate understanding with strength, and, conversely, see that discouragement, weakness, and weariness are to be associated with ignorance and foolishness, and realize that the healing of depression and inefficiency lies in spiritual understanding.

True self-sufficiency

Perfect freedom, that comes through knowing, manifests as divine, non-resistant independence of all earthly authority and all earthly forms, ceremonies, dogmas, and creeds. All knowledge must be looked for within oneself, and no matter who or what says a thing, when that authority is outside our own heart and mind we are only to accept it as the Spirit in us bears witness to it that it is true. Jesus says, "I receive not testimony from man" (John 5 134); and he also says, "Follow me."—

Luke 9:59. So, since Jesus receives not the testimony of man, and we would follow him, neither are we to receive the testimony of man, but listen to the Father within, just as he did. "All thy children shall be taught of God."—Is. 54:13. "Every man therefore that hath heard, and hath learned of the Father, cometh unto me," says Jesus (John 6:45).

The day, prophesied by Jeremiah, in which a man may say that he knows of himself that this is true, and does not believe it because of what any good man or any good book says, but because of the Christ in him, is now here. "After those days, saith the Lord, I will put my law in their inward parts and write it in their hearts; and will be their God, and they shall be my people. And they shall teach no more every man his neighbor, and every man his brother, saying, Know the Lord: for they shall all know me, from the least of them unto the greatest of them, saith the Lord."— Jer. 31:33, 34.

Divine understanding gives one power to discern all teachings, and ability to divide the wheat from the chaff and keep only that which is true and spiritually profitable. You must trust to the "inspiration of the Almighty" (Job 32:8) in you in reading all books and in listening to all men. Trust in the omnipresent and omnipotent Truth makes us fearless and tolerant towards every claim to knowledge, and we cannot be deceived by sophistry nor misled by strange doctrines, for were we even to drink of most poisonous teaching we would receive only the innocent part of it, thus spiritually fulfilling the Christ-promise, "If they drink any deadly thing, it shall not hurt them."—Mark 16:18.

Bible study

The two greatest aids to an understanding of Scriptural tests are (1) the practice of applying Truth to all the common experiences of daily life and interpreting events from the standpoint of mental causation, and (2) listening to the Holy Spirit within you. Thus you can have every passage in the Scriptures explained, and you will see how all the apparently contradictory passages can be reconciled.

The Spirit of Truth is with you now, that Spirit that was promised by Jesus, and of which he said, "He dwelleth with you, and shall be in you" (John 14:17), and also "he will guide you into all truth" (John 16: 13); moreover "he shall teach you all things" (John 14:26), and will "abide with you forever" (John 14: 16). This Spirit tells you the meaning of all Scripture, and whenever a text or story is interpreted truly through any other student, this Spirit will corroborate it, filling your heart with warm, harmonious assurances of its trueness.

How does the Spirit reconcile "God is angry with the wicked every day" (Ps. 7:11) with the Christ- thought, "he is kind unto the unthankful and to the evil" (Luke 6:35)? In this way: As long as people think they can act wickedly and contrary to the will of God, just so long will they believe that God is a God of wrath and punishment, or as John the Baptist preached, "He that believeth not the Son shall not see life; but the wrath of God abideth on him."—John 3:36. But Christ came to change men's beliefs about God and show them the loving Father instead of the angry God, and whoever believes the Christ-self, and follows His direction, will know God to be pure Love in which there is no anger ever.

The spirit of understanding shows us that all Scriptural passages which represent God as having passions like mortal men, and doing as men do, are an account of God's being and action as it appears to them— men's ideas about God. When men repent, then God seems to repent, as in the case of Nineveh (Jonah 3:10). When men are tempted of their own lusts they, ascribing evil to God, say they are tempted of God (Jas. I:i3, 14). When men are hard and severe, rigid in discipline, and revengeful, their God is the same character to them. He that is loving and forgiving has a loving and forgiving father as his God.

God knows no evil.

God knows no evil and therefore does not permit evil. For God to recognize evil would be for God to think an evil thought, and to think with God is to give life and reality to the thought and to perpetuate it forever, for no thought of God's can ever be destroyed. God's mind is too pure to behold iniquity. "Thou art of purer eyes than to behold evil, and canst not look on iniquity."—Hab. 1:13. God does not see the evil and imperfection in you, but only that which is the Good and the True in your being. Therefore it is with joy that we know, "Thou God seest me," and not with fear and shame.

It is because you are continually in the mind and heart of God that you are immortal. Your life is perpetually sustained by God loving you all the time. To recognize this to be reconciled to God, spoken of so much in the Bible. To be reconciled to God is to see God and love Him, even as He sees and loves us. Since God does not recognize sin and evil it is not true to say that God permits these things to be. Such is the right view of God, and it stops all that useless questioning as to "why God lets so much sin and suffering be in the world." It is because God is not recognizing these things that their time is short and their apparent power temporal.

Predestination

Can God ever be sorrowful or helpless in the presence of evil? No. Yet one of these would be true if the good God were to behold evil and not annihilate it. "To the pure all things are pure."— Titus 1:15. Who is so pure as God? God sees you as you really are—pure, holy, true, sinless—and this seeing is your salvation. God sees all things working together for His glory and honor, and His predestation and fore-ordination is that He has ordained that the Divine in each shall prove itself of His nature and being, and that the false and the untrue shall be proven pure nothingness, without place or power in the realm of appearances, even as in the realm of the Real. God knows all things that were, and are, and are to be, and He knows, and has always known, that the Real in us would triumph and be glorified, and that the false would finally take its place in "outer darkness," in nothingness.

The "elect" and the "chosen," spoken of in Scripture, is that One in each of us that came from God, and returns to God, and is in God now. It is the only One that enters into Heaven. "No man ascendeth up to heaven, but he that came down from heaven, even the Son of man, which is in heaven."— John 3:13.

The "son of perdition" (John 17:i2) is the false one of each of us, the personality, the man of flesh, the carnal. This one is cast away in Peter and in John just as much as in Judas. It was the son of perdition in Peter that Jesus spoke to when he said, "Get thee behind me, Satan: thou art an offence unto me: for thou savorest not the things that be of God, but those that be of men" (Matt. 16:23), and it was the Son of God in Peter to whom Jesus spoke words the very opposite in kind just previously: "Blessed art thou, Simon Barjona: for flesh and blood hath not revealed it unto thee, but my Father which is in heaven."— Matt. 16:17.

Other names for "that man of sin" (2 Thes. 2:3) are "sons of Belial" (Judges 20:12, 13), which the children of Israel were called when in error; "children of the devil" (John 8:44); and "children of the wicked one" (Matt. 13:38), spoken of by Jesus in the parable of the wheat and the tares. God sows the divine Self, the children of the Kingdom, and apparently right beside this Real One is sown the false self, whose father is a lie (deception). These both grow together until the harvest, when the wheat (all the Truth in each) is gathered into His barns (the Kingdom of Heaven), and the false (the tares) in each of us is gathered together and burned in Love, the everlasting fires of God. This judgment is being passed continuously, and ever the True, the Good, is being separated from the false, the evil, and the Lord God in you is saying to the false, "Depart from me, I know you not whence ye are" (Luke 13:25, 27), and to the true, "Enter thou into the joy of thy Lord."—Matt. 25:23. In the parable of the shepherd and his flock (Matt. 25:32), the sheep represent the pure, innocent, meek, gentle, peaceful thoughts; the goats, the wild, unruly, aggressive, willful thoughts.

Into outer darkness (the nothing) and the bottomless pit (the nothing) are cast (Rev. 21:8) all fearful thoughts, all doubts (the unbelieving), all angry thoughts, all lies, and everything that "loveth and maketh a lie.'"—Rev. 22:15. Who is not glad to see this carried out in himself? "Purge me with hyssop, and I shall be clean: wash me, and I shall be whiter than snow."—Ps. 51 7.

No superiority or inferiority

There is no superiority and inferiority in God—we are all One, we are all equal, the first is as the last, and the greatest as the least. It is only when we look at ourselves as separate personalities that and we see someone superior or inferior. All that was in Jesus is in you now, and all that is in you is in every magdalen that walks the land. The One that is equal in us all is the Christ, the only One.

Self-depreciation has no place in the true Self. Do not compare yourself with others, nor contrast the followers of Truth. Speak the truth each man to his neighbor and of his neighbor, which is: "There is only One in you that knows, and that One is the same in me and in all, and that One knows all things."

The cross

When the disciples went out upon their first ministry they had no dogma or creed to preach. Their first sending forth was by Jesus while he was yet with them, so they could not preach about a crucifixion upon Golgotha, nor the necessity of believing in such an event in order to be saved. Then what was their "preaching of the cross," as Paul expressed it in I Corinthians, first chapter, eighteenth verse? What was Paul's preaching of it? Was it a historical event he was talking about, or did he see that the crucifixion of Jesus was a symbol, just as he saw that the Jewish sacrifices of rams and bullocks were symbols?

The "preaching of the cross" with all the true disciples of Jesus was just the same as that of Jesus himself. And that preaching is found embodied in his words, "If any man will come after me, let him deny himself, and take up his cross, and follow me."—Matt. 16:24. The preaching of the cross is the teaching of the denial of the personality, the material universe, and the principle of evil, or, in ecclesiastical language, it is the denial of "the world, the flesh, and the devil." That which is the means by which you deny is

191

called the Cross. To "cross out" is to cancel, and as long as there seems to be anything to be cancelled we must have our cross with us, which Paul calls "the power of God."

When you successfully deny yourself by right mental practice and a selfless life, you reach that place where you can lay down your body at will, and you can take it up again. "I have power to lay it down, and I have power to take it again."— John 10:18. Then "take up your cross"—in this case your personality (the body is often called the cross), that by which you are visible to mortals, and by which you can deny in the hearing and sight of men— "and follow me." That is, "Behold, I cast out devils, and I do cures to-day and tomorrow, and the third day I shall be perfected. Nevertheless I must walk to-day and tomorrow, and the day following."—Luke 13: 32, 33. To follow Christ we must "walk" until we realize the word of the Father, "I have finished the work which thou gavest me to do."—John 17:4. This is to know, in the flesh, our perfection, the glory which we had with the Father before the world was. To take up the cross daily is to deny something of the world, the personality, and evil every day.

It is well not to have any preference between denial and affirmation, but to see that these each and both be used. Cross and crown they are. If one does not deny the false self, its world, and its evil, then one cannot effectually affirm the true Self, its kingdom, and its righteousness. The wise have said, "No cross, no crown."

Death overcome

Dominion over disease and decay and freedom from sinning ultimate in victory over death. Dying is no part of life, and, according to the Genesis account, was not in the experience of men until they were disobedient to the divine instruction: "The tree of the knowledge of good and evil, thou shalt not eat of it: for in the day that thou eatest thereof thou shalt surely die."—Gen. 2:17.

The greatest work of Jesus' ministry was the triumph over death, his other works, such as healing diseases and emancipating from sin, being subservient to that end and necessary first-steps in the great demonstration.

When asked to give a sign peculiar to his teaching (Matt. 12:38-41) Jesus gave Jonah's deliverance from hell and death as an example of the one sign that should be given by him to mankind. He allowed himself to be murdered, dying the most disgraceful death a criminal can suffer. "No man taketh it [my life] from me, but I lay it down of myself. I have power to lay it down, and I have power to take it again. This commandment have I received of my Father."—John 10:18. This he did that there might be a recorded proof of man's dominion over death. So that even if a spiritually instructed man from any cause become hypnotized into death, he there may remember himself, and break the mesmeric spell, and resuscitate himself by the power of God in him.

Through unfaith the professors of Christianity during these many centuries have lost or obscured this masterly teaching of the Lord Christ by attributing his promises of life eternal to a future world. If one reads his words upon this divine gift and power of everlasting life (John 6:31-63) with the true light upon them, he will see that Jesus did not mean "spiritual death" at all. He says, "Your fathers did eat manna in the wilderness, and are dead." Did he mean that Moses, Joshua, Caleb, Aaron, and many other righteous Israelites were spiritually dead? No. He referred to their physical death. "I am the living bread which came down from heaven: if any man eat of this bread, he shall live forever."—John 6:51. He said to Martha: "I am the resurrection, and the life: he that believeth in me, though he were dead, yet shall he live: and whosoever liveth and believeth in me shall never die. Believest thou this?"—John 11:25, 26. Yet Martha, type of Christian stolidity, did not understand. Instead of grasping his great teaching about victory over death, she but reiterated her convictions of his Christhood.

Putting on incorruption

"Putting on incorruption" is the term with which Paul describes the divine alchemy that takes place in the human body which is going through the regeneration and transmutation of each cell from a center of change and decay to one of purity and life. All the tissues, fluids, and elements of the physical body are subject to every thought of mind. As the mind realizes the unsubstantiality of matter and the readiness of flesh to obey thought, ideas will be held that will beautify even the earthly form, causing it to express grace, youthfulness, strength, purity, according to the individual desire of the one it represents. It can be retained in the sight of men and function in the midst of humanity as long as its possessor wishes, and, when its master wills, disappear as the mirage withdraws with the setting of the sun.

Figuratively speaking, you are the sun, and the physical body is but one of the many pictures your imagining power is forming, revealing, and causing to disappear.

It is the "man of sin" of whom it is said that his "years are three-score years and ten."— Ps. 90:10. As we journey back to our Eden ("and truly, if they had been mindful of that country from whence they came out, they might have had opportunity to have returned" —Heb. 11:15) we shall return to the great age of the patriarchs, as it is promised, "For as the days of a tree are the days of my people, and mine elect shall long enjoy the work of their hands."—Is. 65:22.

The apostle Paul taught the transmutation of the body, and that we rise from the dead while still in the garment of flesh (I Cor. 15 47-58). "We shall not all sleep, but we shall all be changed."—I Cor. 15:51. "For we that are in this tabernacle do groan, being burdened: not for that we would be unclothed, but clothed upon, that mortality might be swallowed up of life."—2 Cor. 5 14. "Therefore if any man be in Christ, he is a new creature: old things are passed away; behold, all things are become new."—2 Cor. 5:11. "Ourselves also, which have the first fruits of the Spirit, even we ourselves groan within ourselves, waiting for the adoption, to wit the redemption of our body."—Rom. 8:23. "And I pray God your whole spirit and soul and body be preserved blameless unto the coming of our Lord Jesus Christ."—I Thes. 5:23.

Those who have "passed away" from the physical plane, the so-called dead, are not barred from the teachings of Truth thereby. They have simply retired into the mental regions of the world. Yet they are not in- advance of the rest of humanity because of their experience. If they will but receive the Truth as it is given in their own realm of thinking they, too, can identify themselves with the Highest, overcome mortality's errors and await in peaceful trust the consummation of the healing of the whole world, when the veil that separates the psychic realm from the physical shall be rent in twain, and the two become as one. This is the age to come, called the Second Coming of Christ, when each shall be God's Christ, even as Jesus was and is.

Forms and ceremonies

The forms and ceremonies of the church are all symbolical of interior processes. As external forms they are nothing at all, and have no power in themselves. Taken alone they are "the letter that killeth." The reality is in the heart and mind. Ceremonies without accompanying heart correspondences are like words without thought, and of them the assassin-king in Hamlet says when trying to pray:

My words fly up, my thoughts remain below: Words without thoughts, never to heaven go.

The real baptism is within, and no rite of baptism is effectual that is not one with the same process performed in the heart (Lesson 2). No one need to be externally baptized unless he be led of the Holy Spirit so to do.

194

Nevertheless if one wishes to be baptized, let no one stand in that one's way. So also with every other ordinance and form of the church.

The true communion of the Lord's Supper is eating the words of Truth and drinking the words of Life. To eat and drink of the flesh and blood of Jesus Christ is to let his spirit fill you, and to lead his Life by keeping his sayings in thought, word, and deed.

In the great lesson which he gave upon the communion (John 6:47-63) Jesus plainly reveals his mystic statement, "Except ye eat the flesh of the Son of man and drink his blood ye have no life in you," by the closing words of his discourse, "It is the spirit that quickeneth; the flesh profiteth nothing: the words that I speak unto you, they are spirit and they are life."

He who eats and drinks the words of Christ partakes of the communion daily. Every time he eats and drinks outwardly he can sup with the Lord by realizing that he does not eat material food, but in spirit and in truth is receiving and incorporating into his very being the substance of God.

Every act of the life can be holy. "Whatsoever ye do, do it from the soul, as unto the Lord, and not unto men."—Col. 3:23. He that realizes the cleansing of the word of Truth is baptized every time he washes his hands or enters his bath. The true "grace" to breathe before each meal is the consciousness that in reality one is identifying himself with the substance (spirit) and creative power (life) of God.

The fasting of the saints arose from their continual denial of the world, the flesh, and the devil. When filled with the bread and wine of the Spirit the devotee often finds himself having no appetite for material food, and so does not eat, nor care to eat. Then the world sees him fasting. He is not fasting to become spiritual, but because he has become spiritual he is fasting. "Is not this the fast that I have chosen? to loose the bands of wickedness, to undo the heavy burdens, and to let the oppressed go free, and that ye break every yoke? . . . Is it not to deal thy bread to the hungry, and that thou bring the poor that are cast out to thy house? when thou seest the naked, that thou cover him; and that thou hide not thyself from thine own flesh?"—Is. 58:6, 7.

Practice

It is divine understanding that enables us to see all things in their true light, and to rely upon ourselves for all teaching and interpretation. As we look within for all our instruction, we shall see that all the world is contributing to us of its wealth of knowledge without our seeking it or asking for it, for outward teachers, whether they are persons or books, are symbols of certain thoughts held in the mind. Say to yourself, "God reveals that to me," and soon some person comes along and speaks the very word you are to hear—it may be a sentence, or a course of lectures. Say to yourself, "God reveals that to me," and you pick up just the book you should, or read the very article in magazine or newspaper you should. It is wisdom not to ascribe any of your learning to an earthly teacher or an earthly book, but continue in the thought forever, "I am taught of God only."

There are no burdens in the spiritual consciousness. "Cast thy burden on the Lord" (Ps. 55 -.22) and know that by so doing you make nothing of it, for God is not burdened with heavy cares and weary work. To cast your burden upon the Lord is as though it were dropped into the bottomless pit. When you have thus thrown off this sense of weighty responsibility see that you do not take it again.

"Bear ye one another's burdens" by making nothing of them.

If, at times, you find yourself in the "slough of despond" and cannot account for your state of mind, you may be reflecting some one's despondency, and you can come quickly out by sending the word of courage, strength, and knowledge to some one who appears to be under the cloud of sorrow or misfortune. If you know no such one, then radiate quickening, invigorating beams of wisdom to the whole world, and some drooping heart will receive refreshment, and return an answering chord of relief that will set you free.

If you ever feel discouraged over a case, treat your patient for secret discouragement, or yourself for the belief of the lack of knowledge and of power.

In the regular order of six-day course of treatment this is the fifth stage of unfoldment, generally an appearance of weakness, weariness, and discouragement, and therefore the especial word is that which brings realization of the inner source of strength and knowledge, the inexhaustible supply of life, health, and goodness, the freedom from every burden.

"Be not weary in well doing."—2 Thes. 3:13.

LESSON XII. DIVINE COMPLETENESS, OUR SATISFACTION.

The awakened soul

ALL language descriptive of God and the Soul is, at best, but figurative. So the enlightened man does not cavil at the use of limited terms to express spiritual processes. He knows that,

The tau [the word] that can be tau-ed [worded] is not the Eternal Tau [The Word].

Lao-Tze.

The name that can be named is not the Eternal Name. And he can speak of the changeless verities of God as he wills, and not be deceived by the words he uses. Thus, much is said by inspired teachers of the awakening of the Soul, yet the Soul never sleeps. The Psalmist cries, "Awake, why sleepest thou, O Lord?" (Ps. 44:23), and yet he truly knows, "He that keepeth Israel shall neither slumber nor sleep."—Ps. 121 -.4. The true Self is ever awake and conscious of itself and the Truth. This knowledge is eternal peace and bliss, and to abide in it is rest and satisfaction always, as it is written, "I shall be satisfied when I awake with thy likeness." —Ps. 17:15.

To awaken is to come to the consciousness of who we are and where we are. We are now awake to the knowledge that we are holy, spiritual Being, and that we are surrounded by the Kingdom of Heaven, that we have ever been what we are now, and God's perfect world is the only true realm, and in it is nothing of wrong or of injury and pain. It is restful joy to maintain this true cognition of our Self, and dissatisfaction is impossible to him who remembers his divinity and its omnipotence.

The Soul knows that it is free from the delusions of sense, that illusion has never deceived it, and therefore it has neither been attracted nor repelled by the changeable, unreal forms of mortality. The Soul does not need experiences in matter in order to receive knowledge. She knows all things now. Nothing is true of your Soul that is not true of God. God is not evolved, neither are you. God, the Perfect, does not progress from a state of ignorance and not-being to one of knowledge and being, neither do you. Progression is an appearance, the representation of that eternal joyous going from glory to glory, the "many mansions" of our "Father's house," those manifestations whose number is infinity and whose beauties are transcendently varied and yet all One, that is, God.

The emancipated devotee

As the panorama of existence passes before the gaze of the emancipated devotee he sees: "I am all that I have ever loved in this: I am the beautiful, the noble, the pure, the grand that is mirrored about me. In the great harmonies, I sing; in the weavings of the sunlight through hue and form, I glide; in every heart that loves, I am the lover; in every dear one, I am the beloved. I laugh in the innocent child, I think in the masterful reasoner. All men love me and there is none unloved of me. Life is a great symphony, and I am the musician; an enchanting romance, and I am the romancer.

"I am in my story or not, as I will—never entangled, yet lavishing my whole being upon my holy creation; doing nothing by halves, for my Love gives its whole life, service, and being to its Beloved. In peace and in joy, henceforth, shall I lead my own to the heights of bliss. By comforting words, by easy paths, shall I invite and guide each and every heart which seeks that which I am into the happiness which is mine, 'eternal in the heavens."

Then is it revealed to the devotee how he, too, has been led all the way along to his deliverance. He learns that all nature is in a friendly conspiracy to assist him and to contribute to his happiness, and to the ultimate emancipation of all.

Nothing happens by chance

Nothing happens by chance in man's life. Great laws are back of every movement he makes. What you did that time when you took the step that has seemed such a mistake was the outcome of the myriads of thoughts that went before. The tendencies of character obey that natural law, so familiar in mechanics, of moving along the line of the least resistance. With the desires you had, and the knowledge you possessed, you could not have done otherwise than you did. Nevertheless, even of our mistakes the Good can and does make advantages to us.

Watch for the Good in all the events of your life. Be alert to discover what new realization the Spirit is presenting to you, that your joy may be increased. Every personality that walks beside you in life's journey is as a jewel casket holding an entrancing treasure which now and then is opened for whomsoever will to see. Whoever sees the priceless interior of any nature, be its external even passingly foolish or uncouth, will never forget, but will love that one, and having truly loved once, will love "unto the end."—John 13:1.

Love is life

The Christ in giving life to the world gives Love. It wells up in the heart spontaneously, and as your cup runs over with its bounty your eyes are opened to see the ideal in some one, and you exalt that one to the very throne of deity. Your ecstasy is holy, and in your wisdom you see that this loved one is a means of holding the great overflow of divine joy, as glasses hold the effervescing wine, until such time as the great love can be lifted up into the Universal Presence wherein all are loved with the same fervor and bliss. The highest office of the earthly institution of marriage is to afford an orderly, serene, happy way up which the human love may mount to that all-absorbing divine Love of God, that unspeakable happiness about whose charms poet and prophet have never ceased to sing since first Love said, "Let there be light."

The Hindu scriptures say: Verily a husband is not dear that you may love the husband, but that you may love the self, for that is a husband dear. Verily a wife is not dear that you may love the wife, but that you may love the self, for that is the wife dear. Verily the worlds are not dear that you may love the worlds, but that you may love the self, for that are the worlds dear. Verily creatures are not dear that you may love the creatures, but that you may love the self, for that are creatures dear.

He who would increase in spirituality and in powers to do the works of Christ, let him increase in love, for greater than knowing is love, greater than faith is love. There is nothing that love cannot do. Your whole being is filled with love now— you are a concentration of desire, which is but a form of love. Desire brought you into manifestation, and holds you there, and governs all your steps—just give avenues and vehicle to the great love which you have. "Love is of God; and every one that loveth is born of God, and knoweth God."—1 John 4:7.

The Soul is complete

The Soul is complete. It is not dual, it is One. It has never been divided into sexes, and therefore it is not seeking a mate. The appearance of sex is a delusion, part of the masquerading in which the Self is denied and the claim of being separated from our Beloved is set up. The petty differences that lie in the mind associated with belief in duality fall away, and we rise above the weaknesses of sexuality as we see our Soul. The wild, eager search of men and women for companions who shall understand them and appreciate their true nature is really the search after God. And satisfaction comes only as God is found, and the Holy One seen to be our real bride, our real husband. "For thy Maker is thine husband; the Lord of Hosts is his name; and thy Redeemer the Holy One of Israel; The God of the whole earth shall he be called."—Is. 54:5.

The earthly marriage can represent the heavenly union, and if those who find themselves in this relation but exalt its every department to the highest and holiest place, they can make of it a perpetual sacrament and a means of developing the hidden beauties of their nature through abiding in chastity, gentleness, love-service, patience, and reverence towards the Lord in each.

Those who give all their desires and powers to God no longer generate after the flesh but after the Spirit, which is the re-generation. Birth, marriage, and death are but different forms of the same proceeding. Each has a mystical significance describing a spiritual reality. You are Spirit, therefore, in reality, you were never born, neither do you marry, neither shall you die any more, even as the Lord Christ has said: "They which shall be accounted worthy to obtain that world, and the resurrection from the dead, neither marry nor are given in marriage: neither can they die anymore; for they are equal unto the angels; and are the children of God." — Luke 20:35, 36.

Paradoxical statements

Wise men, inspired of the One, have taught that the Lord of all is the Unnameable, and that no one name can comprehend all that It is, and that no one statement of Truth can convey the knowledge and beauty of the Divine Presence. The mind that is the most efficient vehicle in bringing one to the apprehension of Deity must be supremely elastic and supple in its dealings with the many contradictory statements made concerning "Him that is without a second."

The mind swings between such extreme utterances as "God is All" and "God is the Nothing," and finds the unity of the extremes, and rests in conscious poise and ecstasy of realization. It sees that there is only God, and the Nothing is the receptivity of the divine nature, the Motherhood of God, and the All is the Fatherhood of God. The All is ever filling the Nothing, and this full-filling is manifestation and creation. Nature is the holy Mother, pure nothingness, the void, without whom there could be no bringing forth. She is God, the immaculate Virgin that all womanhood typifies. Her emptiness ever draws the divine substance into manifestation. She is never known as the Nothing, but by the name of her Lord. All creation reveals her mystery; the sap rushes up the trees because her vacuum precedes it, the breath flows into the lungs because of the emptiness, there is no movement of currents of air or water, of rock or fire, but must have a vacancy to cause its motion. Of this sweet Mother of us all the mystic sings:

There was something chaotic in nature which existed before heaven and earth. It was still. It was void. It stood alone, and was not changed. It pervaded everywhere, and was not endangered. It may be regarded as the Mother of the Universe. I know not its name; but I give it the title of "Tau." Lao-Tze.

The heavenly Nothing is manifest in us as humility and meekness and lowliness of heart. This is the philosophy of taking the lowest place, and thereby being exalted; of truly retiring, and in consequence being made prominent; of the honor conferred upon the modest; of the lowly being raised up. When the feminine (the negative) of your nature is discovered, the masculine (the positive) cannot be suppressed; creation is inevitable.

He who knows the masculine and keeps the feminine, will be the whole world's channel, (i. e., the center of universal attraction.) Tao-teh-king, with translator's commentary.

All Good rushes to you, all manifestation seeks to express its joy, its richness, its goodness through you.

Eckhart, an illuminate of the thirteenth century, says:

Whatever is receptive or whatever is to take in must be naked and empty. Having nothing will permit the water to flow. A cup being perfectly empty, even of air, would forget itself and be drawn into Heaven. Therefore, when the spirit is free, in right loneliness, it forces God. Therefore, in order to come to the pure, absolute beholding of the Divine, we must get beyond all fixed doctrine, beyond the Holy Scripture, and even beyond the human Christ. I declare by good truth and truth everlasting, that in every man who hath utterly abandoned self, God must communicate Himself, according to all His power, so completely that He retains nothing in His life, in His essence, in His nature, in His Godhead—He must communicate all to the bringing forth of fruit.

Uniting the high and the low, the without and the within, so that only God is seen, Man is instrumental in revealing Heaven upon earth, as is prophesied in sayings ascribed to Christ by the early Christians:

"Unless ye make the right as the left, the left as the right, the top as the bottom, and the front as the backward, ye shall not know the kingdom of God." "If you do not make your low things high, and your crooked things straight, ye shall not enter into my kingdom." "For the Lord himself being asked by a certain person when his kingdom should come answered, When two shall be one, and that which is without as that which is within; and the male with the female, neither male nor female."

The consciousness that realizes the point of unity between opposites so fully that all sense of opposition utterly disappears, transcends the realm of appearances, and of him it is said that he can "go in and out and find pasture."—John 10:9. He can dwell in realities and also in appearances, and eat of the good things of whichever realm he chooses; he is safe, he cannot be deceived.

Perfection

Even while appearing to use processes through which to make spiritual attainment, the wise student ever is reminding himself that he is there now. Holiness is the natural state of the Soul, innocence and purity emanating from her like a perfume, and causing all things that enter into her presence to feel pure and guileless. Right religious methods uncover this precious sanctum, and in their turn the methods must be dissolved, that the True may be all in all. While using methods, be not attached to them. Be unattached at all points. While doing benevolent deeds, care not for the fruits of them. While zealously engaged in unselfish, even great works, care nothing for recognition or gratitude. No rest is more soul-satisfying than this realization embodied in the words of one of our greatest teachers of Truth:

Knowing all things, doing all things, I am identified with nothing; I am free. Emma (Curtis) Hopkins.

All things in your world are now consecrated to God, and the seal of holiness is upon everything. All the heavenly messengers that respond to your behests and speed your Good to you in all ways and forms sing ever the one refrain, "Holy, Holy, Holy" (Is. 6:3). As priest to your world you hear and obey the injunctions of your Lord: "Every devoted thing is most holy unto the Lord. . . . He [the priest] shall not search whether it be good or bad."—Lev. 27128, 33. "What God hath cleansed, that call not thou common. . . . God hath shewed me that I should not call any man common or unclean."—Acts 10:15, 28.

The Day of the Lord

"Be still, and know that I am God."—Ps. 46:10. The thought of God swallows up all other thinking. Man ceases to reason, ceases even to think, when immersed in the illumination called in Scripture the "Day of the Lord." Control of the physical consciousness and the stilling of all the thoughts of the mind give one opportunity to look through illusion and see the Soul at the depths, as one sees the bottom of the lake when its waters are clear and at rest. This ability to rest in yourself, blissful, serene, knowing God only, is called by the Hindus Yoga, and the state itself, Samahdi.

Whoever knows how to enter into his own Soul can also get to the heart or soul of anything he wishes, and there are no secrets to him. He is able to perform a samyama, or complete concentration, upon anything, and not only its very essence will be his, but all its properties, such as strength, warmth, solidity, rarity, smallness, lightness, and so forth, can be used by him. This is the ultimate of education. Knowing God, you know all things.

Truth is very simple

Truth is very simple and easy to be understood by the simple in heart. Some who are seeking to enter into the Way are encumbered with the idea that there is so much to learn and so much to do. But this is not true. All the cumbersomeness arises from man's ignorance, from his belief that much learning and many works and manifold experiences are necessary in order to enter into eternal life. Everything in the spiritual Life has been worked out for us, and we can reap where others have sown. The prophets and wise men of old are like the first astronomers. Their strivings and wrestlings can be compared to the work of the astronomers, who, when they wished to compute the times and relations of the stars, occupied days, even years, in calculating, using many figures and methods. We, as heirs of the ages, are like the little children in the common schools who to-day accomplish the same results in mathematics in a few minutes with a few figures, so simple have become what were once such abstruse problems.

So, though it may seem that divine doctrine is full of mystery, and close application and continual practice are required in order to manifest the fruits of the Spirit, yet it shall seem simpler and simpler to the faithful one, until to say "Be" is all-sufficient for the manifestation of the works of God.

The natural unfoldment of the spiritual understanding may be compared to a child who, in learning arithmetic, studies the multiplication table, and according to the teacher's instructions repeats it over and over. When he begins to apply his knowledge to the working of problems he perhaps finds it slow work to remember all the answers to the combinations of figures. When he wishes to remember how much 3 X 4 is, he must "run over" in his child-mind, "3 X 1 = 3, 3X2 = 6, 3X3 = 9. 3 X 4= 12," before he realizes what 3 X 4 is. But there comes a time when the moment he sees three and four associated in multiplication he knows the answer instantly. This is because of faithfulness to the principle of mathematics. Let us apply this parable to the Life of the faithful student of God:

As Christ, your teacher, reveals to you the Allness of God and the unreality of evil, you apply yourself to the law and the commandments, even as it is written (Deut. 6:6-9). You acknowledge the presence of God only, and deny the reality of that which is not God.

Perhaps when there is an opportunity to apply your principles it does not seem easy.

Perhaps the problem is a sorrow, and you do not readily realize the peace of God. Perhaps you must repeat your affirmations and denials some time before the delusion disappears. But you are faithful, and soon the day is upon you when for you to look upon sorrow is to cause it to flee away, and no word of human language need be spoken.

No effort put forth in the name of God is ever lost. Never think your past aspirations toward God, and your efforts, your strivings, blind though they might have been, were useless and to be regretted. Not so. Those were the days of Moses and the prophets. "Elias truly shall first come, and restore all things." —Matt. 17:11. You are simply continuing, but now in the straight and narrow Way that leads into life.

In the world, not of it.

This is your satisfaction, to watch the Lord win the victory. Be in the world but not of it. Be among the sinful and sick but not of them, but be holy and healthy. Be walking through sorrow and affliction, not disturbed by it, or overcome by it, but walking over it, as Jesus walked over the sea. While you are in the world you will meet these things, but they will be no more to you than the storms, the winds, and the floods that beat against the house that was founded upon the rock. The one who is in that house rejoices when the storms beat and the winds howl around, because he is so safe. So with the one who is hid with Christ in God when pestilence stalks the land, and persecutions arise, and slanders, and sorrows, and temptations. "These things have I spoken unto you, that ye should not be offended."— John 16:1. These are not necessary for you to go through. We do not learn by any experience in evil, and one way to avoid these experiences is to believe that they are not necessary. Take as little notice of them as possible. Do not recount them to another unless for the help and encouragement of that other. Do not expect any particular evil. "Every man's work shall be revealed by fire" (I Cor. 3:13), but the fire need not bum him nor hurt one hair of his head. "These things have I spoken unto you, that in ME ye might have peace. In the world ye shall have tribulation: but be of good cheer; I have overcome the world." —John 16:33.

God is eternally satisfied, and you as the image and likeness of God, are, in your real Self, now satisfied. "Awake, thou that sleepest!"—Eph. 5:14. Think of your true Self and speak from your Soul:

"I am satisfied."

Put down every clamorous desire with

"I am satisfied."

Hush every complaining voice in you with

"I am satisfied."

Thus is brought forth that still, placid state that is the Rest of God.

For the mortal to stop its thinking is to be thought by God. God thinking in you is omnipotence, and "He shall give thee the desires of thine heart."—Ps. 37:4.

The last treatment to give a patient is called the Spiritual Baptism, in which is expressed the patient's complete unity with the Good everywhere.

Most of it consists in affirmations of the presence of Good. This last word completes the circle of manifestation. Just as six days represent the week of creation, so there are given six days' treatment corresponding to each day of the week. The crown of creation is the image and likeness of the Creator, which was the sixth day's work. So the Spiritual Baptism is giving to the recipient all the most spiritual and healing affirmations that can come into your mind.

The seventh day of this healing week you rest in the consciousness that it is finished, and, if in your judgment it is best, you can again conduct the case through another creative week, or you can give a rest for a season, and then resume that patient's healing; in all this looking to God for guidance and direction.

In the treatment make a statement as to the complete perfection of the divine One in your hearer. Then declare the Good that flows to that One from All, and the Good that flows from that One to All. Declare the presence of the pure and perfect Spirit, mind, heart and body, closing with a spiritual benediction.

After this manner speak:

Child of our Heavenly Father, listen to me. Remember who you are— now and forever, the pure and perfect child of the living God. You are noble, grand, beautiful, and holy in every part of your being. You are filled with the Spirit of Almighty God, and the life which you now lead is the free, loving, healthful, joyous Life of God. In unchanging bliss you live, and move, and have your being—restful, glorified—through all eternity.

You are strong with the strength of omnipotence. You are established forever in endless health and harmony. You are fearless and free.

All Good is flowing to you from every direction and from every one. All the universe gives you Good. All the wisdom, love, power, strength, and prosperity of God's world pours round about you, and uplifts you, and bears you along in peace and joy.

All the holiness and sweetness, peace, gentleness, and goodness of all the Host of Heaven ministers to you, and watches over you, and blesses you.

The glory of God shines round about you.

Everyone sees you well and strong, wise and loving, true and good. You are a source of joy to all you meet. You give good to all. You are just, you are unselfish, you are honest, you are generous, you are merciful and forgiving, you are perfect even as your Father in Heaven is perfect.

You are pure Spirit—your body is spiritual, incorruptible, clear, and white with the light of Heaven. You are pure Love. Your heart is filled with the undying fire of God's holy love. You are pure Wisdom. Your mind dwells in the meekness and simplicity of the little child. God thinks all your thoughts; your judgment is sound; your knowledge, profound.

And now, O Father, glorify thy Son with thine own Self, with the glory which he had with Thee before the world was.

It is finished.

In the name and by the power of the Father, and of the Son, and of the Holy Ghost, I pronounce you whole and strong, sound and well in every part, now and forever more. Amen.

You are a living witness of the power of the Word of Truth to set free.

IT IS FINISHED.

BOOK FOUR.
PROSPERITY: THROUGH THE KNOWLEDGE AND POWER OF MIND

LECTURES AND MENTAL TREATMENTS

Delivered in London, New York, Chicago, San Francisco and Los Angeles In the years between 1900 and 1913

Thou shall remember the Lord thy God: for it is he that giveth thee power to get wealth. Deut. 8:18.

FOREWORD

This hand-book of PROSPERITY was written from the basis, that thought is a substantial influence in the world like electricity, steam, heat and light. That man can control, direct, transform and dissipate his thoughts in the same way that he manipulates the forces that are evident to his five senses.

If the man who takes this book has studied psychology and metaphysics from this viewpoint, he doubtless has had proof of this thought-power. If he has not, then let him approach this book with a fair mind willing to investigate and not to judge until all the evidence is in, and a thorough trial has been given to the practices and applications, recommended.

In many cases, the simple perusal of the book will be sufficient to bring about a marked change for the better in one's affairs.

But the most earnest desire of the Author is, not that one shall be merely prospered in his worldly affairs by this volume, but that the little book shall prove the door of a new life. And that the reader shall go on, studying other works, of like nature, until he knows all the joy and freedom, that have come to the many, who have found their peace and happiness by living the principles, that are here upheld.

The Author will always be glad to hear from those who have been benefited by these teachings.

Los Angeles, Cal A. R. M.

Easter, 1913.

PART I. PRINCIPLES AND PRACTICE

I. Prosperity and Spirituality.

"Both riches and honor come of thee and thou reignest over all; and in thine hand is power and might and in thine hand it is to make great and to give strength unto all." — I Chron. 29:12.

It is now established in the minds of many people that health of body is a legitimate result of spiritual knowledge, and eventually will be one of the signs of a practical follower of Christ, but these same ardent believers, many of them, find it difficult to believe that health of circumstances can be demonstrated in the same way, and is as legitimate and true a sign of the understanding of spiritual law, as the healing of the body.

Approaching the subject of riches with a fair unprejudiced mind, we shall understand why it is, that they have been largely in the possession of the unspiritual, instead of the children of God, to whom the heritage rightfully belongs.

Worldly riches have been feared, despised, condemned and even hated by spiritual aspirants, because of ignorance of how to be in them, and yet not of them — to possess them, and not be possessed by them. Doubtless this attitude is less deceiving than the other error: greed, worship and the fear of losing riches. But the really Wise avoid both attitudes through knowing world-wealth to be but a reflection of the real riches, which must be sought first, last and always. Having found the richness of heaven you cannot escape the richness of earth unless you purposely repudiate it.

The rich state of being is The Promised Land that belongs to the people of God. Its occupancy by the selfish and carnal is like the Hittites, Canaanites, etc., possessing The Promised Land, at the time the Israelites began their march, under Moses, out of Egypt to regain their own country. The land according to the spiritual spies (Num. 13) was most desirable, a land flowing with milk and honey, a land of the olive and the vine. This innocent land was sweet and pure and goodly even though exploited by the heathen. So are worldly riches, impersonal, good, useful, commanding the world's respect.

Let us be true and not despise that which shadows a divine blessing, nor yet, on the other hand, lust for that which is not the real riches, for "how hardly do they that trust in riches enter the kingdom of heaven!" a saying that applies to the eager, anxious poor, as well as the besotted rich. It is not money itself that is the root of all evil money is nothing of itself but a symbol. It is the love of money that makes the terrible trouble in families and between friends, and spoils the candidate for spiritual powers and illumination.

The first step in prosperous attainment is to have the right attitude of mind and heart towards world wealth. To see that prosperity and spirituality must be wedded here upon the earth and Man must be the word that makes the marriage.

Too long has prosperity been looked upon as material and carnal, like the untrue wife described in Hosea II. Forgetting the source of her riches, "she did not know that I gave her corn and wine and oil and multiplied her silver and gold" a Dame Fortune, the scarlet woman, fickle and false.

Too long has spirituality like an austere monk, ascetic, condemnatory, impractical and exclusive, repudiated her and not known "whom God hath joined" man cannot keep asunder. That old spirituality is dead all hail to the New, that does not put off the kingdom of heaven to a state after death, but realizes that, here and now, is the place and time for the riches of the kingdom to be made manifest.

Man, like an officiating priest, marries these that have seemed two, and even in opposition, by (1) believing in their union, (2) by revealing their true character. Prosperity is spiritual, and Spirituality prospers.

Prosperity is of God, like Life, Health and Strength. It is man's privilege to use these divine gifts as he wills; he may use his strength to knock another down; he may use his health to impose his appetites on others, but these uses do not lessen the fact that strength and health are the gifts of God.

Man may misuse his prosperity, may ascribe it to sources, dishonest and selfish, but those are his mistakes the truth is still that that which is universally good in itself is of like origin, the Good, and prosperity originates with the All-Prosperous One, who makes all things good and very good and never knows failure.

There is not one good that man pursues but, when regarded in its purity and from the highest viewpoint, cannot be identified with God. "I am the Lord thy God which brought thee out of the . . . house of bondage" (Ex. 20:2). I am the Lord your Good that delivered you from that great trouble, that saved you from that mistake, failure, or other liability the evil that beset you.

Prosperity is the presence of God. It is that expression of comfort, power, beauty and freedom, that is always associated with the kingdom of heaven, and whenever the advent of the Christ-reign is described, the language of earthly richness is used, and the scriptures teem with heavenly attributes and comparisons, drawn from the prosperous things and men of the world.

Identifying Prosperity with God, we see this to be the truth of its being: that it is omnipresent and universal. Being everywhere, one does not need to go from place to place to get it. Find it within. Then you carry it with you you are yourself prosperity. Like Whitman you can say "I seek not fortune, I myself am good fortune." You find it in the business you have now, you fulfill the promise declared of him who delights "in the law of the Lord and in his law doth he meditate day and night . . . whatsoever he doeth shall prosper." (Ps. 1:2, 3.)

Being universal, the prosperity that is one with God expresses itself in everything and through everyone. It manifests in your life as general good luck. All the kingdoms of the world yield their best to you. In the vegetable kingdom your plants are healthy, your crops are abundant and not subject to drought, frost, pest, or blight; in the mineral kingdom, the gold and silver, the treasures in the rocks: diamonds, coal and oil are uncovered to you; in the animal kingdom, your cattle increase and keep in fine condition; in the kingdom of man, you are magnetic, blessed with friends, initiative, executive, efficient.

Prosperity, seen to be one with God, is not temporal and changeable. It is eternal. It is not limited in its expression. It is manifest not only in the ordinary ways of the world, but also it includes prosperity in health and in strength, in honors and in pleasures, in love and in ^learning.

The prosperity of the worldly-minded has the proverbial wings, and always there is a skeleton at the feast of the unprincipled and ignorant rich. How superstitious they are! They build fine houses and dare not move into them, because forsooth! rich men have died on being snugly settled in new houses! How fearful they are of competitors! How discontent with the amount they have! How little hold they have upon health and life and their loved ones! Riches without spirituality are Dead Sea fruit. The substance and lasting joy of riches is knowledge of Truth.

Let us return to the statement that spirituality prospers one and consider how it does so. First, it gives insight into human character, so that one knows with whom to associate in business, what are the things that men want, how to please. Second, it inspires confidence within, and invites the confidence of others in us. Third, it increases the fellowship feeling, gives a lively interest in the welfare of even strangers, making one magnetic. Fourth, it gives a clear head, sober judgment, common sense. Fifth, it gives poise, and trust as to the future. These are a few of the reasons, others will be disclosed as we pursue the subject.

Good luck is not a thing of chance. It is not a fatality, nor a matter of our stars or our karma, but its cause lies in a law, fulfilled either consciously or unconsciously, the latter with most people, the former with the enlightened.

One of these laws is Acknowledgment of 'the Real Source of our fortune. This law was fulfilled by Abraham, who would not receive anything from the king of Sodom, "even to a shoe-latchet and that I will not take anything that is thine, lest thou shouldst say, I have made Abram rich" (Gen. 14:23) and this law was enjoined strictly upon all the Hebrews. For the tendency of the mortal is to ascribe his success to his own skill or labor, foresight or energy, forgetting that even these are gifts of God, and that they are being applied daily by others, but without success.

Our God dwells within us, our real I AM. It is likewise the I AM of everyone else, and cannot be claimed by any mortal ego as his exclusively. It is the same One in us today, that spoke to the ancient Israelites, and now gives us warning of the way to be eternally prosperous, that

"When thou hast eaten and art full, then thou shalt bless the Lord thy God for the good land which he hath given thee.

Beware that thou forget not the Lord thy God, in not keeping his commandments.

Lest when thou hast eaten and art full, and hast built goodly houses, and dwelt therein;

And when thy herds and thy flocks multiply, and thy silver and thy gold is multiplied, and all that thou hast is multiplied;

Then thine heart be lifted up and thou forget the Lord thy God,

And thou say in thine heart, My power and the might of mine hand hath gotten me this wealth.

But thou shalt remember the Lord thy God; for it is he that giveth thee power to get wealth." Deut. 8:1014, 17, 18.

Cultivating an intimate communion with the divine I AM within us, we are led from one expression of prosperity to another, along a sure road whose every step is scientific and inspired. This inner guide is called the Holy Spirit by Jesus Christ, again the Spirit of Truth and the Comforter. It is impersonal and universal, and yet, its Voice can be heard unmistakably by those who will not give it a personal cast (as when it is called "spirits" what tricks and folly, and even outrages, have been perpetrated in such delusion!) nor ignore its great commandments, given through the prophets.

This inner Guide has been called by a variety of names such as "something in me," "my impression," intuition, business sense and even it has been called the "prosperity-microbe" by a well-known American wit, who says that he never could be rich because he never had had the "microbe." That once, many years ago when Bell, the telephone inventor, was first placing his stock on the market, he saw that it was a good investment. He therefore drew out all he had in the bank it was only $30,000 and was on his way to buy preferred Bell Telephone shares, when he was met by an officious friend, who laughed scornfully at his simplicity and persuaded him to return with his money to the bank. "And so I just escaped being a multi-millionaire, because I did not have the microbe" he mournfully concluded. He had it, but did not know Its Name and nature.

A young Chicago broker, who enjoyed an ephemeral Napoleonic flight among the bulls and bears on the Exchange, was besieged to give his secret of knowing when and how much to buy, and sell, that was making him such a phenomenal success. He confessed that it was no exact system that he could define, but impressions, "Something in me prompts me to do it and it is irresistible!" he said. But his power was of short duration, for he did not know that it was the Holy Spirit, and therefore he did not seek knowledge of it, so as to know when to abandon those foolish pawns, which are nothing to the Spirit that chooses the nobler instruments of men's hearts and minds, instead of stocks and bonds. When ethical laws are ignored and crossed, no ordinary illumination can keep the novice in spiritual powers from making a failure.

It is possible to ascend great heights of success, under the tutelage of the Holy Spirit, and never become falsely entangled with the moral law, as witness one beautiful character, who was led to the discovery of remarkable mines in Wisconsin, and to establishing a beautiful home in one of the most favored spots in California, where she had a chapel and healed many sick people. She heard the inner Voice from her youth and, like Abraham, she had been assured from the beginning, that if she were obedient to all its instructions, that great riches would be hers and, like Abraham, when she became rich she acknowledged the One Spirit, Lord God of the whole earth, as the Source of her prosperity. I refer to Mrs. Chynoweth of Edenvale near San Jose, who published a most interesting paper for years, describing her wonderful, indeed thrilling, and romantic guidance and protection by the Spirit.

Settling it in one's heart that the law which the Master gave, "Seek ye first the kingdom of God and his righteousness and all these things after which the nations seek shall be added" is sound, scientific counsel for the establishment of eternal prosperity, let us proceed to fulfill the injunction. And let us, early in the pursuit, strictly regard that First. So shall we discover that, in a new sense, shall the "First be the Last," in that, to seek first the kingdom of God truly, we must make it our last or final search, and our only pursuit.

This means that we are not in Truth for its perquisites but for Itself. It means a certain indifference to "the things added" even to a carelessness as to how long they seem in coming, utter disregard whether they ever come such is the paradoxical state of mind of one, who knows such riches inevitable.

Meditate daily upon the pure Being of God, both under the name of Prosperity and under all the other names, as one with Prosperity:

GOD IS

1. Prosperity. 2. Omnipresence. 3. Omnipotence. 4. The Good. 5. Life. 6. Health. 7. Love. 8. Wisdom. 9. Peace. 10. Purity. 11. Faith. 12. Truth.

ALL ONE.

Copy the above upon a card, to be put in some convenient place for ready reference.

Begin some definite practices. as follows:

I. Keep a handy little note-book, to jot down helpful thoughts, original and otherwise.

II. Identify Prosperity (1) with all the other names of God (2) to (12) not all at once but from time to time and watch what masterful thoughts will arise. Thus we reason: Since God is Prosperity (1) and God is Omnipresence (2) therefore Prosperity is Omnipresence, that is, prosperity is everywhere, in all I meet, in my business, in whatever I put my hand to. I do not need to move from place to place. Yet I can go and prosperity will follow me. Everything and everybody prospers me.

Since God is Prosperity (1) and God is Omnipotence (3) Prosperity is Omnipotence, my prosperity is all-powerful, even though it seem but a grain of mustard seed, yet it can move mountains. Nothing can keep it from me. It prospers itself. Nothing succeeds so like success.

Since God is Prosperity and God is the Good (4) therefore Prosperity is the Good, that is, in the Highest, prosperity will bring me good only. It will not bring me pride or folly. It will not mislead me or make me unspiritual. True prosperity prospers others, being of the same nature as the one who makes two blades of grass grow where only one grew before. My prosperity benefits my neighbor it is not parasitical, it is the presence of God.

Since God is Prosperity (1) and God is Life (5) Prosperity is Life, that is, there is life through my affairs. There is no waiting for the death of any thing or any one to bring me prosperity.

Prosperity (1) is one with Health (6), that is, there is no exhaustion of vitality and energy in bringing prosperity. Prosperity (1) is one with Love (7). In the Highest, universal unchangeable love, not selfishness and greed, is the key to prosperity.

Reason in this way ad libitum, always taking each name in its highest, ideal meaning.

III. Combine Omnipresence (2) -with every one that follows from (3) to (12).

IV. Combine Omnipotence (3) with each that follows from (4) to (12). And so go through the list.

What is here recommended is a practice, that has ever been given by spiritual teachers from the most ancient Oriental times, and especially endorsed by Jesus Christ in his words "Watch and pray always," and his direction, "that men ought always to pray and never to faint."

If the Orientals thought prayer always meant a beseeching and asking for something, then Paul would never have given the instruction "Pray without ceasing." He knew that it meant communion with the omnipresent One, our Life and Very Self, and a communication of the vital blessed gifts of God.

The worldly-wise man who grows rich, thinks money, prices, property, ways and means, devices, night and day, for a prosperity that is but as a breath of wind. The man who would know eternal prosperity thinks God, night and day, until he sees and knows nought else but that one supreme blissful presence.

II. The Magic of Meekness.

"Blessed are the meek: for they shall inherit the earth" Matt. 5:5. "Happy are the dispassionate: for they shall inherit the earth." [Another Translation].

When abstinence from theft in mind [envy and covetousness] and act is complete in the devotee, he has power to obtain all material wealth. "- Yoga Aphorisms of Patanjali.

We have long been willing to acknowledge the powerful place that mind occupies in our affairs, that is, through its objective phases, not subjectively. Men point to inventions and arts, writings and buildings, business and science, as the noble fruits of man's intellect, and the necessary means, with other externalized thoughts, by which mind influences the world. But to think that there is a way for thought to work more directly upon these outer affairs is as difficult for some, as it would have been once for one to believe that an electric current could be used without a conductor, definitely placed by the hands of man. Just as the Marconi telegrams do have conductors, though invisible to men's eyes, so thought-force is conducted and applied, though the avenues are still unsensed by mortal man.

Science is slowly working with thought, experimenting and collecting data. And certain ones in the van can hardly restrain themselves from publishing their own convictions, that thoughts can be felt and measured, analyzed and described, as heat and electricity have been, by their effects. But science is conservative. It is philosophy, now beginning to acknowledge intuition as a v factor in acquiring knowledge, that will keep men abreast of the times, and be the best handmaiden of the new thought and theology, whose influence can no longer be denied.

Sufficient for us, that all over the world men and women are proving that thoughts are the greatest means and substance upon the whole earth; that thoughts can be read, and their vibrations felt, most distinctly; that they create atmospheres that are attractive or repulsive according to their character; that it is a crying necessity that men be educated in this field, so that they shall not be exploited by the unscrupulous, nor fall into such errors themselves, but join the great thought-forces that make for righteousness, that is, the health and happiness, wealth and freedom of a man's neighbor as well as himself.

The word, silent or audible, is the conductor of thought, and the trained mind knows what words to use, and what thoughts to make positive, and what negative; and how to keep the true thoughts free from adulteration of false notions, opinions, sentiments and fears.

In the last chapter we dwelt upon the thoughts that constitute the true positive attitude of the mind, that makes for success through spirituality. But not only' must we know the right positive way of thinking, but also we must know the right negative way of thinking. For in the realm of appearances, there are both the positive and negative to be correctly manifest, in order to rightly reflect the things that are. To try to fill our mentalities with true thoughts, while clinging to old false ideas, is like trying to fill a full ink-bottle with milk, without emptying out the ink, with the result of having neither ink nor milk but a useless liquid.

Out of the many affirmations of the last lesson, let us select these, "God is omnipresent" and "God is good."

Combining them we have "Good is omnipresent," the first great axiom of the true Science of God. It is as simple as two and two are four and it is as important. It is the scientific basis of the true and lasting optimism.

When the mind has "a reason for the hope" that is in it, then hope can pass into certainty, and even, at the times when experience and the senses would utterly sweep away a groundless optimism, one can abide in cheerfulness, until its wisdom and its effectiveness are proven. Prosperity and cheerfulness are boon companions and one always attracts the other. "Plenty and good cheer" has passed into proverb.

That the realization, "Good is omnipresent," may be with one continually, the mind must be given over to that kind of thinking, night and day. The old scriptural instructions, to "love God with all your heart, soul, mind and strength" and to "meditate on His Law night and day" to "pray without ceasing 11 and to "acknowledge Him in all thy ways" can be fulfilled only by determined refusal to entertain the opposite thoughts and feelings. Thus the mind refuses to meditate upon evil and failures, wrongs and losses, fears and worriments.

Every time an unhappy thought arises, wisdom displaces it with a silent statement of the allness of the Good. Reason becomes the schoolmaster, and the sense-testimonies are set aside. Not only do we remember the Lord our "God, for it is He that giveth thee power to get wealth," but we learn to forget the old ways of ascribing our riches to material sources and personal efforts. In remembering the Lord our God, we are reminding ourselves of the All Good, and this means a forgetting of evil.

There are people, who are suffering from conditions of poverty, because their minds are filled with memories of losses and failures. If you think about loss, you produce what you think about. Sometimes it is not a meditation on the loss of money and things, but upon the loss of friends, or reputation, or some other good, that seems to have no connection with one's financial welfare.

Socrates says "He that grieves much is a magnet to attract waste of property." Cease to grieve, or entertain sad memories of any kind. One student of truth had a revelation as to the cause of her failures, upon hearing these words of Socrates. She could trace the beginning of the long time of hard luck to the day, when she was overwhelmed by the loss of a darling son. She grieved and grieved, although she was in the truth, and knew that she was not loyal to her principles in continuing such indulgence. But with this awakening, she resolved to put away her sorrow, and remember that her son lived throughout eternity, and no longer deny the presence of the All-Good. And from the day of that resolution, her affairs revived, so that today she has a deep-seated consciousness of God's eternal supply, and demonstrates it daily.

Our thinking is assisted by our speech, so let our determination be to speak on the bright side and refrain from talking about "hard times" and "money being scarce," and other forms of financial straits.

Man himself decides the character of the times by his mental attitude. Man controls the currency, he can make it free, or congested, at will, and sometimes one man can be the key-log of a whole situation, continuing the "jam" by his own stolidity, or causing an easy flow by his freedom.

As an illustration of the difference it makes to an individual, whether he talks "hard times," or simply refrains from such speech, a gentleman told me the following as an actual experience:

There were two merchants in a town in Southern California, both in a flourishing state, until a time of financial panic, which put the character of each to the test. One talked of the bank failures and the gloomy outlook, the other was full of assurance that it could not last, and had only cheery answers to all the pessimistic speculations, and never indulged himself in any talk on the negative side.

About twenty miles from that town, lived a young man on a ranch, which he was developing, while depending for his living upon a monthly remittance, which came from his home in England. He knew of nothing that was taking place in the rest of the world, as he had no newspapers, receiving his mail only when he drove to town, which was at long intervals of time. On such visits he always laid in a good store of provisions.

In the midst of the panic-time he went to town, stopped at the store of the optimistic merchant, and "stocked up 1 ' liberally. Then he went over to the other merchant's place where he intended to buy just as freely. He found 'that merchant standing idly at his door, and exclaimed- at finding such a dearth of customers. Thereupon the merchant launched forth with his tale of woe, which so affected the young man, that he ceased all further purchasing, and soon started for his ranch, resolving to hold to his money, although England at the time was not in the least moved by the local stringencies of America. And he said, the optimist went through the hard times with little falling away, while the other merchant did not recover his old status until long after the panic had passed.

It is as foolish for men to hold back their money at a time of national, financial difficulties, as for the motorist to shut down on his power before ascending a hill. But what could change this natural action of self-preservation but spiritual insight, and regard for one's neighbor's welfare, equal to the regard for one's own.

Three dominant ways of carnal thought must be emptied out of the mind: (1) the belief in evil; (2) in materiality; (3) in the mortal self; and daily, three dominant spiritual ideas must take their place: (1) the belief in the All-Good; (2) in Mind as the one substance and cause; (3) in the God-Self as All in All.

The power to set aside one's human self-hood, through realizing the Self that is divine is called Meekness. This word is not commonly understood, being generally associated with weakness and lack of spiritedness. Whereas no one can be truly meek who is not strong and spirited.

Moses has been cited as the most marked example of the meekness that inherits the earth. Full of fire, and charged with power, he did not use these for his own personal advantage. But he wished all to stand at the same place that he had reached. One of his followers, Joshua, once grew very jealous for his master's glory and power, and asked permission to stop certain young men in the camp from prophesying, because they had not been ordained to that work by the great Moses. But the mighty man replied to his disciple in these noble words:

"Enviest thou for my sake? Would God that all the Lord's people were prophets, and that the Lord would put his spirit upon them!" Numbers 11:29.

There are people, who do not go on to their prosperity, because they are so full of the earthly selfhood all the time thinking of their rights, and seeking to exalt themselves, and demanding acknowledgment from others of their righteousness and ability. Pride prevents them from doing work for which they are especially adapted, and which they could honor and exalt, if they entered into it with the right spirit. Egotism makes them insufferable to others even to those who would otherwise be glad to prosper them. Envy makes them bitter, and even malicious, in their action and speech so that men, who are in a position to choose their associates, avoid them. Covetousness and greed make them overreach the mark, in placing value on their goods, from which, again, fear may make them run to the other extreme and undervalue their work and cheapen themselves. Ambition blinds them, and after many failures, leaves them stranded, wallowing in pessimism and poverty. All because they did not know how to let go of that mortal self -hood, the "little I," and so enter into the power of their mighty Meekness.

Meekness is freedom from pride, envy, greed and egotism. It is a certain emptiness that has a wonderful drawing power.

The principle of Meekness is the same as that of the vacuum. It is that which keeps all good in circulation. What the vacuum is in nature, meekness is with the rich Substance of God. Without a vacuum, that continually demands filling, the movements of nature would cease. It is the vacuum that draws the air into the lungs, that pulls the sap up the trees. And in mechanics it is the secret of the useful pump and the mighty steam engine. O, the mystery of the vacuum! who can compass it?

Even when men have but a little of this Meekness, it has made them rich. It is the key to the prosperity of many a "self-made man." With small beginnings, letting no pride stand in his way, he has gone steadily ahead, often quite free from envy before the success of others, and even, when at the pinnacle, so free from vanity as to do menial things, if exigency requires it, and not think himself lowered by anything he does. Yet, again, he may lose that meekness he may forget and let pride and egotism arrest his development, all because his meekness was not grounded in knowledge but was an unconscious gift from his God-Being.

When one's God-given meekness continues through life, then one's prosperity includes, with riches, great honor and position. The world loves to honor the man who loses himself in the Cause for which he stands. It was this quality in General Grant that made it easy for the world to honor the United States, in honoring him.

His silence, his freedom from egotism, his modesty and freedom from all demands as U. S. Grant, opened wide the gates for the inrush of praise and gifts. The world lay at his feet. He needed only the Christ-knowledge to have placed him forever beyond the reach of failure.

The full Meekness of the Christ is established in the consciousness, that is right valuation. In it there is ever the seeking first the kingdom of God, and there is a perfect deliverance from the pursuit of material things. They follow, they seek him. He does not need to run after them, they are drawn to him as fervently as steel to the magnet, for he has the Substance which they shadow. Those who pursue material things are always just missing them, and not until they do not care, and may even have forgotten their ardent desire for them, do they come and settle down in their world. The Talmud says "Who runs after greatness, greatness runs away from, but who runs away from greatness, greatness runs after."

Turn that rich desire-nature of yours into realization, that there is nothing for you really to pursue. All that you have sought, all that is worth the having, you already have, you already are. Awake! arise! Come to yourself and rest in the great Truth of the ages, that the one desire of our heart is, and always has been, GOD. And God we have, and God we are. For there is naught else to have or to be. Perceiving this, you fulfill the injunctions of old for very joy's sake, "hearkening diligently unto the Voice of the Lord" wherever uttered, upon the lips of fools or in the oracles of masters, in song of bird or of poet, in the roar of the earthquake or in the still small voice within. And ever hearing and obeying, the prophecy is fulfilled in your life:

"And all these blessings shall come on thee, and overtake thee. 1 '

"Blessed shalt thou be in the city, and blessed shall thou be in the field."

"Blessed shall be thy basket and thy store."

"Blessed shalt thou be when thou comest in, and blessed shalt thou be when thou goest out."

"And the Lord shall make thee plenteous in goods, in the fruit of thy body, and in the fruit of thy cattle, and in the fruit of thy ground."

"The Lord shall open unto thee his good treasure, the heaven to give the rain unto thy land in his season, and to bless all the work of thine hand." Deut. 28:2, 3, 5, 6, 11, 12.

In conjunction with the meditation, given at the close of the last lesson, meditate daily upon the following, learning the words by heart, and repeating them, until there is an answering thrill within you at each repetition:

I AM THAT I AM, the rich fountain of your abundant supply within 'you. By the power of the Spirit, my rich substance is now overflowing into every avenue and expression of your Life.

My presence and my power, working all things together for good, is felt and seen in everything you put your hand to.

I AM THAT I AM, your Very Self, Ming your whole being and all your world. Where I AM, there is only Good, and therefore I declare, there is no place in all being for evil; there never can be any failure; there is nothing to fear.

Where I AM, there is only pure Spirit, divine Mind, the eternal rich Substance of God. Therefore I declare the nothingness of material things. They have no power to attract or bind Me. I know no greed for possessions. I have all that is real, and I covet nothing that passes away.

Where I AM, there is only Love, that loves and gives to All, and therefore I know no envy or jealousy, no pride or selfishness.

"Come unto Me all ye that labor and are heavy laden and I will give you rest."

"Take My yoke upon you and learn of Me; for f AM MEEK and lowly in heart: and ye shall find rest unto your souls."

"For My yoke is easy and My burden is light."

III. Confidence Through Knowledge of Truth.

"Be sure you're right, then go ahead."

"Because thou hast asked this thing ... I have given thee a wise and understanding heart . . . and I have also given thee that which thou hast not asked, both riches and honor. '' I Kings 3:11, 12, 13.

One of the most essential concomitants to prosperity is confidence self-confidence and confidence in others, trust in the outcome of an undertaking, and assurance that one is in the right, and bound to win. Without this deep, interior faith, one cannot draw the confidence of others, and so have the co-operation of all those, whose aid and abetting, can give actual standing in the business world.

Everything works for, and to the credit of, those who "know in whom they have believed," and who have great principles for the foundation of their confidence in themselves, and in their enterprise.

Credit is one of the greatest business factors, if not the greatest, in the world today. It would be impossible to carry on the commerce and trade which are so general, active and immense throughout this world, if it were not for the great credit system. There is not enough money coined to be the medium of exchange necessary to, and equal to the ratio of, the business transacted even in one day, nor is there time, or facilities, to affect the exchanges, that even the banks would require, if suddenly all credit were removed from affairs.

So potent is Credit, that even the touch of the hem of its garment, has been known to save a man from financial death. A story is told of the power that the Rothschilds yield in the realm of Credit, that once a man whose business was on the very verge of ruin but who, with a little restraint put upon his creditors, could pass by the crisis in his affairs, appealed to one of the great Rothschilds (who knew him but slightly yet believed his story), for a word, an endorsement, a loan, that would pilot him through the dangerous straits. The giant-financier said to him:

"My friend, I have an errand down the street, just take my arm and walk with me."

And so, as intimate business friends, they passed among the brokers of Paris. It was enough. His creditors stayed their claims, the crisis was passed, and the man's business was saved. It was Thought that did the work, the greatest power in the world.

To know when to have confidence, where to place it, and how to retain it, these are some of the questions. There are those who are not succeeding, because of an undue caution and a lack of trust. Or, in giving credit, they have lacked judgment, or dealt with a slack hand, or get into bondage because of fear.

Then there are those, who think they cannot trust anybody that all men are dishonest, and they will trust no one, until he, or she, has been proven trust-worthy. Experience has been their hard and bitter teacher.

In this world of appearances, there are two kinds of trust, a positive, and a negative. The latter is the trust of the ignorant, and unless there comes wisdom and understanding, theirs may prove even a false trust, which will and must finally pass away. Innocence can trust and be justified, for innocence is divine. Ignorance and innocence are not synonyms, as some suppose; there is no perfect innocence that is not based upon intuitive knowledge. It is when the innocent one begins to mix with worldly knowledge that failure follows. Then their trust in people becomes a mere looking to the mortal, and their trust in God is in a being, who is far away, with partialities, and of uncertain character. And presently their faith is tried, and it cannot stand because their knowledge, being of a worldly nature, is according to appearances, and has not real foundation.

True Trust, the positive confidence, that nothing can take from you, is trust in the Godhood of everybody, and everything. You trust yourself, because you let your Divine Self guide you. You know that the Lord in you can do everything, and you let It's wisdom direct you, and give you skill and insight, inspiration and understanding. You may need to remind yourself often of the One in whom you trust, if you have hitherto lacked confidence. Or, if your old confidence was a kind of self-conceit, brazen yet weak, when you pass like the apostle Paul, from the old boldness to the new meek, yet fearless, confidence, it will be good to say, "I can do all things through Christ which strengthened me," Phil. 4:13.

This is the Wisdom, of which Solomon sung and wrote, whose price is above rubies, "For the merchandise of it is better than the merchandise of silver, and the gain thereof than fine gold," Prov. 3:14. It was this understanding, that brought to that king all his riches and honor. With it, you cannot be poor. Mines of rich ore are discovered by it. Timely inventions spring forth from it. Secrets of nature come with it. Business foresight, judgment as to human efficiency, right valuations as to land and commodities, are some of its gifts. The category of advantages, that accrue with divine understanding, is too long and universal to be written about in these lessons only taste and see.

By this light, you look for the divinity in everyone, even the dishonest, and that One will come forward. By having your eye single to that One you will also be able to discern as to the errors that hide it, and there will be no confusion in your mind, as to human nature. You'll not put your "trust in the flesh," nor "in princes," but ever in the One that is trust worthy.

Be sure the Lord is on your side. Your sense of righteousness is keen enough for that. Business ethics are not different from others. Business is not business with the Spirit left out. It is only a dead and cold Moloch that in the end will consume the fairest and dearest that you hold in life. If you abandon scruples and conscience you must not sink, but rise on the wings of your Godhood, a law unto yourself, and the Supreme Benefactor of the whole human race.

Certain good people fear to be rich, lest they should fall into the snare of riches, and miss their way into eternal happiness. Learn to pray that you be "not led into the temptations" of any God-gift. The Spirit can protect you from every liability, if you but remember. The saying, "How hard it is for them that trust in riches to enter into the kingdom of God" (Mark 10:24), applies to the poor as well as the rich, for many are the poverty-stricken who labor under the delusion, that they would be completely happy if they were only rich. It is our attitude towards riches that determines whether they are a stumbling-block or not. Good people! search the Scriptures, and gather together the many texts that show that riches belong to the righteous! No longer deceive yourselves into thinking Jesus was poor! At any moment he could have had all the wealth of 'the world at his command. Compare two statements which Paul makes about the Master as to his poverty and his sin, that both were but an appearance:

"For he made him to be sin for us, who knew no sin; that we might be made the righteousness of God in him," 2 Cor. 5:21.

"Ye know the grace of our Lord Jesus Christ that though he was rich, he became poor that ye through his poverty might be rich," 2 Cor. 8:9.

It is not money that is the root of all evil, but the love of it. Let money be nothing to you; and let us not talk of "wanting to be rich because of the good we could do," but let us see we wish to be rich because it is right, and it belongs to the daughters of the King, and the princes of God.

There is never any occasion in all one's life for losing faith, or for entertaining doubt. The man who "doubts not in his heart," according to the Master, can "have whatsoever he saith," Mark 11:23.

Faith is persistency, which is rooted in the knowledge that "this good is for you, and you can have it." When Jesus wished to illustrate the faith that wins, he chose an example of persistency, that won its way because of its own nature, and not because of justice, or love, or any other reason. He cites the case of a Judge who neither feared God nor regarded man; and a widow came to him, demanding that justice be done her in a certain cause. At first the Judge pays no attention but the widow troubles him so with her determined claims, that at last he yields to the widow, "lest by her continual coming she weary me."

By this analogy, the Master would give insight as to a Law, by which one can receive his own, even though neither merit nor love have succeeded in bringing it to him. Another peculiar parable to illustrate this power of persistent prayer is given in Luke 11:5 to 10, "because of his importunity."

When tempted to complain and to say, "I've always tried to do right, and to be good, and I've never wronged anyone; I don't see why I should be so poor and suffer so close your lips on that utterance before it can come forth, and rise in your mind above the law of cause and effect, of reward and punishment and take fresh hold of the thought:

"My Good is for me, whether I deserve it, or not, and I can have it now, and I do have it this moment in Spirit, and now, it can manifest!"

Once a young woman came to San Francisco from a country town, an orphan and friendless, desiring to get work. She soon found that her lack of experience in work handicapped her sadly. She was unattractive and without tact, silent and colorless. But she had a marvellous tenacity. .At last she got a position in the United States Mint, a most difficult thing to do, unless one has excellent endorsement. She remained there three years, because her political sponsor was such a man of influence. Someone inquired one day as to his personal character, and she replied, "I know little,

224

or nothing, about him beyond the brief conversations, that I had with him before getting my position." And then she told her simple story of how she succeeded, where hundreds had failed.

When she heard that women worked in the Mint, she went to the Superintendent to ask for a position. He was a polite man, and answered her courteously, that there were no vacancies. In a few days she applied again. Receiving the same answer she left a self-addressed envelope, asking the Superintendent to let her know when there would be a vacancy. She presented herself, after that, numbers of times every few days. At last the Superintendent must have pitied her ignorance, and perhaps admired her simplicity, for he condescended to explain to her that without "influence" the endorsement of some statesman or other man of great public power, or position she could not be accepted. She asked him to name such a man. It happened that a certain Congressman had arrived in the City that very day. She went to see him, took his specious promises in earnest, and haunted his office day after day, until at last to get rid of her he wrote the letter that gave her the place. It is the story of the Widow and the Judge repeated, Luke 18: 2 to 7,

Many a man, and woman, has succeeded by just such simple faith. It was not the mere going; nor by a bold impertinent annoyance; nor was it an ordinary aggressiveness, but a deep childlike trust that took every one at his word and knew no failure.

It is wise never to approach another with the idea of non-success. If you have such impression, either recover from that lack of faith on your own part, or make no attempt to see the person.

Faith in the good-will of people, when it is based upon your respect for their True Self, often forces them, for very peace of mind and self-respect, to show forth their better side. So well is the law recognized today in trade, that clerks and other employees are being educated by their employers to welcome all with a pleasant face, and, whether customers buy or not, whether they are polite or not, to be invariably courteous and agreeable themselves. Such is good, common business-sense.

A noted merchant-prince of Chicago had the following printed, and freely distributed among his patrons and employees, as the ruling "Idea" of his great store:

"To do the right thing at the right time, in the right way; to do some things better than they were ever done before; to eliminate errors; to know both sides of the question; to be courteous; to be an example; to work for love of the work; to anticipate requirements; to develop resources; to recognize no impediments; to master circumstances; to act from reason rather than rule; to be satisfied with nothing short of perfection!'

The finishing and sealing of eternal Confidence in your self, your fellow-man, and your world, lie in the realization of the Truth of these two master thoughts: 1st That your Richness is a blessing to all creation; and, 2nd That it is the Will of the true God, that you shall be a great Success on earth, as well as in heaven.

The old thought, that one cannot be rich but at the expense of his neighbor, must pass away, and every practice that has had that thought for its basis. True prosperity adds to the richness of the whole earth, like the benefit conferred by the man who makes two trees grow where only one grew before. The parasitical belief of prospering by the sacrifices of others has no place in the mind that thinks true. My benefit is your benefit, your success is my welfare, should be the basis of our wealth.

It is the divine will, that you shall be a self-reliant, self-supporting being, strong, upright, efficient, a nobleman of God's realm, able to command all the elements, and to use and beautify all creation, through knowledge of the Self and union with God.

It was in man's disobedient view of the Lord, that he judged Him a harsh, austere task-master over poor slaves. Now we know that we do not honor God with such a view, but we see Him as He is, the lover of all; the true God, who wills that everyone shall enter into joy and freedom, while yet on the earth, by co-operating with the only Will there is, which seeks always and everywhere the Good and Happiness of the whole.

IV. Inspiration in Work.

" Whatsoever thy hand findeth to do, do it with thy might. " Ecclesiastes 9:10.

"Not by might nor by power but by my Spirit, saith the Lord of hosts" [Forces]. Zech. 4:6.

Every human being is a dynamo of concentrated, creative energy, ever seeking avenues of expression. And when the right avenues have been found, and there is nothing that prevents the free and full manifestation of that energy, then heavenly joy is realized, and continues, as the fruits of that work return and glorify their source.

Work is divine, and everyone who is normal in mind and body, loves work not labor, but work, for there is a distinction between work and labor. The first is the creative activity of God, congenial, united with love, inspired, one with play and one with rest. True work is subject to our choice, never obligatory, nor limited by time or space. It is done from the heart, and there is no curse upon it, for the worker obeys the inner Voice, and ever seeks Its sanction in all he does. But labor is work, mixed with false thoughts and feelings, and therefore its fruits are not happiness and freedom.

It is ignorance of one's divine origin, and unspiritual living, that bring man to the place where he must labor in the sweat of his face, become- a slave to others, and have imposition, cruelty and injustice heaped upon him. To escape the misery and degradation of undesirable and brutish labor, man must get knowledge about himself and his fellow-beings, and above all, know the true God, and the reason of Jesus Christ's coming, and the Way to live his Life.

Men may change their environments and their masters, may seek new work, and make new laws, but as long as they are content to sit in spiritual darkness, and ignore the God within, the problem of labor will go unsolved. Social and economic systems grow out of man's views of life, and the passions that dominate them. If these are radically wrong, then the systems are false, and only as Christ-ideals are held uppermost in mind, and human passions are turned from earthly power and money the passions of the poor, as well as the rich can new systems rise, true laws be enacted, and the curse of the old order pass away.

Every one has a congenial work; it is that, which men can do most happily and successfully; wherein they can feel themselves in tune with their own soul, and the souls of their fellow-beings.

The most direct way to that work is by The Rule of the Word.

To the novitiate in spiritual methods, this will need explanation and enlargement.

First of all, let us understand, and agree upon this, that All is Mind; that matter and motion; the two components into which scientists classify all the parts and phrases of creation, are, in other words, mind-stuff and its play upon itself in the Highest, God-Substance and God-working.

Thought is mind in motion, and every activity upon this earth began as a secret thought. The nature of an activity can be decided by the quality of the thought that was its origin, and the thoughts which followed and were its modifiers. When a thought comes out of abstraction into the definite form of a word, it is like captured electricity, and can be conserved, directed and used, as its speaker wills.

As iron-moulds determine the forms of the melted metal that is poured into them, so the Word decides the outer form, which thoughts are to take in the realm of appearances.

As moulds are patterned after certain ideals in the mind of their creator, so our words should be spoken from our higher consciousness the heavenly ideals that are now true in God.

The Rule of the Word is to speak ever, in the present tense, the Truth as it is in God, using positive affirmations with the Good only, and negative statements as to evil. It is to look to the Word as the God-appointed means of bringing into the visible our Good, which still seems invisible to our earthly senses.

There is a direct line between you and the work that you desire to do, the position which you can best fill. That line remains ever the same, and you move along it by the power of your True Word, and the Truth you speak is that which applies to your divine Self, which is ever in its right place and doing its harmonious and happy work.

Following this Rule you declare:

"I am now in my right place!'

"I am now doing the work I love to do!'

According to appearances, these words may seem untrue. But you are not 'speaking from that view-point, but from the realm of the Real. "But," you may say, "if words are such powers, will not such statements keep me in my present position and work, which are both so undesirable?"

Not unless that position and work are quite transformed, and become truly representative of your heavenly state and activity. This sometimes takes place under the Word.

As you continue gathering spiritual thoughts, and ruling your silent mental speech, as well as your audible words, according to the highest ideals, you may discover that you are where you are, to redeem certain traits of character that militate against your spiritual advancement, and therefore interfere with your earthly prosperity also. Then you will be wise, to cast yourself fervently upon the Divine Presence to move you and to place you, just when, and where, the Supernal Will decrees, while you still hold the True Word.

By so doing, one saves oneself many unnecessary, even painful, experiences, the result of the unregenerate nature interfering.

Often one does not know just what work would be most congenial, or may even feel that one is not yet fitted for the work that would most appeal;

in either case, the Christ-abandonment to the Divine Will is wisdom, and perfect trust in the love of our heavenly Father, the surest road to that wherein lies our supreme success.

Eliminate every false thought from the work in which you are now engaged, and whether you be employer or employee often meditate upon such thoughts as these:

I cannot grow weary in well-doing. I cannot be overworked. No mortal can enslave me. No person or institution can bind me. I am fearless and free. No false system can use me or abuse me, I am God's free man, I am God's noble man.

I "labor not for the meat that perisheth but for that meat which endureth unto everlasting life which the Son of man shall give unto" me. Nothing is laborious to me. I am not an hireling. Money is no object to me.

I serve the Lord in All, lovingly, faithfully, abundantly, and I trust the Lord in All to serve me richly, honorably, truly.

I am redeemed from every curse of labor. I am not duty-bound.

In secret, as well as openly, I do my best. All my work is on honor.

Competition is nothing to me. Another's success can

not take my success away. My own comes to me. I have no rivals. I know no enemies. I rejoice in my neighbor s success.

Slander cannot hurt me, for I envy no man. Bitterness and stride have no place in my affairs. Only the elements of harmony can enter into my business. I draw to me those that love truth and honor.

I fear no lack for my Loved Ones. They attract prosperity even as I do.

I gravitate to the highest, most valuable, most useful and happiest position and work, which I can now fulfill to the honor of man and the glory of God.

Emerson says in SPIRITUAL LAWS: "Each man has his own vocation. The talent is the call. There is one direction in which space is open to him. He has faculties silently inviting him thither to endless exertion. He is like a ship in a river; he runs against obstructions on every side but one; on that side all obstruction is taken away, and he sweeps serenely over God's depths into an infinite sea. By doing his work he makes the need felt which he can supply. He creates the taste by which he is enjoyed. He provokes the wants to which he can minister. By doing his own work, he unfolds himself."

When one has no position at all, and everything is crying out in him, and through those near and dear to him, for the sustenance which he still feels must come by the law of cause and effect, as he seems not yet to realize the Absolute, what then?

The same Rule of the Word applies to him, as to others, but more than anything else, let him attend to the Spirit of rich service and divine guidance within him.

Perhaps there has been too much running to and fro, and whipping oneself into strenuous search after work with, all the time, a sense of the uselessness of it. Then it is wise to stay, like Mary of Bethany, "still in the house" until the inner message is brought "The Master is come and calleth for -thee." An illustration of this in a Truth-student's experience will serve best to convey the instruction intended:

A man whose wife had been healed of a severe case of rheumatism, had long been out of work because of his appetite for drink, which had not only caused his discharge from many good positions, but had drawn upon him most bitter invectives from his last employer, who had suffered certain losses through his failing. This "Captain" (he was called) swore at him, and told him never to show his face in his (the Captain's) place again.

But the man had been wholly healed of his intemperance, through his wife's spiritual treatments, and all appetite for liquor had left him forever. Nevertheless, as he went to and fro through the City looking for work, no one would take him, because, as they would say, "You said before you had sworn off and would never drink again. We cannot trust you."

The wife was trying to help with her word, but she was young in the thought and, needing more instruction, came to me to ask what to do next.

"He has gone everywhere he knows," she said, "and is ready to go more, although he feels it will not be any use, and that there must be another way."

Since he was beginning to get this impression, I said:

"Now he is ready to 'stand still and see the salvation of the Lord!' Let him not go out of the house again for work, unless he has a strong impression from within, but let him speak the Word: 'I have my true position, I am now in my right work.' v

He did so. It required fortitude and strength of character to abide by it. But he knew enough of the principles of Truth to wait and trust.

In a day or so, the mail brought a letter from that same Captain, to whom he had not presumed to go, after the terrible dismissal he had received, couched in polite language, saying that he had heard that he (the man) had been looking for a position, and that there was an opening in his old place, if he desired to come back. He took the old position, where he remained many years after, until he finally went into business for himself.

Fill the heart and mind with desire to serve, regardless of whether there be recognition of your value, or just recompense for your good work, and there will gather within you a rich quality, which can always be sensed by a man of large outlook, making him respect your application even when ignoring ordinary demands.

A successful man in Vancouver, who was attending a Prosperity Course which I was giving in that city, furnished me with an example of the success of this method in his own experience as an employer: A few days before, as he was loading, or rather superintending the loading, as stevedore, of a great number of barges with lumber, two men came to him, one after the other, asking for work. It was not uncommon, and would have passed by unnoticed, as he told them he had all the men he wanted, but for two incidents. The first was, that each did the same thing though strangers to each other. After receiving the short, quick dismissal of the stevedore, who was exceedingly busy with a "rush" order, the first man went and sat on a pile of lumber to watch the workers; the second did the same thing, sitting down near the first one.

As a great load was being swung around by a derrick, it began slipping, and the stevedore shouted for the other men to come to the rescue. Some were excited, some were slow, and as the stevedore called for more, the man who had been second to ask him for work, sprang forward with the rest, and gave his best, not only then, but continued working on for the rest of the day. At the close of the day, the stevedore touched him on the shoulder, and said, "Come tomorrow, my man, I want men like you!" And he gave him the position next day, with the thought that he would keep an eye on that man. While the first applicant was lost to him as a pebble dropped among many others.

Further points to be considered in obtaining employment, will be brought out in our next lesson, which will also be devoted to the way out of debt, and aiding others to pay their indebtedness to us.

Through all the success that comes to us in our worldly business, let us never forget that we came to this earth on one Special Errand alone, and, in as much as we accomplish that charge, are we really successful. Truly there is but one Business in all God's world, that is, to prove our own divinity, and the Godhood of the whole race, in proving that God is All there really is.

V. Freedom from Debt.

Owe no man anything but to love one another; for he that loveth another hath fulfilled the law. Love worketh no ill to his neighbor: therefore, love is the fulfilling of the law. The Apostle Paul.

Wherever there is a sense of indebtedness there also is honor; and where honor abides, wealth and power are near at hand, for in Spirit they are never separated: "Both riches and honor come of thee and thou reignest over all; and in thy hand is power and might; and in thine hand it is to make great, and to give strength unto all," 1 Chron. 29:12. And so surely as a debtor gets understanding, by which he can keep his trust as well as his honor, he will never be harassed by his creditors, nor be brought to shame or want.

It is a matter of wonderment to some people that they are" trusted so implicitly by their creditors. Yet the reason is simple. Men are continually reading each other's thoughts, and when there is a determination to do right by one's neighbor, this state of mind is written upon the face and in the actions, as well as radiating through the aura, and if the creditor will but trust his impressions bi c debtor then becomes simply a good investment.

As that wise Jew, Paul, declared and a spiritual Jew is a masterly financier the key to freedom from debt is Love that seeks the good of his neighbor first, last and always. For with Love is that respect, that honor that is a perpetual magnet for riches, even though they are passed along as rapidly as received, and one may not appear to be rich through accumulation. The truly rich are those who have plenty to spend, and spend that plenty, not those who have plenty to save, and save it. The miser is not rich. The prodigal is nearer to prosperity, even in his ignorance, than the thrifty who never learns to spend.

Perfect love casts out fear as to one's continuance in prosperity, and guides one into the Way where indebtedness is no burden, but a convenient and harmonious arrangement, where each is benefited, and each is sure of the outcome.

But the debts that we made in folly and selfishness, that hang over us like a pall, and drag upon us from the past, so that there seems no deliverance! What of these? And those that, it would seem, could only be paid with a life-time of labor, and yet no prospect of funds lies ahead of us?

"Though your sins be as scarlet, they shall be as white as snow." Though your debts be "scarlet," they shall all be cancelled, for such debts in the affairs are like sins in the character, and the Christ-law must be known, and applied, to bring perfect freedom. In the prayer which Jesus gave to his disciples, as a pattern, we have this law, embedded in the words, "Forgive us our debts as we forgive our debtors."

As you open the way by which your debtors can be free to pay you, or not, according to the great equity of God, the way of your freedom will be revealed. Let us consider the mental philosophy of "forgiving our debtors," so that they may be helped to pay us, if not with money, by something valuable to us. It may be revealed to us that an old score in some former existence has been balanced, and they really owe us nothing. At any rate, it is not true for us to hold any thought or feeling against our neighbors, no matter how false their attitude towards us, but at all times to have such a state of mind regarding them, that they shall feel comfortable in our presence, and even glad to think of us.

People often keep others from paying them, because of mentally harassing their debtors. They wonder with indignation why so and so does not pay that bill, and perhaps they talk him (or her) over with a mutual acquaintance, until, if character were clothes, he would not have a rag to his back. Perhaps one hears that the debtor is spending money freely buying luxuries and the rumor adds fuel to the flames.

In the meantime the debtor is exceedingly uncomfortable every time the thought of that creditor comes into mind, and he shuns him. If he sees him coming, he will cross the street, or in some way avoid a meeting. He may even hate him. Finally, he succeeds in so dismissing that creditor from his mind that, when he is ready to pay his debts, that one does not come into mind at all. This sense of uncomfortableness is also the reason why one who has received a favor of money loaned, is so often not a good friend after that the burden of obligation chafes him.

If, because of Truth, you will not think evil of your debtor,- that he is dishonest, or untrue, or selfish, or weak, or poverty-stricken, but will hold him in his noble, honorable, true being, you will easily and happily come into his mind, just at the right time, with the desire to do the right thing by you, and also the ability. This was literally demonstrated in the experience of a lady, a student of Truth, who, among many others, had loaned a man a sum of money who made a failure in the venture, in which all the money had been sunk.

He left the town, followed by anathemas from all his creditors but this lady. She kept her mind upon his true self, and whenever the subject of his delinquencies was broached, she never spoke against him, but always, "He will pay me. I have no fear. I trust him," or words of like meaning.

Then news came that he had "struck it rich" in Alaska, but it brought no hope to those creditors who had decided that he was thoroughly bad. But the lady soon received a letter with the full amount of her loan in it, and the words, "You have never said one word against me, and so I pay you first. The others can wait." This lady exercised the real forgiveness, which is not a sentiment but a power. She forgave or gave-for the false appearance of fraud, the true thought of the Real Man, with the result of proving that what she declared was true.

Our debts are forgiven us by the same process of the Law of the Good substituting freedom-from-all-indebtedness for the former bondage; and healing the cause, our weakness or ignorance and bringing forward our good judgment and insight.

With the new mind, many errors fall away, that have not been seen as errors, although their basis was some limitation, or belief in evil. Thus one ceases to hold back money from fear, or save it up for "a rainy day." When there comes an over-flow of money, then to bank the surplus may be a matter of convenience, and not fear.

There should be no waiting for others to pay us before we will consider paying our debts. Doing our part may supply the impetus for our debtor to do his, as when a single $5 piece has been known to pay $20 indebtedness in a family by being circulated at the right moment.

Pride and conventionality are displaced, and debts may be paid in very small sums at a time, and inspiration guides us as to whom payment should be made first. Sometimes a hard thought is being held against one, so that it is like a curse, preventing the free flow of one's blessings. A true step taken may relieve the whole situation. A dollar paid to. a man who thinks what you owe him is a bad debt, may relieve a congestion in the thought-causes back of your affairs.

A lady had been owing her music-teacher for her last lessons over a year, because she never had the amount, fifteen dollars, on hand when she thought of him. She resolved to put aside her pride and fixed ideas of how he should be paid, and send him a dollar at a time until the debt was cancelled. After mailing a letter of apology enclosing the dollar, she received a most cordial reply full of protestations that she did not owe him anything, begging her to dismiss all thought about it, as she had paid him many times more than that amount in pupils, to whom she had recommended him. The attempt she had made well repaid her; for not only was the debt cancelled, but the expression of appreciation that she received was a surprise and a delight, as she had not considered the favor she was doing him, but only the benefit she was conferring on those who became his pupils.

Through meditating on the divine desire within you to bless your neighbors, there will rise a joy in paying them. Also, a faith that others enjoy paying you, and you will not dread, nor hate, to present a bill.

Sometimes letters and other papers are so embued with the false thoughts which are held when they were being prepared, that they come like a blow, or an insult, and quite miss their intention. An illustration of this fact was given me by a member of one of my classes: Miss M., a healer and teacher, had given many treatments and lessons to a wealthy lady, who had made no movement towards payment, and finally Miss M. concluded that she was waiting for a bill. Feeling it to be thoughtless on the part of her patient to wait for a bill, and with a combination of resentment, impatience and indignation, she sat down and wrote the bill and mailed it. Now the lady was generous and just, and also, a good student of Truth. If she had not been, Miss M. would have waited long for her money.

"For," the lady said, "the moment I took the bill in my hand, I had such a feeling of resentment, impatience and indignation against you, that I almost threw the bill into the waste-basket, with the vow that I wouldn't pay you for a month! Then I remembered my principles, and instantly I knew that those were your feelings about me, and I had been reflecting them, and I immediately came down here to pay you. Be careful, young lady, what you think, when you send out bills!"

The question has sometimes risen, ought we to contract debts when there is no money in sight to pay them? Unless there is the true supreme assurance from within, that the money to pay such debts is already on the way, it is better to fast and pray until such assurance come, than to put oneself to too great a test. The demonstration of faith is not the venturing into debts, but the realization of the means to meet debts, even before they are contracted.

In accordance with the statement given in our last lesson, I will herewith give some further thoughts about obtaining employment.

Keep well in mind the understanding that you are no mere machine, but always a brother, and a fellowman a sister and a member of God's family. There is nothing so interesting to personalities as personality, and especially a personality that is also interested in personalities. Approach those from whom you expect favors with interest in your face, that has sprung from communing with the Spirit within them, and whether the favor be granted or not, take the decision as from the Spirit at that moment not necessarily final and so maintain a high standard of respect between you. It will not be forgotten and next time you apply, it will be easier to get into the "good graces" of the one in power.

Some good advice was given to a young man, who had been spending days looking for work, until he was greatly discouraged. The man who gave the advice, had just made the stereotyped reply, "Sorry, but I've nothing for you," and as the young fellow was turning sadly away, he added:

"But young man, I can give you a piece of advice, which, if you take it, will get you a position soon. It is this. Never again approach an employer with that gloomy face. Smile, look cheerful and you'll succeed."

The young man thanked him and put it into practice. As he kept thinking upon cheerfulness, and smilingly received one refusal after another, he grew light-hearted until, at the last place he applied a coal yard as the same old answer was given him, he turned and went through the yard whistling a merry tune. The man called him back.

"You seem to be a pretty cheerful fellow! I like such men round me. Come here tomorrow, and T think I can make a place for you."

He received work from that time, and never forgot the valuable advice of his stranger-friend.

Never expect to succeed by appealing to another's pity or sympathy; nor by bringing forward your need or lack, weakness or ignorance. Let your main thought ever be, "How can I serve you?"

A few aphorisms are added for your meditation:

Riches are a state of mind. Richness should circulate through our affairs as air does in the lungs.

Nothing succeeds so well as success; nothing prospers so well as prosperity; therefore never put on a "poor mouth."

Freedom in giving and receiving is the law of healthy supply. The Lord [Prosperity] loveth a cheerful giver.

Do not save up for a "rainy day"; for they will come as long as you prepare for them.

Money must not be clutched. It loves freedom. Carry yourself as one who owns the earth, for you do.

Business instinct is spiritual intuition applied to affairs.

Money invested in spiritual things is not loss, but gain, an hundred-fold.

"Consider the lilies how they grow." They have a law within themselves by which they draw to themselves their own sustenance.

Get into the current of the stream of Prosperity and your boat will be carried along all right without interfering with your neighbor.

VI. The Rich Mentality.

Lay up for yourselves treasures in heaven. Matt. 6:20.

A good man out of the good treasure of the heart bringeth forth good things. Matt. 12:35.

They shall prosper that love thee. Ps. 122:6.

Then shalt thou prosper if thou takest heed to fulfill the statutes and judgments. 1 Chron. 22:13,

Why transgress ye the commandments of the Lord that ye cannot prosper? because ye have forsaken the Lord he hath also forsaken you. 2 Chron. 24:20.

Acquaint now thyself with him and be at peace: thereby shall good come unto thee. Receive I pray thee the law from his mouth and lay up his words in thine heart. If thou return to the Almighty thou shalt be built up ... Then shalt thou lay up gold as dust and the gold of Ophir as the stones of the brooks. Yea, the Almighty shall be thy defense and thou shalt have plenty of silver. Job 22:21 to 25.

Riches are primarily a state of mind and not a matter of accumulation of money or things. Having a rich mind will necessarily be represented by plenty of the world's goods, either in possession, or at command; but to have millions, and to lack the fertility of mind to place them, is to be like the mule that bears rich ore on his back out of the mine he knows only the burden of it and none of the richness.

Men and women of assured income, who have not known the interior wealth, have led miserable lives of fear, lest thieves should rob them of everything, and some have gone insane with the dread of poverty, and spent the last days of their earthly existence in hourly expectation of being sent to the poor house because of their indigency. Paupers in mind, they cannot recognize riches when they stare them in the face.

Therefore the wisdom of the great Philosopher of Life: Seek first to be rich towards God and let the earthly riches follow. For then is the problem taken hold of at the right end, at its source, and one escapes the folly of so many poor ones who have put the cart before the horse, seeking riches first and the spiritual life last.

Everyone who comes into the world has a rich aura, the gift of his heavenly Father it is his "living" from the Source of all wealth. Most of us seem to have been prodigal sons, letting our rich consciousness be frittered away by the delusions of sense, until we find ourselves bound to mortality, and far from happiness, heaven, our home. But we know that even then, if we only remember and "come to ourselves," we can return to the rich consciousness by keeping our face steadily towards our Father's house, that is, "seeking first the kingdom of God and his righteousness."

The rich aura that surrounds and fills each of us, is the reflection of the Divine Mind, and it contains all the elements of every expression of richness upon the face of the whole earth. Its thoughts of goodness are the reality of gold; its consciousness of freedom lies back of the silver; its purity is the substance of the diamond and all its virtues are portrayed in the gems of the earth. Its life fructifies the very soil, its beauty and grace determine the forms of fruit and flower. Its culture pictures forth in the arts of man, according to what development man has given himself towards that Rich Mentality.

As long as man looks outside himself for all the causes of his fortune or misfortune, he does not find this law of thought and feeling, by which he may be prospered. In man's attitude towards this Rich Mentality, which is in truth his Divine Mind, lies the explanation of many an unusual experience in his life.

Certain habitual thoughts and feelings towards God and the spiritual life have made a man's fields yield more richly than his neighbors, although in every other respect the soil and the seed were the same. Crops have been delivered from pests, and also protected, so that a blight or frost or other enemy could not harm them. Illustrating this, a story was told the writer by a student, about his father, who had a remarkable proof that a "praying man" comes under divine protection, even in his fields.

This gentleman said that his father, Mr. N., was a successful farmer in England, who, in raising potatoes, had united with a number of his neighbors in leasing a long strip of land, dividing it so that every farmer had two long rows of potato-hills. They bought seed together, ploughed and sowed at the same time. Mr. N. had a most practical idea of the presence and power of God in a man's affairs, and so while planting his seed, he invoked the blessing of the Almighty upon it, for he believed' that all his prosperity came through remembering God in all his ways.

When the time came to gather the potatoes, the farmers found that a potato disease called "dry-rot," which appeared that year for the first time in England, had attacked every tuber, making almost a total loss to each farmer but Mr. N. For when he turned over the soil in the two long rows of hillocks, not one potato in the whole of his tract had been touched. This made a very deep impression upon all the country round, especially as Mr. N. ascribed his protection to the goodness of God in answering his direct and believing prayers for the yield of his field.

All that one puts his hand to comes into this Divine Aura, and if a man consciously, or unconsciously, cooperates with it and fulfills its laws, that will take place, that is written (Ps. 1:23) "whatsoever he doeth shall prosper."

This Rich Mentality might be compared to g, field of rich soil which each one owns. If it seems unyielding as to prosperity, then it is not recognized and cultivated. It may be like a wilderness, full of weeds, yet yielding a certain increase. Such are the fields of the spendthrift, the sordid and the care-ridden. Perhaps it is unwatered, like the Great American Desert, which has been proven to be so fertile when well irrigated. Then ignorance of this great law. of prosperity is the cause, or a forgetting the truth about oneself, one's source and powers.

The desire in the heart of a man to be self-supporting and independent is because such is the divine intention. The revelation of this inner eternal supply establishes the consciousness of endless prosperity. "As the Father hath life in himself; so hath he given to the Son to have life in himself," John 5:26.

Richness circulates through the body of one's affairs, as air in the body of flesh. And as, through intelligence and power, one controls the breath, so should the welfare of our circumstances be subject to our mind.

A lady in Southern California realized this power of control once, to the great advantage of an important crop. Her home was in the midst of a large orange grove which was then in full bearing, and promising a fine revenue that winter, with which they hoped to recuperate their fortune, and once more be on their feet. She had a neighbor whose financial history had been almost identical with her own, for both, with their husbands, had invested in adjoining lands, planted and raised orange trees, which had already yielded several crops. But the neighbor did not believe in the power of mind, but scoffed and antagonized so much, that the lady ceased to refer to the Truth and its powers in her presence.

One night a report was carried through the town, that they were liable to have a black frost before morning, and that every man had better "smudge" and so save his orchard. "Smudging" (some may not know), is producing a smoke from specially built fires, thus warming the air and keeping it moving so that the cold air cannot bite the tender fruit. Now it so happened that the husbands of both ladies were away. The neighbor came in wringing her hands and crying, "What shall we do! No one to help us we cannot do it alone our crop will be ruined!"

The lady, Mrs. R., tried to console her but her own heart was heavy, and she had little success. After the neighbor returned, she walked the floor trying to calm herself with Truth, repeating over statements as to the allness of good, and the nothingness of evil, in every variety of declaration, that came to her. Presently her faithfulness was rewarded. She remembered what her teacher had said, as to the power of Mind to go forth and heal the plants, and she spoke aloud: "God can protect my orchard! The presence of God is there, and even now folds it round about, and keeps it from every harmful thing." She remembered "there shall no evil come nigh thy dwelling"; she recited the 91st Psalm; she remembered the words spoken to Job beginning, "He shall deliver thee in six troubles" including "neither shalt thou be afraid of destruction" and ending "the beasts of the field shall be at peace with thee" (Job 5:19 to 23) and she was filled with trust and a mighty consciousness of power. An impression came to her of her orchard, being covered over, as with a great canvas, and she lay down upon her pillow and slept like a child until morning.

The black frost came, and every orchard, that had not been smudged, came woefully under the blight. Every orchard but that of Mrs. R. in which not one orange was touched, although her neighbor's crop was a total loss.

It was a nine-days wonder and many were the congratulations. She was young in the thought, and told no one of her prayers, although her neighbor suspected the source of her victory, for she never again scoffed at her belief.

When discouragement and despondency settle down upon a man, or when discord, misunderstanding or bitterness distract and tear the inner man, his very cattle and his other creatures show forth his state of mind in their condition. Lift up your mind, get hold of the Spirit, throw off those mean feelings as you would shake off the flakes of snow before entering a warm room.

Practice repeating words of cheer and spiritual promises, and meditate upon the very opposite thoughts to those that drag you down, until there comes an inner change. And the longer it takes you, the more should be your persistence the fact of its taking so long shows how sadly you needed the practice. Remove the curse from that unrented house, by mentally filling it with loving, attractive thoughts, changing its atmosphere from that deadening, repelling character that people feel, even as they approach a place, making them decide against it before examining it. Read Isaiah 35 and 11:1 to 9 and 65:16 to 25 and give your mind and heart to the fairest pictures of concord and harmony that they raise.

You are not building up this Rich Mentality. It is already there in all its fullness and perfection. It is your part to uncover it, to co-operate with it, to believe in it. Then like the lilies of the field, the law that is within you can operate and draw your own to you.

We perpetually remember that the one who is prospered by a knowledge of Truth brings prosperity to the whole earth, for he draws heaven into the earth, and Love is the law of his life, causing him ever to lead his fellow-beings to the same law within themselves that he has found in himself.

As vines that are pruned, only bear the better and fuller fruits, so let us see all the forms of hardship and wrong and failure through which we may have passed in former days, but as the times of our pruning, and because we are alive let us know that Life to be Prosperity itself, the Rich Mentality, containing the greatest fortune that earth has ever known. And now is the time and here is the place that we prove ourselves the masterful Word of the Almighty, pressing the Kingdom of Heaven into the earth, until poverty shall be known no more, nor any poor, but all shall come to their thrones, glorified Sons and Daughters of the Most High.

PART II. SIX SPIRITUAL TREATMENTS

EXPLANATORY

In the following Treatments, the first thing that is considered is the right attitude that one should take in the home-life, so that the Truth may work in our secret thoughts and feelings, when our life seems separated from business and we are not being put to the test in strenuous affairs.

The second consists of a meditation to read, letting the ideas sink into the heart, and bring forth original observations, of which the student should make notes in a convenient note-book.

The third is the Treatment which is to be read for oneself, as though the Inner Voice was uttering the words, and our spiritual reason confirming them.

The Treatments proper always begin with Listen to Me!

Not only read them for yourself, but silently read them to others, who are feeling stress in their circumstances. Be orderly in this, and write down the names of those whom you are treating, and the times of treatment. And seek to realize what you are saying to them.

In giving these treatments to yourself or to others, pause with impressive realization at each mark, and if the Word is doing its work, there will come a definite feeling of power and satisfaction, both to the healer and the one being healed.

Even though this feeling does not come at first, the Truth in the words will do the work, often to the surprise of the young student, whose faith is weak or undeveloped.

Remember the virtue there is in Repetition and as one progresses more rapidly in learning a language, or

acquiring an art, by having the lessons close together and the practice constant, so it is in the spiritual acquisition of the prospering power. Missionaries give the first two years of their noviate almost all the waking hours of each day to learning the language of those whom they have come to save. The human mind seems slow. Let us possess ourselves in patience and in due time we shall reap.

VII. In the Quiet of the Home

The real Home of each one of us is Heaven and the bitter home-sickness of so many of the race will never be healed until Heaven is found within.

For the longing of men and women for a spot that they can call "home" is but a form of spiritual homesickness. And the Student of Truth is wise who will not seek the healing of that malady through acquiring the outer home, for, without the conscious union with Heaven within, they will only acquire burdens with the house, that they desire to be their home.

But by developing the home-realization within, every place where they shall relax and spend the quiet hours of their lives, will be a happy nest a sheltering abode drawing others with its home-charm, as well as expressing their own deep, holy peace.

In the quiet of your abiding place, be it a flat or a garret, farm-house or hotel, bungalow or hall-bedroom, radiate the richness of- your Soul, until the transformation of your room, will reveal the achievement of your true thoughts.

Never take the worries of your business into the family life. Take your faith there, when you consult your loved ones as to your affairs. The only connection, that there should be between your business and your home, is that of spiritual cheer and an abiding scientific optimism.

As you stand at your front door say, "Peace be unto this house!" And be sure that you never let your peace depart from you! Hold your peace forever!

TREATMENT I. THE HIGHROAD OF PROSPERITY.

Meditation. "Come, let us reason together!" God is the true source of all the riches in the earth "The silver is mine and the gold is mine, saith the Lord of hosts" (Haggai 2:8) and you are the offspring of the Most High, heir of all the richness of God and you are here to express that richness through this body and in this world.

There is a Highway of Prosperity the King's Highway the road up the Mountain of supreme success, that has an easy grade, where the travel is ever smooth, and where they that walk therein know no more worry or fear, or strife or hard times, or slavish work or failure. They live and let live, and they are consciously secure, forever, from all sense of deprivation or lack.

The uninstructed follow by-paths in seeking their wealth, where there is much stumbling and blindness of chance, where burdens pile up, but the travellers never reach the heights. All these sidetracks end in gullies and pits., for all that is gained must eventually be given up. Men enter them as short-cuts to wealth, and though some of them cross the real Road, so intoxicated are these wanderers, that they know not the Way even when their feet press its fair track, long miles at a time.

The right view of Prosperity as God's own presence, not to be refused or despised, but to be seen as the legitimate expression of the spiritual life, comes to "the man whose eyes are open" and he seeks understanding so as to think and feel, speak and act according to the Law that operates, to make bodies healthy and circumstances wealthy, as one and the same work. The body is wealthy that has health, and the - circumstances are healthy that have wealth.

Listen to me! The Highroad of God's Prosperity is unlimited wealth, riches that are eternal and the Life that is endless ease and comfort. This blessed Road is not far from you; it is not divided and set off from your life or the life of anyone. "For it is the Omnipresence of God."

Because this Highroad to prosperity is the omnipresence of God, "you are in it now, you cannot miss the Way." Your mind is set right now. And mind being the cause of all that manifests in your life, its right thinking will show forth right conditions in your affairs. Your Father is rich. "Your Father has "enough and to spare" and His decree is that you shall prosper in whatsoever you put your hand to."

Your heritage is boundless wealth and the Wise One within you reveals to you the laws "by which your own comes to you." Jesus knew the deep laws of Spirit "by which he could pay his taxes, furnish the finest wines for the feast, and feed multitudes with overflowing abundance. You have the same Intelligence in you, for it is the Mind of God opening up the Way of your supply.

Now you are on the Highroad to the riches that will never fail. You are coming out of mortality's dream. As a mortal you have been rich a thousand times in lives gone by. What did it profit you? Nothing. Now temporal richness is finished. Enter into the riches "prepared for you from the foundation of the world." Because you seek the riches of God first, you must have the other also. It is the law. You have the Word of Christ for it. Being rich towards God, rich in loving service to humanity, "rich in goodness of character, rich in holy wisdom and devotion to God and His Christ," you cannot miss the riches of the world.

God's prosperity flows to you without effort. It is the divine gift. It comes, not by hard work of head or hand, but by the Spirit. Inspiration leads you to your expression of happy usefulness. You find the work you love to do, and it pays.

Debts are no part of your life.

The light of the Christ-mind shines on your Way, and shows you how to cancel every debt. Spirit keeps your mind at ease. You need never worry. Worry never does anything. Now you let trust-in-the- Almighty-Good displace all anxiety, and give you rest. What is to be of God's good state and accomplishment, is done already. Therefore your debts are already paid in the divine Mind. Honor and equity take you out of indebtedness. You are not a debtor, you are a good investment. You make rich returns. You are a Bank, not a bankrupt. The law of the Spirit in Christ Jesus makes you free.

Every day brings you fresh inspiration. Every night brings you innocent sleep and righteous rest.

Every experience means the closer communion with God. Nothing can daunt you. Nothing can discourage you. You touch the Highroad of God's prosperity ^ and you are wafted along the Way on winged feet. Honor and riches are yours, and your peace no man can take from you now and forever more.

IT IS DONE.

VIII. Prosperity Begins at Home

Every household can prove itself a center for the expression of God's prosperity, no matter how small its beginnings may be. As a mighty oak is but a spindling twig at first, but, through faith in itself, and the loving encouragement and protection of nature, becomes the tower of strength, that is the admiration of all that behold it, so one's spiritual demonstration of prosperity may seem a weakling at first. But, if you temper the winds of fierce race-suggestions of the reality of poverty, and keep your faith steadily centered in the rich God-life that dwells within, your prosperity will prove itself an established presence, that no fluctuations among the nations, or untrueness among individuals, can move or destroy your wealth, like your health, will be eternal.

But let no home work for itself alone, and neglect its neighbor. For the joy of demonstrating God's presence, in any form, is that that consciousness can be given to our world. Sometimes one must consider one's world first, in order to come to one's individual expression of prosperity; for there is always a stage, where selfishness must pass away, that one may go on into greater power and prosperity.

It may seem that selfishness has given people prosperity, but that manifestation is crossed and recrossed with decay and death, and only the spiritually ignorant will walk that path. What are millions to you if they cannot save your life, or heal you of blindness, or bring you love? Yet thousands are dying, or going into insane asylums, or leading a life of sorrow, whom the world envy because of their wealth.

The riches that come through Truth are permanent, and are companioned by all the joys of heaven, because they are not confined to property and affairs, but are universal, and express themselves through every department of our being.

TREATMENT II. RICHES, THE GIFT OF GOD.

Meditation. The Laws of Spiritual Prosperity are the very reverse of the laws of worldly prosperity. In divine economy, you do not gain by "saving up for rainy days," you do not lose by spending, the more you give away the more you have. You do not earn divine riches, therefore you do not have to work hard for them, either mentally or physically.

It belongs to your creative consciousness to love to work, and by fearlessness concerning supply and support, you can gravitate to your congenial work, which will be valued highly by the world because art will enter into it. "Art is love for one's work" Elbert Hubbard.

Time and wages belong to slaves. We come out of Egypt by ceasing "to work for a living" in our mind. Whatever work you are engaged in now, become an artist in it, by putting soul into your service. Educate yourself to find divinity in your work and in your associates, whether employer or employees. When you have learned your lesson, you will graduate easily into a congenial, because your own, vocation.

The Spirit knows spirit only, and in its realm there is no bargaining, no buying and selling, no wages, no hirelings, no laborers, no rewards or punishments, no merit or demerit, no deserving, and no unworthy, ones.

All is Love, and everything is done for Love, and all the fruits of Love are gifts.

Listen to me! The substance of Prosperity is spiritual and it enfolds you and fills you, breath of your breath and the fullness and perfection of your life. This rich substance is a gift to you, it came with you into the world; you never earned it ^ and so it can never be taken from you.

Riches are yours whether you deserve it or not. You are a Prince with God. Princes are rich without earning their wealth. You are heir with Christ, and all, that the Father hath, is yours. The silver and the gold are mine saith the Lord ^ and all that the Father hath is mine, saith the Christ.

Your Good takes care of you. As you were nourished and protected from the beginning, so now. You came with a world of wealth. Now by the power of God within you, you draw it into manifestation.

You lay up riches in your heart. God gives you Trust in place of worriment. God gives you Faith in place of fear. God gives you Forgiveness to take the place of bitterness. God gives you Inspiration and takes away plodding. God gives you Insight instead of scheming. God gives you Interest-in-your neighbor in place of selfishness. God gives you Honest Ways to replace all trickery.

You rise above the plane, and law, of cause and effect. You dismiss from your mind all sense of injury. Mortal man is nothing to you. Wrongdoing on his part cannot make you suffer. The Spirit rights all wrongs. You do the right thing by your fellow-man. No one's curse or hatred can keep you from your own. You look not to man ^ for your support. God is your sufficiency and the source of all your riches. God is for you what can man do against you? ^

You live in a world of freedom and you give everybody and everything freedom. You give money freedom. You do not clutch money. You let go and trust. Stand still and see the salvation of the Lord!

You go to your happiest work. By the Spirit within, you find your place. Your Genius goes before you and makes channels to express itself.

Angels of prosperity surround you. Angels of prosperity work for you. Everything you put your hand to, prospers.

You are now opening the Way, by which your riches can take tangible forms in your world.

Prosperity seeks you, and must find you. You are in its Way and it cannot miss you.

You bear witness to the presence of prosperity, by your carriage, you hold your head up; by your poise, r your back is not bowed; by your courage ^ you put your best foot forward.

You are in the Current of Prosperity. All things in your affairs move smoothly, with the Current. And your heart is at rest, for your prosperity is sure.

ABIDE IN PEACE.

IX. The Home Refurnished

The home is the bulwark of the nation, and anything that builds up the home and contributes to its ideals, strengthens the race, both within and without. For the home is also the place to picture forth heaven, and often it is the training-school for wild, crude mortality wherein it learns the joys of peace, order and loving service, a preparation for heaven here on the earth.

Each home that is consecrated to this ministry of the Christ message and healing, becomes an example of purity and harmony to those seeking heaven on the earth. Perhaps your ministry cannot yet be an open one, but it can do a silent work by its hospitality, comfort, restfulness and love. The very walls can sing of goodness and truth. The common furniture can caress us, the homely fare can give us sweetest satisfaction.

Fill your home with blessing. Remove every suggestion of discontent. If there is a room that savours of selfishness, or of impurity, or of deadness, in its mental atmosphere, heal it. You can do it by a half-hour of silence in it each day, in which you meditate upon the omnipresence of heaven, declaring for some special expression of heaven, centering there.

The richness of- your spirit must enter the place where you reside, even though it be a cellar or a hall bed-room, and permeate it. The ease and comfort of a rich consciousness must radiate from your personality.

For riches draw riches, and prosperity gravitates to the things and the people that are like it, especially when backed by principle. There are people who look prosperous, and yet, are undermining themselves by a false state of mind; and there are people who are rich but do not look prosperous, and they are missing some of the good things that belong to them.

The kingdom of heaven appears, when there is a perfect harmony and unity between the without and the within.

In proving God to be the health of your circumstances, see to it that your home does not contradict your faith. There is a great law fulfilled in "putting one's best foot forward." Business men know that it is a good investment, for the later success of their projects, to have a good office, well furnished. The habit of beginning with poor equipment makes new enterprises long and slow in reaching success.

When an instrument is tuned too low like a harp, violin or guitar then one string is raised to a proper pitch and the rest keyed up to it. Sometimes one can raise the whole vibration of a house, and the household, by introducing some rich, up-to-date feature, and then keying all the rest of the establishment up to that vibration, even though many days go by before it is finished.

Act wealthy, talk prosperously. Be a free avenue through which riches may pass to all. The world needs to learn the spiritual science of wealth, and your home can be a class room.

TREATMENT III. BLESS, PRAISE, GIVE THANKS.

Meditation. There is no greater prospering power than the word of Blessing, of genuine praise and of thanks from the heart- especially towards those people, and about those things and events, that have seemed to curse us.

As these utterances must not be merely from the lips, it will require skill, discernment, inspiration and a prophetic sense to find that, which one can praise in our enemies, be thankful for in misfortune and bless in treachery. And the very exercise itself will enrich one, like the sons, in the fable, of the wise old father, who had four lazy sons, and in dying, told them that he had nothing to leave them but a field. But in that field was buried a treasure. So when he died they vigorously dug up that field. But they found no treasure. The next crops, however, that grew in that ground yielded four times the ordinary crop, and then the sons knew that the treasure in the field was what they had put into it their own energy and faith.

Practice skill and discernment in finding the good in the people who have injured you, and the failures that have burdened you. Let the Spirit inspire your thanksgiving and open your prophetic sense, to see the blessing that is coming out of it all. The exercise is enriching, both spiritually and materially.

Listen to the Divine Voice within you. It guides you. It cheers you. It shows you the Way of righteousness and eternal prosperity.

The divine approval overshadows you and protects you. Your heavenly Father awaits lovingly your return ^ to the spiritual life and its ways ^ and runs to meet you, saying, Thou art my beloved in whom I am well-pleased.

The blessing of the Lord it maketh rich. The Lord in you blesses your whole world ^ and the act enriches you. You give your heart and mind to blessing everybody and everything.

You bless them that curse you. You do good to them that hate you. You know no rivals. You have no competition. All that is done against you, helps you.

Your destiny is to know the secret of prosperity. You cannot fail. Your success is decreed ^ from the foundation of the world.

The Spirit opens your eyes to see the Way of it. There is a straight line ^ between you and the next successful step, and you go forward upon it.

Fear passes utterly away. You are calm and trusting. Your confidence inspires confidence.

You lay up treasures in heaven. You do good and forget it. You give freely your tenth your tithe. And you reap an hundred fold. Bring ye all the tithes into the storehouse that there may be meat [substance] in mine house, and prove me now, herewith saith the Lord of hosts 'if I will not open you the windows of heaven and pour you out a blessing, that there shall not be room enough to receive it'.

No anger can undermine you. No envy can corrode your affairs. No selfishness can rust you. No greed can overload you. You are God's free instrument of distribution.

Riches flow to you and through you to bless all the world. You freely receive and you freely give. No foolish accumulation burdens you. No loss disturbs you.

You bring faith into the storehouse of Plenty. You bring love into the storehouse of Opulence. You bring knowledge into the storehouse of Abundance. You bring goodness into the storehouse of all your Prosperity. And they return to you in all the world's forms of wealth ^ unlimited, unceasing, full, perfect and free.

REST IN DIVINE BOUNTY.

X. Our Unlimited Capacity

Contentment is one of the richest jewels that a home can have, and when its foundation is knowledge of Truth, it abides forever, and becomes a powerful magnet, to draw to itself, the best in people and in things.

When contentment is mated with poverty, there is usually some false reason at the root of the matter. Sometimes it is a yielding to circumstances as inevitable a kind of fatalism, but oftener it takes its rise from the religious training, especially the doctrine that Christianity and poverty are logical associates, and that the Greatest of all the Christians, himself, was poor, having "no place to lay his head."

We know now that we cannot call Jesus Christ poor, any more than we can think of the king of England as poor, simply because he has no money in his pocket. Jesus had command of forces, that could have made him a Croesus in a moment, but he would not be cumbered with property.

If one chooses to go without, all right. But to be forced to go without, and even to be in debt, is not a free state and therefore not true Christianity. For has not the Christ said, "Ye shall know the Truth and the Truth shall make you free?"

The old preaching from the pulpit, that one cannot expect to be rich in this life, was often from a certain text, as a favorite quotation from which to expound the.-e views. It is found in Hebrews 13:5, and according to

the old King James Version, it reads: "And be ye content with such things as ye have." But according to a learned prelate of the Church of England, the translation should read: "Be ye conscious, that ye have contained within yourselves all capacity " which version is more in keeping with the context, "For he hath said, I will never leave thee nor forsake thee, so that we may boldly say, The Lord is my helper, and I will not fear what man shall do unto me."

"Contentment," "contain" and "contents" are all of the same family of words. Our true Contentment is ability to contain all the blessings that the good God shall pour out upon us.

The story of Elisha" s increasing the widow's pot of oil, is illustrative of the point that Paul was teaching, concerning our capacity. There was a widow, who appealed to Elisha to save her two sons from being sold for debt, that is, becoming slaves in order to pay a debt. Elisha asked her what she had in the house, and she answered "Nothing but a pot of oil." Then he told her to go and borrow all the vessels she could from her neighbors. "Borrow not a few," was his instruction. And then she was to pour oil from that little pot of oil, until all were filled. She procured all that she could, and the oil increased until the last vessel was full, and then "the oil stayed." "Then she came and told the man of God. And he said, Go, sell the oil, and pay thy debt and live thou and thy children of the rest."

Here was an instance of a woman, enriched by the law of God, to the exent of her receptive capacity, which was limited. Paul reminds us that our capacity is unlimited, and we must be conscious of it.

Let us practice removing every limitation, which we have been prone to put upon ourselves, either as to receiving or disbursing. We do not need to depend upon our neighbors for our increase, the Lord within us is our support, who shall limit us?

TREATMENT IV. "MY CUP RUNNETH OVER."

Meditation. In the temporal prosperity which comes from worldly methods, it is considered good judgment to gauge the amount of one's spending by the extent of one's income; and that is good sense, when one has a material basis of prosperity.

But the spiritual law is stated, "With what measure ye mete, it shall be measured unto you." "Give, and it shall be given unto you." In other words, learn to spend. Not recklessly, nor in a meaningless way, but with the wisdom of one who is being educated to disseminate riches like seed, breaking down fear and sense of limitation, and cultivating faith and consciousness of the all capacity in one.

To illustrate, one may start out to buy a garment for $20, but finds one just suitable for $25. In the old way of thinking the extra $5 would debar that garment from one, although the money might lie in the purse. If then, from trust in the Divine Bounty, the extra amount is paid, the purchaser will not be lacking in that sum of $5, but on the contrary, will have entered into a new current of receptivity, and, if alert, will be able to see the unexpected increase, when it comes, in obedience to the great law.

When one intends to make a gift of money, according to a certain amount, and then mentally lessens it, he is lessening his own receiving capacity. A homely illustration of this law is the good milch cow, that, as long as all she has to give is taken from her, keeps up her capacity of receiving, but if her milker, in a foolish moment, should think to save her by not stripping her milk, she would give him that much less next time, even though he milked her dry.

Practice distributing freely because of trust in your unlimited Source of Supply.

Listen to me! You have the capacity to receive all riches and you disburse them by inspiration and wisdom. It is nothing to you how mortals feel about the times. You are not under the law of limitation. The income and the outgo are perfectly balanced. The more comes in, the more you spend and the more you spend the more comes in. The more you spend the more comes in.

You gauge your own capacity. No one can limit you. You enlarge your horizon of expenditure.

The best is none too good for you, You are a prince with God. Our Father is rich. His children are a credit to his bounty.

You find no fault. You make no complaint. You never whine. You blame no one. You are not a beggar. You are not a dependent. You are cheery and free. You are courageous. You are a magnet to draw your own. No one loses, who gives to you. Everyone gains by prospering you. And they know it. And they know it.

You live in the realm of Love, where giving freely, and receiving graciously, is the law. The commercial belief cannot influence you; it cannot use you or bind you. You do your best at all times. You give yourself to the Divinity in all. Your work calls forth rich appreciation, which takes form as money, and the things the world values.

Make channels for your divine prosperity. Make channels for Love to express itself through you. Love and eternal prosperity are one and they are yours now.

Where others give pennies, you give nickels; where others give nickels, you give quarters; where others give quarters, you give dollars.

"Make channels for the streams of Love,

Where they may broadly run;

And Love has overflowing streams,

To fill them every one.

For we must share, if we would keep

That blessing from above.

Ceasing to give, we cease to have,

Such is the law of Love."

XI. The Age of Miracles Still Here

Magical laws are to be found in the realm of spiritual prosperity, and when their operations are not viewed with superstition, or as miraculous, in the sense of doing violence to natural law, they will be more frequently seen. Moses received and understood these laws, both from his Egyptian tutors, the soothsayers and magicians of Pharaoh, and from his spiritual Instructor, great Jehovah.

It is for us to prove that our supply is not fixed by the Rule of Three, but, there is a living principle back of our silver and our gold, that is one with God, and to touch it, is to open a way by which our material supply will increase, as seeds will sprout if the right elements are brought to them.

In the booklet, The Quiet Hour, by S. D. Gordon, published by Fleming H. Revell Co., New York City, there is a story of miraculous increase, of which the following is a condensed account. It is called

FINNISH GOLD STORY. "It was a winter's night up in Stockholm. The evening meeting was over, and a number of Christian friends were gathered about the supper table. We were talking as we ate, of our experiences of God's goodness. One lady present was induced to tell through interpretation, a story of the unusual experience of a friend of hers in Finland.

It was about a woman who had to pay an unjust bill for lumber used in building a little chapel. She hadn't money enough; all efforts to get more failed; legal action threatened; then during prayer the money in her little treasure box increased in amount until there was enough to pay the claim. That is the bones of the story.

It quite startled every one who heard it. Such a thing was unheard of in modern times. And doubt was freely expressed by some of the most earnest and thoughtful ones present. The doubt was not of God's power to do such a thing, but of the accuracy of the story. The woman in her excitement must have made a mistake. Some friend was secretly helping, it was thought. Was she used to counting money? Was the box locked up so that no one else could get access to it? She was probably a good woman, but rather excitable. So question and comment ran.

As I listened to the story, then to the comments, I thought that if it were true and our friend who told it to us, and who personally knew the woman in it, seemed quite assured herself of its being so it should not be told until it could be thoroughly verified, but that if it could indeed be verified, it should be told, and told widely."

Here the author tells of how he and his wife prayed, that, if the story were true, they might be led to Finland and meet the woman and speak in the little chapel. It is exceedingly interesting to read of how the Spirit opened the way, so that they went to the village and were with the woman two days, having an excellent interpreter, who also came in answer to prayer.

The woman is the postmistress of the village, or rather railroad junction, a very important post which she has occupied over twenty years. It is a position of great responsibility, as there are no banks in Finland and much money passes through the mails. Something like $800,000 passed through her hands some years.

"Her books were as carefully kept as any bank account books I have ever examined in my earlier banking days; not only with painstaking accuracy, but with neatness of a skilled accountant. This seems sufficient answer to the comments I heard when the story was told in Stockholm."

There was need of a chapel, and the woman, a quiet, unassuming body, undertook to lead and be responsible for its building. Free-will offerings constituted the supply. While the building was going on, there came a bill for lumber, which had been bought and received. But the charge was larger than it should have been. With the bill came a peremptory demand for immediate payment of the money, $150, threatening legal proceedings. It is customary in Finland to provide long credit, and the chapel funds were not equal to that payment. The people were poor, and there had been much opposition on the part of the Church people to the chapel being built.

She made every effort to get the money, but it was all fruitless. The final time of payment drew near. She made one last journey to a near-by town. "The man she hoped to see was abroad; his wife thought she ought not to have begun building till she had the money."

On her way back, as she was in prayer, a thought came to her that had been coming, more or less, all through this trial. It was of how Jesus increased the loaves and fishes. She thought, "God can touch my slender chapel funds and do as in the desert, make them sufficient for the need."

"On her return home, as soon as she could get time from her work, she went to the drawer to get the little box where the chapel funds were kept. She had counted the money before that last journey and she found she had just $70 (350 marks in Finnish money)." She had $18 of her own. She was all alone, and she poured the money on the table and put her own meager store with it, and covering it with her hands, prayed in simple childlike language:

"Lord Jesus bless Thy money as Thou dist bless the loaves in the wilderness. I will put my loaves too in Thy hands, and do Thou let them, with Thine, meet this need; let this money cover the amount of this bill."

Then she counted the money, and it was exactly 751 marks ($150) and she noticed there was now much gold, though there had not been much gold in the box.

She sent word to the collector that he could come for the money. Before he arrived she again spread the money out to count it, this time feeling an impulse to take out her own little store of 90 marks ($18) and the remainder amounted again to the 751 marks ($150). With a heart overflowing with thanksgiving she awaited the collector.

When he came she told him her wonderful experience, and he was much moved. As the money was counted again before him, there were a few silver coins over, and the bill was duly paid, and the officer gave her the receipt.

The author goes into many details, to show the unmistakable character of the wonder-work, and gives it as a message from the prayer-answering God.

The law that was fulfilled in this increase, can be known with the same exactness, with which we understand the laws of the telephone; and scientific men are preparing to study these laws, with the same zeal and profound passion of the devoted astronomers, who have sought out, and found the laws of the planets.

TREATMENT V. GODLINESS, THE SUBSTANCE OF RICHES

Meditation. "He shall be like a tree planted by the rivers of water, that bringeth forth his fruit in his season; his leaf also shall not wither; and whatsoever he doeth shall prosper" (Ps. 1:3). Thus is the godly man described a*s to his good fortune.

There are certain of us, who did not come into this existence "with a silver spoon in our mouths." It seems to us, that all our goodness has been fruitless, that fate is against us, and that there is no use trying.

If we have started this life like bankrupt men, then there must be the more resolution and determination, and a courage that knows no defeat.

The law of Christ, like the laws of bankruptcy, removes the past burdens and debts that destiny (or karma) may have loaded upon our infant shoulders. No matter what bad luck may have seemed to be ours from birth, this day we come under the law of our Christ-self, and believe in the God-promise that our Goodness shall take tangible form, here and now.

Exercise a patience, that is one with Absolute Trust, and never, even in the secret of your own chamber, acknowledge the slowness or the failure, as real or lasting.

The treasures that you have laid up in heaven the within are destined to take form as the treasures of earth. With most people, they do not appear until another incarnation, when they are said "to be born with a silver spoon in their mouth." You do not need to wait for another incarnation, but your goodness of today can be expressed here and now, in this incarnation, as overflowing plenteousness of the world's goods.

Listen to me, O! Offspring of pure Goodness! You know how to bring forth into this world all the goodness there is in you.

The Spirit instructs you in what ways to express your Love. It takes universal form, overflowing to all.

Your magnetic quality is irresistible. Humanity loves to bask in the sunshine of your presence. Its value is high. There is a market for it everywhere.

Your Goodness overflows in generous service to all.

Your Goodness draws forth Goodness.

Your talent is uncovered and appreciated with financial expressions.

Your ingenuity and power of invention come to the fore.

You are invaluable to humanity.

Your Goodness makes others feel good. Your generosity makes others generous. You are a seed in the soil of Richness, drawing whatever prospers you, to yourself. You flourish like the lilies of the field without care or fear, without anxiety or hard work. You are a law unto yourself. You are independent of man-made laws, of personalities, of corporations and of systems. These serve you and bless you, but cannot enslave you. You look to One only as the source of your Prosperity.

You are self-made, made by the One Self Creator of all. You are not vain-glorious, no mortal pride can trip you up ^* no mistake of the past can keep you down. No foolish pride can keep you from your own. You have Self-respect, not pride ^* and you hold your head up, and keep your back straight, and your step firm.

Nothing can discourage you. The wrong-doings of others cannot make you bitter. The successes of others cannot make you envious. You radiate the Goodness of God.

You are an ever-flowing fountain of resourcefulness. You are in connection with the Fountain-Head on High. You are the power of God, to translate divine, invisible substance, into tangible, visible forms.

Your faith is unlimited because it is based on reason and knowledge. You can do all things by the God-power in you. Divine Wisdom guides you, you are kept from folly. You do not waste yourself, your time, your substance or your life. Good judgment attends you ever. Divine Intelligence keeps you from foolish ways and foolish things. Inspiration lifts you out of all entanglements and sets your feet firm in Wisdom's Ways.

Your gentle goodness cannot be preyed upon. It is one with the Lamb of God and no wolf of commercial greed can seize you. The folly of others cannot deceive you. Deceitful words and deeds cannot move you. You cannot be ensnared by greed or ignorance. No one's craftiness can beguile you. You are true to yourself, and your trueness defends you.

The Goodness of God fills your whole life. Goodness fills and covers all that is yours. All that you put your hand to, prospers. All that you touch turns to riches. Surely goodness and mercy shall follow you all the days of your life and you shall dwell in the house of the Lord forever.

IT IS ESTABLISHED.

XII. Jesus Christ in the Business Man

On the matter of business, Jesus Christ gave many directions and much teaching. For Jesus Christ was very practical, coming to a people that were masters of finance, many of them, yet missing the main thing; and, on the other hand, eagerly zealous in righteousness and good works, but making a failure financially. He taught the Way that is One, for both these extremes.

He knew there was but one business for everybody, who had come to this earth -his heavenly Father's business, i. e., to bear witness to the Truth, prove oneself immortal and divine, and make heaven on earth for one's neighbor. He made his disciples successful fishermen, and then said, "Come, I will make you fishers of men." So now, Jesus Christ in you will make you a success where you are, and at the same time call you to gather men and women into the Kingdom.

"I will make you builders of men's character and health and happiness," he says to the carpenters and contractors and others who are constructing.

"I will make you promoters of men's spiritual nature," he says to those who are developing business, and earth's products.

"I will make you feeders of men's souls, and clothiers that bring forth bodies worthy of God's children."

"I will make you bankers of men, laying up saved men as gold."

What greater work can be done for the Kingdom of Heaven, than making a success in the business life, and proving to men that you did it by the power of the Holy Spirit within you!

You cannot serve God and mammon at the same time. You have proven it. You cannot give your whole heart to mammon. You have a Conscience that no man can kill, either in you, or in himself. He may drug it with sophistries for years, and even think he has no Conscience; but he will find his mistake. For Conscience is simply one's knowing, the exercise of one's Supreme Intelligence, and it will not down. It is immortal.

People grow rich with a quasi-worship of mammon. They do unscrupulous things for a long time, and think they can bluff their great Soul-Self. But they only fool themselves. Their wealth is as sand and ashes in their mouth. Something has been missed.

Better to be a lamb, thrown from one wolfs maw to another, imposed upon, fleeced again and again, than to win riches at the expense of that tender, holy, rich love-nature, that eventuates in the Eternal Joy which is independent of time and space.

But it is possible to keep the Lamb-quality, and receive all the powers and substance that are now owned and exploited by the wolves. Jesus Christ has given the Way and by the Holy Spirit, one may gather together all his teachings about prosperity, and the records of his deeds, which especially relate to the way to succeed, and use this masterly key into the Kingdom of Eternal Wealth.

Jesus did not despise either money or business. He appointed a treasurer for the disciples, in Judas. He taught them to "gather up the fragments that remain, that nothing be lost," he taught them not to be slack.

But he inculcated a new value sense. He told the money-loving Pharisees, that " that which is highly esteemed among men is abomination in the sight of God." "For what is a man advantaged if he gain the whole world and lose himself?" he said. Like another Alexander, who at the age of thirty had conquered the whole world, and yet died in a drunken bout.

He paid tribute to Caesar and to the synagogue, using occult laws by which to procure the money.

But the plainest teaching of all was when, on two occasions, he directed his disciples, who had been toiling all night at their fisheries without success, just where to drop their nets, so as to make hauls that would soon, if repeated a few times, make a man rich.

Jesus did not hesitate to use his deeper senses to promote earthly prosperity. He had the true business sense, which comes by the Holy Spirit. And this Master stands in your heart today, and if you will hear his Voice and be guided. by his principles, you shall be the fulfillment of the great promises: "Delight thyself in the Lord; and he shall give thee the desires of thine heart," "they that seek the Lord shall not want any good thing."

TREATMENT VI. CHRIST IN ME, MY PROSPERING POWER

Listen to me! The Christ in you is your clear insight, your true business sense, and your inspired guidance into success.

You are in business to save the world. Your integrity pervades your whole world. It directs your vision to the region of richness. Jesus Christ in you superintends all your investments, affairs and dealings.

You work for the Kingdom of God alone. This is your first concern. You are enthusiastic in your Way of working. The Holy Spirit infuses you with a new imagination about your affairs. You are initiative. You are original. You find new ways to serve humanity. You discover the wealth producing regions of the earth. You uncover the most valuable powers in human beings.

You save other men in their business. By the Christ in you, you point out the Way they can be prospered. You give freely any counsel or discovery that will prosper others. No commercialism can interfere with your inspiration. The Spirit protects you from greed and imposition.

Jesus Christ in you reveals the errors to be removed, that you may be receptive to all wealth. You put your hand to the Christ-plough, and you do not look back. You banish all memory of losses. You do not meditate upon losses of any kind. You spend no time in grieving. You deliberately forget all mistakes your own as well as others. You give all appearances of weakness, poor judgment, vices, ignorance, folly and ill-luck into the care of the Holy Spirit.

You practice the presence of God. You remember to meditate upon the godlike thing to do. You do what Jesus Christ would do. You are Jesus Christ in the business world. You preach the good news of the Way to prosper forever. You preach silently, by your life, by your methods, by your character.

The Inspired One in you uncovers the Secret laws of increase and transmutation. You have the holy Divining- Art. You know the way to find gold in the bowels of the earth. You know the place of the watersprings. The elements yield you their secrets. Yon are the irresistible conqueror of the planet. Everything yields you its best, by the Law of Love. You are the Lover of All, and draw to you all the gifts of Love.

You sit still in the Christ-consciousness and all the ends of the earth seek you to serve you and bless you. You are at peace with all and the satisfaction of the Richest Being in the universe centers in you and showers blessings through you upon the whole world. "

Serene I fold my hands and wait,

Nor care for wind, or tide, or sea;

I rave no more 'gainst time or fate,

For lo! my own shall come to me.

The waters know their own, and draw

The brook that springs in yonder height;

So flows the good, with equal law

Unto the soul of pure delight.

The stars come nightly to the sky,

The tidal wave unto the sea;

Nor time, nor space, nor deep, nor high.

Can keep my own away from me.

BOOK FIVE.
ALL THINGS ARE POSSIBLE TO THEM THAT BELIEVE

I. ALL THINGS ARE POSSIBLE TO THEM THAT BELIEVE

WHEN the disciples of Jesus asked, "What must we do that we may work the works of God?" all the reply that Jesus gave was, "Believe," and this was the substance of all his instruction. Set your thoughts in a certain direction; make your mind to hold thoughts that believe in the Good as possible. That is all that is necessary for us to do to increase our belief, to extend the boundaries of what we believe to be possible.

All that we are now is the result of our believing; every action and word shows forth what we have been believing, and are now holding in mind.

When you life down at night you believe you will arise in the morning; when you walk, every step you take you do so through the exercise of faith, believing that you will be supported: so all things that you do are simply pictures of your faith, or what you are believing in.

Your powers of believing are exercised in three ways: by thinking, by speaking, by doing. Thought is the causative power, words and deeds are the fruit of your thinking.

Keep the thoughts upon believing in the Good, and your words and deeds will conform to your thoughts. These should be one and the same always. It is not enough to think aright, but also we must speak aright, and act aright. When you are trying to believe in the reality of the presence of your desire, do not let the lips speak as though there were any other presence than Good. See that all your words and deeds are consistent with your thoughts.

"What things soever ye desire, when ye pray, believe that ye receive them."

What things soever. That is, it makes no difference for what you ask; if you will believe, you shall receive.

But if you are doubting in your heart as to whether God is willing you should receive, then indeed you will not receive. Have no doubt in your mind of God's willingness to give you any good thing that you would give yourself. Jesus taught us to think that God is just as willing to give us good gifts as is any earthly father. If you, as a child, were asking yourself, as a father, for any good thing, and the father in you would be willing to grant you that which you ask, then you must also think God is willing to give you what you desire. Cannot the same power that grants you your wish protect you from any evil that might seem to come through receiving the good you desire? Have no doubt of any kind in the heart, no doubt of the reasonableness of your request or whether it is good in God's eyes, no doubt of God's willingness to give — " for verily I say unto you, That whosoever shall say unto this mountain. Be thou removed, and be thou cast into the sea; and shall not doubt in his heart, but shall believe that those things which he saith shall come to pass; he shall have whatsoever he saith."

Our faith must be such that it cannot be moved by appearances, and it must persist when impossibilities seem to face us. (^'Lord, I believe; help thou my unbelief " is our prayer, and it means, put away from us all doubt, all distrust, all discouragement, and establish us in the belief in the presence of All-Good.,

There was once a woman who demonstrated just what was the belief that we must have in order to get the answer to our prayer. It is said of her that she was blind — totally without sight. She heard of a man whose prayers were healing all for whom he prayed, and when she heard of him a strong faith arose in her heart that his prayer would heal her. Her faith was stupendous, and so strongly did it possess her soul that at last she said that she must go to him. He lived in a town some miles distant — an obscure shoemaker plying his trade daily, and praying for all who asked him. She went to him with a heart strong in the belief that immediately after his prayer she would see. He prayed. She opened her eyes fully expecting to see, but she did not. She was amazed, stunned — she could not understand it.

She left the shoemaker in a dazed state of mind, pondering over the Master's words, "Whatsoever things ye desire, pray, believing, and ye shall receive." All the long journey home she tried to find wherein her faith had been lacking, when suddenly she realized that her believing had found its limit because of appearances, and she had held it only because of something that was to come by it, whereas she must have faith no matter what the appearances, and not be moved. So she determined to believe that God had healed her, and she would hold to the thought "I can see" forever, and never let appearances move her from believing that God had given her her sight.

She went home, and was met by her expectant family, to whose inquiry she answered, ** I can see," and great was their rejoicing. But soon they saw she was just the same after her return as before she went to the healer.

To their questions as to why she said such things when she did not manifest sight, she replied, *' I am following my Master's instructions to believe that I have received what I desire, and I shall never speak or act contrary to what I am determined to believe." So she went on, and would never let any one speak to her, or act toward her as though she were blind. At times it seemed almost more than she could do, but never would she be moved, she declared, if she had to go on believing against appearances all the rest of her natural life. At times the family feared her mind had been affected, and she had much to do to withstand their fears for her sanity.

One night not very long after her return home, as she was lying in bed thinking upon her determination to believe in spite of all opposition, suddenly there was a glimmer before her eyes. She leaped up in bed and cried, " I see! indeed, I see! Bring a light, for I do see." The family thought, "Now she has gone crazy." But they brought the light, and she proved then and there that she saw, and she has been seeing ever since.

That was the faith she had to manifest — to know no limit to her faith; no appearances could cause her to doubt, or to let disappointment or discouragement possess her and displace her beautiful faith. (If you have asked God for anything and you have not received, do not think God refuses it to you. No, the only trouble is you have not asked aright. "Ye ask, and receive not, because ye ask amiss." God has not heard you, for it is written, " God heareth not sinners " — that is. He hears not mistaken prayers.

Do not stop praying, but change your prayers. Pray without ceasing, pray in every right way you can think of; at last you will speak the words that reach God, the words that are the substance out of which the answer to your prayer is made. For this is true: Out of your own words are formed the manifestation you desire to show forth.

Never give up praying — ^never give up believing in the possibility of having that which you desire. "Increase our faith." Increase our beliefs in the possibility of all good things being now manifest. Break down the boundaries of our belief. No matter how great our faith may seem to be, make it a little greater, and then look out that our words and actions are consistent with what we are determined to believe.

All things are possible to him that will believe

" He that believeth on me, the works that I do shall he do also."

This is the whole doctrine of Jesus: Believe,

As you will believe, so it is unto you. As a man believeth in his heart, so is he.

II. THOU SHALT DECREE

Thou shalt also decree a thing, and it shall be established unto thee, — Job xxii: 28.

All the good that is to be manifest in a man's life is already an accomplished fact in the divine Mind.

The knowledge of God cannot be added to nor taken away from, and He knows all that is to be as that which always has been, and is now the complete Truth of Being.

It lies with Man to call into manifestation that which already is an absolute and established creation in God.

Man is the image and likeness of God, therefore he is spiritual and perfect. He, in his true being, works after the same manner as God. Inspiration tells us that God creates all things by the Word of his mouth, that He says "Be," and it is so.

Man, the Son of God, does all things as he sees his Father do, and what he decrees comes to pass. When he decrees healing, health springs forth speedily; when he speaks "Life," deadness disappears; when he declares the powerlessness of wickedness, vice melts to uselessness before his word.

Because his inspiration is not from flesh and blood (Matt, xvi: 17) but from the Father within he has the key to Heaven, and he decrees a thing to come to pass upon the earth that has already been determined upon in Heaven, in accordance with the Christ prophecy: " And I will give unto thee the keys of the kingdom of the heavens; and whatsoever thou mayest bind upon the earth shall have been bound in the heavens, and whatsoever thou mayest loose upon the earth shall have been loosed in the heavens " (Matt, xvi: 19, Rotherham's translation).

In ancient times the disciple who was instructed into the arcana of Egyptian magic was told at a certain stage in his development how to accomplish his wishes and do wonder-works by pronouncing the two little words: "It is," He was taught to lead a very pure and unselfish life of self-control that he might always know the will of the gods and conform all his wishes thereto.

The man who seeks no will but the Will of the Great God of all can declare concerning any of his desires "/< is" and his words will come true, for his will is omnipotent. "He doeth according to his will in the army of heaven, and among the inhabitants of the earth: and none can stay his hand" (Dan. iv: 35).

"The will of the just man is the will of God." It is the desire of every just man that you shall have perfect health. It is the wish of good men and women that you shall be free from debt, and live in comfortable circumstances. Every true heart desires you to be pure and loving, intelligent and free. It is the will of God that you shall manifest every quality and condition on the earth that belong to the Kingdom of Heaven. "... God our Saviour; who will have all men to be saved, and to come unto the knowledge of the truth" (1Tim.ii:3,4).

To every such true and good wish of your heart say: "It is."

"Then when you have thus decreed your Good, begin to conduct yourself in speech and action as though you had already received it, and it was apparent to the eyes of all.

For your Word of decree is just like a seed which you have put into the ground, and all that you need to do is to keep it from being trampled upon by doubts and fears and worry, and to see that the sun and dew of an active faith nourish it until it come to fruition. "And he said. So is the kingdom of God, as if a man should cast seed into the ground; and should sleep, and rise night and day, and the seed should spring and grow up, he knoweth not how. For the earth bringeth forth fruit of herself; first the blade, then the ear, after that the full com in the ear. But when the fruit is brought forth, immediately he putteth in the sickle, because the harvest is come" (Mark iv: 26-29).

The tongue that can decree effectually never voices an evil wish. Its words are upon the good, the beautiful, and the true. It does not describe disease, for " the tongue of the wise is health" (Pro v. xii: 18). It does not linger on accounts of death, accidents, poverty, or sins, for its words are precious, since they are to bring to pass the Kingdom of Heaven in our midst.

" They that observe lying vanities forsake their own mercy" (Jonah ii: 8).

"Speak ye every man the truth to his neighbor; ... and let none of you imagine evil in your hearts against his neighbor" (Zech. viii: 16, 17).

" Thou shalt not bear false witness against thy neighbor " is fulfilled as we do not hear witness to the false in our neighbor, but talk only of the true. The object of this commandment is to train the speech of the aspirant to heavenly powers so that his words will never curse the earth, but every word, though not a conscious decree, shall bless by simply being uttered.

"By the establishment of truthfulness, the yogi gets the power of attaining for himself and others the fruits of work without the works" (Yoga Aphorisms of Patanjali), and commenting upon this Swami Vivekananda says: " When this power of truth will be established with you, then even in dream you will never tell an untruth; in thought, word or deed, whatever you say will be truth. You may say to a man ' Be blessed,' and that man will be blessed. If a man is diseased, and you say to him, ' Be thou cured,' he will be cured immediately."

"So shall my word be that goeth forth out of my mouth: it shall not return unto me void, but it shall accomplish that which I please, and it shall prosper in the thing whereto I sent it " (Is. Iv: 11).

"If ye abide in me, and my words abide in you, ye shall ask what ye will, and it shall be done unto you. Herein is my Father glorified, that ye bear much fruit; so shall ye be my disciples " (John xv: 7, 8).

Dwell continually in the consciousness of being the Son of the Most High, and let your mouth be filled with good words, both audible and silent. Then glorify God by bringing forth fruits of healing of yourself and others, of sinless living, of peace, prosperity, and happiness for all through your silent, immutable decrees.

You are God's Living Decree of Good to this world. Let your light shine. " Thou shall decree," See this as a commandment, as imperative as any one of the Decalogue.

And God said, Let them have dominion over the earth. The hour cometh, and now is, when divine man, he that overcomes, takes to himself his mighty prerogatives, and whatever he wishes he brings to pass by pronouncing the magical words

BOOK SIX.
SPIRITUAL HOUSEKEEPING

INTRODUCTION

IT has been claimed by certain occult teachers that one cannot advance in spiritual life so long as one is in business or in any way engaged in material affairs. This is one of those half-truths that so often discourage the young student and cause him to take fanatical steps or utterly abandon the pursuit of the spiritual life through believing it is not for him.

It is true that one who is given over to money-getting or mentally enslaved to drudgery cannot expect to attain heavenly heights. Indeed, he is not seeking such attainment. But the one who does desire it should realize that he can begin just where he is, and can make his work a mighty means of advancement, turning it from being a hindrance into a stepping-stone. His mind must be set right regarding his work until all sense of its burden and materiality has passed away, and those features in it that are untrue, dishonest, and unworthy of a man of God have been redeemed.

Man decides the nature of work, making it noble or degrading according to his attitude in it and toward it. Any work that is for the good of humanity, even the most menial, can be elevated by the workman who serves the divine One in all.

The following talks upon housework and its meaning in the spiritual life apply to all manner of work. The topic, Housekeeping, is chosen to make the application less abstract, but those who can read between the lines can see themselves all housekeepers, men as well as women; the women of leisure as well as the busy housewives, all keepers of the temple of God. Your body is your house; your mentality is your garden; your character is your earth. All these are subject to your spirit, the Master of the House.

In this temple-house of God your thoughts and feelings as well as the members of your body can hold devotional services daily by doing all things for the Lord only. There is no piece of work but what may be a sacrament and an opportunity for bringing forward the high and holy One who is on His way proving Himself All in All.

As this study upon concentration is presented under the headings of the days of the week a word as to the significance of this division of time will not be amiss.

The formation of the seven-day week, while having a certain natural cause in the changing phases of the moon, these have been arbitrarily numbered four, whereas there could be as many phases as a compass has points), is essentially religious, and symbolizes a perfect round of devotion. Among the pagans the days were consecrated to the gods of the seven planets: Sun, Moon, Mars, Jupiter, Mercury, Venus, and Saturn, but among the Israelites, the God-illumined people, they were devoted to the One.

It is ancient teaching that there are seven aspects of Deity (the seven spirits or angels) and that Man, as the image of God, is a sevenfold being. The Bible teems with symbols of seven in connection with God, from the seven days of Genesis to the seven angels of Revelation.

When the seer who gave us the account of creation in Genesis described his vision he presented the different manifestations or aspects of God's presence in the terms of days of the week. These are given as sequential stages, but spiritual perception reveals God as ever creating or manifesting Himself in all His aspects simultaneously, as seven rays of light are flashed at once from a fixed star. The old belief that God created a world in a week and then abandoned it to its fate, as a clockmaker might do with a clock, is passing away, and spiritual reasoning portrays the omnipresent changeless God as ever manifesting His wholeness throughout eternity.

Each day of the seven is a period of illumination from and upon one of the aspects of our divinity. Therefore to fill a week with right meditation is to have a rounded period of enlightenment concerning one's own true Being.

For this reason a week of concentration practices is described. Continuation in these practices must eventually reveal the Supreme Master enthroned within the devotee, who, when acknowledged and obeyed will keep the mind poised and strong in perfect power of concentration without effort and finally without practice.

Annie Rix Militz.

Sierra Madre, California. January, 1910.

THE FIRST DAY. Sunday— Rest Day

THIS is the day of beginnings, wherein we take a fresh start. " Old things are passed away; behold, I make all things new." It is the resurrection day, this Sabbath of the Christians, and it was chosen to take the place of the old Jewish Sabbath for the benefit of the early Christian converts, who still clung to the idea that one day must be esteemed especially holy, and could not receive the liberty of the Christ, who knows all days to be alike holy.

The seventh day was the Sabbath of the old dispensation; the first day is the Sabbath of the new. This day will continue to be set apart so long as men feel work to be a burden and a curse, and so long as men work for something and some one else besides the ideal. But to him who has found the truth that work is joy, and activity which blesses others is ever divine, there is no need of a special day of rest, for he rests in working, never knowing weariness or bondage.

"The sabbath was made for man, and not man for the sabbath " (Mark ii, 27), and was intended from the first to be a reminder to man that " there remaineth a rest for him," a final attainment of perpetual rest in the midst of, and one with, ceaseless activity— the divine paradox, identity of rest and activity.

The spiritual quality for which each day stands permeates and fills all the other days in the well-ordered, harmonious life. The Sunday is the day of serenity, stillness, poise, repose, and these qualities in truth overshadow and bless all the week days.

Sunday's word is Peace. " Thou wilt keep him in perfect peace, whose mind is stayed on thee, because he trusteth in thee " (Is. xxvi, 3). " For thus saith the Lord God, the Holy One of Israel: In returning and rest shall ye be saved; in quietness and confidence is your strength " (Is. xxx, 15).

Early Sunday morning let us fill our hearts with meditation upon Peace, and let the thought run all through our week that all our activities shall begin with Peace. The first practice of right concentration is the stilling of the mind. The human mentality is like a mirror whose reflections can be perfect only as the mirror is still; or like a lake, which must be smooth and still, without a ripple, in order to reflect the objects upon its surface.

Sabbath stillness should begin every day— not planning and hurrying with sense of so much to do and so little time to do it in. Five minutes with this Truth of God, that all things are now done and finished in the divine Mind; that there is nothing to do, no one to set right, no problems to solve, will work like a charm upon your faculties, and, instead of being tired even when you begin your day, everything will work so smoothly, fairly " doing themselves," that when evening comes you will be just as fresh as you were in the morning, and you will lay your head upon your pillow like a baby, which has no sense of weariness, but only readiness for refreshing

Let us remember:

Every day is a fresh beginning,

Every morn is the world made new.

The great Creator of all that really is ever creates and manifests true Being, which is bright and fresh and new; nothing is stale or dull in God's world. This source of your originality, invention, and skill is your divinity. " All things were made by him; and without him was not anything made that was made" (John i,3).

"And God saw everything that he had made, and behold, it was very good " (Gen. i, 31). From these statements of Scripture we logically conclude that that which is not good is not really made— all that offends, the corrupt, the decaying, the ugly and the inharmonious are outside the realm of the true (Matt, xiii, 41).

The newness of God's kingdom we indicate by arraying ourselves in new, fresh garments on Sunday, and while we don these our silent prayer can be worded, "Behold! I make all things new." New garments typify new minds, new hearts, new bodies. The New Man of the resurrection is the theme for concentration on the First Day of this holy week— the new creature whose formation or regeneration is not with striving and hard work, but in peace and by inspiration.

Sunday is the day of light and brightness, as the name signifies. Sabbaths are a thing of the past, " an abomination unto me; . . . even the solemn meetings" (Is.i,i3).

Each day of the week is named after a god who it was believed presided over a planet. Sunday is the day of the sun, Monday, the day of the moon, Saturday, the day of Saturn. In our meditations we will sail our mental ships upon the current of these ancient beliefs, for even our work of to-day is arranged along the lines of these pagan devotions. And we will take these symbols out of the darkness and superstition of paganism into the light of truth. Thus, the sun stands for the one God, the universal Good, who is the real light of the world. 11 Ye are the light of the world," the sun of righteousness with healing in its beams.

Sunday's work is like the shining of the sun, which fructifies and blesses by simply being, without strife or effort. So the inspiration and the joy of truth redeem us from the curse associated with work, and all we do is accomplished by the divine One within us. " My Father worketh hitherto, and I work."

"Sanctify my Sabbaths." We fulfill the spirit of the fourth commandment by making every day holy unto the Lord, knowing it is lawful to do good every day, and that all days are the Lord's Day. Like yeast in the flour, so shall the ideal day of union between rest and work leaven all the days. Already here is a perpetual Sabbath observed the world around, for Christians worship God on Sunday, Grecian zealots hallow Monday, Tuesday, Persians spend in prayer, Assyrians, Wednesday revere. Egyptians, Thursday; Friday, Turks, On Saturday, no Hebrew works.

But as the true worshipers worship God in Spirit and in truth every day of the week so the First Day simply becomes a time to express that worship in a certain way, the Second Day in another way, and so on through the Sacred Seven.

The true holy day is a holiday, a time for recreation, a time to realize the innocence of pleasure, and to know that all real enjoyment is spiritual. Knowledge of Truth enters us into the Spirit of work and play alike, and then whatever we do glorifies God and honors man. It is said that Jesus, one day, seeing a man working on the Sabbath, said to him, " Man, if thou knowest what thou doest, blessed art thou. But if thou knowest not what thou doest, cursed art thou, and a transgressor of the law." Paul expresses somewhat of the same idea, " Happy is he who condemneth not himself in that thing which he alloweth " (Rom. xiv, 22).

Throughout Sunday let your practice of concentration be serenity, oneness of mind; let a radiance of peace fill your aura. Excitable natures often find it difficult to concentrate; such should consciously have a Sabbatical some part of every day.

'A lady who was all wrought up one day in the midst of moving out of a house while some one else was moving in at the same time, and whose goods must be removed within a short space of time, recognized that she had reached the place where distraction and confusion were holding carnival in her mentality, and deliberately she dropped everything, and calmly sat down in the midst of the confusion, and for five minutes withdrew her mind utterly from her surroundings, turning to the Spirit with the words, " Thou wilt keep him in perfect peace whose mind is stayed on thee." The rest and recuperation of those five minutes were beyond description. She arose a new woman, with fresh powers, and her whole work was transformed.

You whose muscles become tense, whose nerves get on edge, relax often, let go, remember your divine Being, as you silently and slowly breathe these words: " The serene, calm, restful, trustful Self now accomplishes everything in and through me perfectly and without effort."

Look not into the future, dwell not upon the past. The present is the only time with Spirit. Train your thoughts to remain in the present and not stand a-tiptoe peering into the future, and hopping about from one worn-out subject to another. Then your plans will come through your prophetic sense, then your reviews will have a profitable bearing upon the present. Dignity and majesty mark the nature whose power of concentration is perfect. Get withal childlike and simple, with a joy that gives no reason for being— plasticity and stability united.

Let the endless sabbath of your soul baptize your whole being and give a holy gladness to every day of the year.

THE SECOND DAY. Monday— Freedom Day

MONDAY is the day of the moon, shown in the derivation of the word not only in the English language, but also in the French, Landi, and the German, Montag. It therefore belongs to the traditions of our ancestors that this day, being devoted to the goddess who presided over the moon and thence over the waters of the earth, is the lucky day upon which to engage in the employments associated with water. Hence, Monday, the world around, is " wash day." It is a scientific fact that the waters of the great oceans are governed by the moon, as demonstrated in the tides, and the alchemists held that the very moisture of the human body came under its influence.

And now we come to the significance of water, and to that of which we can be reminded every Monday in our concentration practice.

Water symbolizes the great negative power of the Spirit, the power of annulling and destroying evil. Water has had an important part in the rites of all the is great religions, as witness the baptisms, holy water, and feet-washings of the Christians, the lustrations of the Essenes, the sacred baths of the Hindus, the purification waters of the Hebrews.

Water stands for the loosening, cleansing, and freeing power of Truth. The denials of Christian metaphysics have this effect, and mental washing is accomplished by the free use of the word of denial.

The affirmations of Truth, such as " God the Good is all there is," and " I am one with God, therefore I am spiritual and immortal, pure and perfect Being," and "All the presence and power there is is Health, Love, Life,

Wisdom, Peace, and Prosperity," have the effect of establishing and confirming our consciousness in and of Truth. But sometimes false beliefs are in the way, and it is needful that they be removed in order to make room for the grand affirmations of Spirit.

An old untrue supposition about life is like an old building that stands upon the ground where we desire to construct a new one. To attempt to realize these new true statements of life while still clinging to our old views is like trying to erect a new building over the old. Certain students of Truth have attempted this, and then they wonder why their affirmations do not heal and bring them their desires.

Let us learn to clear out the old accumulations of false thoughts by the right use of denials. Good judgment must be exercised with the words of denial, just as the good laundress has common sense in the use of water. Some denial statements are strong, such as " There is no evil," " There is no personality," " There is no matter," and the effect is often quick, and there also seems a great stir and dust, and the appearance for the time being is that evil is more real than ever, selfishness is rife, and materiality rampant. So it is when an old structure is being torn down; it quick and strong ways and means are used the ground, covered with debris, looks hopeless except to the builder. "And they shall gather out of his kingdom all things that offend," said that MasterBuilder, Jesus the Christ.

Certain denials are tempered in their expression, such as " There is no reality in evil," and " sin has no real power"; " nothing is material, all is mind"; "God never made disease, therefore it is not an entity "; " in heaven there is no sorrow, no pain, no poverty, and heaven is here." And the wise practitioner will apply them to the states of mind where the more drastic forms might be antagonizing. The skillful housewife does not pour boiling water upon the flannel garments, nor use strong soaps with delicate fabrics.

The correspondence between water and the great negative announcements of Truth is perfect. The words which describe water are negative: pure water is colorless, odorless, tasteless. Like the moon her patroness, water is a good reflector— a mirror is a good reflector when it is nothing of itself. The negative mentality— called the mortal or carnal mind— is at its best when, like pure, still water, it is a clear reflector of the ideas held over it. Herein, according to the Hindu teaching of Yoga, is a key to the power of perfect concentration. The turbid, restless mentality must become clear and quiet, like the stormy waves of Galilee when calmed by the Master's command, " Peace! be still."

The virgin Diana was the Greek goddess of the moon, pure, chaste, and cold. The life of denial makes the ascetic. The true Christian is not an ascetic only, but, while all pure within, she is clothed with the warm fructifying Sun, putting the Moon-nature (ascetic and psychic) under her feet, "a great wonder in heaven; a woman clothed with the sun, and the moon under her feet " (Rev. xii, i). The same truth is embodied in the symbolism of the " wedding at Cana of Galilee " (John ii, i-ii). When the Christ is an invited guest at the true wedding of the positive and negative elements of our nature He turns the cold, sterile waters of our old faith, found in the purification jars of the old religion, into the warm, exhilarating wine of the Spirit which we drink anew with the Christ in the kingdom of heaven within. All our life can be this marriage feast, where we are making the union between the positive good of our spiritual Being and the negative good of our earthly experiences. The Christ can be our perpetual guest, ever changing the water of our barren commonplace work into the wine of ecstatic communion with God. Let us know no drudgery, nothing common or unclean.

Teach me, my God and King,

In all things Thee to see,

And what I do in anything

To do it as for Thee.

All may of Thee partake,

Nothing can be so mean

Which with this tincture (for Thy sake)

Will not grow bright and clean.

A servant with this clause

Makes drudgery divine;

Who sweeps a room, as for Thy laws,

Makes that and the action fine.

— George Herbert.

Thus let us approach all the uses of water. We may not all serve by washing clothes, but we are using water in multifold other ways, washing dishes, watering plants, giving drink to animals, bathing the children or ourselves, and so forth.

The thought to associate with water is Freedom. This is the word for Monday.

Early in the morning your devotions can begin with your bath. Then you can realize the work the Spirit is doing for you in cleansing and freeing you from the thoughts and feelings that distract and interfere with your peace and power of concentration. At this time you can silently voice your desires for freedom as already accomplished in the divine Mind:

" The Spirit now sets me free from all that binds and clogs; I am cleansed from every impure suggestion; the Truth loosens from me every burden; I am free from selfishness; I am free from jealousy, bitterness, and so forth."

Full freedom springs from within. It is the freedom that gives freedom to others. Therefore, what we declare and wish for ourselves let us seek to make manifest for others.

When Jesus washed the feet of his disciples he indicated the power he was exercising through his silent word. He followed the act with the definite statement as to what was the real cleansing power.

" Now are ye clean through the words which I have spoken unto you."

The Spiritual householder and houseckeeper fulfills a like office for all that come under her charge or even into her mind— her family is the whole race –silently speaking the cleansing word as she goes about her daily work.

As the clothes are gathered together to be washed realize that garments stand for the thoughts, words, ideas that clothe the I Am. We read in Scripture of the garments of praise, of righteousness, of " purple and fine linen," signifying external power and the outer form of purity.

Again, the clothing can mean to us character, traits, habits; some fine, some strong, some durable — every garment fit to wear has some virtue in it that can be applied to the inner nature.

The family wash typifies the process of freeing the family from false beliefs, and as the concentrated worker applies herself she can realize that it is the Spirit that is doing this work, and it is not a mere matter of muscle and physical hard work. Remember to let God work through you, and mark the new features that will come into your work, the skill, the ease, the good judgment with which you will uplift what has been a laborious task.

We are now redeeming " blue Monday," that state of exhaustion, depression, and gloom which so often followed a Sunday in which the clergyman of the old school made such an intellectual effort that " brain-fag " laid him low, or he gave sermons which were such a strain upon his feelings (his inspiration being so largely through his psychic senses and the whole sustained by a strenuous working of human will) that depletion almost to nervous prostration followed, and all his family were covered and saturated with his heavy and exhausted aura. The maids reflected the heads of the household with irritated and impatient feelings, and with words that have given wash-day a bad reputation, even in such old folk-songs as

The little kittens on the hearth

They dare not even play,

For it's up with a thump and many a bump

All on a washing-day.

 It's scold, scold, it's thump, thump,

It's scold, scold away

And not a bit of comfort here,

All on a washing-day.

To such mentalities the word " freedom " applied to wash-day seems veritable irony. Yet here is rich soil in which to plant our seed of freedom-thought. Duty sense makes bondage —doing things because one is duty-bound. Let us bring forth the love-thought, and dismiss forever that false cause, duty. You are free Spirit, and there is a deep, true love-reason back of all that you do. Find it. When we see that there is some- \ thing within us that loves to serve, and that work is best) done by inspiration, not effort, then we also find an original and initiative Spirit with us, and all manner of devices and labor-saving ways and means spring up in our minds. So labor grows light in every Way, and the blueness of Monday scintillates with starry hopes, and merry songs and tripping steps make a holiday of what was once a hard labor day. The same joy and freedom that marks the work of the happy laundress can be ours, and all the sting and weariness pass away.

Let me say, right here, to the suggestion that one might become fixed in material work by being content with it that it is a fact of observation that in almost every instance where rebellion has ceased because of principle, and where work which chafed has become nothing to one, it passes utterly out of one's experience and never enters again except it be by one's deliberate choice.

And now, dear Martha of the family, let Mary's good part enter into your work. Wash away the family sins by the power of the Christ-life working through you.

" Though your sins be as scarlet they shall be white as snow " (Is. i, 18). But for the most part the family sins are not the deep-dyed ones, but the errors are worriment and fear, tempers, common selfishness, quarreling, unkind teasing, tardiness, disobedience, forgetfulness — bad habits which demand daily correcting until the higher Self is invoked and trusted. Each garment that is handled can remind one of a word of Truth to be spoken for its owner. As you wash little Johnny's stockings you will see how the Spirit is working within him to give the love of being helpful and thoughtful for others; as you wash little Mary's apron, that habit of carelessness and untidiness will receive its cleansing and come forth the clean garment of a spontaneous orderliness that will charm while yet years rest lightly upon her.

Great can be the ministry of the household priest and savior if she will, like Mary, sit at the feet of Truth and remember that whatever she gives and does for anyone in the name of the Christ she gives and does to the Christ within herself —so entering and abiding perpetually in the kingdom of heaven while here on the earth. " Ye shall know the truth, and the truth shall make you free." " If the Son [the Truth] therefore shall make you free, ye shall be free indeed."

THE THIRD DAY Tuesday— The LOVE "Day

THE origin of the Anglo-Saxon name of the third day of the week is Tiwes, the fire god of our Teutonic ancestors, the same as the war god of the Greeks and Romans, Mars, from whose name the French word for Tuesday is derived, that is, Mardi.

In the olden time the god of fire was also the god of war, wrath, revenge, and destruction, and even to-day the astrologer enlarges upon the fighting, raging, stinging influences of the planet Mars, although he acknowledges there is a propitious, even beneficent, aspect of this star that is expressed as energy, refining power, skill, and zeal.

Fire symbolizes Love. The Hebrews described their God as " a consuming fire " (Deut. iv, 24), and St. John said, "God is love" (I John iv, 8)

The primitive concept of the divine passion was based upon the belief in the reality of both good and evil, therefore supreme Love implied and included extreme hatred, and if aught opposed or disobeyed the God-love it then became God-wrath, which burned with equal intensity. And in the dark days of their disobedience and sin the children of Israel imaged only the fierce anger of their God, so suffering torment, disease, and defeat until Christ came, teaching a God of love in whom was no wrath at all. The destructive nature of fire portrays the former idea of holy Love, destroying all that is not like itself —selfishness, corruption, whatever is offensive and useless. This aspect of the God-love is called hell fire in the New

Testament—" gehenna," from the garbage-burning outside the walls of the city, Jerusalem. Into this were cast certain of the refuse of the city, especially from the sacrificial animals, and also the dead bodies of criminals.

All applications of fire by the spiritual householder can be compared to the workings of Love in the realm of appearances. Often we make holocausts of the things which we see should cease to cumber our earth, like old letters and relics. If there are associations of sadness, regrets, mourning and evil memories, then as the flames consume the pile let the heart breathe, " Thus love dissipates all memory of evil," recollecting that all the happiness connected with these is eternal and self -renewing, to be finally manifest with no mixture of sin or sorrow.

Again, when the dust heap is burning the weeds from the garden, and other forms of rubbish, then our silent prayer can be of acknowledgment of the inner fire of God's love able to destroy each false trait of character, naming them specifically.

Our pagan ancestors gave us this custom of devoting Tuesday to using the element that belonged to Mars, the god of that day. Let us devote it to the real God of all days, and let every use of fire be to us symbolic of the Spirit's work of love.

Monday is wash day, Tuesday is ironing day. The clothes in drying have been bathed in sunshine and air, types of universal love and inspiration, and as they are gathered together and sorted the angel within whispers to us of its mission of harvesting (Matt, xiii, 38, 39), separating ^the tares from the wheat.

Some garments are like conventional beliefs, all stiff with pride and self-assertiveness, and so needing the sprinkling of the gentle waters of humility, preparatory to the refining, polishing work of love to round the character.

Asceticism, like a severe washing, leaves some natures dry and withered, others harsh and " scratchy " with criticism, and only a new baptism of meekness and a strong and skillful application of the smoothing iron of love can make them comfortable to contact. " Thee must be dipped again," an old Quaker used to say to certain of his Christian brothers whose zeal was awry, " Thee must be dipped again!"

The flatiron stands for the word of the Spirit, our silent voicing of Truth. As the iron presses and gives the shine, we can remember the power of love to harmonize and smooth the ways of the family. Some natures are happy and useful "rough-dry"; though blunt and outspoken, not given to conventionalities, they are clean-minded: and wise is the house mother who knows how to be content to have such natures about, not finding fault because they do not receive the polish of which other natures are capable. Then there are those whose positiveness in truth must be established because they seem limp and weak in their self-depreciation. As some stiffly starched garment is being ironed for them tell them of the courageous, strong self within them, able to go forward truly and wisely. But perhaps another may be too assertive, then the skillful flatiron of the Word can round the sharp corners and gently bring to mind the unobtrusive Christ-Self that is there.

As the delicate and beautiful have their part in the harmonious home, and require skillful handling with intelligence, so there are temperaments, like filmy lace and silken mesh, that seem impractical and sentimental, and yet have a deep, rich presence which, rightly appreciated, would be the lasting joy of the family.

Sensitive children, like woollen garments, should receive considerate treatment, not scorching by injudicious counsel or untimely and excessive punishment.

Every nature and disposition in a family is represented in the garments, and the consecrated worker, intent on carrying the good news, will find a message to deliver with every piece that is ironed.

When building a fire, meditation upon the encouragement of the interior nature is in place. Faith in human nature may seem cold and weak, and there needs to be a patient upbuilding and persistent lighting from the stores of love. Sometimes a fire will not burn because ashes lie accumulated, or the flues are choked with soot. So, unforgiveness, disappointed ambitions, unrequited loves seem to prevent inspiration and free realization, and as the ashes are removed let us perceive the power of the Spirit to remove all old thoughts that interfere with its currents of blessing, and to burn up the soot of materialism, doubts, procrastination, impurity and impatience.

There are the lamps to be cleaned and filled. The Wise Virgins of the parable give us the clew to this work, as it is in the Spirit. The oil for their lamps (Matt, xxv, 4) was kept in plentiful supply, so that when the bridegroom — the cosmic consciousness— came, though in a way and at a time unlooked for, they were ready. In the regeneration the illumination that we have within must receive daily reenforcement through prayer and communion with God, and the wick of our Soul's lamp must be kept free from old accretions of deadness and obtuseness through fasting from those material pursuits and sense-pleasures which make us forget God and fall into unlovely ways. As the globes are dusted or cleansed think of how they represent the body, which by right thought is pure and true, so that the light of the Soul is seen clearly shining through.

Love keeps the furnace of God's dwelling house steady in its genial hospitality, tempered in its zeal, universal in its comfort. The faithful heart that is janitor and stoker receives appreciation and honor from the mind that exalts all service to the holy place.

All in the family contribute in some way to the love and harmony that warms and cheers, from the little lad who fills the wood box to the father, who, standing for the great Source of supply, pays the bills of gas and electricity, wood and coal.

When the heat of the day, or of the stove, or of un usual work, seems to press upon one, then is the time to realize oneself the crucible in the magic laboratory of the Spirit where divine alchemy is redeeming some grossness and transmuting it into the fine gold of high and noble character. By calm cooperation with the heat it will never overpower you, but will find you vibrating evenly with it, not fainting but exhilarate, not exhausted but uplifted and inspired. This fierce influence has been called the anger of the Lord, but the wrath of God is passing into myth through the knowledge of the Love which is God; and our human anger, impatience, and irritability shall pass away through being lifted up into our God-self in such trying moments, so letting serenity reign supreme.

The homely tasks of ironing day may be marked by an occasional burn upon the body while yet we are in the days of our spiritual greenness, and then comes an opportunity for one of those demonstrations which in its simplicity and completeness is such a convincing proof of the power of mind. Perceiving instantly: " The flesh feels nothing— it is the mind that feels, and I am Spirit, and cannot be burned," is to be delivered from the pain and blister, and to see wholeness and freedom in place of sores and scars. A student of Truth who kept a restaurant in San Diego, California, covered her hand with scalding potato soup as she was moving a kettle of it, full to the brim, from one part of the range to another. The cook and waitresses who witnessed it were filled with horror, and in a panic began running for flour and oil to assuage the burning, but the lady calmly wiped the potato off her hand, refusing their remedies with a smile, saying, " I have better medicine within me." Standing still, and lifting her thoughts above her surroundings, she remembered, "I am Spirit, Mind, above all this, and nothing shall by any means harm me," and the burning sensation wholly passed away in a few minutes. Then she looked at her hand which had become a fiery red and saw that it was beginning to blister, and instantly she reasoned, " The same power that delivered me from the pain now keeps my hand from blistering," and all the redness and blistering disappeared. The afternoon of that same day she showed me the hand as white and whole as the other, while a waitress standing by said, " Yes, and I saw it, and it was wonderful! I am going to look into this new teaching." What a lesson was given there! It could not soon be forgotten.

"Love lightens labor" is an old maxim, and how true it is many a devotee to " New Thought " can testify. Weariness takes to itself wings. The hard task grows easy, the burden becomes light, as service to humanity is seen to be service to God, and that everything is an opportunity to rise above the belief in slavery and bondage to the flesh, and enter into the original, magical power of The Word, when to speak our wish is to see even things inanimate as well as animate respond with loving eagerness, hastening to do our pleasure, as the listening winds and waves joyed in quick obedience to the voice of the Master of Love who proved by a life of perfect service that " All power is given unto me in heaven and in earth."

THE FOURTH DAY. Wednesday — Wisdom Day

THE aspect of divinity which the middle day of the week presents is that of the power of thought from the heights of intelligence called Wisdom, and the works which are the consequence of it.

The word Wednesday is derived from Woden, the chief god of our Anglo-Saxon ancestors. His character, office, and functions were much the same as the Roman god, Mercury, called by the Greeks, Hermes, and by the Egyptians, Thoth, the deity that presided over thoughts, and the works of thought. The Latin races obtain their name for this day from the god Mercury, as in the French, Mercredi.

To those who have been making the powers and nature of mind an ardent study Wednesday offers manifold suggestion about thought and its creative aspects. Under the old gods thought has a subtle history, and there are marvelous tales of the magical quickness of Mercury, this fleet message-bearer of the gods.

" Quick as a thought " is our superlative for speed. We call quicksilver mercury, because of its movement, and the first characteristic of the planet Mercury is its swift revolution about the sun. The mercurial temperament among the people of the United States, bright, alert, sprightly, has been held by astrologers to be proof that this country is ruled beneficently by the planet Mercury.

All these intimations we can, like Mary, " ponder in our hearts " while remembering the Christ that redeems these attributes from their old perversions for which Mercury was notorious among the gods, thieving, mischief-making, cunning, fickleness, and double-dealing.

With winged head and feet, bearing the mystic rod, serpent-entwined, Mercury well symbolizes our mysterious thinking power. But as the gods dwelt among the clouds and seldom favored mortals with their gifts, so thought has been, in the centuries past, relegated by the majority to the realm of fancy and untrained imagination, and only as the one God, the Christ-Self, redeems the thinking faculty from its falsities and impositions can it be reinstated, and come to its original recognition as to place and power. Under the guidance of the Christ human thought is purified, lifted into the realm of divinity and made an instrument for the establishing of the Kingdom of Heaven on the earth.

As one with intelligence all expression is possible to the thought of man. Wisdom and creation are one in the divine realm, " The Lord by wisdom hath founded the earth" (Prov. iii, 19). " O Lord, how manifold are thy works! in wisdom thou hast made them all " (Ps. civ, 24) . Because the supreme intention for man is that he shall create, like his Heavenly Father, the progressive races have been imbued with the idea of the necessity of education, the bringing forth of intelligence from within the child:

" The Lord possessed me [Wisdom] in the beginning of his way, before his works of old. I was set up from everlasting, from the beginning or ever the earth was " (Prov. vii, 22, 23).

The one appointed to instructing, whether schoolteacher, guardian, or parent, should remember that all schooling is for the one end of bringing forth the Godman who walks in the footsteps of the Heavenly Father — " for what things soever he doeth, these also doeth the Son likewise " (John v, 19).

Children are our young thoughts —innocent, spiritual ideas in their incipiency, only needing faith in them and development through love in order to be the avenue along which can come every blessing to the earth.

Wednesday is the day in which to meditate on the perpetual creation— one with supreme intelligence. It is sewing day, and new garments are planned and put together. Other days also may be occupied with new creations, and in great variety and diversity from the knitting of a sock to the building of a house, yet they can all be viewed in the same light with which we shall consider this day's sewing and mending.

Inspiration can be in every piece of our creating through seeking to do it perfectly, for the Truth's sake, and because of the principle within one.

Nothing makes the soul so pure, so religious, as the endeavor to create something perfect; for God is perfection, and whoever strives for it, strives for something Godlike.— Michel Angelo.

" Whatsoever thy hand findeth to do, do it with thy might" (Eccles. ix, 10). Do it with spirit, not because you are obliged to do it, not for money or reward, not for praise, but for your Soul, for the kingdom of heaven's sake. The rich zeal and interest and integrity that you put into your work, when done for Truth's sake, give you a mighty impetus along the lines of your Soul's accomplishments; it is laying up heavenly treasures that many a praying recluse is missing in his sense of separation from humanity and indifference to their needs and the service he could render them.

"But how can I be energetic and work with a vim when my body is so heavy and I am so easily exhausted and tired? " cries one who perhaps has bemoaned her " laziness," and suffered acute mortification as her own uselessness has been contrasted with others' activity. Remember there are no " lazy " in God's kingdom. Laziness is a disease which is not healed by condemnation, and if we will never accuse another of laziness we will not come under that ban from our own thought or that of others. As one wisely and lovingly seeks a remedy for a disease, so laziness should receive our intelligent and successful healing. The rigor of enforced labor and stinging stripes of others' rebukes and our own self-contempt has only served to make the condition more evident, and it has brought confusion as to judgment in training an inchoate humanity out of its weakness into its strength. Tramps are the offspring of self -ignorance and rebellion against a false civilization.

One's body is heavy and lax because the thoughts are material and sensual, or surcharged with anxiety and sense of the reality of evil, or, again, because one has dwelt in dreams and ideals which he has separated from the earth consciousness. Centering the mind in the God-Self in the midst of one and regarding every being in its spirituality and lovableness brings one to the balanced place in the body so that the body is not felt at all, and your activity is as easy and effectual as the resilient step of the youthful foot. If that foot were twisted in its shoe its steps would be halting and painful, and the youth might seem lazy and abnormal until the mistake was corrected and comfort restored. So false views of life, whether they be selfish indulgence of passions, negative wills, or merely not-knowing, twist the mentality, and a new view must be taken for relief.

Our bodies are made " to fit "—let us keep a good center in them through perpetual cooperation with our God-Self. Meet the slightest suggestion of being tired with a spirited " I cannot grow weary in well doing," and never let the tempter suggest " overwork " or " thankless doing," or allow any other thought to crush you with a sense of injustice and wrong.

Keep your faith in Good inviolate, it holds the key of perpetual renewal of joy and youthful interest.

There is upon Life 's hand a magic ring,

The ring of faith-in-good, Life 's gold of gold.

Remove it not lest all Life 's charm take wing,

Remove it not, lest straightway you behold

Life 's cheek fall in and every earthly thing

Grow unutterably old.

One of the works of the Christ is to give " the garment of praise for the spirit of heaviness " (Is. lxi, 3), to raise up those who are cast down, the discouraged, self-depreciative natures, with words of loving interest and approval breathed silently while working upon their garments, and audibly whenever the words can be fitly spoken.

This is the day for mending, and the spiritual devotee can remember the power to heal misunderstanding as her needle joins the torn places. Mending the worn parts may stand for the mending of one's ways. As the needle weaves back and forth in darning the heart can cooperate with the Spirit in speaking the word that substitutes strong, positive, wholesome habits for the weakness that is appearing in the one to whom the garment belongs.

The dressmaker who will bless her customer while fitting her, and send her messages of peace and goodness while sewing, will prove herself a minister of the gospel without stirring from her workrooms. How often the message of patience and thoughtfulness, of love and harmony, of satisfaction and poise could transform a troublesome patron into a happy cooperating sister in Truth!

Mechanical and uninteresting pieces of work become alive and even charming as we work blessed realizations of Truth into them. A lady who crochets much has learned to find sentences of Truth to take the place of empty counting. Having to make seven stitches very often in a certain doily, she substituted "God the Good is all there is " for the old monotonous repetition, and it was a joy to her to write this line when sending her gift: "This work comes to you filled with words of Truth, and every stitch carries a blessing and a reminder of the almighty Good that is working in and through our lives." It is this human element of love and goodness that makes hand-wrought articles so much more valuable to the people of taste than the machine-made, soulless and without thought. Our quality is charging all that we contact whether we know it or not, and there are senses in mankind that discern these qualities, and characters can be read from the subtle emanations and vibrations of things that have been in intimate association with them. Letters have revealed the nature of their contents before they are opened, handkerchiefs have shown the secret thoughts of their owners. It was this knowledge that was with the woman who said, " If I may but touch his garment I shall be whole " (Matt, ix, 21). Truly it was her own receptive trust that opened her to the benefit of that touch, for no others of the crowd that pressed upon the Master were healed in that way. The virtue (goodness) of Jesus Christ has gone forth into all the earth so that he who touches a stone in faith touches God. " Lift the stone, and there am I."

Everything in your world must be imbued with the best of you. The sewing machine you use can receive your calmness and patience as well as your skill and expedition. You take out of the instruments you use what you put into them. Engineers often feel their locomotives to be like living, throbbing, sensitive creatures, requiring all the wise handling that must be given a high-mettled horse. Barbers tell of tired razors whose dull edge no honing can make keen. They lay them on the shelf for a week or two and their power is restored. Violins are loved and caressed and made to respond to such sweet harmonies for so long that their very frames become vibrant and sensitive to the most delicate touch and emotions of their loving masters. Flowers grow and flourish under a fond hand that gives something more than fertilizer or other material elements. Domestic animals thrive in the atmosphere of love that reveals something more in them than mere brute creations.

The garment that is made over represents the reforming powers of Truth working with the elements of a character or system at the place where it finds them, and bringing forth a fair work even from material judged hopeless. There is an enthusiasm with some mentalities in exercising their skill to make much out of little; it is akin to that of the magician who with the wand of his word can bring into appearance that which was invisible, so seeming to make something out of nothing. All joy is ours, that of the mind full of devices for remaking, and that of the one who delights in perfectly new material upon which to exploit his original powers.

When engaged in any process of reconstruction let us remember how the body is being transformed by the renewal of the mind. New cells replace the old by the same Breath of Life in whose presence and by whose moving the originals were made manifest. New thoughts make new bodies.

Some of the works that engage our interest have come under the ban of uselessness because they have been made for beauty and pleasure, and this day we can redeem these works by seeing the usefulness of beauty as well as the beauty of usefulness, and that pleasure is life, and one of the chief works of life is to give pleasure. Thus, while trimming a hat one can remember that crown of a glorious life for which it stands; while dressing the hair the thought can dwell on the halo of Spirit whose radiance becomes very visible when the heart is filled with love-memories of our first glory. Jewels stand for the treasures of the Kingdom, the Soul's grace is as an ornament to the neck, diamonds are the emblems of chastity and purity, and often they have been substituted for the consciousness of the reality and brought a quasi-temporal satisfaction.

The fancy-work of leisure moments can be redeemed from sense of folly by keeping the imagination (fancy) pure and high at such times, guiding conversation out of meanderings along scandal, malice, and foolish gossip. Much good vacation work can be done by a wholesome mind resting in the midst of the vaporings of mentalities that have not yet "found themselves." The angel presence of a true thinker on the summer porch or at the winter resort has been the leaven of the Kingdom of Heaven in the meal of negative brain centers, and has brought men and women to themselves, and started them on the way back to their Father's house.

Wisdom is strength, folly is weakness. " My people perish for lack of knowledge." Many a frivolous, weak, senseless pursuit will be abandoned, and the dear one arrested from going on a path of degeneracy by reminding him (or her) that such signifies lack of intelligence.

In the Book of Proverbs Wisdom is personified as a woman most desirable for life-companionship, while sense delusion, worldly wisdom, sophistry, maya, the folly of isms— materialism, atheism, sensualism— are personified as the strange woman that befools the unwary, and leads them to failure, shame, and misery.

If mistakes are made in building, or any other act of construction, waste no time in vain regrets. Speak the word quickly for accuracy and trueness, such as, "The Spirit makes me always sure and true," " I do everything

286

exactly right," "Nothing can go wrong, for God makes good." Keep your eye on the true I and you will go where you look. One who was learning to ride the bicycle and whose mind was alert for all the lessons of life found himself continually running into the pillars of the rink where he was being taught. The teacher observing his mistakes called to him, " Young man, don't look at the posts unless you want to run into them, for you will always go where you look!" And he thought, "How that describes the power of one's mind!"

" That thou seest, that thou beest." Keep your eye on the mark of the high calling of Christ Jesus.

At times one is kept to a work by the powers that bless until a certain quality is developed, and the quickest way out of an undesirable position is to do your very best in it.

" Why is my talented son obliged to work in a position where his gift has no opportunity for development?

He has a fine genius for the violin, but he is working laboriously at braking on freight trains, and he likes it, too, "• said a fond mother to a Truth-teacher one day.

"Perhaps there is some trait that must be established in him," was the reply, "before he is ready to take up his talent and use it. For instance, he may lack continuity."

" You are right!" she exclaimed, " that is just what he has lacked, so that he never would practice as he should. But he cannot indulge that weakness as a brakeman, and it is wonderful how he forces himself to rise exactly on time and keeps himself alert to do everything in his work with order and dispatch. It makes me quite contented now that I see there may be a purpose in it all."

The word for Wednesday is " God works and wills in and through me, and in and through all things for good."

Wisdom works wisdom's way, all beauty and usefulness, all blessing and all delight.

THE FIFTH DAY. Thursday — POWER Day

THOR, the Norse deity, whose name is the origin of Thursday, or Thor's-day, was the God-Man of the northern mythology— the human being whose powers and works were manifested through being overshadowed by his divinity. This Man has ever been recognized by the dominant races of the planet and some, like the Greeks and the Hindus, have seen this master expressed in many forms, although with one Spirit. Such were Hercules and Achilles, Krishna and Ram, the Egyptian Osiris; and even the Aztecs of Mexico and the Peruvians of South America had their God-hero whose office and character partook of certain marked traits belonging to this manifestation.

This God-Man is always a Savior of His people. One has twelve labors to perform in delivering the oppressed; certain have human mothers and a divine father; all commune with the gods; most of them have a vulnerable point that makes them subject to death; they heal diseases, they join the gods, and are immortalized in the memory of their people.

The cross was a symbol common to all the nations to whom religion was an important part of life. By the cross Osiris " gave light eternal to the Spirits of the Just "; the cross, according to Prescott, was found by the Spaniards in the temples of Mexico as an object of worship; and in the form of a hammer it was the magic wand of Thor. With it, according to Scandinavian legends, Thor crushed the head of Mitgaard, the serpent, destroyed giants, restored to life the dead goats which ever after drew his car, and consecrated the pyre of Baldur.

Thus we see that Thursday is the day of the Christ-Man, the power of Almighty God in the flesh. In the wonderful Nazarene all these symbols and works were rescued from myths and gathered together in a human life, which was to represent, to the end of time, the Way out of the maze of mortality, and the Life that sets us free from the seductions of the sense serpent.

The story of Jesus Christ is not a myth compounded from the legends of the race but a witness to the marvelous power of the Holy (Whole) Spirit to picture forth in the flesh the great paradox of the Cross, that is, the victory and glory of the Real Self through the humiliation and complete denial of the petty self.

Thursday is an open day in the communities that have observed a regular routine of housework, and it is devoted to a great variety of employments according to the neighborhood, city, or country, and the interests of the individual householders. There is gardening and letter-writing, making calls and receiving them; there are extra and unusual departments, such as cellar and garret to receive attention; there is " The Club;" there are the lessons in music, painting, and so forth; there is the philanthropic work; and in many places it is the day that the maid takes for her holiday.

This is Individual Day, wherein the powers of one's divinity can be the special meditation that will serve to gather one's human radiations to a focusing center of strength, so that even with the infinite variety of demands that may be made upon one there will be no confusing distraction or scattering, but a glorious expression of talent and genius, the reality of the individual Idea which we are in the divine Mind.

Your individuality is your soul, and you are here to express it in fullness, the hero and heroine that you are, the original, beautiful, noble Self — that Idea of you in the Mind of God, equal with God, and God's own Being. The fear of the loss of one's individuality disappears through knowledge of Truth, for the Soul Sense is restored, and one knows one's self to be eternal Soul, as impossible to be lost as for God to cease to be. No soul can be lost — it is the sense of being Soul that has been obscured, and which returns by the saving power of the Christ-Self.

Individuality is not demonstrated by separation, opposition, competition, or difference. This is the mistaken view of mortals, who thus hope to be individual by eccentricity, egotism, and exclusiveness.

There is but one true Individual God, and we are all That. As personalities grow impersonal and universal, putting away the petty differences of race, family, position, sex, and so forth, forgetting the little I, they show forth the character and powers of their Godhood, and join even the world's immortals. The hero who performs a great deed forgets himself, and even his family and everything but the Cause which he has espoused, and for which he is ready to die if it must be. The sense of personality utterly melts before the cosmic consciousness, yet individuality is intensely clear and full, and immortality is an assurance forever beyond question.

As the worker is engaged among the plants of her garden let her remember the plants of the Lord's planting (read Jer. xvii, 7, 8), the precious one in the people of her world. And as she loves, trains, and nourishes each vine and shrub let her meditate upon the tender, watchful work of the Spirit toward every human being, pruning it, cleansing it, giving it the soil (environment) best fitted to develop it. Let her remember that Eden garden of her soul and the deeds of true thinking and feeling implanted within her consciousness. The power of the Christ transcends time, and spiritual seeds can produce quickly " fruit after their kind."

The word for Thursday is "All power is "given unto Me," and also " God's grace is sufficient for Me," messages which radiate from the Christ-consciousness within. Divine power is not violent or resistant. It is effortless and peaceful, yet mighty and effectual— it cannot be separated from Grace.

Whenever strength is needed in one's affairs this Christ-power should be invoked, for by it wonderworks have been performed. A little woman found herself at a place in a work of cleaning up her belongings and getting them ready for moving where she needed a strong arm to lift a dentist's chair. She was alone, having been recently widowed, there was no man near, yet all her work would be delayed if this heavy iron chair was not moved. She breathed a silent prayer: " I can do all things through Christ which strengtheneth me," and she lifted that chair, and its weight was no more to her than a child's high-chair —indeed, it seemed to be as light as a balloon as she raised it off the rug that she had rolled up. Afterward it required two men to carry it out of the house.

All power is given to you, the Christ-Self, in heaven and on earth, and that power overshadows, surrounds, upholds and fills the earth-man as he lets it. And this power cannot be limited by any earthly law; it is not upon a basis of ethics; it is above cause and effect, the Grace that ever works good because of love that sees only "My Beloved."

In this light we understand the comfort and promise which Paul received when he heard " My grace is sufficient for thee"; that is, the sweet graciousness of his own divinity would set him free from the rigid laws of reaping what he had sown by giving him power to forgive his enemies and cast out all bitterness, resentment, and desire for revenge.

The gracious man or woman is the one who is considerate, gentle, patient, kind to poor and rich alike, saint and sinner equally, knowing neither high nor low, but only: this is a human being, therefore one to be respected.

The forms of salutation even in our letters, the ceremonies of polite society, the etiquette and courtesies observed by the aspiring members of the human family have their foundation in sincere actions of love and respect. Without these principles they become mere affectations and hypocrisy, or at best cold forms. It is in the power of the truth-lover to restore the dead letter of manners and customs to their original Spirit by doing all these things from the heart, and thinking of how one can bless and serve another in place of what is due to oneself.

Thus, when one is making calls or receiving them, instead of dreading to meet certain ones, begin to meet them in Soul before the outward approach. Look through that shell, the mere external, and silently talk to the inner one while commonplace remarks about the weather and health, relations and current events are exchanged. You will find original remarks rising to your lips, displacing these trite hacks of effete conversation. To you every human being then becomes a treasure-box to be opened and made to reveal the precious jewels there which may even surprise their owners. Each one, even the most repulsive and uncongenial, stands for a heavenly Idea. Exercise yourself to find what they represent in divine Mind— perhaps it is the very opposite to what they appear, and it will yet be proven so to you.

Writing letters represents the Spirit's eternal act of sending forth the Word, therefore they can go forth with inspiration. Holding to the Christ-power to word your epistles will make them easy in style, rich in substance and able to convey truly what was intended. Giving this act to God will prevent writing when in a passion, or under any thought-pressure of evil. And also it will cause some letters to remain unsent. Again, it will send messages between the lines that will make the letter food and drink to the spiritually hungry.

" Do all things unto the glory of God." When you go to the Club, be the sweet gracious thought that heals gossip and envying, that harmonizes factions and promotes usefulness, and though you are silent, some member will voice your thought in a way acceptable and helpful in expressing the real purpose of the organization. If you go to the theater, find the Spirit there and see how it is giving light and joy to the soul. If you attend a dance, let the grace of your Spirit lift men's thoughts above the mere sensuous into the heights where Miriam dwelt with David when they danced before the Lord. If you play cards, redeem them from the earth-passion and condemnation, and as you let your intelligence and skill testify to a power greater than ordinary, silently give all praise to the One. Every game has an innocent origin— cards were even Scripture to the people who first used them, they claiming their invention to be from the gods. Whatever is pernicious in games will not pass by condemnation but by redemption.

Taking and giving lessons in art, science, language, or any work may be associated with the soul's power of imparting itself; knowing, without strenuous study, doing, without arduous practice. All thought of stupidity and inability must be swallowed up in the memory of the source of power and intelligence. Dismiss every suggestion of " can't " with the realization of "I-can-and-I-will" by the power and grace of your God-Self. As a teacher you can imbue your pupil. As a student you can be so baptized by your Supreme Self.

This day of grace that knows neither high nor low is a fit one in which to give the servant her holiday, honoring her desires and considering her welfare as you would be blessed were you in her place. Seeing one life in all makes it possible for one to appreciate the needs and wishes of another whose tastes may be quite different from our own. We may discover them to be more delicate on certain points, and where they seem to be inferior we can respect their right and not despise or judge superficially. "Shall the eye say to the hand, I have no need of thee?" We are members of one body, and each member is to be honored according to its view of what is fit and desirable. There are servants who " know their place" and love to keep it and to have it recognized graciously and wisely, and there are servants who desire to be treated as members of the family, and the true master and mistress of the household know how to bring that wish to pass to the comfort and well-being of all. We are all servants in love, one with Him who came not to be served but to serve.

And now we come to the philanthropic work to which you may pay special attention on some days even though every day be tinctured with some form of it. In the first place we lift it all out of the old view of "charity," the thought that we give to others that which was not theirs but by our favor — the act of a superior to an inferior. Such is an abomination in the sight of the Lord.

We realize that all belongs to the One, who is in all, and we never give to another aught but his own, and our part is but to be wise stewards in this demesne of the Father of us all, giving by the Spirit and withholding by the Spirit. Until you can give the true thought with your money you have not fulfilled your part. The wise one gives to the Christ in all and does not regard the appearance — looks through the drunkard, the grime and the wickedness to the One that God sent, " the light which lighteth every man." To him there are no tramps, no beggars, no imposters. He thinks not of need nor poverty, as he gives to the rich one that is there, the worthy one, the honest, the able, the true One. And with that thought he draws forth the man of God. Only those who are prompted by the Christ within can appeal to you as you hold yourself to be God's Hand to dispense His bounty, and you can say with all your heart to every one whose case draws forth your sympathy, " Blessed is he that cometh in the name of the Lord." Indiscriminate charity is a weakness and often a thoughtless make-shift of ignorance, that thinks itself unselfish when it is only superficially easing its own discomfort at the sight of pain and want. Give your impulses to inspiration and not be prompted so much by the sense of the reality of the evil as by the joy of distributing the plenty God has given you.

A lady of New York City determined one winter to literally " give to everyone that asked" her. By the end of the winter her house had become " a tramp's boarding house"— so her cook said. The following winter she followed the same rule and she found her income hardly sufficient for her own living, besides her servants greatly taxed. Nevertheless she kept bravely on, and when the third winter started and the same horde began to come— men of previous years returning again and again, having her place marked and listed on their memoranda, she was led to seek counsel of a teacher of divine Mind power. The latter asked her:

" To whom have you been giving? To the tramp, the beggar, the drunkard?"

" O, yes!" she promptly replied, "to everyone that has come."

"Then, hereafter do not give to them, but to your brothers, to the Christ in them, and silently say to everyone, ' I give to the true One in you, and the honest, temperate, pure One in you uses this gift to the glory of your Godhood. , Moreover have this realization for yourself, expressed in the words of Christ, ' No man can come to me except the Father which hath sent me, draw him.',"

She took this advice, and the magical result was a class of applicants whose number and character she could serve easily and satisfactorily with the sense that she was truly blessing and not " hindering them on their upward way."

One of the most remarkable proofs of the power of a silent blessing accompanying a gift, with a spoken word of good to seal it, was shown in the following instance:

It was a drizzly winter day in Los Angeles when a man who would be called a typical hobo, dirty, unshaven, unkempt, with breath redolent of liquor, presented himself at the kitchen-door of a lady who had begun to take the true attitude towards all humanity, asking for money. A very strict law had been passed in Los Angeles to arrest such creatures, and this lady could have handed him over to a policeman who happened to be nearby, but she did not. She answered simply:

" Very well, wait a minute," and went to get her purse to find a small coin. There was nothing less than a fifty-cent piece in it.

" This is too much," she thought. Then, " No, I will give it with a message to his soul."

So, holding it in the palm of her hand, she blessed it, and said:

" Go with him and tell him, he is a child of the Most High God, pure and holy, loving noble things and able to live an honorable, manly life, honest and true!"

Then she put the coin into his hand, speaking aloud the words, as she looked him in the eye:

" I believe in you!"

As he hurried down the hill he was filled with glee as he thought of the treat that he and his tramp-chums would have down among the hogsheads where they had been having their open-air lodgings. As his bleary eyes brightened at the thoughts of the prospective " beers" another thought would come athwart these, and he would say:

" I wonder what she meant by saying ' I believe in you!'"

The words kept coming. At the corner of Fourth and Spring streets he went into a cellar where the Salvation Army was holding a meeting, so as to be out of the rain and enjoy his good luck. The Salvation people were telling of the work they had procured for a number of men, and they were inviting any who were there to come forward and list their names for employment and they would do for them what they could. A strong feeling came over this man to take up a clean life, and he found himself in the aisle going up to be an applicant. The outcome was an invitation from the Salvationists to work around their barracks for his room and board until they could procure him a place. This he did. At the end of a month he obtained a job, proved competent, was promoted, and six months from that drizzly day he presented himself at the door of that lady's house, a fine handsome man, both within and without, seeking to know why she said, " I believe in you."

" How far doth a little candle send its rays!" 11 Let your light so shine before men that they may see your good works and glorify your Father which is in heaven."

THE SIXTH DAY. Friday— Day of Purity

ERIDAY, the "sweeping-day" throughout the realm of the orderly housewives, has of old been under the auspices of that goddess of love who was all grace, beauty and purity, Frigga, the Venus of the Norse mythology. These three attributes belong to the Love that is Divine, and where any one is missing it must be supplied, that the expression of love on the earth may be perfect— grace that is the height of unselfishness, beauty, the natural radiance of love and purity, the unalloyed freedom of true hearts.

Early on Friday morning every thing is astir for a good sweeping and dusting. The windows are thrown open, as indeed they are every morning, and as the fresh, sweet billows of new-day sunshine and air roll in we remember why we love and embrace them so. It means our union with our world, our enlarging the areas of our earth-consciousness.

The reason why we love the great out-doors so much, flinging aside draperies and swinging our casements wide open, is because it represents the Spirit's universality, rising above the selfish interests, and breaking forth into joy in the life of the whole. But if some one is fearful of the drafts, and compels us to sleep in a room tight-closed, it is our privilege to remember we carry an aura of soul-breath of which we can partake at such moments, exercising one of the powers of our divinity to extract the wholesome from the foul, the pure from the impure. The Hindu devotee that has this power is called a pa.ra.mha.msa. — the great Swan, because of the tradition that if you put a drink of milk and water before a swan it has the power to sup the milk and leave the water. Never let the thought of a close room annoy or pain you. You breathe the breath of the Almighty, and nothing can stifle you or make you faint or give you headache— you are greater than any earthly air.

As the merry little housewife goes about brushing the curtains and pinning them up, dusting the ornaments and putting them under covers, sweeping the walls and mouldings and picture-frames, beating dust out of cushions, dusting and moving out furniture, all preparatory to the thorough sweeping of the floor, rugs and carpets, let her meditate upon the grace and beauty and purity of that inner home of love, our heaven.

Some of the carvings and scrolleries may test her patience, but let love reveal how she is uncovering some of the hidden subtle beauties of soul by her persistent word — the dust-cloth is " the word" as also the broom, and all the different implements of sweeping. As her new thoughts work with her busy hands she may see that some of the ornaments are anything but ornamental—they are old-fashioned, they have not kept in line with her own development in taste and the march of the race as to standards of beauty — they are faded or broken, and simply cumber the room. Then she can cull them out, realizing she is renewing her youth as she is willing to put away these old useless sentiments and break down attachment to relics which in some cases she has kept because of the donor who "will be more honored in the breach than in the observance" of these respectful memories.

Learn to pass along things you have outgrown but which may still give someone else pleasure or benefit. Instead of cluttering your attic with heaps of cast-off clothing or piles of ornaments and furniture that are passe give them to those of your little sisters who will receive them as from a sister. There are always the settlement-workers, the Salvation Army, the kindergarten philanthropists, and individuals who carry magazines to hospitals, teach the ignorant to make homes, and work privately in multifold ways for the negative members of our world-family who will be glad to get a message from you, asking them to place these articles which are still good, and which you feel to pass along.

Bless everything that you dust, especially the old and ugly. Cease to fret because things so poorly represent your ideals. Change the tendency of finding fault with the furniture and walls into habits of meditating on the forms that would better portray the ideas they represent. Thus a chair stands for the idea of rest, and if the chair is broken or ugly, uncomfortable or weak, then as you dust it, call it God's Rest, and declare, " God's Rest is perfect and beautiful, full of comfort and strength, and It is here." If no correspondence comes to mind, silently affirm in a general way, "This stands for an idea of God, the Good. All God's ideas are true and full of grace, pure and beautiful."

A lady who was burdened with the sense of the oldness and unfit character of her furniture took up this method of blessing and thanksgiving, because she saw it was the true attitude of mind, with the result of being able to dispose of all her old furniture, and, while moving into a new apartment, to get new furnishings throughout, having demonstrated the way and the means of procuring these by the Truth to which she was conforming her whole life. And today she is a prosperous, independent healer, owning her own home, all through living this life, this special feature beginning with the day that she blessed her belongings instead of cursing them by finding fault and hating them.

Harmony in the mind finds expression in harmony of the home-furnishings, but sometimes the tune is pitched too low, and it is not music but silence, and the key must be raised to higher tones. As when a guitar is tuned too low, and you raise one string to the right pitch and then the others to harmonize, so sometimes a new piece of furniture can become the key to new furnishings throughout, everything beginning to "live up to" the latest import. And the money comes and the way opens where there is a will founded upon principle.

This is the day of cleanliness, that of the within as well as the without. "Cleanliness is next to godliness," but it may be the "miss that is as good as a mile" if kindness and unselfishness are forgotten. For godliness means happiness, comfort and peace, and if one's cleanliness is such as to make oneself unhappy at the sight of dirt or make others uncomfortable, then it is far from godliness, and one needs to go often by oneself and "clean house" interiorly, putting away the belief in the reality of uncleanliness, and the pride in one's order and immaculate neatness. While outwardly all should be sweet, spotless and clean, inwardly there should be the same consciousness, so that the mind is at rest and withdrawn from detecting dirt and seeing disorder at untimely moments. To go about continually putting in order, wiping up mud-stains, brushing up litter with ubiquitous dustpan and brush in hand is a sign of disorder in the mentality, where the real correction must begin. All the efforts to keep clean should be so effectually hidden that things will seem to keep themselves neat and orderly.

No one's thoughtless untidiness should distract you nor bring scolding, nagging words to your lips. The latter are more out of order than the former. "But," you may ask, "how shall these careless habits in the family be corrected?" By silent communion with the One who is in us all that ever calls forth harmony out of chaos. By faithful belief in the true One in the growing child there will come to the mind ways and devices which are pleasant and even entertaining by which they are reminded to hang up their hats, or wipe the mud from their shoes, and to attend to all those regularities, even in trifles, the observance of which so largely makes a happy household. At most these early years of selfish savagery, the remains of race chaos, are but few. Be patient, and trust, and never lose your peace.

The gentle art of housekeeping includes within itself a happy abandonment in its working that puts all at ease, skillfully covering any noise or friction of the "machinery." So inspired has been the generalship of many a successful house-mother that families have been born, raised and married before their members have dreamed of the masterly management that made their home to be a home, and some have never found it out. Revelations await us along these lines of unwritten history.

As the good housewife on this, Frigga's day, wields her broom with short, strong strokes or light ones, let her be reminded of the Spirit sweeping from her mentality and out of her life all the useless dust and accumulations of false thinking and feeling, especially all memory of impurities in herself and others. To see and talk about impurity is to have lodged in the cells of one's brain and other organs what the physicians call "dirt," and clean thinking sweeps out the foreign matter from our cells and saves us from the diseases resulting from it.

The dust rolled up in tiny, grey clouds of down, lying in quiet corners on the floor, outpictures idle thoughts, materialistic and worldly. The large damp cloth that gathers them from day to day is the gentle, vigilant word of Spirit that daily frees us from the world while yet we are in it.

Idle thoughts Emerson, in one of his essays, compares to flies, and by such similies we often find correspondences between the inner and the outer, and herein we have a hint of what we are driving out from our mentalities when we swing the fly-driver. One of the problems of housekeeping is the dealing with ants, moths and other insects, so as to be free from them, and not appear to destroy life. Every form of vermin, like the "disease microbe," is subject to the will of man, and though the forms be destroyed, the instructed truth-student should never hold that life has been taken, else he will bind himself, and come under the whip of conscience. "Happy is the man that condemneth not himself in that thing which he alloweth," and if because of ignorance of any better way he destroys the form of a snake or a scorpion, a man-eating tiger or a mouse, he should realize that the life of each is as safe as his own, and even then begins to form another body and seek ingress for it to the outer world. But the best of all is to win the victory by the skill of knowing. The wonderful intelligence that marks the ant has been so identified with the highest intelligence that silent reasoning with it has resulted in turning ants from a house to the outside field.

No expression of life is an enemy to the one who understands and seeks the friendship of all. This is the key to the success of the bee-keeper who can handle his charges and never be stung. All insects that intrude upon man can be seen in their best light, each an aspirant for a higher form that is admirable to their Lord, man, and which is of a harmless nature and even more, a benefit.

There are no parasites in the kingdom of heaven, and every such appearance can be transmuted by the magical thought of man who can raise a form, without destroying it, from a low, selfish vibration to a high, beautiful form of a brilliant color and graceful movement. The lovely butterfly is the ideal of the moth, the brilliant dragon-fly of the mosquito, the green-gold beetles and honored scarabse are the high marks for the despised parasites of their own family. All creation rises by pleasing man, the Lord of creation.

When cleaning house in the spring or fall, the presiding consciousness of loving, and peaceful purity, can take away the sense of confusion, and attract comfort and joyous cooperation on the part of all the members of the household. The pneumatic and electric devices for cleaning have come to us because man is letting inspiration and invention raise the work of the race out of the Adamic curse to the Christ-plane where all work becomes a joy. Willingness to try new ways and purchase the latest labor-saving implements which have been proven belongs to the youthful realization that renews the body and keeps one abreast with the times. The Spirit ever lives in the Now. Every form of work that freshens up the old, brightens with polish, decorates and renovates, stands for the power of the Self to bring forth the heavenly treasures both old and new. Spirituality prevents all crudity and bad taste in this refurbishing of the old and making acquisitions of the new. Standards of beauty and grace in furniture come forth from the mentalities of those who combine art with work because of inspiration and love of creating. And whoever makes the selection of his house furnishings a matter of spiritual importance will be of the same mind as the most artistic of his time. And it will not always be a matter of expense, for some of the most artistic furniture has cost little money and has often been the work of the home-maker, who has become cabinet-worker for the time being, to the lasting pleasure and profit of the family.

All the employments that combine the useful and the beautiful are opportunities for the overshadowing by high ideals that minister to the best in customers, and destroy vanity-thoughts, and set aside the weaknesses, follies and deceptions of those that seek your service and what you have. The questions of integrity and honor that arise between employer and employed can be silently met with Principle, so that demands cannot be made upon you that are unjust or dishonest. Meet the direction to misrepresent given you by your superior (in worldly position) with the silent declaration, "You love honor, and you ask only the honorable thing of me," and two results will follow your divine word: first, such suggestions will cease to come your way; second, your own God-powers will "make good" your representation. You are then the healing word for the crooked ways of the business-world, and the ignorant and shameful methods fall away before the strong light of Principle that brooks no compromise.

Silent appeals to the soul of a man succeed where preachments fail. If your superior has a superior who in turn has his, who is responsible for such orders, then you can mentally go to headquarters and heal the bitter waters at their source. There is no phase of human life that needs healing more than business, and whoever will stay by his post, radiating the warm light of his own pure ideals without antagonism or condemnation, will correct and transform the worldly code of business dealings by simply being, as the sun breaks up the darkness, about which it knows nothing, by steadfastly shining.

There is a monotony about some employments that is very trying, handling the same things, repeating the same words, doing some one thing hour after hour. The devotee of Truth will here find a special advantage in the power of the Spirit to ring infinite variations through the one theme. As illustration: a young woman had many chairs to dust— nearly two hundred— usually a long, tedious work. One day she conceived the idea of giving a blessing to all those who should next occupy those chairs, and she varied the blessing with each chair she handled, and the work became alive to her and ceased to be merely mechanical. Workers in factories and piece-workers can mentally go forth into the world with every piece they handle, touching with messages of "the good tidings" the distant islands and zones of arctic cold and tropic heat. All sense of being a ma chine passes away with the incoming of the rich Spirit that gives real value to all work.

The word for Friday is Purity.

" Unto the pure all things are pure " (Titus i, 15).

"Blessed are the pure in heart, for they shall see God" (Matt, v, 8).

" Thou art of purer eyes than to behold evil " (Hab. i, 13).

" I know, and am persuaded by the Lord Jesus that there is nothing unclean of itself " (Rom. xiv, 14).

" Behold, all things are clean unto you " (Luke xi, 41;.

Special attention can be paid this day to eliminating from the personal and the race consciousness all belief in the reality of impurity. The human mentality, like a lake, reflects whatever is brought into right relation for reflection, and in order to be a good reflector this mind must be still and clear. We have already considered the stillness, now let us think upon the clearness. If the water is muddy there is a poor reflection, so poor that few eyes can see it, but where water is pure from mud and other foreign elements the reflections are so perfect that the scene within the water is the same as that without, though inverted. Pure thoughts are the clearness of the mind, but beliefs in impurity are as mud to the mentality, and picture forth as corruption in the body.

Not only must one realize oneself pure, but all things that one can see or recognize in any way must be viewed only in their purity.

The false suggestions of adultery, of the reality of the unchaste, of all unholiness, and every form of uncleanness must be swept from the mind by the free, fresh winds of spiritual insight. It may require a daily use of the mental broom and duster of the true word to cleanse the family mind from the daily contact of newspaper reports of " horrors, " and so forth, but no better work can be done for yourself and them.

While purity is the principal thought maintained on this day of Venus the other thoughts of beauty and grace must often be remembered, for the meditation upon purity alone has been cold and severe, like the snows that are piled on our sidewalks in winter. Even the old ascetic thought of purity must be swept aside by the true thought, which is one with beauty and grace, and if it falls to your lot to sweep away the snow from steps and paths carry the love-consciousness that warms you to the work with its memory of the whole trinity of love in form, beauty, grace and purity.

As you go from room to room on this day with the sweet contentment of reviewing all the outward cleanness stand in the center of each one and radiate the inward praise of your sunny soul, giving to each room that special blessing that redeems it from some limitations or make universal some special goodness that belongs to it. Thus, if it is too dark, breathe a blessing of God's light shining there— who knows? perhaps some one will think of putting a little window in the roof or high in the wall or some fit place that will be the outpicturing of your silent prayer. Another room may be all that is ideal in its appointments, and as you stand in the center of that room radiate its rich spirit to the thousands of homes round about that are void of that comfort and beauty; some receptive heart will catch the message and the spirit, and another home will grow towards heaven because of your loving prayer.

" In my Father's house are many mansions," many manifestations of harmony and every other good—" I go to prepare a place for you." The Christ ever goes forth to prepare yours for you, mine for me, and all for all. You do likewise who build a happy home, not for yourself alone, but for all, not for time alone, but for all eternity.

THE SEVENTH DAY. Saturday — Perfection

SEVEN is the number of the perfect Man, who has made the complete union between the human and the Divine, therefore the day was pronounced sacred to the finished work of the Creator, a day to celebrate, a holy day and a holiday, which are one in Spirit and true manifestation.

When the Christ in Jesus blessed every day of the week, and made them all holy, there were some of his Hebrew followers who still " esteemed one day above another." For their sake the resurrection-day became the Lord's Day, nevertheless Saturday, as the Sabbath, was not wholly abolished among the Jewish Christians, and it was of them that Paul wrote (Rom. xiv, 5): " One man esteemeth one day above another: another esteemeth every day alike. Let every man be fully persuaded in his own mind." At this time every Christian knew himself to be a priest of God, a " Levite," ready to serve the Lord in each with roast sacrifices of lamb and beeves, and sacred bread and honored wine. Their communions were love-feasts where some would come with large appetites and exhibit unseemly greed, so that Paul felt the need of ministering such rebukes as in the eleventh chapter of First Corinthians, twenty-first, thirty-third and thirty-fourth verses, counselling them to take the edge off their hunger before coming to the table of the Lord, lest they eat with forgetfulness.

There was so much to do in these servings that special officers were appointed for the work, the very first one being the great Stephen, " a man full of faith, and the Holy Ghost," and power, doing "great wonders and miracles among the people " (Acts vi, 2-8). He proved that a lover of Truth can serve tables and minister the Word, do great works most effectually, reason with intellectual rulers, have the face of an angel (Acts vi, 15), and endure martyrdom, realizing the glory of the cosmic vision in his passing hour (Acts vii, 55, 56).

In the old dispensation the Sabbath was the busiest day of the week for the priests, for there was so much to do of sacred service, and the natural descendant of that Levitical labor is the strenuous finishing work of our old time housewives on Saturday. And the orthodox clergy of to-day find their Sabbath the most laborious day of the week, for they, too, cling to the old dispensation, the " esteeming one day above another." It is in our power to unite the rich-providing work of the old living with the light merrymaking of the new, and make of our Saturdays both a rounding fullness of a week well-lived and an overflowing holiday of care-free frolic, thus most happily wedding work and play at this meeting of the ways of the old week and the new.

Saturday is the day of Saturn, or Satan, the ancient god of wrath, whose reign was finished with the incoming of the Christ. This is the god whose subtle, secret revenge upon his enemies has been so well depicted in that mythological character after whom the planet Saturn was named, and which is said to have astrological influences — cold, cruel, selfish and deceitful— upon those in opposition, but beneficent to those who know how to " agree with their adversary " and to be still before it, and more subtle, mounting to God in their selfness, and able always to lift up every serpent in the wilderness.

Interesting declarations are made for these times by spiritual astrologers, who tell us that as a race we have passed from the dominant ruling of Saturn to that of Uranus, and whereas our most successful men have been of the saturnine temperament— cool, calculating and secretive — the men who will succeed in this age, and for coming centuries, will be of the Uranian temperament— bold and radical, frank and original, willing to trust their impressions, and acknowledge psychical powers; and certainly the men who are the rising rulers of the hour are largely fulfilling that description— exeunt the Rockefeller type of success, enter the Roosevelt manner of leaders. "All the world's a stage," and every actor has his day.

Saturday is the day in which we redeem every remaining evil belief, beginning with that god of evil called Satan, the devil, " that old serpent."

When the children of Israel were journeying from Egypt to the Land of Promise, they became rebellious and complaining, and old desires for their former slave life came upon them, for then they could also enjoy some of the rich dishes of their masters. Their fault-findings and bitter loathings took form as serpents that turned upon their creators and stung them to death. Then Moses prayed for knowledge of the way to deliver his people, and was told to make an image of a serpent from brass in such a fashion that it could glow with the heat and light of fire within it, then to lift this upon a pole, or cross, and it would follow that all who would listen and obey should be healed by simply lifting their eyes to the image which had been moulded under the directions of the Holy Spirit, and they repented and were healed.

The same method was advised for those Philistines whose capture and retention of the ark of the Lord in their midst seemed to work them evil instead of good, because they could not live up to it. They became afflicted with boils, and their fields were overrun with a pest of mice. They returned the ark, and sought counsel of the Israelites, and were told to make images of the mice and of the boils in gold, and present them to the Lord, and they did so, and were healed in body and in their land.

A wonderful principle is involved in these strange performances, and it is for us not to miss the secret power of deliverance that comes through understanding how to make a mental image of our infliction under the guidance of the Spirit, so that we can lift up our eyes, our perception, and be healed.

The " abomination of desolation," or the most hateful and destructive agency in our lives, must come to the holy place of the high and noble recognition of the goodness there before the end of the old condition can come to pass. To love your enemy you must find God there.

Satan is the reverse side of God, called in the Old Testament, " the anger of the Lord," as is shown by comparing II Samuel, twenty-fourth chapter and first verse with I Chronicles, twenty-first chapter and first verse. It is that view of God that gives deity all the false characteristics of the mortal, such as deception, killing, revenge, hate, and all those degrading traits that the illuminated have said must be destroyed in man that he may please

God. But this view of God had its good effect in arresting certain degeneration through a wholesome fear, until the Christ consciousness should reveal the God of love, through the love that knows that what the Great One rebukes in man cannot be in Itself.

Satan is that aspect of divinity which is a terror to evil-doers, and a tester to those on the upward way. No mere pretender can pass its examination successfully, but the true candidate for celestial degrees realizes the nature of its examinations, and comes through with honors. And yet so advanced is the knowledge of divinity now that it is possible to be " honorably promoted,"* not having the necessity of examination, or testing, to prove us worthy. Thus are our daily prayers answered, "Lead us not into temptation." Satan, the seventh angel of the Lord (called in Isaiah eleventh chapter, third verse, " the fear of the Lord ") came among the Sons of God (Job i, 6) when they assembled to consider that master, Job, and his fitness for further blessings. He tries Job even as he tested Jesus— the one

passed through quickly without failure, the other becomes a type of the long trial through which so many are passing— long because of ignorance, yet triumphant in the end, so that the candidate has honors and riches many fold more than in the beginning. Satan redeemed becomes the mystery of Godliness, that open door to the infinite variety, the unexpected, the eccentric that ever allows the unusual, the rare, the unconventional to be expressed in harmony with the whole.

Saturday in its employments is a combination of contradictions, being a holiday for some, the hardest workday of the week for others, and sabbath-day for others still. It is a day in which to deify that which has been our cross, our sorrow, grievance, humiliation, and so remove the sting, and be healed of the bite. Work itself may be our Satan, yet it may have a grand ripening mission for us in preparing us for our own place, just as Saturday prepares for Sunday. Instead of running away from it, hating it, and rebelling, let us use the subtle policy of Jesus Christ, who threw himself whole-heartedly into the earth life until he made it yield up its sweetness and richness to all. It is possible to finish quickly with a hard and uncongenial piece of work by getting from it for oneself and others all that which God intended.

The principle work of Saturday is baking and cooking in general, and the meditations which we will associate with this day's work we can connect with every meal that is prepared throughout the week.

Right here it is well to call attention to the fact that many times one will be so absorbed in one's work that no special spiritual thinking will come to mind, then the habit of associating elevated ideas with that work in particular will imbue the whole with spirituality and make it a joyous, free expression wherein the Good only is remembered. It is not necessary always to think upon exact ideals, but rather to have one's whole activity idealized by perpetual recognition of the beautiful, the good and the true everywhere.

What one cooks partakes of one's nature, and the more of one's quality of goodness, such as love and kindly care and thought, one puts into food the more it is relished. It is not always that the cook thinks about the food she is preparing— sometimes she gives it no special thought —but it is to have a certain radiance of goodness that is sympathetic and interesting in its quality.

Home cooking is enjoyed because mother-love is put into it. A rich sympathetic human interest enters into such food which is missing when the food is machine-made, or when the mind of the cook is filled with commercial dryness and dead indifference. It is the hearty, genuine interest in people that makes the success of the public caterer, especially when combined with fearlessness and a correct sense of values.

Nothing is more prolific of symbolical suggestion than food. It is much favored in the Bible to indicate heavenly truths that nourish the spiritual man; meat is used for strong statements of truth, milk for elementary teaching (Heb. v, 12-14). So also fruit, bread, wine, butter and honey are used for truths which are to be appropriated and assimilated.

When making bread, remember Jesus' comparison of the Kingdom of Heaven to the three measures of meal which a woman takes in preparing loaves for the baking. The Master was wonderfully familiar with the common tasks of lowly life, and almost all his metaphors are drawn from domestic and field life. And nothing shows this better than this figure (Matt, xiii, 33). First the yeast (the truth) is put into a small measure of flour (the twelve disciples) until that measure is thoroughly leavened. Then it is mixed with the next measure (the Christians of the past centuries) and now the third measure is receiving its working. So with the three-fold individual man, the measures may be named, soul, body and affairs. Long has the human soul, or character, been under the influence of the Christ message, until now the next measure, the physical body, is being electrified with vitality, and ultimately the grand old world will respond to its persistent love-leavening.

In the home the family can be changed from discontent and dissatisfaction by cooking the food with the true thought. A complaining mood spoils digestion more than material things. " Better is a dinner of herbs where love is than a stalled ox and hatred therewith" (Prov. xv, 17). A certain hausfrau had much difficulty in satisfying her large hungry family of six grown sons and their father. With old-fashioned German lavishness she provided the best and plenty for ordinary appetites, but her men had extraordinary appetites. In vain she increased the quantity— they were never quite satisfied. When she received the understanding that their real hunger was for spiritual food she silently bespoke for each the true satisfaction. The result was almost startling. They became normal, and her cooking was no longer a burden, and sweet content reigned in her house.

Every meal can be a communion. " This do in remembrance of Me." Eat and drink of the spiritual body—" a body hast thou prepared for me" — by remembering that man liveth not by bread alone, but by the Word, which he is in the mouth of the Lord. The silent grace before eating sanctifies all the food so that nothing can by any means harm you. Discern the body of the Lord in everything that is set before you. Often invoke the power of the Spirit to reveal its presence in all that you eat.

Discern for me, O, Spirit, The body of my Lord;

I eat thee, I drink thee, I live by thy Word.

He that is of a merry heart hath a continual feast (Prov. xv, 15). Nothing worrisome or vexatious should ever be discussed at meal time. A silent invocation for the realization of their Good working in and through their lives should be breathed for those who come to breakfast with a scowl and a complaint, and it is often in the power of the captain of the house-ship to steer her charge clear from the reefs and rocks of inharmonious conversation.

One of the opportunities for the cultivation of patience and self-control is in dish-washing. Certain truth-students have found that they get their most inspiring thoughts when engaged in this common task. The very mechanical nature of their work allows them to dismiss the material thoughts, and to be open to the Spirit. But this is not day-dreaming. By their fruits you can know the difference. Spiritual meditation takes no goodness from the work, but makes all bright and clean, while idle day-dreaming is shown in the neglected and careless results. Special thought can be held for the good of the family appetites when washing dishes. One then can be cleansing away greed, intemperance and idolatry of food.

No day should be given wholly over to material work from morning to night. Recreation is just as true activity as work, and Saturday is the day to remember planning some interesting entertainment, so that the day may demonstrate that divine unity of zealous accomplishment and merry-making that marks the graceful expression of a happy life.

Certain thoughts are working throughout the nation that will solve the servant question. One of them is a recognition of the necessity of making the kitchen, which is the most trying place in the house, a realm of peace and comfort to be respected by all. The loving heart and hand that makes the servant's room as pleasant as any in the house will never lack for efficient help. To the kitchen gravitates naturally the thoughts that are the by-products of the family life, and the wise mistress can often save a situation when her servant is at a height of irritation by a silent blessing and a helping hand of love. The Golden Rule is the best one to remember in connection with all that serve you.

The word for Saturday is Perfection, that perfection which is above the opposites of mortal sense, above the good and evil of human judgment, that holiness beyond the ethics of virtue and vice — that perfection which has not evolved, but has ever been and always will be perfect, the same yesterday, to-day and forever.

Fill up the measure with a sinless life of love, wholly blameless, sanctified even as Christ is sanctified. " Be ye perfect, even as your Father in heaven is perfect." I am perfect, for my source is Perfection itself.

"All things are now ready." " Enter ye into the joy of your Lord." Meet every unredeemed state with the declaration, " It is finished." Identify every form of good with its perfection in God. Uplift your whole world by the power of truth, and so finish the work which your Father has given you to do.

CLOSING WORD

THE vision of Truth is of one day, endless, all light, in which all expression is gloriously complete. Its creative method is blissful wishing that is perpetually gratified. The out-breathings and in-breathings of the Almighty Expressor are effortless and irresistible Love.

The Realm of the inspired and inspiring Word is here, and you sit upon Its throne. The elements rush eagerly to serve You. You say, "Be!" and it is so. As toys in the hands of a babe, as skillful tools in the hands of an artisan, as magical words on the lips of the Christ, so do You use the omnipotent forces that bring all things to pass. With a touch You move what You will, with a look You command all things. The dream of toil has passed like a fleck of mist, and You are awake in the Christ-consciousness, Lord of All.

BOOK SEVEN.
ALL THE WAY

A Handbook for Those who have entered the Path and have determined to walk all the Way with Christ to the Heights of the Ascension

Foreword

THOSE who have made up their minds to go on to the Ascension, taking all the steps essential to that attainment, should read each chapter and verse carefully and prayerfully. For there is a teaching for each Candidate which is beneath the words and unwritten and, to catch that instruction, there must be a conscious openness to the TEACHER WITHIN.

The writing of this Handbook on ALL THE Way has not been by subject or by any fixed order that human intellect might dictate, but on the contrary. For each chapter was written as the substance came to me with apparent repetitions, and some disconnected and irrelevant presentations, because of leaving the construction wholly to the Spirit that guides the Candidate into all the truth that belongs to achieving the Christ goal.

The paragraphs are numbered as well as the chapters for convenience in referring to specific instruction,

God grant that many will be led to commune with themselves and, by the power of their own great Self, determine to reach the Heights. Any communication from you, dear Reader, as to your experiences and aspirations as well as obstacles in the Path upon which your feet shall henceforth walk, will be welcome and held in sacred confidence.

Let us ever remember that none could make this attainment in his own strength. It is God that walks the Way in us and is our Almighty Power to attain the Heights. To him only belongs the glory.

Annie Rix Militz, Sierra Madre, Calif.

I.

And there went great multitudes with him: and he turned, and said unto them.

If any man come to me and hate not his father, and mother, and wife, and children, and brethren, and sisters, yea, and his own life also, he cannot be my disciple.

And whosoever doth not bear his cross, and come after me, cannot be my disciple.

For which of you, intending to build a tower, sitteth not down first, and counteth the cost, whether he have sufficient to finish it?

Lest haply, after he hath laid the foundation, and is not able to finish it, all that behold it begin to mock him.

Saying, This man began to build, and was not able to finish.

Or what king, going to make war against another king, sitteth not down first, and consulteth whether he be able with ten thousand to meet him that cometh against him with twenty thousand?

Or else, while the other is yet a great way off, he sendeth an embassage, and desiretk conditions of peace.

So likewise, whosoever he be of you that forsaketh not all that he hath, he cannot be my disciple. — Luke 14:25-33.

EVERYONE who is contemplating going forward in the Christ Life to its glorious ultimate must begin to consider all that it means. It means all for All.

2 Therefore Jesus presents it very strongly, that unless you can, in seeking to do the will and work of Christ, be indifferent to relatives, even to the one who has been dearest, and indifferent to your own life, you cannot follow the Master to the heights.

3 Holding to one's possessions, to one's pleasures, to one's duty to relatives, has kept many an earnest heart from making the attainment — the price, "all that he hath," has been kept back.

4 He who sets out upon the Way of the Christ begins to lay the foundation of a Tower, which is the new body, the incorruptible body in which he can achieve the Ascension. To build upon that foundation a finished structure, he must have every stone of the Christ doctrine, alert to reject none lest he miss "the head of the corner," and therefore find himself among the many who shall strive to enter in and shall not be able,

5 This Walk with God means a consciousness in the outer (the body) and a consciousness within (the character). The king, your aspiring self, must consider whether it has the equipment to fight the carnal self that seems so strong. And if there seems something lacking one must either fight like David about to meet Goliath, casting oneself wholly upon God, or must take the whole message of the Christ of non-resistance and "agreeing with thine adversary," not warring at all but winning over evil with good.

6 The Christ Way is bearing your cross instead of rebelling and fighting it. The carnal self seems to cross the self that is aspiring to be one with the true Self. The old, violent way was to fight it, beating and otherwise punishing it unmercifully — the crucifixion that ended in death of the body. But Jesus was crucified literally once for all people, and we who follow him to the Ascension now "take up (elevate) our cross and follow" him.

7 So also other things that humiliate, persecute and torment one are crosses, not to be fought nor run away from, but to be lifted as Moses lifted the brazen serpent in the wilderness under the Lord's direction, and it healed all those who had been bitten by serpents, when they obediently "looked up" to it.

8 Every relative, friend or other personality must be secondary to the Life. The measure of one's freedom from relatives and other people is indicated by the amount of disturbance that is made within us by the contemplation of their disapproval or misunderstanding of us, or their loss through defection, treachery or death. Can we still realize the immortal Life of them and ourselves? Do we continue to hold our peace and trust the Best in them? Let go I Give up! Loosen every chain.

9 "Who is my mother, or my brethren? Whosoever shall do the will of God, the same is my brother, my sister, and my mother,"

(Mark 3:33-35). "And call no man your father upon the earth: for one is your Father, which is in heaven," (Matt. 23:9).

10 "If any man come to me and hate not his . . ." (Luke 14:26); the word "hate" is not a good translation of the Greek word which means "to love less." For these relatives are our "neighbors" whom we are enjoined to love as ourselves, the Second Commandment, which "is like unto the First."

The significance is this, that when it comes to a choice, and we take our love for, or duty to, our relatives instead of the Way which is plainly to follow some direction of the Christ, then we cannot follow him all the Way.

11 Duty, even what seems a most sacred duty, must not interfere. Nothing was more binding in the heart of a filial Hebrew than to observe

the last sacred rites in the burial of a parent. Yet the Master commanded one of his followers to

"Let the dead bury their dead, but go thou and preach the kingdom of God," (Luke 9:59, 60).

12 Not even sentiment shall enter in, not old observances of the ceremonies and habits that connect one with the former relationships shall interfere with the direct call to go forward in this upward Way.

13 Another follower of Jesus wished to turn back, to ceremoniously bid his people farewell, thus making himself liable to their influence and placing a stumblingblock in his way. To him Jesus replies:

"No man, having put his hand to the plough, and looking back, is fit for the kingdom of God," (Luke 9:62).

14 "Go thou and preach the kingdom of God," is the word to all who are learning there is but one business in life, our heavenly Father's business. "Wist ye not that I must be about my Father's business?" (Luke 2:49).

15 "Labour not for the meat that perisheth, but for that meat which endureth unto everlasting life" (John 6:27), and he called his disciples from their fish nets and they dropped them where they were and followed him. He said to Matthew, the publican, as he sat at the money-changer's table, "Follow me," and he rose then and there and left his table as it was, and followed him.

16 No earthly business must stand in the way when the Master calls, even though that business be one's very life. No cares of the household should keep one from sitting at the Master's feet and serving him in the way he would be served, in ministering Truth to a hungry world.

17 We remember Jesus' rebuke of the fretful and complaining Martha, burdened with much serving, when she would take Mary away from listening to the message of Truth: "Martha, Martha, thou art careful and troubled about many things: but one thing is needful: and Mary hath chosen that good part, which shall not be taken away from her," (Luke 10:38-42).

18 There is but one work for those who are walking the earthly road for the last time, and the sooner and the fuller such enter into this work of teaching the nations the Christ life, the more quickly they will advance in the heavenly Way and finish all earth's sorrows and hardships.

19 Meditation upon Jesus' words as our very own establishes the state of mind that will outpicture in the most direct and easiest way, the means and method of external accomplishment:

"To this end was I born, and for this cause came I into the world, that I should bear witness unto the truth. Every one that is of the truth heareth my voice," (John 18:37).

"I must work the works of him that sent me, while it is day: the night cometh when no man can work," (John 9:4).

"Say not ye, There are yet four months, and then cometh harvest. Behold, I say unto you, Lift up your eyes and look on the fields; for they are white already to harvest."

"The harvest truly is great, but the labourers

are few: pray ye therefore the Lord of the harvest, that he would send forth labourers into his harvest," {John 4:35 and Luke 10:2).

"My Father worketh hitherto and I work," (John 5:17).

"Take no thought how or what ye shall speak: for it shall be given you in that same hour what ye shall speak. For it is not ye that speak, but the Spirit of your Father which speaketh in you," (Matt. 10:19, 20).

"The words that I speak unto you, I speak not of myself: but the Father that dwelleth in me, he doeth the works," (John 14:10).

"My meat is to do the will of him that sent me and to finish his work," (John 4:34).

"It is finished," (John 19:30).

20 And the work which Christ has given you to do? Six directions were given to the original twelve with the injunction that they were to teach others to do all that he had told them to do: "Go ye therefore and teach all nations . . . teaching them to observe all things whatsoever I have commanded you," (Matt. 28:19, 20).

The six directions are (Matt. 10:7, 8):

1 Go, preach, saying, The kingdom of

of heaven is at hand.

2 Heal the sick.

3 Cleanse the lepers.

4 Raise the dead.

5 Cast out devils.

6 Freely ye have received, freely give.

21 The direction "Freely give" is especially stressed by the Master. For each one that enters the Way must learn early that God alone is our support and the means of our supply, and that all that we do should be without a thought of compensation from those benefited.

22 This going forth into the highways and byways of the world without thought of whereby we shall be fed, clothed or housed is a splendid adventure more fraught with surprises and marvellous achievements than those of the knights of old, whether Crusaders or mere adventurers.

23 We need no backing but the Holy Spirit, none to call us and ordain us but the Voice of Jesus Christ within us. And God will make our word and our work, good.

24 In all ways we loosen our minds from dependence upon worldly methods for our support and from looking to personalities to supply us or uphold us. We free ourselves from looking to our own work, whether spiritual or material, as our means of supply.

25 All attachment to money ceases with those who walk the Way; every one holding himself ready, no matter how great or how small or how precious his possessions may be, to "sell that ye have and give alms." Such a state of mind provides a perpetual wealth, "bags that wax not old, a treasure in the heavens that faileth not," (Luke 12:33).

26 We cannot be divided in our thoughts, feelings and works between worldly things and methods and those of the Spirit, one or the other will suffer neglect and we shall make a success of neither. "No man can serve two masters: for either he will hate the one and love the other; or else he will hold to the one and despise the other. Ye cannot serve God and mammon. Therefore I say unto you, Take no thought for your life, what ye shall eat or what ye shall drink; nor yet for your body what ye shall put on," (Matt. 6:24, 25).

27 Of the two masters God is the one and money is the other. To try to serve both results in being indifferent to God ("hating the One") and worshipping money or giving it power and respect ("loving the other") or on the other hand, to try to serve both God and money, will be to attempt to live the spiritual life ("hold to the One") and to have such a contempt for money ("despise the other") as to be impractical in demonstrating prosperity.

28 The only way is to give all power, all thought, all respect and all place to God and let money follow that true consciousness as its natural shadow. So shall you be "seeking first the kingdom of God and his righteousness" and seeing "all these things" after which the worldly people seek "added unto you," (Matt. 6:33).

II

Behold I skew you a mystery; We shall not all sleep, but we shall all be changed.

In a moment, in the twinkling of an eye, at the last trump: far the trumpet shall sound, and the dead shall be raised incorruptible, and we shall be changed.

For this corruptible must put on incorruption, and this mortal must put on immortality.

So when this corruptible shall have put on incorruption, and this mortal shall have put on immortality, then shall be brought to pass the saying that is written, Death is swallowed up in victory.

O death, where is thy sting? O grave, where is thy victory?

The sting of death is sin; and the strength of sin is the taw.

But thanks be to God, which giveth us the victory through our Lord Jesus Christ.

Therefore, my beloved brethren, be ye steadfast, un- ' moveable, always abounding in the work of the Lord, for as much as ye know that your labour is not vain in the Lord.— I Cor. 15:51-58.

1 The Way of the Christ is called in Isaiah 35:8, "The way of holiness." The prophet declares that "the unclean shall not pass over it but it shall be for those," that is, whoever enters that path of regeneration begins to be clean with his first step and, in order to progress ("pass over it") he must grow cleaner with every step.

2 Health is one of the requisites of the Candidate: every cell that has been liable to corruption must be cleansed of all such tendency and become, in form and substance, absolutely without corruption.

3 Therefore an education of complete purity begins in the feeling and thinking nature. Every lustful thought is arrested instantly. "You are none of mine," said one faithful student who began to see that the unwelcome suggestions coming to him did not originate with him. And the thoughts receded like the voice of a dream.

4 Every involuntary response in the body to a lustful suggestion is arrested, while communion begins silently with the Holy One within, our incorruptible Self.

5 Such an inner work begins the cleansing of the cells of the body. Whatever appearance of corruption may then force itself upon one's notice must be treated as though it were the whole body, rising from the dead.

6 A faithful demonstration with a single cell, is the uplifting (raising up or resurrection) of all the cells — the whole body. Therefore walk honestly, in purity and in strength, from one incorruptible expression to another, until this whole body is "clothed upon with our house which is from heaven," (2 Cor. 5:2).

7 Perpetual youth is another requisite of those who are Candidates for the Christ attainment. "His flesh shall be fresher than a child's: he shall return to the days of his youth," (Job 33:25).

8 It matters not how many years may seem to have accumulated, let the Candidate but become young in heart and mind through remembering that the True Self is ever youthful (even while it is the Ancient of Days) and thereupon the body will begin to show renewal, and the whole being be filled with interest, enthusiasm, joy and strength.

9 It is promised that those who serve their God-Self shall renew their strength (Is. 40:31); they shall know no weariness; they shall cast their burdens upon the Lord; they shall not fail nor faint nor lose courage, but they "shall renew their youth like the eagle's" (the phoenix); and all these things are looked for in this Path of wisdom.

10 For the Way of the Christ is a joyous road wherein all the world's pleasures return to their innocence, purity and full zest. "They shall obtain joy and gladness, and sorrow and sighing shall flee away," (Is. 35:10). For Christ's way is truly the path of Wisdom, of whom it is written, "Her ways are ways of pleasantness and all her paths are peace," (Prov. 3:17).

11 Take every tear as a sign that some of the old life remains, and begin to purge the memory of its gloomy pictures and imaginations; heal the feelings of false sensitiveness, self-pity and the sense of the reality of the wrongs and griefs of mortality. Tenderness and sweet sympathy and compassion are Christ powers that act most perfectly when free from the weakness of tears.

12 The Way of Christ is all joy and all that walk it should walk in peace and happiness, adhering as faithfully to these expressions of the true Life, as the ancient religionists held to morality and goodness.

13 "In the way of righteousness is life; and in the pathway thereof there is no death" (Prov. 12:28) and all meditation upon death is finished. There is no looking forward to it as a release, nor is there any fear of death and what will follow.

14 "I AM the Door" and "I Am the Life," says the Christ, therefore Life is the Door and not death. Every Candidate should press on ardently to the Door of the Christ Life to pass quickly to the powers of the Ascension. For

none can serve God and humanity; so effectually and efficiently as those who are free to function with their whole being upon any, and all, planes, a power in which Jesus Christ dwells now who, describing that state, declared "All power is given unto me in heaven and in earth," (Matt. 28:18).

'15 "But some doubt," questioning their ability to reach the goal. Let them then seek to live the long life, even the patriarchal age, and use each year with all faithfulness to surmount unbelief and let God work out his own divine desire concerning them.

16 More than anything else, seek to be infused with the divine breath called the Holy Spirit. This is the baptism that brings about all things. It is the instantaneous and universal working of the whole of Heaven in Man.

17 Prayer is the one supreme instrument given to man by God for all attainment. "Pray without ceasing." "Watch and pray always." "This Spirit itself maketh intercession for us."

18 Prayer is the Word of God. It is God speaking to God. It is the Breath of God that is back of our physical breath, and when we are alert in consciousness of prayer or breathing from God, if our physical breath were suspended, we would continue life in this physical form through the Soul-breath until the physical breath should again be free.

19 "Tarry ye in the city of Jerusalem" — abide in spiritual and moral form and trueness, "until ye be endued with power from on high," (Luke 24:52). "Then returned they unto Jerusalem" and "all continued with one accord in prayer and supplication" (Acts 1:12, 14) "and when the day of Pentecost was fully come, they were all with one accord in one place, and suddenly there came a sound from heaven as of a rushing mighty wind, and it filled all the house where they were sitting. And there appeared unto them cloven tongues like as of fire and it sat upon each of them. And they were all filled with the Holy Ghost," (Acts 2:1 to 4).

"If ye then being evil know how to give good gifts to your children: how much more shall your heavenly Father give the Holy Spirit to them that ask him."

20 Forty days had the disciples communed with the resurrected Jesus Christ, upon the "things pertaining to the kingdom of God," (Acts 1:3), and then they witnessed his "taking up." And, following his command, they stayed close in Jerusalem abiding and praying with one accord for ten days, and on the Fiftieth Day after the Passover week (from the day of the Resurrection) the same baptism descended upon the disciples that came upon Jesus as he went up out of the waterbaptism of John the Baptist, (Mark 1:10, 11).

Meditate upon this initiation of those who walk all the way with Christ, and pray and commune with the Spirit and wait on the Lord until you know yourself "endued with power from on high."

III

They which shall be accounted worthy to obtain that world, and the resurrection from the dead, neither marry, nor are given in marriage. — Luke 20:35.

Behold the bridegroom cometh; go ye out to meet him. —Matt. 25:6.

Let your loins be girded about, and your lights burning; and ye yourselves like unto men that wait for their Lord, when he will return from the wedding; that when he cometh and knocketh, they may open unto him immediately.— Luke 12:35, 36.

And the Spirit and the bride say. Come. And let him that heareth say, Come. — Rev. 22:17.

All men cannot receive this saying, save they to whom it is given. For there are some eunuchs, which were so born from their mother's womb: and there are some eunuchs, which were made eunuchs of men: and there be eunuchs, which have made themselves eunuchs for the kingdom of heaven's sake. He that is able to receive it, let him receive it. — Matt. 19:11, 12.

Strive to enter in at the strait gate; for many, I say unto you, will seek to enter in, and shall not be able. — Luke 13:24.

I am the Way.— John 14:6.

I am the Door.— John 10:7, 9.

By me if any man enter in, he shall be saved, and shall go in and out and find pasture. — John 10:9.

Enter ye in at the strait gate: for wide is the gate, and broad is the way, that leadeth to destruction, and many there be which go in thereat. Because strait is the gate, and narrow is the way which leadeth unto life, and few there be that find it. — Matt. 7:13, 14.

To him that overcometh will I grant to sit with me on my throne. . . Behold I have set before thee an open door, and no man can shut it. — Rev. 3:21, 8.

1 Ability to make the Heights, living to, and in, the New Age and overcoming death, is especially indicated by one's freedom from the thought of marriage and turning wholly from marrying or being given in marriage.

2 All expectancy of happiness through finding a mate on the earth must be turned to Christ, as the one spiritual Bridegroom, to God, as the one Husband. "Thy maker is thy husband," (Is. 54:5).

3 In the regeneration, every woman is to the candidate, his Mother or Sister, every man, her Father or Brother, and these relationships are with the Christ within each.

4 The union with the Universal is realized through giving the closest relationship, that human beings can have, to God, Christ and the Holy Spirit, finding the Bridegroom in these, likewise the Bride.

5 The portals of immortality are opened only to Virginity, which is first a consciousness, completed by the outer form of being sealed unto the Lord.

6 The heart and mind receive the seal when all one's generative powers are turned from flesh use and carnal pleasure. Then the psychical nature is sealed from astral imposition, as we read in Ezekiel 9:4 ("the mark," according to Tertullian was X tne Tau Cross) and Rev. 7:3. "Sealed in their foreheads" is more literally, in the top of the head, where we are psychically open, as a babe is physically open, until the Master of Regeneration has sealed us, as fruit is sealed with wax and so protected from the fermentation of corruption and death.

7 Then follows the sealing of the body as in a virgin state, so that the physical skin hermetically (so called because of the magic of Hermes or Thoth, god of thought) seals the whole body from the intrusion of death and decomposition. "And after my skin hath compassed this body, in my flesh I shall see God* [immortality]," Job 19:26 — Young's Translation combined with A. V.

8 While one appears to be in a sensual world, in order not to be "of it" there must be a perpetual alertness not to be seduced by the false suggestions of one's own old nature or by false prophets who do not accept Jesus Christ.

9 For more candidates have fallen by the wayside, who were near to their goal, by a false attitude as to sex than by any other error. Theirs is the failure of David, who through the weakness of sex desire became "a man of blood," causing the death of Bathsheba's husband, and so he could not build the house of the Lord, that is, his immortal body on the earth.

10 Keep "oil for your lamps" by conserving your creative powers, increasing in knowledge and in other ways "laying up treasures in heaven"; so shall you be a "wise virgin," ready for the cosmic consciousness when it shall descend upon you.

11 "Gird up your loins" by refraining from loose speech and habits and ways respecting sexual matters, yet "quit you like men" who are virile and free and a law unto themselves.

12 By this fine culture, all the senses grow very refined, alert, delicate and sensitive, so that one hears instantly the gentle knock of the True Self (the Bridegroom) and opens the Door to him immediately.

13 All are being called to this Perfect Life, and he who hears the call should not hesitate to call others as he sees they will listen. But no one is to be pressed to walk all the Way, for only those can enter the path to remain who have the inner urge. All shall be taught of God (John 6:45) eventually, and step upon the great Way. We can invite them to live this life but only God in them can respond to, and accept, this invitation.

14 Those who are able to enter the virgin life and there abide, are divided into three classes, according to Jesus (Matt. 19:12): (1)

Those who from birth have been able to control their sex desire; (2) Those who have continued in the virgin life because circumstances have compelled it. It is as though there had been a secret understanding with their guardian angels, that he or she should be kept from lawless or even lawful carnal intercourse, because the desire to go all the Way would be greater.

15 The third class are those who may have lost their virginity through earthly marriaee, or through ignorant license, or through assault. But when they learn that, to go all the Way they must become as a little child, or youths and maidens whose virginity is inviolate, then their hearts are given to the pure Christ life, and God works with them to deliver them finally from all external temptation and carnal approach.

16 With all the zeal in you, seek to go into the Way by the Absolute Truth and perfect obedience to the Christ. Many are trying to enter into this complete bliss, but only those will succeed who co-operate absolutely with Jesus Christ.

17 For Jesus Christ is the only one who has walked all the Way to translation in the sight of men. Enoch walked with God and pleased God and so was translated, but he took his secret with him. Therefore Jesus is the Way to be translated.

18 But the Ascension is more than translation. Enoch and Elijah were translated into the heavenly realm, but they know not the Way to be translated back into the earthly realm, but this was what Jesus accomplished. "By me if any man enter in he shall be saved and go in and out. I am the Door."

19 The Gate and the Way are so narrow that only one can walk that Way, and only one can enter that Gate or Door. That one is the Christ and to enter that Gate and not be challenged by the Porter (the Cherubims, Gen. 3:24; "To him [the Christ] the porter openeth," John 10:3) we must be able to give the password, "I am the Christ."

20 All mortality is in the broad road that leads to death and destruction. Back and forth, round and round they wander, yet the straight and narrow road runs right through and across the broad way, as the straight line runs through the serpentine "S" in the dollar mark. And any moment the wanderer can enter the Way if he will,

"How far is it to Heaven? Not very far my friend; A single, hearty step Will all your journey end."

21 All roads may lead to Rome but only one road leads to Heaven. Only the Absolute Truth, with no dualism in it, contains all the principles. Only one Master, Jesus Christ, he who walked all the Way and entered in at the Door can guide, all other Masters, Gurus, Prophets, Law-givers and Saviors have left their disciples to wander alone finally to die, falling short of the mark. But Jesus Christ though invisible still walks with his followers, and will continue to do so to the end of time. 22 Bend your whole being with all zeal, prayer, devotion, faithfulness, fullness of love, to co-operate with Christ who has overcome the world, the flesh and the devil; and you will find yourself on the throne of Christ with all power in heaven and on earth, with death under foot and with the Hosts of Heaven and the inhabitants of the earth glorifying God, that he has given such power and honor to men.

IV

Whosoever will come after me, let him deny himself and take up his cross and follow me. — Mark 8:38.

And he that taieth not his cross, and followeth after me, is not worthy of me. — Matt. 10:38.

Whosoever shall seek to save his life shall lose it; and whosoever shall lose his life shall preserve it. — Luke 17:33.

For whosoever will save his life shall lose it-' and whosoever will lose his life for my sake shall find it. — Matt. 16:25.

How can ye believe which receive honour one of another and seek not the honour that cometh from God onlyf — John 5:44.

I receive not honour from men. — John 5:41.

I seek not mine own glory. — John 8:50.

I seek not mine own will. — John 5:30.

I can of mine own self do nothing.— John 5:30.

The son can do nothing of himself. — John 5:19.

I speak not of myself. — John 14:10.

He that speaketh of himself seeketh his own glory: but he that seeketh his glory that sent him, the same is true and no unrighteousness is in him. — John 7:18.

Be not ye called Rabbi: for one is your Master, even Christ; and all ye are brethren. Neither be ye called masters: for one is your Master, even Christ. — Matt. 23:8, 10.

Why callest thou me good? There is none good but one, that is, God.— Matt. 19:17.

When ye have done all those things which are commanded you, say, We are unprofitable servants: we have done that which was our duty to do. — Luke 17:1 0.

For thine is the kingdom, and the power, and the glory, for ever. Amen. — Matt. 6:13.

Put off . . . the old man which is corrupt . . . and be renewed in the spirit of your mind, and . . . put on the new man which after God is created in righteousness and true holiness. — Eph. 4:22, 23, 24.

Ye have put off the old man with his deeds, and have put on the new man which is renewed in knowledge after the image of him that created him. — Col. 3:9, 10.

1 The selfless life is the magical power to draw God and to be rilled with one's Divinity.

2 The human I am must become utterly nothing to human sense while the divine I AM takes its place.

3 This is an accomplishment utterly impossible without the conscious co-operation of Jesus Christ, who brings it to pass by his Godknowledge and power.

4 Perpetual, silent prayer to the Father to remove and dissolve the human selfhood must be the ready weapon of him who would make the attainment.

5 To annul and neutralize the subtle assertion of the human self means alertness, watchfulness and unceasing communion with one's Divinity.

6 For the little I am merges so completely into the great I AM that ultimately all that is declared applies (to human sense) to both, and no sharp line of distinction can be drawn.

7 Previous to that conscious at-one-ment, the little I am must be thoroughly cleansed of all sense of separate selfhood, which expresses itself as vanity, self-conceit, egotism, self* praise and pride.

8 Close the lips when tempted to tell something to one's own credit, or that will draw forth the admiration of others.

9 And if unconsciously you have told that which brings a response of praise from others, silently repeat "Thine the glory," "Thine the glory," until all personal feeling of self-satisfaction has subsided and become still.

10 For we can do and be nothing of ourselves. All the intelligence we have is God shining through. All the beauty is God-presence. All the skill, bravery, strength, wit, talent, genius, are from the Christ-self, and nothing comes from our human self.

1 1 Watch that no comparisons rise in your thoughts and so begin to voice through your lips, between yourself and others, such as "I would never do that."

12 Ordinary boasting, the spiritual know how to avoid, but the subtle tributes to one's human position, name, ability, etc. — all, one must learn to repudiate, and this silently, lest even this act draw forth further expressions to be overcome. And the silent reminder can be, "Thou only! Thou only!"

13 Pride of family passes away. Is not the Divine in all humanity our family? We have but one Father, but one Ancestor, God. Every form of pride is put under foot by the power of the Spirit

14 Arrogance may He crouching quite unknown to us. If so, then we draw crosses. We are misunderstood, snubbed, blamed unjustly, neglected, insulted. When these appear, instead of resenting them, secretly rejoice that, by your non-resistance, some secret error is being dissolved and passing away forever.

15 Embrace every cross. Do not run away from your problems. Walk up to them and make yourself one with them through prayer and conscious co-operation with Christ, your yoke-fellow.

16 Be skillful so as not to antagonize others with your goody-goodness. Let not your good make others feel evil.

17 Let not your unselfishness hide from you the common forms of selfishness that rise from our beliefs in what are "our rights" and what "is

due us." Watch self-congratulation upon "getting the best" of another, also the resentment and "blues" when another gets an advantage over you.

18 Not "What is there in it for me?" but "How can I serve another?" Not "Where do I come in?" but "What can I do for you?"

19 It is not enough to be unselfish. Let us break down all indifference to the welfare of our fellow beings. Let us love as Christ loves. It is Christ in us that does that. Pray for it

20 Are you afraid to lose an advantage, a pleasure, some measure of praise, something that is your very life? Can you lose anything in reality? If you think you can, then lose it this moment in Christ. Let it go. Loose it.

21 Loose from your mind every sense of loss and be free. Then you'll find the reality of what you prize abiding with you forever and taking form after form.

22 Be fearless before public opinion. Be rightly indifferent to what "they say," so long as you know you are being true to your principles.

23 When you discover yourself thinking how you can please the ear of man and call forth his praise, fly to your heavenly Father, seeking his pleasure, to be honored only by him. Herein lies a secret of enlarging one's faith and power to believe.

24 Be finished with titles and the desire to be a leader, or to excel others in anything. Let your desire to excel be only to please God and honor the Truth.

25 As we walk all the way we shed the old life, form, loves and ways as the old leaves of the live-oak fall to earth with the coming of the new growth. We know with Paul, "I live, yet not I — it is Christ that lives in me."

V

By this shall all men know that ye are my disciples, if ye have love one to another. — John 13:35.

A new commandment I give unto you. That ye love one another; as I have loved you, that ye also love one another. As the Father hath loved me, so have I loved you.— John 13:34-15:9.

Love your enemies, bless them that curse you, do good to them that hate you and pray for them which despite' fully use you and persecute you. — Matt. 5:44.

For if ye love them which love you, what thank have ye for sinners also love those that love them. — Luke 6:32.

And if ye do good to them which do good to you what thank have ye for sinners also do even the same. — Luke 6:33.

And as ye would that men should do to you, do ye also to them likewise. — Luke 6:31.

Give to him that asketh thee, and from him that would borrow of thee turn not thou away. — Matt 5:42.

And if ye lend to them of whom ye hope to receive, what thank have ye for sinners also lend to sinners, to receive as much again. — Luke 6:34.

And unto him that smiteth thee on the one cheek offer also the other; and him that taketh away thy cloak forbid not to take thy coat also. — Luke 6:29.

And why beholdest thou the mote that is in thy brother's eye, but perceivest not the beam that is in thine own eye?— Luke 6:41.

Either how canst thou say to thy brother, Brother, let me pull out the mote that is in thine eye, when thou beholdest not the beam that is in thine own eye? Thou hypocrite cast out first the beam that is in thine own eye, then shall thou see clearly to pall out the mote that is in thy brother's eye. — Luke 6:42.

Forgive and ye shall be forgiven. I say not unto thee. Until seven times: but until seventy times seven. — Luke 6:37, Matt. 18:22.

Father forgive them, they know not what they do. — Luke 23:34.

Judge not and ye shall not be judged: condemn not and ye shall not be condemned: forgive and ye shall be forgiven. — Luke 6:37.

For if ye forgive men their trespasses, your heavenly Father will also forgive you. So likewise will my heavenly Father do also unto you, if ye from your hearts forgive not every one his brother their trespasses. — Matt. 6:14, Matt. 18:35.

1 Loving is the one supreme sign that one is in the Way. Though one have a correct belief, a faith that works miracles, a morality unimpeachable, a name for greatest philanthropy, yet if Love is not complete the attainment will not be made.

2 This Love is a gift of God and it rests in us as the presence of our heavenly Father. By faith in it and prayer for it, this Love is uncovered and expresses itself to perfection.

3 It draws no line with anyone. It does not wait to find lovableness but with every enemy finds only a larger opportunity to love — not in theory but actual love from day to day until success comes — the enmity has gone forever.

4 For every unkind thought another is sending, radiate a genuinely approving thought For every malicious word spoken to one's face, or reported as having been said, give a good word back either silently or audibly. Feel these in your heart by the help of God.

5 Those who are hating you, take special steps to do something good to them or for them — do it so secretly that none shall know until everything secret shall be revealed.

6 If anyone is treating you unjustly, snubbing you or ignoring you, holding you in contempt, scandalizing you or in any way tormenting, take each act as a pressure upon you to exude more of the perfume of your soul.

7 It is easy to love those who are loving to us, we can whirl in a circle of contentment when no opposition comes into our lives. Progress comes when opposition presses us out of our smug contentment with mediocrity.

8 Those who are degenerating can do good to those who are good to them. But regeneration means doing good to those who know us not, who cannot make any return even to the extent of expressing appreciation.

9 All things are from the Lord, and if there be any opposition take it as from the Lord and all sting will be gone — peace only reigns.

10 Remember that all belongs to all and in giving, you are but passing one's own along to him. In such giving there is no loss. Who gives to the Lord, gains.

11 It is written, Thou shalt lend to many, but borrow from none. Who lends to the Christ without thought of return shall be delivered from imposition.

12 Take from your mind and heart all opposition, resentment, resistance and revenge, and the Way will become smooth so that you will walk it as upon winged feet.

13 If you can draw into your life a lawsuit make nothing of it. Trust the Spirit to defend you and if judgment goes against you, let not a ripple disturb your peace. Rather, run out to meet the demand upon you by giving more than is demanded. All these things are finished in mind.

14 What is well done in mind may never — if, to the world, not desirable — take place outwardly. Abraham's perfect surrender of Isaac in heart prevented the surrender of Isaac's form.

15 The eye that renews its youth becomes innocent of faultfinding; the mind, that remains sane, harbors no criticism. We remove the motes from the eye of our brother by making nothing of them.

16 Our world is a mirror. Let us remove every belief in the reality of evil from our consciousness, and our world shall be free from evil, even as our thought.

17 To walk every step of the fair Way to the Ascension, every wrong done to us must be forgotten never to come into mind again.

18 Substituting for the false belief about self, the Truth about the real Self of another, which is incapable of wronging anyone, is the forgiveness that heals.

19 Lift up your eyes from every untrue appearance, and fill them with the Christview, so shall your eyes be to the shadows of wrong as the sun to darkness.

20 Forgive forever and to the uttermost. Let no thought place limitation upon your forgiving power.

21 Let your forgiveness be more than a sentiment; see it as Power, the dynamo that dispels the darkness by replacing it with the light of Truth.

22 Who judges not according to appearance, judges not at all. For appearances are the combination of good and evil. Seeing no evil we have nothing to judge.

23 Condemnation is death — a mental stoning that in the end slays the slayer, therefore in the Way of Life there is no condemnation, because in the Way of Life there is no death.

VI

No man can serve two masters: for either he will hate the one, and love the other; or else he will hold to the one, and despise the other. Ye cannot serve God and mammon. —Matt. 6:24.

Take heed and beware of covetousness: for a man's life consisteth not in the abundance of the things which he possesseth. — Luke 12:15.

And he sent them to preach the kingdom of God, and to heal the sick. And he said unto them. Take nothing for your journey, neither staves, nor scrip, neither bread, neither money; neither have two coats apiece. — Luke 9:23.

Thus said Jesus unto his disciples. Verily I say unto you. That a rich man shall hardly enter into the kingdom of God. And again I say unto you. It is easier for a camel to go through the eye of a needle than for a rich man to enter into the kingdom of God. — Matt. 19:23, 24.

So is he that layeth up treasure for himself and is not rich toward God. — Luke 12:21.

Jesus said unto him. If thou wilt be perfect, go and tell that thou hast, and give to the poor, and thou shalt have treasure in heaven; and come and follow me. — Matt. 19:21.

Sell that ye have, and give alms; provide yourselves bags which wax not old, a treasure in the heavens that faileth not.— Luke 12:33.

And why call ye me. Lord, Lord, and do not the things which I say? Whosoever cometh to me and heareth my sayings and doeth them, I will show you to whom he is like:

He is like a man which built an house, and digged deep, and laid the foundation on a rock: and when the flood arose, the stream beat vehemently upon that house, and could not shake it: for it was founded upon a rock.

But he that heareth, and doeth not, is like a man that without a foundation built an house upon the earth; against which the stream did beat vehemently, and immediately it fell; and the ruin of that house was great. — Luke 6:46-49.

For ye know the grace of our Lord Jesus Christ, that though he was rich yet for your sokes he became poor, that ye through his poverty might be rick. — 2 Cor. 8:9.

I have given you an example, that ye should do as I have done to you. — John 13:15.

Who then is a faithful and wise servant, whom his lord hath made ruler over his household, to give them meat in due seasont

Blessed is that servant, whom his lord when he Cometh shall find so doing.

Verily I say unto you. That he shall make him ruler over all his goods. — Matt. 24:45-48.

1 The love of money cannot exist in the heart of the devotee who desires to love God and humanity with his whole heart.

2 Therefore do nothing for the sake of money. Give no respect or consideration to it; nor let it, or the lack of it, be the reason for any of your movements or of your stillness.

3 God is the only Power; all the power that money seems to have is what man gives it, and is but a reflected or secondary power. Acknowledge God as the only Reason and Power in all your ways.

4 Early you must decide whether you shall be influenced by money or by God; and all the Way, the consideration of money must be put into the background and under foot.

5 He who would run, or progress rapidly, in the Way of the Christ must know how to slip his wealth into the perpetual use and benefit of humanity.

6 So shall a man's stewardship remain, and he himself mount to the Highest.

7 All desire for possessions is transmuted to one supreme Desire for God.

8 Neither the loss nor the gain of things disturbs or excites the one who abides in Christ, for his peace and joy remaineth in him.

9 All our circumstances and associates are tools in God's hands, training us to be indifferent to worldly riches and independent of them.

10 Miraculous provision is one of the delights of the Way.

11 Accumulations of wealth act as the dust and stone under which to bury the bodies of their owners.

12 The shame of dying rich is the final fruit of the pride of living rich.

13 He who walks the Way must acquire the skill of the Christ, to distribute all that comes to him to his neighbors who have need, giving not only one-tenth but all that he has, and yet remain independent himself.

14 Trust-in-riches is secretly and faithfully transmuted in the heart of the Christ candidate to trust-in-God.

15 The "bags that wax not old" and the "house founded upon the rock" is the Body, immortal and efficient, that develops for the candidate who gives all for all and, not only listens to the Christ directions, but also practices them.

16 In the Way of the Christ, is also the highway of prosperity for it is the Path of Wisdom, in "whose right hand is length of days and in whose left hand are riches and honour."

17 The glorious insignia of God's prosperity are the enrichment, comfort and freedom that it brings to others beside the Candidate, through his service and knowledge of Truth.

18 To be rich and yet to appear to be in moderate circumstances, that others may be comfortable, is to walk with Jesus Christ who laid his own wealth on the altar that all might be rich.

19 The servant or steward who is "faithful to give his household, meat in due season" begins the distribution in consciousness, giving in mind first and then outwardly.

20 Give to the Christ in every one, those who seem unworthy as well as the worthy. There is only One to give to in every one, the Christ.

21 The generous giver wisely withholds until the first gift is made — the true thought:

"You are not poor; you are not a beggar; you are not deceiving; you are not worthless. You are God's Beloved, you are the Christ."

22 The Inner Voice counsels whether to give or to withhold. Be not impulsive, be inspired.

23 It is Christmas day every day, when Christ is the giver and Christ the receiver of your bounty.

24 Be unselfish to the point of selflessness that does not even think of being unselfish.

25 Give in secret and in the open, in season and out of season, regardless of appreciation, gratitude or thanks.

26 And as graciously receive as you give. Bring all things to equity and equality; and know only kings to whom you give and, in turn receive, as kings from kings.

VII

I am come to send five on the earth. — Luke 12:49.

For every one shall be tailed with fire. — Mark 9:49.

Receive ye the Holy Ghost: whose soever sins ye remit, they are remitted unto them; and whose soever sins ye retain, they are retained. — John 20:22, 23.

Judge not and ye shall not be judged: condemn not and ye shall not be condemned; forgive, and ye shall be forgiven. — Luke 6:37.

But I say unto you. All sins will be forgiven the sons of men and evil speaking. But one, speaking evil against the Holy Spirit, may not be forgiven to the end of the age. but is liable to age-lasting judgment. — Literal Translation of Mark 3:28, 29.

Because they said. He hath an unclean spirit. — Mark 3:30.

I judge no man. — John 8:15.

For with what judgment ye judge, ye shall be judged. Matt. 7:2.

Verily, verily, I say unto you, He that heareth my word, and believeth on him that sent me hath everlasting life and shall not come into judgment, but is Passed from death unto life.— John 5 -24.

Howbeit when he, the Spirit of truth, is come, he will guide you into all truth . . . he dwelleth with you and shall be in you. — John 16:13 and 14:17.

The Comforter, which is the Holy Ghost, whom the Father will send in my name, he shall teach you all things. —John 14:26.

Ye shall be baptized with the Holy Ghost not many days hence. — Acts 1:5.

1 In every Candidate for the Ascension there breaks forth the Fire of the Holy Spirit.

2 This Fire is sweet, and a delight to those who will not condemn others nor even judge them.

3 But this same Fire is hell to those who have not learned to refrain from criticizing and judging others, for they come under their own condemnation as well as suffering from the judgment dealt to them by others.

4 Receive this Holy Breath by forgiving to the uttermost and training your whole being to see no evil, hear no evil and speak no evil.

5 By utterly refusing to recognize evil in others you will escape the chief error of calling the Holy Spirit in another, an evil thing.

6 Only the Holy Spirit can teach us the Way to be loosened from our subtlest errors, and to accept the Truth, which we have continually rejected.

7 For as Master Builders we shall find that the rejected Stone, or Truth, becomes the Head of the corner, the finishing of our immortal body.

8 As long as evil is recognized in others, the Holy Breath may seem to leave us for a while — coming and going, as with the early Disciples and even Jesus before Ascension Day.

9 The Holy Spirit must be a permanent Presence to the senses of the Candidate who would escape all suffering and death on the Way to the Ascension Mount.

10 Jesus finished all suffering and death for every one who will understand his teaching, and will believe into his own Godhood here and now. Such have passed already from death to Immortality.

11 For only the Holy Spirit can guide one past the dangerous places where others have fallen.

12 And to hear the slightest whisper of the Inner Voice at any moment that its counsel is needed, the imagination and the hearing must be perfectly defended from evil reports.

13 Ceaseless prayer must be made for the consciousness of hearing the Voice of the Holy Spirit — daily declaration of its speaking within — until your ears are forever opened.

14 Then when the Voice of gentle silence has reached your inner ear, it itself will guide you to listen to it daily.

15 For there must be (1) no uncertainty about it; (2) it must be divinely impersonal; (3) one with the great impersonal Jesus Christ; and (4) wholly without interference from our intellect, feelings or senses.

16 All that Jesus Christ taught about the Inner Voice proves true in the experience of the devotee.

17 Study the Master's words about the Spirit of Truth, called the Comforter, also the Holy Spirit and the Holy Ghost in John, chapters 14, 15 and 16.

18 The Holy Spirit is within you now and is evermore speaking to you as "impressions," conscience, "that something," intuition, etc.

19 The Fire will reveal the work of the Holy Spirit in your life from the day of your first breath to the present moment. Its works last forever.

20 The Holy Breath and the Love Fire open your interior senses of seeing and hearing and your prophetic sense.

21 Waiting for the Holy Spirit to develop these, saves the devotee visions and experiences that are undesirable. "Wait on the Lord and he will bring it to pass."

22 To the life of sincere, faithful devotion come all the revelations, inspirations and other delights of the heavenly realm.

23 Though these gifts may seem long in manifestation, never be impatient nor disappointed. In all ways live, speak, act as though they were present now, for they are. Thereby shall you be ever ready, and never be taken unawares.

VIII

And he spake a parable unto them to this end, that men ought always to pray, and not to faint. — Luke 18:1.

And he said unto them. Which of you shall have a friend, and shall go unto him at midnight, and say unto him. Friend, lend me three haves. . . .

I say unto you, Though he will not rise and give him, because he is his friend, yet because of his importunity he will rise and give him as many as he needeth. — Luke 11:5-8.

And I say unto you Ask, and it shall be given you; seek, and ye shall find; knock, and it shall be opened unto you. — Luke 11:9,

If ye then, being evil, know how to give good gifts unto your children: how much more shall your heavenly Father give the Holy Spirit to them that ask him. — Luke 11:13.

And it came to pass, that, as he was praying in a certain place, when he ceased, one of his disciples said unto him, Lord, teach us to pray, as John also taught his disciples. —Luke 11:1.

And when thou prayest, thou shall not be as the hypocrites are . . . after this manner therefore pray ye. —Matt. 6:5-9.

And when ye stand praying, forgive, if ye have ought against any: that your Father also which is in heaven may forgive you your trespasses. — Mark 1 1:25,

All things whatsoever ye shall ask in prayer, believing, ye shall receive.— Matt. 21 21.

If ye shall ask anything in my name, I will do it. — John 14:14.

Watch ye therefore and pray always, that ye may be accounted worthy to escape all these things that shall come to pass, and to stand before the Son of man. — Luke 21:36.

1 The path direct to God is every step a prayer.

2 Therefore the successful follower of Christ learns to pray without ceasing.

3 Every temptation to fail, he makes an occasion to commune with God upon success.

4 Every suggesion to be sick, to be afraid, to be discouraged, to sin, to let go of life or any good, means to him more determination to talk with his , heavenly Father about Health, Faith, Courage, Love, Life and Good of every kind.

5 He will not be refused. He will never let go. He is the importunity that is irresistible.

6 Three loaves we must have for our Friend, our Divinity when it comes, perfection of body, mind and soul — God only can give us this Perfection.

7 Ask, seek, knock, day after day and believe into this Perfect Triune Man.

8 In its simplicity the fulfillment of every prayer is the receiving of the Holy Spirit of anything one may ask for.

9 Pray to know how to pray.

10 Ask the Holy Spirit to pray in you.

11 Do not pray the way that those do who receive no answers.

12 Change your own way of praying until realization comes; then you can repeat and repeat and it will not be vain, but effectual.

13 If doubt or discouragement begin to confuse or weaken you, then repeat the Lord's Prayer even though it be mechanical.

14 If your prayer is aloud, do not think how it sounds to human cars. Be silent before such thoughts.

15 A steady, faithful silence directed earnestly to God; a breathing, "Father!"; a fervent sentence "Thou knowest"; a stillness of "I believe," resting and waiting in the Presence — these are better than loud cries of feverish unbelief.

16 Study all that Jesus Christ has taught on prayer. Learn his words. Sink into his being, and pray to the Father as Jesus Christ's own self.

17 Above all things, remove all barriers of unforgiveness between yourself and your fellow beings; put away all criticism, all condemnation.

18 Realize you cannot ask for anything that has not already been given you. Prayer wipes out time and space between you and the receiving.

19 One hearty prayer full of faith and realization should be our first expression with expectancy of immediate answer.

20 If the response is not at once, then prayer should be continued not only in words but in new deeds, new thoughts, new feelings and new works of the Christ.

21 To have a body that can bear the new life, a mind strong before the new thoughts, a soul that will stand firm before its Divinity, and that one may escape all the disasters and calamities of the closing age, the Christian must be alert, and so prayer- filled, that he is the very Word itself, by which all things were and are made.

IX

I am the door; he that entereth in by the door is the shepherd of the sheep. To him the porter openeth. — John 10:7, 2, 3.

I am the door: by me if any man enter in he shall be saved and shall go in and out and find pasture. — John 10:9.

I am the living bread which came down from heaven: if any man eat of this bread, he shall live forever. — John 6:51.

My Father giveth you the true bread from heaven. I am the bread of life: he that cometh to me shall never hunger; and he that believeth on me shall never thirst. — John 6:32,35.

Abide in me and I in you. — John 15:4.

He that abideth in me and I in him, the same bringeth forth muck fruit; for without me ye can do nothing. — John 15:5.

IF ye abide in me and my words abide in you, ye shall ask what ye will, and it shall be done unto you. — John 15:7.

That they all may be one; as thou. Father, art in me, and I in thee, that they also may be one in us. — John 17:21.

He that hath seen me hath seen the Father. I and the Father are one.— John 14:9 and 10:30.

Know ye not your own selves, how that Jesus Christ is in you—2 Cor. 13:5.

For as many of you as have been baptized into Christ have put on Christ.— Gal. 3:27.

Put ye on the Lord Jesus Christ— Rom. 13:14.

The mystery which hath been hid from ages . . . which is Christ in you. — Col. 1:26, 27.

Christ is all, and in all.— Col. 3:11.

That we may present every man perfect in Christ Jesus: for in him dwelleth all the fullness of the Godhead bodily and ye are complete in him. — Col. 1:28 and 2:9, 10.

I live; yet not I but Christ liveth in me: and the life which I now live in the flesh, I live by the faith of the Son of God.— Gal. 2:20.

---

1 Man is one being, not a million. And as One Being only can he attain immortality in the flesh and the Ascension.

2 Jesus Christ demonstrated his identity with God and with Man, therefore his is the mind and the heart that thinks and feels truly.

3 Man is making the same achievement, thinks the same thoughts and feels the same feelings.

4 Therefore to cross the portals of Eden, or go through the Door of the Ascension, Man must go as Jesus Christ.

5 The name Jesus Christ is the password; to him that says, "I am Jesus Christ," the sentinel says, "He knows, let him pass."

6 But if he has not the "wedding garment," (Matt. 22:11, 12) the body prepared for the heavenly consciousness, he cannot remain, but is presently back in the ordinary thinking.

7 And none can have the immortal body except those who are fed on, and nourished by, the Truth, the substance and the life ("flesh and blood") of Jesus Christ.

8 We eat this Bread from Heaven by thinking Christ's thoughts, meditating upon his words, making them our very own, and living his life.

9 As baby bees become queen bees through being fed upon royal bee-bread, so those that eat Christ become Christ in the flesh.

10 In truth, we are already Christ. The appearance of becoming Christ is only in the flesh, the realm of demonstration.

1 1 God and Christ are the same. Jesus proved this, and the one who merges himself into Jesus Christ will prove the same truth.

12 Making the union with Jesus Christ is the beginning of unity with all humanity, whereby each is brought to his Father's house, fruits of the heavenly vine.

13 No other Master ever rose to the heights that Jesus achieved, therefore there is none can instruct us in that Way but Jesus. Other Masters may carry us far, but we abandon them for Christ when we aspire to our Godhood while yet in the flesh.

14 All things are possible to the Christ consciousness, and all that such devotees may wish comes to pass while they put their wish into the form of prayer.

15 Only God in you can reveal the truth that you are Christ

16 There is but one God and there is but one Man and he is the God-man, the reality of every human form.

17 Eat and drink the words of Jesus Christ, that have been passed down to us through inspirational memory, and as a special gift of God to his beloved world.

18 He who meditates upon Jesus' words, turning them over and over in mind; using them as his own; studying to get to the essence or spirit of them, will receive new thoughts every day, revelations and inspirations of untold value, making a life of infinite satisfaction.

19 Every tiny cell of your body thinks and can say, "I am." Every one must eventually say, "I am Jesus Christ" in order to show forth the body of immortality.

20 Who loses his individuality in Jesus Christ will truly find it, and he who tries to maintain a separate individuality will fail.

21 Paul became great in the measure that he put on Jesus Christ.

22 To hide your life in Jesus Christ so that none can see you for the light of your Soul, is to find your name written in heaven; and you yourself chosen by God to live, here and now, the immortal life, and be among those to usher in The New Age.

Made in the USA
Monee, IL
07 December 2024

72895152R00187